2273B: Managing and Maintaining a Microsoft® Windows Server™ 2003 Environment

"recommend Book

① Mastering
Windows Server 2003   by Mark Minasi.

D1457115

END-USER LICENSE AGREEMENT FOR OFFICIAL MICROSOFT LEARNING PRODUCTS – STUDENT EDITION

PLEASE READ THIS END-USER LICENSE AGREEMENT ("EULA") CAREFULLY. BY USING THE MATERIALS AND/OR USING OR INSTALLING THE SOFTWARE THAT ACCOMPANIES THIS EULA (COLLECTIVELY, THE "LICENSED CONTENT"), YOU AGREE TO THE TERMS OF THIS EULA. IF YOU DO NOT AGREE, DO NOT USE THE LICENSED CONTENT.

1.　　　**GENERAL.** This EULA is a legal agreement between you (either an individual or a single entity) and Microsoft Corporation ("Microsoft"). This EULA governs the Licensed Content, which includes computer software (including online and electronic documentation), training materials, and any other associated media and printed materials. This EULA applies to updates, supplements, add-on components, and Internet-based services components of the Licensed Content that Microsoft may provide or make available to you unless Microsoft provides other terms with the update, supplement, add-on component, or Internet-based services component. Microsoft reserves the right to discontinue any Internet-based services provided to you or made available to you through the use of the Licensed Content. This EULA also governs any product support services relating to the Licensed Content except as may be included in another agreement between you and Microsoft. An amendment or addendum to this EULA may accompany the Licensed Content.

2.　　　**GENERAL GRANT OF LICENSE.** Microsoft grants you the following rights, conditioned on your compliance with all the terms and conditions of this EULA. Microsoft grants you a limited, non-exclusive, royalty-free license to install and use the Licensed Content solely in conjunction with your participation as a student in an Authorized Training Session (as defined below). You may install and use one copy of the software on a single computer, device, workstation, terminal, or other digital electronic or analog device ("Device"). You may make a second copy of the software and install it on a portable Device for the exclusive use of the person who is the primary user of the first copy of the software. A license for the software may not be shared for use by multiple end users. An "Authorized Training Session" means a training session conducted at a Microsoft Certified Technical Education Center, an IT Academy, via a Microsoft Certified Partner, or such other entity as Microsoft may designate from time to time in writing, by a Microsoft Certified Trainer (for more information on these entities, please visit www.microsoft.com). WITHOUT LIMITING THE FOREGOING, COPYING OR REPRODUCTION OF THE LICENSED CONTENT TO ANY SERVER OR LOCATION FOR FURTHER REPRODUCTION OR REDISTRIBUTION IS EXPRESSLY PROHIBITED.

3.　　　**DESCRIPTION OF OTHER RIGHTS AND LICENSE LIMITATIONS**

　　　3.1　　　*Use of Documentation and Printed Training Materials.*

　　　　　3.1.1　　　The documents and related graphics included in the Licensed Content may include technical inaccuracies or typographical errors. Changes are periodically made to the content. Microsoft may make improvements and/or changes in any of the components of the Licensed Content at any time without notice. The names of companies, products, people, characters and/or data mentioned in the Licensed Content may be fictitious and are in no way intended to represent any real individual, company, product or event, unless otherwise noted.

　　　　　3.1.2　　　Microsoft grants you the right to reproduce portions of documents (such as student workbooks, white papers, press releases, datasheets and FAQs) (the "Documents") provided with the Licensed Content. You may not print any book (either electronic or print version) in its entirety. If you choose to reproduce Documents, you agree that: (a) use of such printed Documents will be solely in conjunction with your personal training use; (b) the Documents will not republished or posted on any network computer or broadcast in any media; (c) any reproduction will include either the Document's original copyright notice or a copyright notice to Microsoft's benefit substantially in the format provided below; and (d) to comply with all terms and conditions of this EULA. In addition, no modifications may made to any Document.

　　　　　Form of Notice:

　　　　　Copyright undefined.

　　　　　© 2005. Reprinted with permission by Microsoft Corporation. All rights reserved.

　　　　　Microsoft and Windows are either registered trademarks or trademarks of Microsoft Corporation in the US and/or other countries. Other product and company names mentioned herein may be the trademarks of their respective owners.

　　　3.2　　　*Use of Media Elements.* The Licensed Content may include certain photographs, clip art, animations, sounds, music, and video clips (together "Media Elements"). You may not modify these Media Elements.

　　　3.3　　　*Use of Sample Code.* In the event that the Licensed Content include sample source code ("Sample Code"), Microsoft grants you a limited, non-exclusive, royalty-free license to use, copy and modify the Sample Code; if you elect to exercise the foregoing rights, you agree to comply with all other terms and conditions of this EULA, including without limitation Sections 3.4, 3.5, and 6.

　　　3.4　　　*Permitted Modifications.* In the event that you exercise any rights provided under this EULA to create modifications of the Licensed Content, you agree that any such modifications: (a) will not be used for providing training where a fee is charged in public or private classes; (b) indemnify, hold harmless, and defend Microsoft from and against any claims or lawsuits, including attorneys' fees, which arise from or result from your use of any modified version of the Licensed Content; and (c) not to transfer or assign any rights to any modified version of the Licensed Content to any third party without the express written permission of Microsoft.

3.5   *Reproduction/Redistribution Licensed Content.* Except as expressly provided in this EULA, you may not reproduce or distribute the Licensed Content or any portion thereof (including any permitted modifications) to any third parties without the express written permission of Microsoft.

4.   **RESERVATION OF RIGHTS AND OWNERSHIP.** Microsoft reserves all rights not expressly granted to you in this EULA. The Licensed Content is protected by copyright and other intellectual property laws and treaties. Microsoft or its suppliers own the title, copyright, and other intellectual property rights in the Licensed Content. You may not remove or obscure any copyright, trademark or patent notices that appear on the Licensed Content, or any components thereof, as delivered to you. **The Licensed Content is licensed, not sold.**

5.   **LIMITATIONS ON REVERSE ENGINEERING, DECOMPILATION, AND DISASSEMBLY.** You may not reverse engineer, decompile, or disassemble the Software or Media Elements, except and only to the extent that such activity is expressly permitted by applicable law notwithstanding this limitation.

6.   **LIMITATIONS ON SALE, RENTAL, ETC. AND CERTAIN ASSIGNMENTS.** You may not provide commercial hosting services with, sell, rent, lease, lend, sublicense, or assign copies of the Licensed Content, or any portion thereof (including any permitted modifications thereof) on a stand-alone basis or as part of any collection, product or service.

7.   **CONSENT TO USE OF DATA.** You agree that Microsoft and its affiliates may collect and use technical information gathered as part of the product support services provided to you, if any, related to the Licensed Content. Microsoft may use this information solely to improve our products or to provide customized services or technologies to you and will not disclose this information in a form that personally identifies you.

8.   **LINKS TO THIRD PARTY SITES.** You may link to third party sites through the use of the Licensed Content. The third party sites are not under the control of Microsoft, and Microsoft is not responsible for the contents of any third party sites, any links contained in third party sites, or any changes or updates to third party sites. Microsoft is not responsible for webcasting or any other form of transmission received from any third party sites. Microsoft is providing these links to third party sites to you only as a convenience, and the inclusion of any link does not imply an endorsement by Microsoft of the third party site.

9.   **ADDITIONAL LICENSED CONTENT/SERVICES.** This EULA applies to updates, supplements, add-on components, or Internet-based services components, of the Licensed Content that Microsoft may provide to you or make available to you after the date you obtain your initial copy of the Licensed Content, unless we provide other terms along with the update, supplement, add-on component, or Internet-based services component. Microsoft reserves the right to discontinue any Internet-based services provided to you or made available to you through the use of the Licensed Content.

10.   **U.S. GOVERNMENT LICENSE RIGHTS**. All software provided to the U.S. Government pursuant to solicitations issued on or after December 1, 1995 is provided with the commercial license rights and restrictions described elsewhere herein. All software provided to the U.S. Government pursuant to solicitations issued prior to December 1, 1995 is provided with "Restricted Rights" as provided for in FAR, 48 CFR 52.227-14 (JUNE 1987) or DFAR, 48 CFR 252.227-7013 (OCT 1988), as applicable.

11.   **EXPORT RESTRICTIONS**. You acknowledge that the Licensed Content is subject to U.S. export jurisdiction. You agree to comply with all applicable international and national laws that apply to the Licensed Content, including the U.S. Export Administration Regulations, as well as end-user, end-use, and destination restrictions issued by U.S. and other governments. For additional information see <http://www.microsoft.com/exporting/>.

12.   **TRANSFER.** The initial user of the Licensed Content may make a one-time permanent transfer of this EULA and Licensed Content to another end user, provided the initial user retains no copies of the Licensed Content. The transfer may not be an indirect transfer, such as a consignment. Prior to the transfer, the end user receiving the Licensed Content must agree to all the EULA terms.

13.   **"NOT FOR RESALE" LICENSED CONTENT.** Licensed Content identified as "Not For Resale" or "NFR," may not be sold or otherwise transferred for value, or used for any purpose other than demonstration, test or evaluation.

14.   **TERMINATION.** Without prejudice to any other rights, Microsoft may terminate this EULA if you fail to comply with the terms and conditions of this EULA. In such event, you must destroy all copies of the Licensed Content and all of its component parts.

15.   <u>DISCLAIMER OF WARRANTIES.</u> **TO THE MAXIMUM EXTENT PERMITTED BY APPLICABLE LAW, MICROSOFT AND ITS SUPPLIERS PROVIDE THE LICENSED CONTENT AND SUPPORT SERVICES (IF ANY) *AS IS AND WITH ALL FAULTS,* AND MICROSOFT AND ITS SUPPLIERS HEREBY DISCLAIM ALL OTHER WARRANTIES AND CONDITIONS, WHETHER EXPRESS, IMPLIED OR STATUTORY, INCLUDING, BUT NOT LIMITED TO, ANY (IF ANY) IMPLIED WARRANTIES, DUTIES OR CONDITIONS OF MERCHANTABILITY, OF FITNESS FOR A PARTICULAR PURPOSE, OF RELIABILITY OR AVAILABILITY, OF ACCURACY OR COMPLETENESS OF RESPONSES, OF RESULTS, OF WORKMANLIKE EFFORT, OF LACK OF VIRUSES, AND OF LACK OF NEGLIGENCE, ALL WITH REGARD TO THE LICENSED CONTENT, AND THE PROVISION OF OR FAILURE TO PROVIDE SUPPORT OR OTHER SERVICES, INFORMATION, SOFTWARE, AND RELATED CONTENT THROUGH THE LICENSED CONTENT, OR OTHERWISE ARISING OUT OF THE USE OF THE LICENSED CONTENT. ALSO, THERE IS NO WARRANTY OR CONDITION OF TITLE, QUIET ENJOYMENT, QUIET POSSESSION, CORRESPONDENCE TO DESCRIPTION OR NON-INFRINGEMENT WITH REGARD TO THE LICENSED CONTENT. THE ENTIRE RISK AS TO THE QUALITY, OR ARISING OUT OF THE USE OR PERFORMANCE OF THE LICENSED CONTENT, AND ANY SUPPORT SERVICES, REMAINS WITH YOU.**

16.   <u>EXCLUSION OF INCIDENTAL, CONSEQUENTIAL AND CERTAIN OTHER DAMAGES.</u> **TO THE MAXIMUM EXTENT PERMITTED BY APPLICABLE LAW, IN NO EVENT SHALL MICROSOFT OR ITS SUPPLIERS BE LIABLE FOR ANY SPECIAL, INCIDENTAL, PUNITIVE, INDIRECT, OR CONSEQUENTIAL DAMAGES WHATSOEVER (INCLUDING, BUT NOT**

LIMITED TO, DAMAGES FOR LOSS OF PROFITS OR CONFIDENTIAL OR OTHER INFORMATION, FOR BUSINESS INTERRUPTION, FOR PERSONAL INJURY, FOR LOSS OF PRIVACY, FOR FAILURE TO MEET ANY DUTY INCLUDING OF GOOD FAITH OR OF REASONABLE CARE, FOR NEGLIGENCE, AND FOR ANY OTHER PECUNIARY OR OTHER LOSS WHATSOEVER) ARISING OUT OF OR IN ANY WAY RELATED TO THE USE OF OR INABILITY TO USE THE LICENSED CONTENT, THE PROVISION OF OR FAILURE TO PROVIDE SUPPORT OR OTHER SERVICES, INFORMATION, SOFTWARE, AND RELATED CONTENT THROUGH THE LICENSED CONTENT, OR OTHERWISE ARISING OUT OF THE USE OF THE LICENSED CONTENT, OR OTHERWISE UNDER OR IN CONNECTION WITH ANY PROVISION OF THIS EULA, EVEN IN THE EVENT OF THE FAULT, TORT (INCLUDING NEGLIGENCE), MISREPRESENTATION, STRICT LIABILITY, BREACH OF CONTRACT OR BREACH OF WARRANTY OF MICROSOFT OR ANY SUPPLIER, AND EVEN IF MICROSOFT OR ANY SUPPLIER HAS BEEN ADVISED OF THE POSSIBILITY OF SUCH DAMAGES. BECAUSE SOME STATES/JURISDICTIONS DO NOT ALLOW THE EXCLUSION OR LIMITATION OF LIABILITY FOR CONSEQUENTIAL OR INCIDENTAL DAMAGES, THE ABOVE LIMITATION MAY NOT APPLY TO YOU.

17. **LIMITATION OF LIABILITY AND REMEDIES.** NOTWITHSTANDING ANY DAMAGES THAT YOU MIGHT INCUR FOR ANY REASON WHATSOEVER (INCLUDING, WITHOUT LIMITATION, ALL DAMAGES REFERENCED HEREIN AND ALL DIRECT OR GENERAL DAMAGES IN CONTRACT OR ANYTHING ELSE), THE ENTIRE LIABILITY OF MICROSOFT AND ANY OF ITS SUPPLIERS UNDER ANY PROVISION OF THIS EULA AND YOUR EXCLUSIVE REMEDY HEREUNDER SHALL BE LIMITED TO THE GREATER OF THE ACTUAL DAMAGES YOU INCUR IN REASONABLE RELIANCE ON THE LICENSED CONTENT UP TO THE AMOUNT ACTUALLY PAID BY YOU FOR THE LICENSED CONTENT OR US$5.00. THE FOREGOING LIMITATIONS, EXCLUSIONS AND DISCLAIMERS SHALL APPLY TO THE MAXIMUM EXTENT PERMITTED BY APPLICABLE LAW, EVEN IF ANY REMEDY FAILS ITS ESSENTIAL PURPOSE.

18. **APPLICABLE LAW.** If you acquired this Licensed Content in the United States, this EULA is governed by the laws of the State of Washington. If you acquired this Licensed Content in Canada, unless expressly prohibited by local law, this EULA is governed by the laws in force in the Province of Ontario, Canada; and, in respect of any dispute which may arise hereunder, you consent to the jurisdiction of the federal and provincial courts sitting in Toronto, Ontario. If you acquired this Licensed Content in the European Union, Iceland, Norway, or Switzerland, then local law applies. If you acquired this Licensed Content in any other country, then local law may apply.

19. **ENTIRE AGREEMENT; SEVERABILITY.** This EULA (including any addendum or amendment to this EULA which is included with the Licensed Content) are the entire agreement between you and Microsoft relating to the Licensed Content and the support services (if any) and they supersede all prior or contemporaneous oral or written communications, proposals and representations with respect to the Licensed Content or any other subject matter covered by this EULA. To the extent the terms of any Microsoft policies or programs for support services conflict with the terms of this EULA, the terms of this EULA shall control. If any provision of this EULA is held to be void, invalid, unenforceable or illegal, the other provisions shall continue in full force and effect.

Should you have any questions concerning this EULA, or if you desire to contact Microsoft for any reason, please use the address information enclosed in this Licensed Content to contact the Microsoft subsidiary serving your country or visit Microsoft on the World Wide Web at http://www.microsoft.com.

Si vous avez acquis votre Contenu Sous Licence Microsoft au CANADA :

DÉNI DE GARANTIES. Dans la mesure maximale permise par les lois applicables, le Contenu Sous Licence et les services de soutien technique (le cas échéant) sont fournis *TELS QUELS ET AVEC TOUS LES DÉFAUTS* par Microsoft et ses fournisseurs, lesquels par les présentes dénient toutes autres garanties et conditions expresses, implicites ou en vertu de la loi, notamment, mais sans limitation, (le cas échéant) les garanties, devoirs ou conditions implicites de qualité marchande, d'adaptation à une fin usage particulière, de fiabilité ou de disponibilité, d'exactitude ou d'exhaustivité des réponses, des résultats, des efforts déployés selon les règles de l'art, d'absence de virus et d'absence de négligence, le tout à l'égard du Contenu Sous Licence et de la prestation des services de soutien technique ou de l'omission de la 'une telle prestation des services de soutien technique ou à l'égard de la fourniture ou de l'omission de la fourniture de tous autres services, renseignements, Contenus Sous Licence, et contenu qui s'y rapporte grâce au Contenu Sous Licence ou provenant autrement de l'utilisation du Contenu Sous Licence. PAR AILLEURS, IL N'Y A AUCUNE GARANTIE OU CONDITION QUANT AU TITRE DE PROPRIÉTÉ, À LA JOUISSANCE OU LA POSSESSION PAISIBLE, À LA CONCORDANCE À UNE DESCRIPTION NI QUANT À UNE ABSENCE DE CONTREFAÇON CONCERNANT LE CONTENU SOUS LICENCE.

EXCLUSION DES DOMMAGES ACCESSOIRES, INDIRECTS ET DE CERTAINS AUTRES DOMMAGES. DANS LA MESURE MAXIMALE PERMISE PAR LES LOIS APPLICABLES, EN AUCUN CAS MICROSOFT OU SES FOURNISSEURS NE SERONT RESPONSABLES DES DOMMAGES SPÉCIAUX, CONSÉCUTIFS, ACCESSOIRES OU INDIRECTS DE QUELQUE NATURE QUE CE SOIT (NOTAMMENT, LES DOMMAGES À L'ÉGARD DU MANQUE À GAGNER OU DE LA DIVULGATION DE RENSEIGNEMENTS CONFIDENTIELS OU AUTRES, DE LA PERTE D'EXPLOITATION, DE BLESSURES CORPORELLES, DE LA VIOLATION DE LA VIE PRIVÉE, DE L'OMISSION DE REMPLIR TOUT DEVOIR, Y COMPRIS D'AGIR DE BONNE FOI OU D'EXERCER UN SOIN RAISONNABLE, DE LA NÉGLIGENCE ET DE TOUTE AUTRE PERTE PÉCUNIAIRE OU AUTRE PERTE

DE QUELQUE NATURE QUE CE SOIT) SE RAPPORTANT DE QUELQUE MANIÈRE QUE CE SOIT À L'UTILISATION DU CONTENU SOUS LICENCE OU À L'INCAPACITÉ DE S'EN SERVIR, À LA PRESTATION OU À L'OMISSION DE LA 'UNE TELLE PRESTATION DE SERVICES DE SOUTIEN TECHNIQUE OU À LA FOURNITURE OU À L'OMISSION DE LA FOURNITURE DE TOUS AUTRES SERVICES, RENSEIGNEMENTS, CONTENUS SOUS LICENCE, ET CONTENU QUI S'Y RAPPORTE GRÂCE AU CONTENU SOUS LICENCE OU PROVENANT AUTREMENT DE L'UTILISATION DU CONTENU SOUS LICENCE OU AUTREMENT AUX TERMES DE TOUTE DISPOSITION DE LA U PRÉSENTE CONVENTION EULA OU RELATIVEMENT À UNE TELLE DISPOSITION, MÊME EN CAS DE FAUTE, DE DÉLIT CIVIL (Y COMPRIS LA NÉGLIGENCE), DE RESPONSABILITÉ STRICTE, DE VIOLATION DE CONTRAT OU DE VIOLATION DE GARANTIE DE MICROSOFT OU DE TOUT FOURNISSEUR ET MÊME SI MICROSOFT OU TOUT FOURNISSEUR A ÉTÉ AVISÉ DE LA POSSIBILITÉ DE TELS DOMMAGES.

LIMITATION DE RESPONSABILITÉ ET RECOURS. MALGRÉ LES DOMMAGES QUE VOUS PUISSIEZ SUBIR POUR QUELQUE MOTIF QUE CE SOIT (NOTAMMENT, MAIS SANS LIMITATION, TOUS LES DOMMAGES SUSMENTIONNÉS ET TOUS LES DOMMAGES DIRECTS OU GÉNÉRAUX OU AUTRES), LA SEULE RESPONSABILITÉ 'OBLIGATION INTÉGRALE DE MICROSOFT ET DE L'UN OU L'AUTRE DE SES FOURNISSEURS AUX TERMES DE TOUTE DISPOSITION DEU LA PRÉSENTE CONVENTION EULA ET VOTRE RECOURS EXCLUSIF À L'ÉGARD DE TOUT CE QUI PRÉCÈDE SE LIMITE AU PLUS ÉLEVÉ ENTRE LES MONTANTS SUIVANTS : LE MONTANT QUE VOUS AVEZ RÉELLEMENT PAYÉ POUR LE CONTENU SOUS LICENCE OU 5,00 $US. LES LIMITES, EXCLUSIONS ET DÉNIS QUI PRÉCÈDENT (Y COMPRIS LES CLAUSES CI-DESSUS), S'APPLIQUENT DANS LA MESURE MAXIMALE PERMISE PAR LES LOIS APPLICABLES, MÊME SI TOUT RECOURS N'ATTEINT PAS SON BUT ESSENTIEL.

À moins que cela ne soit prohibé par le droit local applicable, la présente Convention est régie par les lois de la province d'Ontario, Canada. Vous consentez Chacune des parties à la présente reconnaît irrévocablement à la compétence des tribunaux fédéraux et provinciaux siégeant à Toronto, dans de la province d'Ontario et consent à instituer tout litige qui pourrait découler de la présente auprès des tribunaux situés dans le district judiciaire de York, province d'Ontario.

Au cas où vous auriez des questions concernant cette licence ou que vous désiriez vous mettre en rapport avec Microsoft pour quelque raison que ce soit, veuillez utiliser l'information contenue dans le Contenu Sous Licence pour contacter la filiale de succursale Microsoft desservant votre pays, dont l'adresse est fournie dans ce produit, ou visitez écrivez à : Microsoft sur le World Wide Web à http://www.microsoft.com

Contents

About This Course

This section provides you with a brief description of the course, audience, suggested prerequisites, and course objectives.

Description

This five-day, instructor-led course provides students with the knowledge and skills to manage accounts and resources in a Microsoft® Windows Server™ 2003 environment. The course is intended for systems administrator and systems engineer candidates who are responsible for managing accounts and resources. These tasks include managing user, computer, and group accounts; managing access to network resources; managing printers; managing an organizational unit in a network based on Active Directory® directory service; and implementing Group Policy to manage users and computers. This course also provides students with the knowledge and skills that are needed to effectively maintain server resources, monitor server performance, and safeguard data on a computer running one of the operating systems in the Microsoft Windows Server 2003 family.

Audience

This course is a combination of the first two courses in the systems administrator and systems engineer tracks for Windows Server 2003 and serves as the entry point for other courses in the Windows Server 2003 curriculum.

Student prerequisites

This course requires that students meet the following prerequisites:

- A+ certification or equivalent knowledge and skills
- Network+ certification or equivalent knowledge and skills

Course objectives

After completing this course, the student will be able to:

- Create and populate organizational units with user and computer accounts.
- Manage user and computer accounts.
- Create and manage groups.
- Manage access to resources.
- Implement printing.
- Manage printing.
- Use organizational units to manage access to objects.
- Implement Group Policy.
- Use Group Policy to manage the user and computer environment.
- Implement administrative templates and audit policy in Windows Server 2003.
- Prepare to administer server resources.
- Configure a server to monitor system performance.
- Monitor system performance.
- Manage device drivers by configuring device driver signing and restoring a device driver.
- Manage hard disks.
- Manage data storage.

- Manage disaster recovery.
- Use Microsoft Windows Server Update Services (WSUS) to maintain software.
- Maintain Windows Server 2003 security.

Student Materials Compact Disc Contents

The Student Materials compact disc (CD) contains the following files and folders:

- *Autorun.inf*. When the CD is inserted into the CD drive, this file opens StartCD.exe.

- *Default.hta*. This file opens the Student Materials Web page. It provides you with resources pertaining to this course, including additional reading, review and lab answers, lab files, multimedia presentations, and course-related Web sites.

- *Readme.txt*. This file explains how to install the software for viewing the Student Materials CD and its contents and how to open the Student Materials Web page.

- *StartCD.exe*. When the CD is inserted into the CD drive, or when you double-click the StartCD.exe file, this file opens the CD and allows you to browse the Trainer Materials DVD.

- *StartCD.ini*. This file contains instructions to launch StartCD.exe.

- *Addread*. This folder contains additional reading pertaining to this course.

- *Appendix*. This folder contains appendix files for this course.

- *Flash*. This folder contains the installer for the Macromedia Flash browser plug-in.

- *Fonts*. This folder contains fonts that might be required to view the Microsoft Word documents that are included with this course.

- *Media*. This folder contains files that are used in multimedia presentations for this course.

- *Mplayer*. This folder contains the setup file to install Microsoft Windows Media® Player.

- *Webfiles*. This folder contains the files that are required to view the course Web page. To open the Web page, open Windows Explorer, and in the root directory of the CD, double-click **StartCD.exe**.

- *Wordview*. This folder contains the Word Viewer that is used to view any Word document (.doc) files that are included on the CD.

Document Conventions

The following conventions are used in course materials to distinguish elements of the text.

Convention	Use
Bold	Represents commands, command options, and syntax that must be typed exactly as shown. It also indicates commands on menus and buttons, dialog box titles and options, and icon and menu names.
Italic	In syntax statements or descriptive text, indicates argument names or placeholders for variable information. Italic is also used for introducing new terms, for book titles, and for emphasis in the text.
Title Capitals	Indicate domain names, user names, computer names, directory names, and folder and file names, except when specifically referring to case-sensitive names. Unless otherwise indicated, you can use lowercase letters when you type a directory name or file name in a dialog box or at a command prompt.
ALL CAPITALS	Indicate the names of keys, key sequences, and key combinations—for example, ALT+SPACEBAR.
`monospace`	Represents code samples or examples of screen text.
[ ]	In syntax statements, enclose optional items. For example, [*filename*] in command syntax indicates that you can choose to type a file name with the command. Type only the information within the brackets, not the brackets themselves.
{ }	In syntax statements, enclose required items. Type only the information within the braces, not the braces themselves.
|	In syntax statements, separates an either/or choice.
▶	Indicates a procedure with sequential steps.
...	In syntax statements, specifies that the preceding item may be repeated.
.	Represents an omitted portion of a code sample.

Introduction

Contents

Introduction

- Name
- Company affiliation
- Title/function
- Job responsibility
- Systems administration experience
- Windows Server operating systems experience
- Expectations for the course

Course Materials

- Name card
- Student workbook
- Student Materials compact disc
- Course evaluation
- Assessments

The following materials are included with your kit:

- *Name card*. Write your name on both sides of the name card.

- *Student workbook*. The student workbook contains the material covered in class, in addition to the hands-on lab exercises.

- *Student Materials compact disc*. The Student Materials compact disc contains a Web page that provides you with links to resources pertaining to this course, including additional readings, review and lab answers, lab files, multimedia presentations, and course-related Web sites.

   Note   To open the Web page, insert the Student Materials compact disc into the CD-ROM drive, and then in the root directory of the compact disc, double-click **StartCD.exe**.

- *Course evaluation*. Near the end of the course, you will have the opportunity to complete an online evaluation to provide feedback on the course, training facility, and instructor.

   To provide additional comments or feedback on the course, send e-mail to support@mscourseware.com. To inquire about the Microsoft Certified Professional program, send e-mail to mcphelp@microsoft.com.

Prerequisites

- A+ Certification or equivalent knowledge and skills
- Network+ Certification or equivalent knowledge and skills

This course requires that you meet the following prerequisites:

- A+ certification or equivalent knowledge and skills
- Network+ certification or equivalent knowledge and skills

Course Outline

* Module 1: Introduction to Administering Accounts and Resources
* Module 2: Managing User and Computer Accounts
* Module 3: Managing Groups
* Module 4: Managing Access to Resources
* Module 5: Managing Access to Objects in Organizational Units
* Module 6: Implementing Group Policy
* Module 7: Managing the User Environment by Using Group Policy

Module 1, "Introduction to Administering Accounts and Resources," introduces the Microsoft® Windows Server™ 2003 family of operating systems and the tasks and tools for administering accounts and resources on computers running Windows Server 2003 in a networked environment.

Module 2, "Managing User and Computer Accounts," explains how to create and modify user and computer accounts on computers running Windows Server 2003 in a networked environment.

Module 3, "Managing Groups," explains how to use groups to simplify domain administration.

Module 4, "Managing Access to Resources," explains how permissions enable resource access. You also learn how to use NT file system (NTFS) permissions to manage access to files and folders, use special permissions to manage access to files and folders, and manage permission inheritance.

Module 5, "Managing Access to Objects in Organizational Units," explains the permissions available for managing access to objects in Active Directory® directory service. You also learn how to move objects between organizational units in the same domain and how to delegate control of an organizational unit.

Module 6, "Implementing Group Policy," explains the purpose and function of Group Policy in a Windows Server 2003 environment. It also explains how to implement and manage Group Policy objects (GPOs).

Module 7, "Managing the User Environment by Using Group Policy," explains how to use Group Policy to configure Folder Redirection, Microsoft Internet Explorer connectivity, and the desktop.

Course Outline *(continued)*

- **Module 8: Implementing Administrative Templates and Audit Policy**
- **Module 9: Preparing to Administer a Server**
- **Module 10: Preparing to Monitor Server Performance**
- **Module 11: Managing Data Storage**
- **Module 12: Managing Disaster Recovery**
- **Module 13: Maintaining Software by Using Windows Server Update Services**
- **Module 14: Securing Windows Server 2003**

Module 8, "Implementing Administrative Templates and Audit Policy," explains how to manage security in an Active Directory domain and how to audit events to ensure the effectiveness of a security strategy.

Module 9, "Preparing to Administer a Server," describes the role of a systems administrator in performing server administration locally and remotely; which tools to use; and which permissions are required to administer a server. It also discusses how to administer remote connections and why that is an important aspect of system administration. This module is the foundation for the rest of the course. After completing this module, you will be able to administer a server to manage all the systems administrator tasks that are discussed in the rest of the course.

Module 10, "Preparing to Monitor Server Performance," is the first of two modules that discuss the concept of performance monitoring, performance objects, and counters, and it explains how to create a baseline to compare server performance. After completing this module, you will be able to create a performance baseline.

Module 11, "Managing Data Storage," discusses file and folder compression and describes how to use them to manage the data that is stored on your network storage devices. This module also covers Encrypted File System (EFS), which is a method that helps secure files and folders against intruders to your systems. It also describes disk quotas and explains how a systems administrator implements disk quotas. After completing this module, you will be able to manage data storage.

Module 12, "Managing Disaster Recovery," provides information about disaster recovery methods. This module explains how to use tools to back up and restore data that is critical to your systems and describes the tools that you can use to start a server if it cannot be started normally. After completing this module, you will be able to manage disaster recovery.

Module 13, "Maintaining Software by Using Windows Server Update Services," explains what Windows Server Update Services (WSUS) is, how it works, and how it can help keep networks up-to-date with the latest service packs that are available from Microsoft. After completing this module, you will be able to use WSUS to maintain software.

Module 14, "Securing Windows Server 2003," provides an overview of securing servers, including implementing core server security, hardening servers for various roles, and using Security Configuration Wizard (SCW) and Microsoft Baseline Security Analyzer (MBSA).

Self-Study Modules

> - Self-Study Module A: Implementing Printing
> - Self-Study Module B: Managing Printing
> - Self-Study Module C: Monitoring Server Performance
> - Self-Study Module D: Maintaining Device Drivers
> - Self-Study Module E: Managing Disks

Self-Study Module A, "Implementing Printing," explains how to install, configure, and manage printers.

Self-Study Module B, "Managing Printing," explains how to set up a network-wide printing strategy to meet the needs of users and how to troubleshoot installation or configuration problems.

Self-Study Module C, "Monitoring Server Performance," discusses collecting performance data by monitoring the four primary server subsystems and their effect on server performance. It also covers how to use the Performance console and Task Manager in Windows Server 2003 to identify system bottlenecks by . After completing this module, you will be able to monitor server performance.

Self-Study Module D, "Maintaining Device Drivers," provides information about device drivers and how they are used with the Windows Server 2003 operating system. This module covers in detail the configuration of device drivers and describes how to use device drivers to prevent startup and stop problems. After completing this module, you will be able to maintain device drivers.

Self-Study Module E, "Managing Disks," discusses partitions, describes how to create and use partitions, explains the differences between basic and dynamic disks, and explains how to use each disk type. This module explains how to use Disk Management and a new command line tool, DiskPart, to manage your disks. This module also covers in detail how to manage volumes. After completing this module, you will be able to manage disks.

In addition to the self-study modules, the Student Materials CD also includes the following appendixes located in the Appendix folder.

Appendix A, "Differences Between Microsoft Windows 2000 Server and Microsoft Windows Server 2003," explains the differences between the operating systems in the context of the tasks in each module. This appendix is provided for students who are familiar with Windows® 2000 Server.

Appendix B, "Administering Microsoft Windows Server 2003 by Using Scripts," provides information about using scripts to perform the administration tasks taught in this course.

Appendix C, "Partition Styles," provides information about the way that information about the partition is stored.

Appendix D, "Foreign Disks Volume Status in Disk Management," describes the types of status that an administrator can encounter when working with foreign disks.

Appendix E, "Which Recovery Tool Do I Use?" is a job aid that describes which disaster recovery tools to use in a disaster.

Setup

---

* The virtual environment is configured as one Windows Server 2003 domain: Contoso.msft
* DEN-DC1 is the domain controller
* DEN-SRV1 and DEN-SRV2 are member servers and are used as additional computers in student labs
* DEN-CL1 is a workstation running Windows XP Professional, Service Pack 2
* Server computers are running Windows Server 2003, Enterprise Edition, Service Pack 1

Classroom setup

Each student machine has Windows XP Professional installed and is running Microsoft Virtual PC 2004.

The name of the domain is contoso.msft. The domain is named after Contoso, Ltd., a fictitious company that has offices worldwide.

The domain controller is named DEN-DC1, and there are two member servers, DEN-SRV1 and DEN-SRV2. These computers are running Windows Server 2003 Enterprise Edition with Service Pack 1 (SP1). The workstation computer is named DEN-CL1 and is running Windows XP Professional with Service Pack 2 (SP2).

The domain has been populated with users, groups, and computer accounts for each administrator to manage.

Important   You will be switching virtual machines after Module 8. The new virtual machines will use the same computer names and be configured for the same roles. The virtual machines for the first eight modules are used in Course 2274, while the virtual machines used in the last six modules are used in Course 2275.

Demonstration: Using Microsoft® Virtual PC

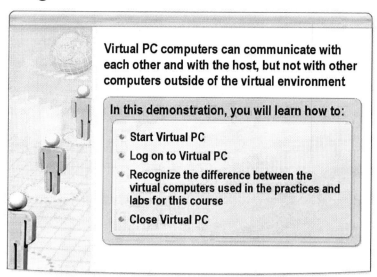

In this demonstration, your instructor will help familiarize you with the Virtual PC environment in which you will work to complete the practices and labs in this course. You will learn:

- How to open Virtual PC.
- How to start Virtual PC.
- How to log on to Virtual PC.
- How to switch between full screen and window modes.
- How to tell the difference between the virtual machines that are used in the practices for this course.
- That the virtual machines can communicate with each other and with the host, but they cannot communicate with other computers that are outside of the virtual environment. (For example, no Internet access is available from the virtual environment.)
- How to close Virtual PC.

Keyboard shortcuts

While working in the Virtual PC environment, you might find it helpful to use keyboard shortcuts. All Virtual PC shortcuts include a key that is referred to as the HOST key or the RIGHT-ALT key. By default, the HOST key is the ALT key on the right side of your keyboard. Some useful shortcuts include:

- ALT+DELETE to log on to the Virtual PC
- ALT+ENTER to switch between full screen mode and window modes
- ALT+RIGHT ARROW to display the next Virtual PC

For more information about Virtual PC, see Virtual PC Help.

Microsoft Learning

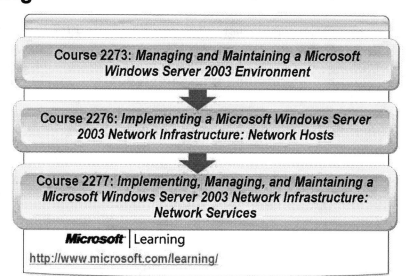

Microsoft Learning develops Official Microsoft Learning Products for computer professionals who design, develop, support, implement, or manage solutions by using Microsoft products and technologies. These learning products provide comprehensive, skills-based training in instructor-led and online formats.

Additional recommended learning products

Each learning product relates in some way to other learning products. A related product might be a prerequisite; a follow-up course, clinic, or workshop in a recommended series, or a learning product that offers additional training.

- Course 2273: *Managing and Maintaining a Microsoft Windows Server 2003 Environment*

- Course 2276: *Implementing a Microsoft Windows Server 2003 Network Infrastructure: Network Hosts*

- Course 2277: *Implementing, Managing, and Maintaining a Microsoft Windows Server 2003 Network Infrastructure: Network Services*

- Course 2278: *Planning and Maintaining a Microsoft Windows Server 2003 Network Infrastructure*

- Course 2279: *Planning, Implementing, and Maintaining a Microsoft Windows Server 2003 Active Directory Infrastructure*

Other related learning products might become available in the future, so for up-to-date information about recommended learning products, visit the Microsoft Learning Web site.

Microsoft Learning information

For more information, visit the Microsoft Learning Web site at http://www.microsoft.com/learning/.

Microsoft Learning Product Types

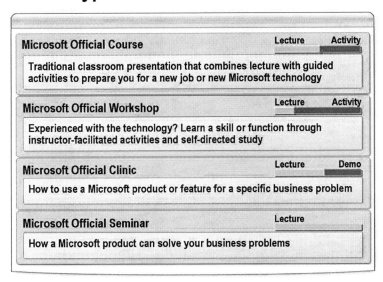

Microsoft Learning offers four types of instructor-led products. Each is specific to a particular audience type and level of experience. The different product types also tend to suit different learning styles. These types are as follows:

- Microsoft Official Courses are for information technology (IT) professionals and developers who are new to a particular product or technology and for experienced individuals who prefer to learn in a traditional classroom format. Courses provide a relevant and guided learning experience that combines lecture and practice to deliver thorough coverage of a Microsoft product or technology. Courses are designed to address the needs of learners engaged in planning, design, implementation, management, and support phases of the technology adoption lifecycle. They provide detailed information by focusing on concepts and principles, reference content, and in-depth hands-on lab activities to ensure knowledge transfer. Typically, the content of a course is broad, addressing a wide range of tasks necessary for the job role.

- Microsoft Official Workshops are for knowledgeable IT professionals and developers who learn best by doing and exploring. Workshops provide a hands-on learning experience in which participants use Microsoft products in a safe and collaborative environment based on real-world scenarios. Workshops are the learning products where students learn by doing through scenario and through troubleshooting hands-on labs, targeted reviews, information resources, and best practices, with instructor facilitation.

- Microsoft Official Clinics are for IT professionals, developers and technical decision makers. Clinics offer a detailed "how to" presentation that describes the features and functionality of an existing or new Microsoft product or technology, and that showcases product demonstrations and solutions. Clinics focus on how specific features will solve business problems.

- Microsoft Official Seminars are for business decision makers. Through featured business scenarios, case studies, and success stories, seminars provide a dynamic presentation of early and relevant information on Microsoft products and technology solutions that enable decision makers to make critical business decisions. Microsoft Official Seminars are concise, engaging, direct-from-the-source learning products that show how emerging Microsoft products and technologies help our customers serve their customers.

Microsoft Certified Professional Program

Exam number and title	Core exam for the following track	Elective exam for the following track
70-290: *Managing and Maintaining a Microsoft Windows Server 2003 Environment*	MCSA	n/a

Microsoft
C E R T I F I E D
Professional
http://www.microsoft.com/learning/

Microsoft Learning offers a variety of certification credentials for developers and IT professionals. The Microsoft Certified Professional (MCP) program is the leading certification program for validating your experience and skills, keeping you competitive in today's changing business environment.

Related certification exams

This course helps students to prepare for Exam 70-290: *Managing and Maintaining a Microsoft Windows Server 2003 Environment*. To prepare for the exam, you should complete both courses.

Exam 70-290 is a core exam for the Microsoft Certified Systems Administrator (MCSA) certification.

MCP certifications

The MCP program includes the following certifications:

■ MCDST on Microsoft Windows XP

The Microsoft Certified Desktop Support Technician (MCDST) certification is designed for professionals who successfully support and educate end users and troubleshoot operating system and application issues on desktop computers running the Windows operating system.

■ MCSA on Microsoft Windows Server 2003

The Microsoft Certified Systems Administrator (MCSA) certification is designed for professionals who implement, manage, and troubleshoot existing network and system environments based on the Windows Server 2003 platform. Implementation responsibilities include installing and configuring parts of systems. Management responsibilities include administering and supporting systems.

■ MCSE on Windows Server 2003

The Microsoft Certified Systems Engineer (MCSE) credential is the premier certification for professionals who analyze business requirements and design and implement infrastructure for business solutions based on the Windows Server 2003 platform. Implementation responsibilities include installing, configuring, and troubleshooting network systems.

- MCAD

  The Microsoft Certified Application Developer (MCAD) for Microsoft .NET credential is appropriate for professionals who use Microsoft technologies to develop and maintain department-level applications, components, Web or desktop clients, or back-end data services, or who work in teams developing enterprise applications. The credential covers job tasks ranging from developing to deploying and maintaining these solutions.

- MCSD

  The Microsoft Certified Solution Developer (MCSD) credential is the premier certification for professionals who design and develop leading-edge business solutions with Microsoft development tools, technologies, platforms, and the Microsoft Windows DNA architecture. The types of applications MCSDs can develop include desktop applications and multi-user, Web-based, N-tier, and transaction-based applications. The credential covers job tasks ranging from analyzing business requirements to maintaining solutions.

- MCDBA on Microsoft SQL Server™ 2000

  The Microsoft Certified Database Administrator (MCDBA) credential is the premier certification for professionals who implement and administer SQL Server databases. The certification is appropriate for individuals who derive physical database designs, develop logical data models, create physical databases, use Transact-SQL to create data services, manage and maintain databases, configure and manage security, monitor and optimize databases, and install and configure SQL Server.

- MCP

  The Microsoft Certified Professional (MCP) credential is for individuals who have the skills to successfully implement a Microsoft product or technology as part of a business solution in an organization. Hands-on experience with the product is necessary to successfully achieve certification.

- MCT

  Microsoft Certified Trainers (MCTs) demonstrate the instructional and technical skills that qualify them to deliver Official Microsoft Learning Products through a Microsoft Certified Partner for Learning Solutions (CPLS).

Certification requirements

Requirements differ for each certification category and are specific to the products and job functions addressed by the certification. To become a Microsoft Certified Professional, you must pass rigorous certification exams that provide a valid and reliable measure of technical proficiency and expertise.

For More Information   See the Microsoft Learning Web site at http://www.microsoft.com/learning/.

You can also send e-mail to mcphelp@microsoft.com if you have specific certification questions.

Acquiring the skills tested by an MCP exam

Official Microsoft Learning Products can help you develop the skills that you need to do your job. They also complement the experience that you gain while working with Microsoft products and technologies. However, no one-to-one correlation exists between Official Microsoft Learning Products and MCP exams. Microsoft does not expect or intend for the courses to be the sole preparation method for passing MCP exams. Practical product knowledge and experience is also necessary to pass MCP exams.

To help prepare for MCP exams, use the preparation guides are available for each exam. Each Exam Preparation Guide contains exam-specific information such as a list of topics on which you will be tested. These guides are available on the Microsoft Learning Web site at http://www.microsoft.com/learning/.

Multimedia: Job Roles in Today's Information Systems Environment

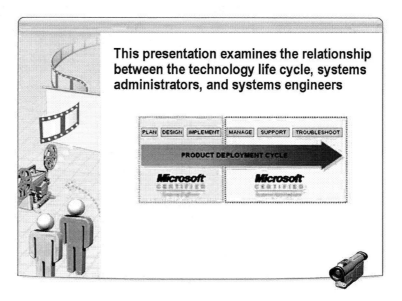

File location

To view the *Job Roles in Today's Information Systems Environment* presentation, open the Web page on the Student Materials compact disc, click **Multimedia**, and then click the title of the presentation. Do not open this presentation unless your instructor tells you to.

Facilities

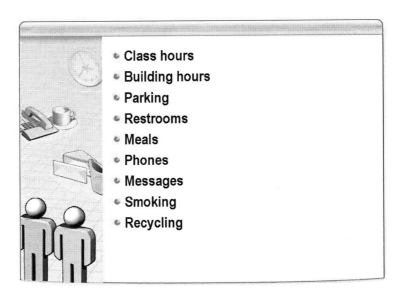

- Class hours
- Building hours
- Parking
- Restrooms
- Meals
- Phones
- Messages
- Smoking
- Recycling

Microsoft®

Module 1: Introduction to Administering Accounts and Resources

Contents

Overview

- **Multimedia: Introduction to Managing a Microsoft Windows Server 2003 Environment**
- **The Windows Server 2003 Environment**
- **Logging On to Windows Server 2003**
- **Using the Run As Feature for Administration**
- **Installing and Configuring Administrative Tools**
- **Creating an Organizational Unit**

Introduction

In this module, you will learn the skills that you need to administer accounts and resources on computers running Microsoft® Windows Server™ 2003 software in a networked environment. These lessons provide information and procedures that you will use throughout the course.

Objectives

After completing this module, you will be able to:

- Describe the Windows Server 2003 environment.
- Log on to a computer running Windows Server 2003.
- Use the **Run as** feature to perform administrative tasks.
- Install and configure the administrative tools.
- Create an organizational unit.

Multimedia: Introduction to Managing a Microsoft Windows Server 2003 Environment

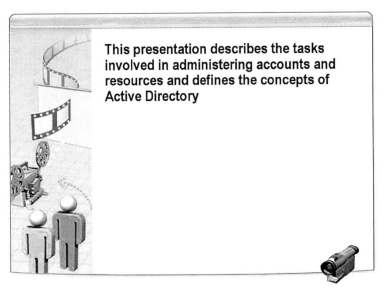

Introduction

In this presentation, you are introduced to the tasks involved in administering accounts and resources in a Windows Server 2003 environment. The tasks and concepts in this presentation are explained in more detail throughout the course.

File location

To view the *Introduction to Managing a Microsoft Windows Server 2003 Environment* presentation, open the Web page on the Student Materials compact disc, click **Multimedia**, and then click the title of the presentation. Do not open this presentation unless the instructor tells you to.

Objective

After completing this lesson, you will be able to describe some common tasks for administering accounts and resources.

Lesson: The Windows Server 2003 Environment

* Computer Roles
* The Windows Server 2003 Family
* What Is a Directory Service?
* Active Directory Terms
* Classroom Setup Review

Introduction

To manage a Windows Server 2003 environment, you must understand which operating system edition is appropriate for different computer roles. You must also understand the purpose of a directory service and how Active Directory® directory service provides a structure for the Windows Server 2003 environment.

Lesson objectives

After completing this lesson, you will be able to:

- Describe the different computer roles in a Windows Server 2003 environment.

- Describe the uses of the different editions of Windows Server 2003.

- Explain the purpose of a directory service.

- Differentiate between the components of an Active Directory structure.

Computer Roles

Introduction

Servers play many roles in the client/server networking environment. Some servers are configured to provide authentication, and others are configured to run applications. Some provide network services that enable users to communicate with other servers and resources in the network. As a systems administrator, you are expected to know the primary types of servers and what functions they perform in your network.

Domain controller (Active Directory)

Domain controllers store directory data and manage communication between users and domains, including user logon processes, authentication, and directory searches. When you install Active Directory on a computer running Windows Server 2003, the computer becomes a domain controller.

> **Note** In a Windows Server 2003 network, all servers in the domain that are not domain controllers are called *member servers*. Servers not associated with a domain are called *workgroup servers*.

File server

A file server provides a central location on your network where you can store and share files with users across your network. When users require an important file such as a project plan, they can access the file on the file server instead of passing the file between their separate computers.

Print server

A print server provides a central location on your network where users can print documents. The print server provides clients with updated printer drivers and handles all print queuing and security.

DNS server

Domain Name System (DNS) is an Internet and TCP/IP standard name service. The DNS service enables client computers on your network to register and resolve DNS domain names. A computer configured to provide DNS services on a network is a DNS server. You must have a DNS server on your network to implement Active Directory.

Application server

An application server provides key infrastructure and services to applications hosted on a system. Typical application servers include the following services:

- Resource pooling (for example, database connection pooling and object pooling)
- Distributed transaction management
- Asynchronous program communication, typically through message queuing
- A just-in-time object activation model
- Automatic Extensible Markup Language (XML) Web Service interfaces to access business objects
- Failover and application health detection services
- Integrated security

Microsoft Internet Information Services (IIS) provides the tools and features necessary to easily manage a secure Web server. If you plan to host Web and File Transfer Protocol (FTP) sites with IIS, configure the server as an application server.

Terminal server

A terminal server provides access to Microsoft Windows®–based programs to remote computers running Windows Server 2003, Standard Edition; Windows Server 2003, Enterprise Edition; or Windows Server 2003, Datacenter Edition. With a terminal server, you install an application at a single point on a single server. Multiple users can then access the application without installing it on their computers. Users can run programs, save files, and use network resources all from a remote location, as if these resources were installed on their own computer.

The Manage Your Server tool

When Windows Server 2003 is installed and a user logs on for the first time, the Manage Your Server tool starts automatically. You use this tool to add or remove server roles. When you add a server role to the computer, the Manage Your Server tool adds this server role to the list of available, configured server roles. After the server role is added to the list, you can use various wizards that help you to manage the specific server role. The Manage Your Server tool also provides Help files specific to the server role that provide checklists and troubleshooting recommendations.

The Windows Server 2003 Family

Windows Server 2003 Edition	Usage Scenario	Sample Roles			
		Web server	File and infrastructure server	Domain controller	Scalable, business-critical applications
Web	Application server	✓			
Small Business Server	Small business with one server	✓	✓	✓	
Standard	Small business or department	✓	✓	✓	
Enterprise	Medium or large organizations	✓	✓	✓	✓
Datacenter	Large organizations	✓	✓	✓	✓

Microsoft **Windows Server System**

Introduction

Windows Server 2003 is available in five editions. Each edition is developed to be used in a specific server role. This enables you to select the operating system edition that provides only the functions and capabilities that your server needs.

Web Edition

Windows Server 2003, Web Edition, is designed to be used specifically as a Web server. It is available only through selected partner channels and is not available for retail. Although computers running Windows Server 2003, Web Edition, can be members of an Active Directory domain, you cannot run Active Directory on Windows Server 2003, Web Edition.

Small Business Server Edition

Windows Server 2003, Small Business Server Edition, delivers a complete business server solution for small businesses with up to 75 workstations and is available in two editions: Standard and Premium. Windows Small Business Server 2003 provides technologies and tools, including e-mail, shared documents and calendars, security-enhanced Internet access and data storage, reliable printing and faxing, and remote administration on a single server.

Standard Edition

Windows Server 2003, Standard Edition, is a reliable network operating system that delivers business solutions quickly and easily. This flexible server is the ideal choice for small businesses and departmental use. Use Windows Server 2003, Standard Edition, when your server does not require the increased hardware support and clustering features of Windows Server 2003, Enterprise Edition.

Enterprise Edition

Windows Server 2003, Enterprise Edition, has all the features in Windows Server 2003, Standard Edition. It also provides features not included in Standard Edition that enhance availability, scalability, and dependability.

Windows Server 2003, Enterprise Edition, is designed for medium to large businesses. It is the recommended operating system for applications, XML Web services, and infrastructure, because it offers high reliability, performance, and superior business value.

The major difference between Windows Server 2003, Enterprise Edition, and Windows Server 2003, Standard Edition, is that Enterprise Edition supports high-performance servers. Windows Server 2003, Enterprise Edition, is recommended for servers running applications for networking, messaging, inventory and customer service systems, databases, and e-commerce Web sites. Also, you can cluster servers running Enterprise Edition to handle larger loads.

Datacenter Edition

Windows Server 2003, Datacenter Edition, is designed for business-critical and mission-critical applications that demand the highest levels of scalability and availability.

The major difference between Windows Server 2003, Datacenter Edition, and Windows Server 2003, Enterprise Edition, is that Datacenter Edition supports more powerful multiprocessing and greater memory. In addition, Windows Server 2003, Datacenter Edition, is available only through the Windows Datacenter Program offered to Original Equipment Manufacturers (OEMs).

Additional reading

For detailed information about each edition's capabilities, see the Windows Server 2003 Product Overviews page on the Microsoft Web site.

What Is a Directory Service?

Identifies resources

Provides a consistent way to:

- Name
- Describe
- Locate
- Access
- Manage
- Secure

Active Directory Benefits
- DNS integration
- Scalability
- Centralized management
- Delegated administration

Introduction

As a user logged on to a network, you might need to connect to a shared folder or send a print job to a printer on the network. How do you find that folder and printer and other network resources?

Definition

A directory service is a network service that identifies all resources on a network and makes that information available to users and applications. Directory services are important, because they provide a consistent way to name, describe, locate, access, manage, and secure information about these resources.

When a user searches for a shared folder on the network, it is the directory service that identifies the resource and provides that information to the user.

Active Directory

Active Directory is the directory service in the Windows Server 2003 family. It extends the basic functionality of a directory service to provide the following benefits:

- Domain Name System integration

  Active Directory uses DNS naming conventions to create a hierarchical structure that provides a familiar, orderly, and scalable view of network relationships. DNS also functions to map host names, such as www.microsoft.com, to numeric TCP/IP addresses, such as 192.168.19.2.

- Scalability

  Active Directory is organized into sections that can store a large number of objects. As a result, Active Directory can expand as an organization grows. An organization that has a single server with a few hundred objects can grow to thousands of servers and millions of objects.

- Centralized management

  Active Directory enables administrators to manage distributed desktops, network services, and applications from a central location, while using a consistent management interface. Active Directory also provides centralized control of access to network resources by enabling users to log on only once to gain full access to resources throughout Active Directory.

- Delegated administration

  The hierarchical structure of Active Directory enables administrative control to be delegated for specific segments of the hierarchy. A user authorized by a higher administrative authority can perform administrative duties in their designated portion of the structure. For example, users might have limited administrative control over their workstation's settings, and a department manager might have the administrative rights to create new users in an organizational unit.

Additional reading

For more information about Active Directory, see *White Paper: Technical Overview of Windows Server 2003 Active Directory* at the Microsoft Web site.

Active Directory Terms

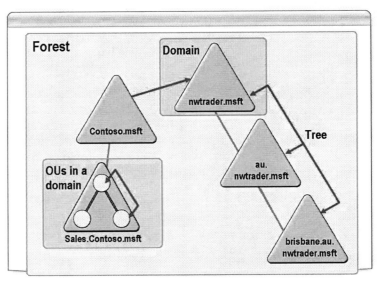

Introduction

The logical structure of Active Directory is flexible and provides a method for designing a hierarchy within Active Directory that is comprehensible to both users and administrators.

Logical components

The logical components of the Active Directory structure include the following:

- *Domain.* The core unit of the logical structure in Active Directory is the domain. A domain is a collection of security principals such as user and computer accounts and other objects like printers and shared folders. The domain objects are defined by an administrator and share a common directory database and a unique name.

- *Organizational unit.* An organizational unit is a type of container object that you use to organize objects within a domain. An organizational unit might contain objects such as user accounts, groups, computers, printers, and other organizational units.

- *Forest.* A forest is one or more domains that share a common configuration, schema, and global catalog.

- *Tree.* A tree consists of domains in a forest that share a contiguous DNS namespace and have a two-way transitive trust relationship between parent and child domains.

Classroom Setup Review

* **The virtual environment is configured as one Windows Server 2003 domain: Contoso.msft**
* **Den-DC1 is the domain controller**
* **Den-SRV1 is a member server and is used as a remote computer for student labs**
* **Den-CL1 is a workstation running Windows XP Professional, Service Pack 2**
* **Server computers are running Windows Server 2003, Enterprise Edition, Service Pack 1**

Introduction

Now that you have been introduced to the basic components of an Active Directory structure, you have a better understanding of the setup of the classroom.

Classroom setup

Each student machine has Microsoft Windows XP Professional installed and is running Microsoft Virtual PC 2004.

The name of the domain is contoso.msft. The domain is named after Contoso, Ltd., a fictitious company that has offices worldwide.

The domain controller is named DEN-DC1, and there is a member server, named DEN-SRV1. Both computers are running Windows Server 2003 Enterprise Edition with Service Pack 1. The workstation computer is named DEN-CL1 and is running Windows XP Professional with Service Pack 2.

The domain has been populated with users, groups, and computer accounts for each administrator to manage.

Lesson: Logging On to Windows Server 2003

* Multimedia: Logon and Authentication
* Logon Dialog Box Options
* What Are User Principal Names?
* Practice: Logging On to Windows Server 2003

Introduction

Windows Server 2003 authenticates a user during the logon process to verify the identity of the user. This mandatory process ensures that only valid users can access resources and data on a computer or the network.

Lesson objectives

After completing this lesson, you will be able to:

- Explain the difference between a local and a domain logon.
- Identify logon dialog box options.
- Describe the function of the user principal name.
- Log on to a local computer and a domain.

Multimedia: Logon and Authentication

* **This activity presents information about:**
  * Local logon process
  * Domain logon process
  * Secondary logon process
  * Smart card logon process
* **Important points to look for:**
  * Difference between local and domain authentication
  * How to perform a secondary logon
  * Contents of an access token

File location

To start the *Logon and Authentication* activity, open the Web page on the Student Materials compact disc, click **Multimedia**, and then click the title of the activity.

Logon Dialog Box Options

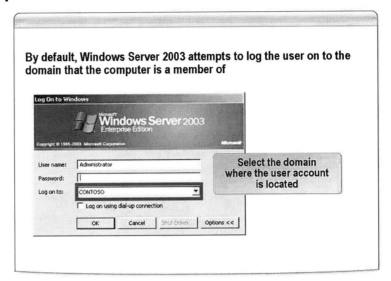

By default, Windows Server 2003 attempts to log the user on to the domain that the computer is a member of

Select the domain where the user account is located

Introduction

The Windows Server 2003 logon dialog box provides an **Options** button for users that are logging on. Clicking the **Options** button displays the **Log on to** dialog box. The **Log on to** list includes the names of all trusted domains and the local machine. The user then has the option of logging on to the local machine by using a local user account or logging on to the domain where that user's account is located. By default, Windows Server 2003 does not show the **Log on to** dialog box at the initial logon but will remember the status of the **Log on to** dialog box from the last logon for subsequent logons.

The logon dialog box

The following table describes all the options in the logon dialog box.

Option	Description
User name	A unique user logon name that is assigned by an administrator. To log on to a domain, this user account must reside in the directory database in Active Directory.
Password	The password that is assigned to the user account. Users must enter a password to prove their identity.
	Passwords are case sensitive. The password appears on the screen as dots (●) to protect it from onlookers. To prevent unauthorized access to resources and data, users must keep passwords secret.

(*continued*)

Option	Description
Log on to	Specifies whether a user logs on to a domain or logs on locally. The user can choose one of the following: • **Domain name**: The user must select the domain that that user's account is in. This list contains all of the domains available in the forest and through trust relationships. • **Computer name**: The name of the computer that the user is logging on to. The user must have a local user account on the computer. The option to log on locally is not available on a domain controller.
Log on using dial-up connection	Permits a user to connect to a server in the domain by using a dial-up network connection. Dial-up networking enables a user to log on and perform work from a remote location.
Shut Down	Closes all files, saves all operating system data, and prepares the computer so that a user can safely turn it off. On a computer running Windows Server 2003, the **Shut Down** button is disabled. This prevents an unauthorized user from using this dialog box to shut down the server. To shut down a server, a user must be able to log on to it.
Options	Switches between the two versions of the **Enter Password** dialog box. One of these two dialog boxes provides the **Log on to** option, which enables the user to select a domain or the local computer.

What Are User Principal Names?

* Provides an alternative logon method
* Is unique within the forest

Example: don@contoso.msft

Introduction

Users can log on to a Windows 2003 domain using two different logon names. For example, you can use your user logon name—for example, **don**—or your User Principal Name (UPN)—for example, Don@Contoso.msft.

Alternative logon

The UPN consists of a logon name and the UPN suffix that must be appended to the name (the text following the @ symbol).

By default, the user has a UPN suffix of @domain_name. When an account is created, it can be assigned a UPN suffix other than the domain name to simplify logon. For example, the user Joe in the Northwest.America.Contoso.msft domain might prefer to use a UPN of **Joe@contoso.msft**.

Why use User Principal Names?

In a multiple-domain environment, users must supply the domain name to log on—for example, **Contoso\Don**. A UPN already includes the domain name, making logon easier. In many cases, the UPN will be the same as the user's e-mail address so that users do not have to remember one name to log on to the network and a different name for e-mail.

Unique within the forest

The UPN must be unique within the forest. A global catalog resolves the UPN if the authentication domain controller does not have knowledge of the account. This happens when a mobile user is logging on to a computer in an office that uses a different domain in the same forest. For the logon to be successful, a global catalog server must be available for the UPN logon to succeed.

Practice: Logging On to Windows Server 2003

In this practice, you will:

* Log on to your workstation by using a local account

* Attempt to access a network share by using a local account

* Log on to your workstation by using a domain account

* Attempt to access a network share by using a domain account

Objective

In this practice you will:

- Log on to your workstation by using a local account.
- Attempt to access a network share by using a local account.
- Log on to your workstation by using a domain account.
- Attempt to access a network share by using a domain account.

Instructions

Ensure that the DEN-DC1 and DEN-CL1 virtual machines are running.

Practice

▶ **Log on to your workstation by using a local account**

1. Make sure that the DEN-CL1 virtual machine is the active window. Press RIGHT ALT+DEL.

2. In the **Log on to Windows** dialog box, in the **User name** text box, type **Paul**.

3. In the **Password** box, type **Pa$$w0rd** (the 0 is a zero).

4. In the **Log on to** box, select **DEN-CL1 (this computer)**, and then click **OK**.

▶ **Attempt to access a network share by using a local account**

1. Click **Start** and then click **Run**.

2. In the **Run** dialog box, type **\\den-dc1\sales_data** and then click **OK**. You should see a logon dialog box asking you to provide credentials to access the domain resource.

3. Provide the credentials of Don Hall, a valid domain user, in the form **contoso\don**. In the **Password** box, type **Pa$$w0rd**. You should see the contents of the shared folder displayed.

4. Close all windows and log off the local computer.

▶ **Log on to your workstation by using a domain account**

1. Press RIGHT ALT+DEL.

2. In the **Log On to Windows** dialog box, in the **User name** box, type **don**.

3. In the **Password** box, type **Pa$$w0rd**.

4. In the **Log on to** box, verify that the **CONTOSO** domain name is displayed, and then click **OK**.

▶ **Attempt to access a network share** by **using a domain account**

1. Click **Start** and then click **Run**.

2. In the **Run** dialog box, type **\\den-dc1\sales_data** to attempt to connect. You should see the contents of the shared folder displayed.

3. Close all windows and log off the domain.

Important   Do not shut down the virtual machines.

Lesson: Using the Run As Feature for Administration

* What Is the Run As Feature?
* Using the Run As Feature

Introduction

In an Active Directory environment, users should not be logged on to workstations with administrative credentials. Instead, users should be logged on with a nonadministrative account and perform administrative tasks using the **Run as** feature. In this lesson, you will learn the function and use of the **Run as** feature.

Lesson objectives

After completing this lesson, you will be able to:

- Describe the function of the **Run as** feature.
- Use the **Run as** feature for administrative tasks.

What Is the Run As Feature?

* Allows a user to run specific tools and programs at any workstation with different permissions than the user's current logon provides
* Can be used in troubleshooting scenarios to perform administrative tasks at the client's workstation without logging off the current user

Introduction

It is a security best practice for administrators to perform routine, nonadministrative tasks using an account with only those permissions that are required to accomplish those tasks. In this way, administrators can reserve the use of accounts with administrative permissions to perform tasks that require administrative privileges. You could accomplish this temporary elevation of privileges by logging off the user account and then logging back on using the administrative account. You can also remain logged on to the user account and then use the **runas** command. This command allows you to exercise privileges associated with an account that is different from the account you are currently logged in as. The **runas** command provides a quick and secure way to run the tools that require the administrative permissions from an account with a reduced set of privileges.

When to use the Run as feature

The use of the **Run as** feature is not restricted to administrator accounts, although that is the most common use. Any user with knowledge of alternative credentials can use the **runas** command to run a program, an MMC console, or a Control Panel item using those credentials. For example, help desk personnel might use the feature to troubleshoot client issues without having to log off the client.

With the **runas** command, you can run programs (.exe), saved MMC consoles (.msc), shortcuts to programs and saved MMC consoles, and Control Panel items. You can run them as an administrator while you are logged on to your computer as a member of another group, such as the Users or Power Users group.

You can use the **runas** command if you provide the appropriate user account and password information and that user account has the ability to log on to the computer, and if the program, MMC console, or Control Panel item is available on the system and to the user account.

Important   Not every administrative task can be accomplished by using the **runas** command. For example, property dialog boxes such as network adapter TCP/IP properties or the Printers folder cannot be accessed as a different user.

Using the Run As Feature

* The Run as feature can be invoked from a shortcut menu
* A desktop shortcut can be configured to use the Run as feature
* The Run as feature can be used from the command line

```
runas /user:domain\domainadmin "mmc %windir%\system32\compmgmt.msc"
```

Introduction

The **Run as** feature can be employed by using various methods. It can be used from the shortcut menu of an executable or MMC. It can be configured as a parameter of a desktop shortcut, or it can be invoked from the command line.

Using Run as from a shortcut menu

To start a program as an administrator from a shortcut menu:

1. From the program's executable or a **Start** menu item, right-click the program icon, and then click **Run as**.

2. In the **Run as** dialog box, type the administrator account name and password that you want to use.

Configuring a desktop shortcut

To configure a desktop shortcut to always use the **Run as** feature:

1. Create a new shortcut that points to the executable.

2. Open the property sheet for the shortcut, and then click the **Shortcut** tab.

3. Click the **Advanced** tab, and then select the **Run with different credentials** check box.

Using the command line

To use the command line to invoke the **Run as** feature, open a command prompt window and use the following syntax:

runas [{*/profile*|*/noprofile* [*/smartcard*] */user*:UserAccountName program

The following table defines the **runas** command-line parameters.

Parameter	Description
/profile or */noprofile*	Specifies whether or not the user profile should be loaded. The default is **/profile**.
/smartcard	Use if credentials are being supplied by a smartcard.
/user	The name of the user whose credentials will be used by the **runas** command. The user name should be in the form *user@domain* or *domain\user*.
program	The path to the executable program that will be started by the **runas** command.

For a complete list of available options, type **runas /?** at a command prompt. For example, to run the Computer Management console as the domain administrator in the Contoso domain, the command would be:

runas /user: Contoso\administrator "mmc %windir%\system32\compmgmt.msc"

Lesson: Installing and Configuring Administrative Tools

* What Are Administrative Tools?
* What Is MMC?
* Practice: Configuring the Administrative Tools
* Guidelines for Resolving Problems with Installing and Configuring Administrative Tools

Introduction

In this lesson, you will learn how to install and configure administrative tools. This lesson also introduces the different types of user accounts and shows how to create them.

Lesson objectives

After completing this lesson, you will be able to:

- Describe the administrative tools.
- Describe the Microsoft Management Console (MMC).
- Configure the administrative tools.
- Resolve problems with installing and configuring administrative tools.

What Are Administrative Tools?

> ● **Commonly used administrative tools:**
>   ● Active Directory Users and Computers
>   ● Active Directory Sites and Services
>   ● Active Directory Domains and Trusts
>   ● Computer Management
>   ● DNS
>   ● Remote Desktops
> ● **Install to perform remote administration**

Introduction

Administrative tools enable network administrators to add, search, and change computer and network settings and Active Directory objects. You can install the administrative tools for managing a Windows Server 2003 environment on computers running Microsoft Windows XP Professional and Windows Server 2003 to remotely administer Active Directory and network settings.

Administrative tools

Some of the more commonly used tools include the following:

- Active Directory Users and Computers

- Active Directory Sites and Services

- Active Directory Domains and Trusts

- Computer Management

- DNS

- Remote Desktops

Installing administrative tools

You must install administrative tools on the computer running Windows XP Professional when you want to remotely manage network resources such as Active Directory or network services such as Windows Internet Name Service (WINS) or Dynamic Host Configuration Protocol (DHCP) from a workstation. If you want to install the administrative tools on a computer running Windows XP Professional, Service Pack 1 or a hotfix from Microsoft Knowledge Base article 329357 must be installed.

> **Tip** Administrative tools are not displayed by default on the **Start** menu on a computer running Windows XP Professional. You can customize the **Start Menu** advanced properties to display them.

Windows Server 2003 includes all the administrative tools as snap-ins that can be added to a custom MMC. This includes all the tools for managing Active Directory but does not include management tools for services that are not installed on the server, such as WINS or DHCP. If you must remotely manage a network service from a computer running Windows Server 2003 and the service is not installed on the computer, you must install the administrative tools.

To install the Windows Server 2003 Administration Tools Pack on a computer running Windows XP Professional, you must have administrative permissions on the local computer. If the computer is joined to a domain, members of the Domain Administrator group are able to perform this procedure. You must have access to the adminpak.msi file. This file is available on the Windows Server 2003 compact disc and in the %windir%/systerm32 folder on any computer running Windows Server 2003.

Note   As a security best practice, do not install Windows Server 2003 Administration Tools Pack if someone who is not an administrator is going to use the computer running Windows XP Professional.

What Is MMC?

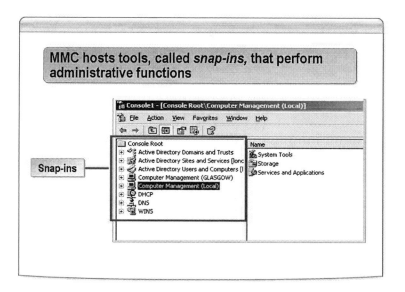

Definition

You use Microsoft Management Console (MMC) to create, save, and open administrative tools, called consoles, which manage the hardware, software, and network components of your Microsoft Windows operating system. MMC runs on all client operating systems that are currently supported.

Creating a custom MMC

You can use MMC to create custom tools and distribute these tools to users. With both Windows XP Professional and Windows Server 2003, you can save these tools so that they are available in the **Administrative Tools** folder. To create a custom MMC, you will use the **runas** command.

What are snap-ins?

A snap-in is a tool that is hosted in MMC. MMC offers a common framework in which various snap-ins can run so that you can manage several services by using a single interface. MMC also enables you to customize the console. By picking and choosing specific snap-ins, you can create management consoles that include only the administrative tools that you need. For example, you can add tools to manage your local computer and remote computers.

Additional reading

For more information about MMC, see *Step-by-Step Guide to the Microsoft Management Console* at the Microsoft Web site.

Practice: Configuring the Administrative Tools

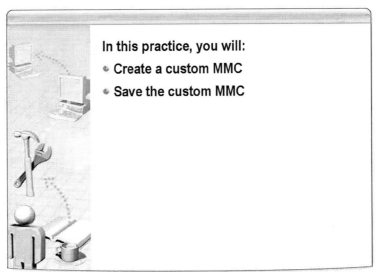

Objective

In this practice, you will:

- Create a custom MMC.
- Save the custom MMC.

Note   This practice focuses on the concepts in this lesson and as a result might not comply with Microsoft security recommendations. For example, this practice does not comply with the recommendation that users log on with a nonadministrative account and use the **runas** command when performing administrative tasks.

Instructions

Ensure that the DEN-DC1 and DEN-CL1 virtual machines are running.

Practice

▶ **Create a custom MMC**

1. Log on to DEN-DC1 as the **Administrator** with the password **Pa$$w0rd**.
2. Click **Start**, click **Run**.
3. In the **Run** dialog box, type **MMC** and then click **OK**.
4. In the Console1 window, click the **File** menu, and then click **Add/Remove Snap-in**.
5. In the **Add/Remove Snap-in** dialog box, click **Add**.
6. In the **Add Standalone Snap-in** dialog box, double-click the items to add as follows.
   a. Add the **Computer Management** snap-in. Ensure that **Local computer** radio button is selected.
   b. Add the **Computer Management** snap-in again and select the **Another computer** radio button, and type **DEN-CL1**.
   c. Add the **Active Directory Users and Computers** snap-in.

7. In the **Add Standalone Snap-in** dialog box, click **Close**.

8. Click **OK**.

▶ **Save the custom MMC**

1. Click the **File** menu and then click **Save As**.

2. Save the MMC on the desktop as **CustomMMC.msc**.

3. Close all open windows.

Important   Do not shut down the virtual machines.

Guidelines for Resolving Problems with Installing and Configuring Administrative Tools

Symptom	Cause	Resolution
Cannot install the administrative tools	Insufficient permissions	You must have administrative permissions on the local computer
	Incorrect operating system	You can install the Windows Server 2003 Administration Tools Pack only on supported operating systems
Broken links in Help files	Both server and client Help systems are required	You can install the Help files for Windows Server 2003 Administration Tools Pack

Introduction

Two common problems that you might encounter when installing and configuring administrative tools are that you cannot install the administrative tools properly and that the Help files contain broken links.

Cannot install

If you have problems installing or configuring administrative tools in Windows Server 2003, verify that you have administrative permissions on the local computer.

Another reason you might not be able to install the administrative tools is that the incorrect operating system is installed. You can install the Windows Server 2003 Administration Tools Pack only on computers running Windows XP Professional or Windows Server 2003.

Broken Help links

When the Windows Server 2003 Administration Tools Pack is installed on a computer running Windows XP Professional, some Help links might appear to be broken. This happens because you must have both server and client Help files for the Windows Server 2003 Administration Tools Pack on Windows XP Professional.

To resolve the problem, you must integrate the server and client Help files for the Windows Server 2003 Administration Tools Pack by installing the server Help files on Windows XP Professional. This is fairly easy to do and should be done after the Windows Server 2003 Administration Tools Pack is installed on Windows XP Professional.

Install Help files

To install Help files from another computer running Windows, or from a CD or disk image:

1. On the **Start** menu, click **Help and Support**.

2. In the **Help and Support Center** window, on the navigation bar, click **Options**.

3. In the left pane, click **Install and share Windows Help**.

4. In the right pane, depending where you want to install Help from, click the link **Install Help content from another Windows computer** or **Install Help content from a CD or disk image**.

5. Type the location of the computer, CD, or disk image, and then click **Find**.

   If you are installing from a CD or disk image, you can click **Browse** to locate the disk containing Help files.

6. When the available Help files appear, click the version of Help that you want, and then click **Install**.

   When the installation is complete, you can switch to the new Help files.

Lesson: Creating an Organizational Unit

- Multimedia: The Organizational Unit Structure
- What Is an Organizational Unit?
- Organizational Unit Hierarchical Models
- Names Associated with Organizational Units
- Practice: Creating an Organizational Unit

Introduction

In this lesson, you will learn how to create an organizational unit.

Lesson objectives

After completing this lesson, you will be able to create an organizational unit, including:

- Describe the organizational unit structure.
- Explain the purpose of an organizational unit.
- Describe organizational unit hierarchical models.
- Identify the names associated with organizational units.
- Create an organizational unit.

Multimedia: The Organizational Unit Structure

File location

To view this presentation, open the Web page on the Student Materials compact disc, click **Multimedia**, and then click the title of the presentation. Do not open this presentation until the instructor tells you to.

What Is an Organizational Unit?

* Organizes objects in a domain
* Allows you to delegate administrative control
* Simplifies the management of commonly grouped resources

Definition

An organizational unit is a particularly useful type of Active Directory object contained in a domain. You can use organizational units to organize hundreds of thousands of objects in the directory into manageable units. You use an organizational unit to group and organize objects for administrative purposes, such as delegating administrative rights and assigning policies to a collection of objects as a single unit.

Benefits of using organizational units

You can use organizational units to:

- Organize objects in a domain.

    Organizational units contain domain objects, such as user and computer accounts and groups. File and printer shares that are published to Active Directory are also found in organizational units.

- Delegate administrative control.

    You can assign either complete administrative control, such as the Full Control permission, over all objects in the organizational unit, or limited administrative control, such as the ability to modify e-mail information, over user objects in the organizational unit. To delegate administrative control, you assign specific permissions on the organizational unit and the objects that the organizational unit contains for one or more users and groups.

- Simplify the management of commonly grouped resources.

    Using organizational units, you can create containers in a domain that represent the hierarchical or logical structures in your organization. You can then use Group Policy settings to manage the configuration of user and computer settings based on your organizational model.

Organizational Unit Hierarchical Models

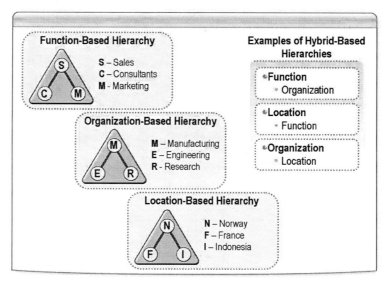

Introduction

As a systems administrator, you do not select the design of the Active Directory structure for your organization. However, it is important to know the characteristics and ramifications of each structure. This knowledge might be critical to you when performing systems administrator tasks within the Active Directory structure. This topic describes the four basic hierarchy designs.

Function-based hierarchy

The function-based hierarchy is based on only the business functions of the organization, without regard to geographical location or departmental or divisional barriers. This approach is chosen only if the IT function is not based on location or organization.

When deciding whether to organize the Active Directory structure by function, consider the following characteristics of function-based designs:

- *Not affected by reorganizations.* A function-based hierarchy is not affected by corporate or organizational reorganizations.

- *Might require additional layers.* When using this structure, you might need to create additional layers in the organizational unit hierarchy to accommodate the administration of users, printers, servers, and network shares.

This structure is appropriate only in small organizations, because functional departments in medium and large organizations are often diverse and cannot be effectively grouped into broad categories.

Organization-based hierarchy

The organization-based hierarchy is based on the departments or divisions in your organization. If the Active Directory structure is organized to reflect the organizational structure, it might be difficult to delegate administrative authority because the objects in Active Directory, such as printers and file shares, might not be grouped in a way that facilitates delegation of administrative authority. Because users rarely see the Active Directory structure, the design should accommodate the administrator instead of the user.

Location-based hierarchy

If the organization is centralized and network management is geographically distributed, you should use a location-based hierarchy. For example, you might decide to create organizational units for New England, Boston, and Hartford in a single domain, such as contoso.msft.

A location-based organizational units or domain hierarchy has the following characteristics:

- *Not affected by reorganizations.* Although divisions and departments might change frequently, location rarely changes in most organizations.

- *Accommodates mergers and expansions.* If an organization merges with or acquires another company, it is simple to integrate the new locations into the existing organizational units and domain hierarchy structure.

- *Might compromise security.* If a location includes multiple divisions or departments, an individual or a group with administrative authority over that domain or over organizational units might also have authority over any child domains or organizational units.

Hybrid-based hierarchy

A hierarchy based on location and then by organization, or any other combination of structure types, is called a hybrid-based hierarchy. The hybrid-based hierarchy combines strengths from several areas to meet the needs of the organization. This type of hierarchy has the following characteristics:

- Accommodates additional growth in geographic, departmental, or divisional areas.

- Creates distinct management boundaries according to department or division.

- Requires cooperation between administrators to ensure the completion of administrative tasks if they are in the same location but in different divisions or departments.

Names Associated with Organizational Units

Name	Example
LDAP relative distinguished name	OU=MyOrganizationalUnit
LDAP distinguished name	OU=MyOrganizationalUnit, DC=microsoft, DC=com
Canonical name	Microsoft.com/MyOrganizationalUnit

Introduction

Each object in Active Directory can be referenced by several types of names that describe the location of the object. Active Directory creates a relative distinguished name, a distinguished name, and a canonical name for each object, based on information that is provided when the object is created or modified.

LDAP relative distinguished name

The Lightweight Directory Access Protocol (LDAP) relative distinguished name uniquely identifies the object in its parent container. For example, the LDAP relative distinguished name of an organizational unit named MyOrganizationalUnit is OU=MyOrganizationalUnit. Relative distinguished names must be unique in an organizational unit. It is important to understand the syntax of the LDAP relative distinguished name when using scripts to query and manage Active Directory.

LDAP distinguished name

Unlike the LDAP relative distinguished name, the LDAP distinguished name is globally unique. An example of the LDAP distinguished name of an organizational unit named MyOrganizationalUnit in the microsoft.com domain is OU=MyOrganizationalUnit, DC=microsoft, DC=com. Systems administrators use the LDAP relative distinguished name and the LDAP distinguished name only when writing administrative scripts or during command-line administration.

Canonical name

The canonical name syntax is constructed in the same way as the LDAP distinguished name, but it is represented by a different notation. The canonical name of the organizational unit named myOrganizationalUnit in the microsoft.com domain is Microsoft.com/MyOrganizationalUnit. Administrators use canonical names in some administrative tools. A canonical name is used to represent a hierarchy in the administrative tools.

Practice: Creating an Organizational Unit

In this practice, you will:

- Install the AdminPak tools
- Use the runas command to launch the command line
- Use the dsadd command and Active Directory Users and Computers to create organizational units

Objective

In this practice you will:

- Install the AdminPak tools.
- Use the **runas** command to launch the command line.
- Use the **dsadd** command and Active Directory Users and Computers to create organizational units.

Instructions

Ensure that the DEN-DC1 and DEN-CL1 virtual machines are running.

Practice: Using a command line

▶ **Install the AdminPak tools**

1. Log on to the domain from the DEN-CL1 machine as the **Administrator** with the password of **Pa$$w0rd**.
2. Click **Start**, and then click **Run**.
3. In the **Run** box, type **\\DEN-DC1\Admin_Tools**.
4. Double-click **adminpak.msi**, and accept all the default settings.
5. Log off as the **Administrator**.

▶ **Create an organizational unit by using dsadd**

1. Log on to the domain from the DEN-CL1 machine as **Judy** with a password of **Pa$$w0rd**.
2. Click **Start**, and then click **Run**.
3. In the **Open** box, type **runas /user:contoso\\*administrator* cmd** and then click **OK**.
4. When prompted for the password, type **Pa$$w0rd** and then press ENTER.

5. At the command prompt, type the following command and then press ENTER:

   dsadd ou "ou=Finance,dc=contoso,dc=msft"

   You should get a **dsadd** succeeded message.

6. Close the command prompt window.

7. Log off of DEN-CL1.

Tip Although double quotation marks are required around the distinguished name only when the name includes spaces, it is a good practice to always use double quotation marks.

Practice: Using Active Directory Users and Computers

▶ **Create an organizational unit by using Active Directory Users and Computers**

1. If necessary, log on to DEN-DC1 as **Administrator** with a password of **Pa$$w0rd**.

2. Click **Start**, point to **Administrative Tools**, and click **Active Directory Users and Computers**.

3. Right-click **contoso.msft**, point to **New**, and then click **Organizational Unit**.

4. In the **New Object – Organizational Unit** dialog box, type **Test OU** in the **Name** field.

5. Click **OK**.

6. Close **Active Directory Users and Computers**.

7. Log off of DEN-DC1.

Important Do not shut down the virtual machines.

Lab: Creating Organizational Units

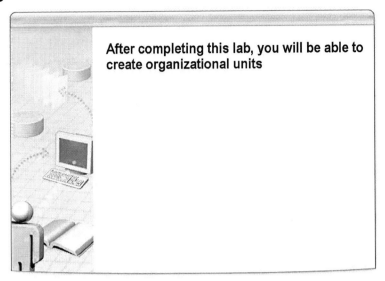

After completing this lab, you will be able to create organizational units

Objective

After completing this lab, you will be able to create organizational units.

Prerequisites

To complete this lab, you must have the following virtual machines:

- DEN-DC1
- DEN-CL1

Lab setup

This section lists the tasks that you must perform before you begin the lab. To complete this lab, you must have reviewed the procedures in the module and successfully completed each practice.

Estimated time to complete this lab: 20 minutes

Exercise 1
Creating Organizational Units from the Workstation

In this exercise, you will log on with a nonadministrative account and create a custom MMC. You will create a desktop shortcut that points to the MMC and uses the **Run as** feature to perform administrative tasks.

Scenario

As a systems administrator for Contoso, Ltd., you have been given the task of creating an organizational unit hierarchy designed by the Contoso Ltd. design team. The organizational unit hierarchy will use a hybrid design that separates business functions by region. You will create the organizational unit hierarchy for the marketing team.

Tasks	Specific Instructions
1. Log on as **Judy Lew**.	▪ On DEN-CL1, log on to the CONTOSO domain as **Judy** with the password of **Pa$$w0rd**.
2. Create a custom MMC with a desktop shortcut that uses the **Run as** feature to launch Active Directory Users and Computers.	a. Create a custom MMC. b. Add the **Active Directory Users and Computers** snap-in. c. Save the custom MMC as **AD_Admin.msc** in the **My Documents** folder. d. Create a desktop shortcut that will launch **AD_Admin.msc**. e. Right-click the **Shortcut to AD_Admin**, and click **Properties**. On the **Shortcut** tab, click **Advanced**, and then select the check box next to **Run with different credentials**. f. Double click **Shortcut to AD_Admin**, to open the AD_Admin console. Provide the domain administrator's credentials: **Contoso\administrator** and a password of **Pa$$w0rd**.
3. Create a Marketing organizational unit and two nested organizational units for the eastern and western regions.	a. Create a new organizational unit named **Marketing** at the domain level. b. Create an organizational unit named **Western Region** inside the Marketing organizational unit. c. Create an organizational unit named **Eastern Region** inside the Marketing organizational units. d. Close the **AD_Admin** console. Do not save changes.
4. Complete the lab exercise.	a. Close all programs and shut down all computers. Do not save changes. b. To prepare for the next module, start the DEN-DC1 and DEN-CL1 virtual computers.

![Microsoft]

Module 2: Managing User and Computer Accounts

Contents

Overview

- Creating User Accounts
- Creating Computer Accounts
- Modifying User and Computer Account Properties
- Creating a User Account Template
- Managing User and Computer Accounts
- Using Queries to Locate User and Computer Accounts in Active Directory

Introduction

One of your functions as a systems administrator is to manage user and computer accounts. These accounts are Active Directory® directory service objects, and you use these accounts to enable individuals to log on to the network and access resources. In this module, you will gain the skills and knowledge that you need to modify user and computer accounts on computers running Microsoft® Windows Server™ 2003 in a networked environment.

Objectives

After completing this module, you will be able to:

- Create user accounts.
- Create computer accounts.
- Modify user and computer account properties.
- Create a user account template.
- Manage user and computer accounts.
- Use queries to locate user and computer accounts in Active Directory.

Lesson: Creating User Accounts

* What Is a User Account?
* Names Associated with Domain User Accounts
* Guidelines for Creating a User Account Naming Convention
* User Account Placement in a Hierarchy
* User Account Password Options
* When to Require or Restrict Password Changes
* Tools to Create User Accounts
* Practice: Creating User Accounts
* Best Practices for Creating User Accounts

Introduction

As a systems administrator, you give users access to various network resources. To do this, you will need to know how to create and configure user accounts and how to establish these accounts within your organization's system. With this knowledge, you will ensure that your Windows Server 2003 network identifies and authenticates users before granting them access to the network.

Lesson objectives

After completing this lesson, you will be able to:

- Explain the purpose of user accounts.
- Describe the types of names associated with domain user accounts.
- Explain guidelines for creating a convention for naming user accounts.
- Describe user account placement in an Active Directory hierarchy.
- Describe user account password options.
- Determine when to require password changes on domain user accounts.
- Describe the tools to create user accounts.
- Create local and domain user accounts.
- Apply best practices when creating user accounts.

What Is a User Account?

Definition

A user account is an object that consists of all the information that defines a user in Windows Server 2003. The account can be either a local or a domain account. A user account includes the user name and password as well as group memberships.

You can use a user account to:

- Enable someone to log on to a computer based on a user account's identity.
- Enable processes and services to run under a specific security context.
- Manage a user's access to resources such as Active Directory objects and their properties, shared folders, files, directories, and printer queues.

Multimedia: Types of User Accounts

To view the *Types of User Accounts* presentation, open the Web page on the Student Materials compact disc, click **Multimedia**, and then click the title of the presentation.

The *Types of User Accounts* presentation explains how using accounts that grant different levels of access to the network meets the requirements of network users.

Names Associated with Domain User Accounts

Name	Example
User logon name	Tadams
Pre—Windows 2000 logon name	contoso\Tadams
User principal logon name	Tadams@contoso.msft
LDAP distinguished name	CN=terry adams,ou=sales,dc=contoso,dc=msft
LDAP relative distinguished name	CN=terry adams

Introduction

Five types of names are associated with domain user accounts. In Active Directory, each user account consists of a user logon name, a pre–Windows 2000 user logon name (Security Accounts Manager account name), a user principal logon name, a Lightweight Directory Access Protocol (LDAP) distinguished name, and a LDAP relative distinguished name.

User logon name

When creating a user account, an administrator types a user logon name. User logon names must be unique in the forest in which the user account is created. Users use this name only during the logon process. The user enters the user logon name, a password, and the domain name in separate fields on the logon screen.

User logon names can:

- Contain up to 20 uppercase and lowercase characters. (The name can be more than 20 characters, but Windows Server 2003 recognizes only 20.)

- Include a combination of special and alphanumeric characters, except the following: " / \ [ ] : ; | = , + * ? < >

- Have any combination of uppercase and lowercase letters. User logon names are case-retained, but not case-sensitive. For example, the user TAdams can enter any combination of uppercase and lowercase letters when logging on.

Some examples of user logon names are **Terryadams** and **Tadams**.

Pre–Windows 2000 logon name

You can use the pre–Windows 2000 network basic input/output system (NetBIOS) user account to log on to a Microsoft Windows® domain from computers running pre–Windows 2000 operating systems by using a name with the *DomainName\UserName* format. You can also use this name to log on to Windows domains from computers running Microsoft Windows 2000 or Microsoft Windows XP or servers running Windows Server 2003. The pre–Windows 2000 logon name must be unique in the domain. Users can use this logon name with the **runas** command or on a secondary logon screen. This name is limited to 15 characters.

User principal logon name

The user principal name (UPN) consists of the user logon name and the user principal name suffix, joined by the at sign (@). The UPN must be unique in the forest.

The second part of the UPN is the user principal name suffix. The user principal name suffix can be the Domain Name System (DNS) domain name, the DNS name of any domain in the forest, or an alternative name that an administrator creates only for logon purposes. Users can use this name to log on with the **runas** command or on a secondary logon screen.

An example of a UPN is **Tadams@contoso.msft**.

LDAP distinguished name

The LDAP distinguished name uniquely identifies the object in the forest. Users never use this name, but administrators use this name to add users to the network from a script or command line. All objects use the same LDAP naming convention, so all LDAP distinguished names must be unique in the forest.

The following are examples of an LDAP distinguished name:

- **CN= terry adams,ou=sales,dc=contoso,dc=msft**
- **CN=computer1,ou=sales,dc=contoso,dc=msft**

LDAP relative distinguished name

The LDAP relative distinguished name uniquely identifies the object within its parent container. The following are examples of an LDAP relative distinguished name:

- **CN= terry adams**
- **CN=computer1**

How names are assigned

From the information provided when a security principal object is created, Windows Server 2003 generates a security ID (SID) and a globally unique ID (GUID) used to identify the security principal. If the object is created using Active Directory Users and Computers, Active Directory also creates an LDAP relative distinguished name, based on the security principal full name. Therefore, the full name must be unique in the container in which the user account is created. An LDAP distinguished name and a canonical name are derived from the relative distinguished name and the names of the domain and container contexts in which the security principal object is created. If an object is created from a script or command line, the LDAP distinguished name is provided and the relative distinguished name and canonical name are derived from it.

If your organization has several domains, you can use the same user name or computer name in different domains. The SID, GUID, LDAP distinguished name, and canonical name generated by Active Directory will uniquely identify each user, computer, or group in the forest. If the security principal object is moved to a different domain, the SID, LDAP relative distinguished name, LDAP distinguished name, and canonical name will change, but the globally unique ID generated by Active Directory will not change.

Guidelines for Creating a User Account Naming Convention

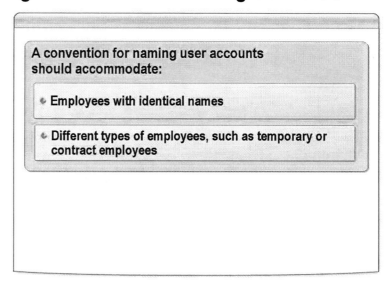

A convention for naming user accounts should accommodate:

* Employees with identical names

* Different types of employees, such as temporary or contract employees

Introduction

A naming convention establishes how user accounts are identified in the domain. A consistent naming convention makes it easier for you to remember user logon names and locate them in lists. It is a good practice to adhere to the naming convention already in use in an existing network that supports a large number of users.

Guidelines

Consider the following guidelines for creating a naming convention:

- Maintain a consistent corporate standard for user names. Accounts adhering to a standard are easier to understand, search for, and create. For example, if your company uses *firstname.lastname* (judy.lew) as the standard, an account created using *firstinitiallastname* (jlew) is confusing.

- If you have a large number of users, your naming convention for user logon names should accommodate employees with identical names. A method to accomplish this is to use the first name and the last initial, and then add additional letters from the last name to accommodate duplicate names. For example, for two users named Judy Lew, one user logon name can be **Judyl** and the other can be **Judyle**.

- In some organizations, it is useful to identify temporary employees by their user accounts. To do so, you can add a prefix to the user logon name, such as a **T** and a hyphen. An example is **T-Judyl**.

- User logon names for domain user accounts must be unique in the forest. Full names for domain user accounts must be unique in the container in which you create the user account.

User Account Placement in a Hierarchy

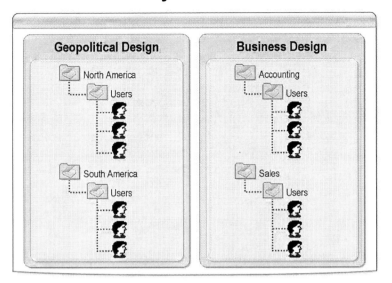

Introduction

You can place domain user accounts in any domain in the forest and any organizational unit in the domain. Typically, account hierarchies are based on geopolitical boundaries or business models.

Place user accounts in an Active Directory hierarchy based on the way the user accounts are managed. For example, security principals that will have similar security requirements, will have the same Group Policy settings, or will be managed by the same administrative personnel can be placed in the same organizational unit hierarchy.

Note The Users container is not an organizational unit. It is a system container that houses the administrative accounts and groups. More importantly, Group Policy objects cannot be directly assigned to the Users container, and the Users container cannot contain any child organizational units. Although you can create user accounts in the Users container, as a best practice the Users container should be reserved for administrative groups and service accounts.

Geopolitical design

In a geopolitical design, you place users in organizational units that match their physical location. You can create an organizational unit hierarchy using parent containers based on city or region.

Business design

When the hierarchy of organizational units is based on business models, you place your sales personnel in a Sales organizational unit and manufacturing personnel in a Manufacturing organizational unit.

Note In many cases, one domain will work for a corporate environment. You can still separate administrative control of users by placing them into organizational units.

User Account Password Options

Account options	Description
User must change password at next logon	Users must change their passwords the next time they log on to the network
User cannot change password	Users do not have the permissions to change their own password
Password never expires	Users' passwords will not expire and do not need to be changed
Account is disabled	Users cannot log on by using the selected account

Introduction

As a systems administrator, you can manage user account password options. These options can be set when the user account is created or in the **Properties** dialog box of a user account.

Password options

The administrator can choose from the following password options to protect access to the domain or a computer:

- **User must change password at the next logon**. Use this option when a new user logs on to a system for the first time or when the administrator resets forgotten passwords for users. This is the default for new user accounts.

- **User cannot change password**. Use this option when you want to prevent a user from changing his or her account password.

- **Password never expires**. This option prevents the password from expiring. To maintain security best practice, do not use this option.

- **Account is disabled**. This option prevents the user from logging on to the selected account.

Default password settings

By default, passwords in a Windows 2003 Active Directory domain must meet several minimum requirements.

- Must not contain all or part of the user's account name.
- Must be at least seven characters in length.
- Must contain characters from three of the following four categories:
  - English uppercase characters (A through Z)
  - English lowercase characters (a through z)
  - Base 10 digits (0 through 9)
  - Nonalphabetic characters (for example, !, $, #, %)

If an administrator changes the password complexity requirements, the new requirements will be enforced the next time passwords are changed or created.

These requirements are not enforced on stand-alone servers for local accounts but are still recommended practices.

When to Require or Restrict Password Changes

Option	Use this option when you:
Require password changes	• Create new domain accounts • Reset passwords
Restrict password changes	• Create local and domain service accounts

Introduction

To create a more secure environment, require password changes on user accounts and restrict password changes on service accounts. The following table describes when you need to restrict or require password changes.

Password modifications options

Option	Use this option when you:
Require password changes	• Create new domain user accounts. Select the check box that requires the user to change the password the first time the user logs on to the domain. • Reset passwords. This option enables the administrator to reset a password when the password expires or if the user forgets it.
Restrict password changes	• Create local or domain service accounts. Service accounts typically have many dependencies on them. As a result, you might want to restrict the password change policy so that service account passwords are changed by the administrator who is responsible for the applications that depend on the service account.

Additional reading

For more information about service accounts, see "Services permissions" on the Microsoft TechNet Web site.

For more information about changing passwords, see:

- Article 324744, "How to Prevent Users from Changing a Password Except When Required in Windows Server 2003," in the Knowledge Base on the Microsoft Help and Support Web site.

- Article 320325, "User May Not Be Able to Change Their Password If You Configure the 'User Must Change Password at Next Logon' Setting," in the Knowledge Base on the Microsoft Help and Support Web site.

Tools to Create User Accounts

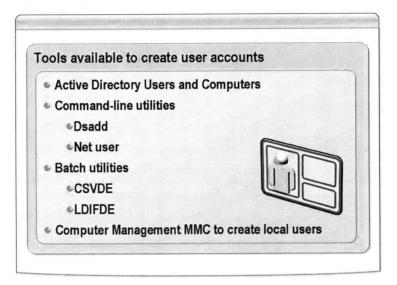

> **Tools available to create user accounts**
>
> - Active Directory Users and Computers
> - Command-line utilities
>   - Dsadd
>   - Net user
> - Batch utilities
>   - CSVDE
>   - LDIFDE
> - Computer Management MMC to create local users

Introduction

Domain user accounts enable users to log on to a domain and access resources anywhere on the network. Local user accounts enable users to log on and access resources only on the computer on which you create the local user account. As a systems administrator, you must create domain and local user accounts to manage your network environment. A number of tools are available for the creation of user accounts, including legacy tools such as User Manager for Domains and command-line and batch utilities.

Using Active Directory Users and Computers

Active Directory Users and Computers is the primary tool used for day-to-day administration of Active Directory. Similar to the file system displayed in Windows Explorer, Active Directory Users and Computers displays Active Directory by using the left pane for a tree view of the domain and the right pane to display the detailed view. You can use Active Directory Users and Computers to create new objects, such as user, group, and computer accounts, and to manage existing objects.

Using a command line

Another way to create a domain user account is to use the **dsadd** command. The **dsadd user** command adds a single user to the directory from a command prompt or batch file.

Type:

dsadd user *UserDN* [**-samid** *SAMName*]
[**-upn** *UPN*] [**-fn** *FirstName*] [**-ln** *LastName*] [**-display** *DisplayName*]
[**-pwd** {*Password*|*}]

Use " " if there is a space in any variable.

Note   For the complete syntax of the **dsadd user** command, at a command prompt, type **dsadd user /?**.

An example of **dsadd user** is shown here:

```
dsadd user "cn=test user,cn=users,dc=contoso,dc=msft" –samid
testuser –upn testuser@contoso.msft –fn test –ln user –display
"test user" –pwd Pa$$w0rd
```

Another way to create a user account is to use **net user** command.

For example, to create a new user named Greg Weber with a password of
Pa$$w0rd, you would type the following command:

net user "Greg Weber" Pa$$w0rd /add

The following example shows the syntax of the **net user** command:

```
net user [username [password | *] [options]] [/domain]
username {password | *} /add [options] [/domain] username
[/delete] [/domain]
```

Important Legacy tools such as **User Manager for Domains** and **net**
commands will place newly created user accounts in the Users container by
default. Also, Microsoft Windows NT® 4.0 domains that have been upgraded to
Windows 2003 Active Directory will place the upgraded user accounts in the
Users container. This default location can be modified by using the **Redirusr**
command. For more information, see article 324949, "Redirecting the users and
computers containers in Windows Server 2003 domains," on the Microsoft
Help and Support Web site.

Using batch utilities

Batch utilities can be used to import user accounts from input files. The
CSVDE utility uses comma-delimited input files and the LDIFDE utility uses
line-delimited files as input to create user accounts and other types of Active
Directory objects.

Note For more information about the CSVDE and the LDIFDE utilities refer
to Course 2279, *Planning, Implementing, and Maintaining a Microsoft
Windows Server 2003 Active Directory Infrastructure.*

**Using the Computer
Management MMC**

You can use the Local Users and Groups snap-in in the Computer Management
Microsoft Management Console (MMC) to create local user accounts.

Important You cannot create local user accounts on a domain controller.

Important A local user name cannot be identical to any other user or group
name on the computer being administered. A local user name can contain up to
20 uppercase or lowercase characters, except for the following:

" / \ [ ] : ; | = , + * ? < >

A user name cannot consist solely of periods or spaces.

Practice: Creating User Accounts

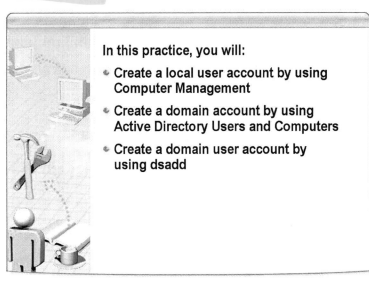

In this practice, you will:

- Create a local user account by using Computer Management
- Create a domain account by using Active Directory Users and Computers
- Create a domain user account by using dsadd

Objectives

In this practice, you will:

- Create a local user account by using Computer Management.
- Create a domain account by using Active Directory Users and Computers.
- Create a domain user account by using **dsadd**.

Instructions

Ensure that the DEN-DC1 virtual machine and the DEN-CL1 virtual machine are running.

Practice

▶ **Create a local user account by using Computer Management**

1. Log on to DEN-CL1 as **Judy** with the password of **Pa$$w0rd**.

2. Click **Start** and then click **Control Panel**.

3. Click **Performance and Maintenance**, and then click **Administrative Tools**.

4. Right-click **Computer Management** and then click **Run as**.

5. Select **The Following user** check box. Log on using **DEN-CL1\administrator** with a password of **Pa$$w0rd**.

6. In **Computer Management**, expand **Local Users and Groups**.

7. Right-click the **Users** folder, and then click **New User**.

8. In the **New User** dialog box, create an account using the following parameters:

- User name: **Service_Backup**
- Description: **Service Account for Backup Software**
- Password: **Pa$$w0rd** (where 0 is zero)
- Confirm password: **Pa$$w0rd**
- User must change password at next logon: **Cleared**
- Password never expires: **Selected**

9. Click **Create** and then click **Close**.

10. Close **Computer Management**, and then close **Administrative Tools**.

11. Log off from DEN-CL1.

▶ **Create a domain account by using Active Directory Users and Computers**

1. Log on to DEN-DC1 as **Administrator** with a password of **Pa$$w0rd**.

2. Click **Start**, point to **Administrative Tools**, and then click **Active Directory Users and Computers**.

3. Right-click the **IT Admin** OU, point to **New** and then click **User**.

4. In the **New Object – User** dialog box, enter the following parameters:

- First name: **Kerim**
- Last name: **Hanif**
- Full name: **Kerim Hanif**
- User logon name: **Kerim**

5. Click **Next**.

6. In the **Password** and **Confirm password** fields, enter **Pa$$w0rd**.

7. Clear the **User must change password at next logon** check box.

8. Click **Next**.

9. Click **Finish**.

10. Close **Active Directory Users and Computers**. Do not log off.

11. Test the user account that you just created by logging on to DEN-CL1 as **Kerim**, with a password of **Pa$$w0rd**.

12. Log off of DEN-CL1.

▶ **Create a domain user account by using dsadd**

1. On DEN-DC1 open a command prompt window.

2. At the command prompt, type the following command and then press ENTER:

   dsadd user "cn=Luis Bonifaz,ou=it admin,dc=contoso,dc=msft" -samid luis -pwd Pa$$w0rd –desc Administrator

   You should see a "dsadd succeeded" message.

3. Close all windows and log off of DEN-DC1. Do not shut down the virtual machines.

Important   If the **dsadd** command does not specify a password and the domain policy requires a password, the account will be created but will be disabled until the password requirements are met. If the Security Accounts Manager (SAM) name (**samid**) is not specified, **dsadd** will use up to the first 20 characters of **CN** to create the SAM account name.

Best Practices for Creating User Accounts

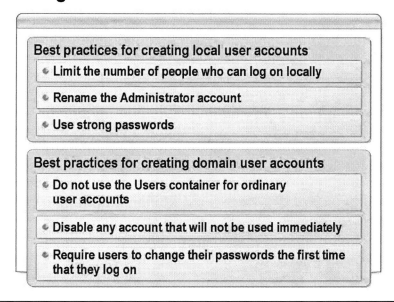

Best practices for creating local user accounts

* Limit the number of people who can log on locally

* Rename the Administrator account

* Use strong passwords

Best practices for creating domain user accounts

* Do not use the Users container for ordinary user accounts

* Disable any account that will not be used immediately

* Require users to change their passwords the first time that they log on

Introduction

Several best practices for creating user accounts reduce security risks in the network environment. Software products change, however, so be sure to review current best practices at www.microsoft.com/security.

Local user accounts

Consider the following best practices when creating local user accounts:

- Do not enable the Guest account.

- Limit the number of people who can log on locally.

- Rename the Administrator account.

- Use strong passwords.

Domain user accounts

Consider the following best practices when creating domain user accounts:

- Avoid using the Users container for ordinary user accounts. The Users container is a system container and should be used to hold administrative groups or accounts and service accounts.

- Disable any account that will not be used immediately.

- Require users to change their passwords the first time that they log on. This will prevent administrators from having access to user passwords. This is the default setting for new user accounts.

- As a security best practice, it is recommended that you do not log on to your computer with administrative credentials.

- When you are logged on to your computer without administrative credentials, it is recommended that you use the **runas** command to accomplish administrative tasks.

- Rename or disable the Administrator and Guest accounts in each domain to reduce the attacks on your domain.

- By default, all traffic on Active Directory administrative tools is signed and encrypted while in transit on the network. Do not disable this feature.

Lesson: Creating Computer Accounts

* What Is a Computer Account?
* Why Create a Computer Account?
* Where Computer Accounts Are Created in a Domain
* Computer Account Options
* Practice: Creating a Computer Account

Introduction

The information in this lesson presents the skills and knowledge that you need to create a computer account.

Lesson objectives

After completing this lesson, you will be able to:

- Define a computer account.
- Describe the purpose of computer accounts.
- Describe where computer accounts are created in a domain.
- Describe the various computer account options.
- Create a computer account.

What Is a Computer Account?

* Identifies a computer in a domain
* Provides a means for authenticating and auditing computer access to the network and to domain resources
* Is required for every computer running:
  * Windows Server 2003
  * Windows XP Professional
  * Windows 2000
  * Windows NT

Introduction

Every computer running Microsoft Windows NT, Windows 2000, Windows XP, or Windows Server 2003 that joins a domain has a computer account. Similar to user accounts, computer accounts provide a means for authenticating and auditing computer access to the network and to domain resources.

What does a computer account do?

In Active Directory, computers are security principals, just like users. This means that computers must have accounts and passwords. To be fully authenticated by Active Directory, a user must have a valid user account, and the user must also log on to the domain from a computer that has a valid computer account.

Note You cannot create computer accounts for computers running Microsoft Windows 95, Microsoft Windows 98, Microsoft Windows Millennium Edition, and Windows XP Home Edition, because their operating systems do not adhere to Active Directory security requirements.

Why Create a Computer Account?

* **Security**
  * Authentication
  * Auditing
* **Management**
  * Software deployment
  * Desktop management
  * Hardware and software inventory through Systems Management Server

Introduction

Computers access network resources to perform key tasks such as authenticating user logons, obtaining an IP address, and receiving security policies. To have full access to these network resources, computers must have valid accounts in Active Directory. The two main functions of a computer account are performing security and management activities.

Authentication

A computer account must be created in Active Directory for users to take full advantage of Active Directory features. When a computer account is created, the computer can use advanced authentication processes such as Kerberos authentication. For each workstation or server running Windows 2000, Windows 2003, or Windows XP that is a member of a domain, there is a discrete communication channel, known as the security channel, with a domain controller. The security channel's password is stored along with the computer account on all domain controllers. The default computer account password change period is every 30 days.

Auditing

The computer also needs a computer account to dictate how auditing is applied and recorded.

Management

Computer accounts help the systems administrator manage the network structure. The systems administrator uses computer accounts to manage the functionality of the desktop environment, automate the deployment of software by using Active Directory, and maintain a hardware and software inventory by using Microsoft Systems Management Server. Computer accounts in the domain are also used to control access to resources.

Where Computer Accounts Are Created in a Domain

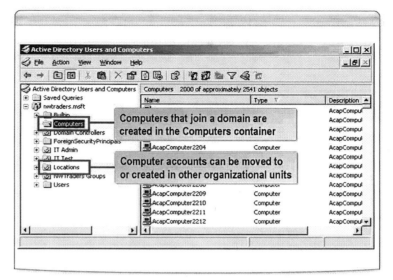

Introduction

When systems administrators create a computer account, they can choose the organizational unit in which to create that account. If a computer joins a domain, the computer account is created in the Computers container, and the administrator can move the account to its proper organizational unit as necessary.

Tip You can change the default location for computers joining the domain by using the **redircmp** command. For more information, see article 324949, "Redirecting the users and computers containers in Windows Server 2003 domains," Microsoft Help and Support Web site.

Who can create computer accounts?

By default, administrators can create computer accounts in any container except the System and NTDS Quotas containers. Computer accounts cannot be created in those containers. The Account Operators group can create computer accounts in the Computers container and in new organizational units. However, they cannot create computer accounts in the Builtin, Domain Controllers, ForeignSecurityPrincipals, LostAndFound, Program Data, System, or Users containers. Also, anyone who has been delegated authority to create computer objects in an organizational unit can create computers accounts in that container.

Users adding computers to the domain

When a user joins a computer to the domain, the computer account is added to the Computers container in Active Directory. This is accomplished through a service that adds the computer account on behalf of the user. The system account also records how many computers each user has added to the domain

By default, Active Directory users can add up to 10 computers to the domain with their user account credentials. This default configuration can be changed. If the systems administrator pre-creates a computer account in Active Directory, a user can join a computer to the domain without using any of the 10 allocated computer accounts.

Pre-staged computer accounts

Adding a computer to the domain by using a previously created account is called pre-staging, which means that computers are added to any organizational unit for which the systems administrator has permissions to add computer accounts. Usually, users do not have the appropriate permissions to pre-stage a computer account, so as an alternative they join a computer to the domain by using a pre-staged account. You can designate which user or group has the right to join the computer to the domain during the creation of the computer account by clicking the **Change** button in the **New Object – Computer** dialog box.

Additional reading

For more information about users adding computer accounts to a domain, see article 251335, "Domain Users Cannot Join Workstation or Server to a Domain," on the Microsoft Help and Support Web site.

Computer Account Options

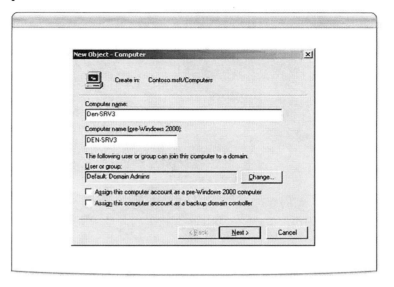

Introduction

You can enable two optional features when creating a computer account. You can assign a computer account as a pre–Windows 2000 computer or as a backup domain controller (BDC).

Pre–Windows 2000

Select the **Assign this computer account as a pre–Windows 2000 computer** check box to assign a password based on the computer name. If you do not select this check box, a random password is assigned as the initial password for the computer account. The password automatically changes every five days. This option guarantees that a pre–Windows 2000 computer will be able to interpret whether the password meets the password requirements.

Backup domain controller

Select the **Assign this computer as a backup domain controller** check box if you intend to use the computer as a backup domain controller. You should use this feature if you are still in a mixed environment with a Window Server 2003 domain controller and Windows NT 4.0 BDC. After the account is created in Active Directory, you can then join the BDC to the domain during the installation of Windows NT 4.0.

Practice: Creating a Computer Account

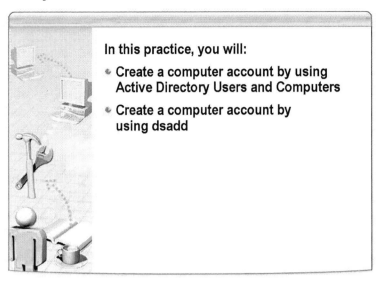

In this practice, you will:

- Create a computer account by using Active Directory Users and Computers
- Create a computer account by using dsadd

Objectives

In this practice, you will

- Create a computer account by using Active Directory Users and Computers.
- Create a computer account by using **dsadd**.

Instructions

Ensure that the DEN-DC1 virtual machine and the DEN-CL1 virtual machine are running.

Practice

▶ **Create a computer account by using Active Directory Users and Computers**

1. Log on to DEN-DC1 by using the **Administrator** account, with a password of **Pa$$w0rd**.

2. Click **Start**, point to **Administrative Tools**, and then click **Active Directory Users and Computers**.

3. Right-click the **Sales** organizational unit, point to **New**, and then click **Computer**.

4. In the **New Object-Computer** dialog box, enter **Sales2** in the **Computer name** field.

5. Under **The following user or group can join this computer to a domain**, click **Change**.

6. In the **Select User or Group** dialog box, type **Judy**, and then click **Check Names**. Click **OK**.

7. Click **Next** twice.

8. Click **Finish**.

9. Close **Active Directory Users and Computers**.

▶ **Create a computer account by using dsadd**

1. Open a command prompt window.

2. At the command prompt, type the following command and then press
   ENTER:

   **dsadd computer "cn=Sales3,ou=sales,dc=contoso,dc=msft" –loc
   downtown**

   You should see a "dsadd succeeded" message.

3. Close all windows and log off of DEN-DC1.

Note   To perform this procedure, you must be a member of the Account
Operators group, the Domain Admins group, or the Enterprise Admins group in
Active Directory, or you must be delegated the appropriate authority. As a
security best practice, consider using **runas** to perform this procedure.

Important   Do not shut down the virtual machines.

Lesson: Modifying User and Computer Account Properties

* When to Modify User and Computer Account Properties
* Properties Associated with User Accounts
* Renaming a User Account
* Properties Associated with Computer Accounts
* Practice: Modifying User and Computer Account Properties

Introduction

This lesson presents the skills and knowledge that you need to modify user and computer accounts.

Lesson objectives

After completing this lesson, you will be able to:

- Determine when to modify user and computer account properties.
- Describe the properties associated with user accounts.
- Describe how to rename user accounts.
- Describe the properties associated with computer accounts.
- Modify user and computer account properties.

When to Modify User and Computer Account Properties

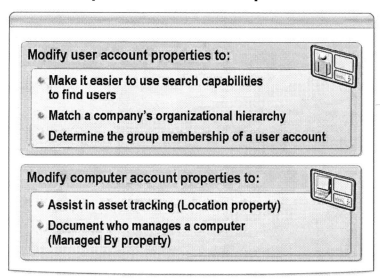

Modify user account properties to:

- Make it easier to use search capabilities to find users
- Match a company's organizational hierarchy
- Determine the group membership of a user account

Modify computer account properties to:

- Assist in asset tracking (Location property)
- Document who manages a computer (Managed By property)

Introduction

As a systems administrator, you might be responsible for creating user and computer accounts in Active Directory. You also might be responsible for maintaining those user and computer accounts. To complete these tasks, you must be very familiar with the various properties for each user and computer account.

User account properties

It is critical that systems administrators are familiar with user account properties so that they can manage the network structure. Users might use the user account properties as a single source of information about other users, like a telephone book, or to search for users based on items such as office location, supervisor, or department name. The systems administrator can use the properties of a user account to determine how the user account behaves in a terminal server session or how the user can gain access to the network through a dial-up connection.

Computer account properties

To maintain computers, you must find the physical location of the computers. The most commonly used properties for computer accounts in Active Directory are the **Location** and **Managed by** properties. The **Location** property can be used to document the computer's physical location in your network. The **Managed By** property lists the individual responsible for the computer. This information can be useful when you have a data center with servers for different departments and you need to perform maintenance on the server. You can call or send e-mail to the person who is responsible for the server before you perform maintenance on the server.

Properties Associated with User Accounts

The Properties dialog box for a user account contains:

Introduction

The **Properties** dialog box for a user account contains information about each user account that is stored in Active Directory. The more complete the information in the **Properties** dialog box, the easier it is to search for users in Active Directory.

User account properties

The following table lists the most commonly used properties for user accounts.

Tab	Properties
General	Name, job description, office location, telephone number, e-mail address, and home page information
Address	Street address, city, state or province, postal zip code, and country
Account	Logon name, account options, unlock account, and account expiration
Profile	Profile path, logon scripts, and home folder
Telephone	Home, pager, mobile phone, fax, and IP telephone numbers
Organization	Title, department, company, manager, and direct reports
Member Of	Groups to which the user belongs
Dial-in	Remote access permissions, callback options, and static IP address and routes
Environment	One or more applications to start and the devices to connect to when a Terminal Services user logs on
Sessions	Terminal Services settings
Remote control	Terminal Services remote control settings
Terminal Services Profile	The user's Terminal Services profile

Renaming a User Account

The Rename User dialog box

Introduction

Occasionally, employees in your organization will need to change their user name for personal or legal reasons. For example, employees who get married and legally change their surnames will need their user account names updated. Instead of deleting the old account and creating a new user, you can rename the original account. Use the following procedure to rename a user account.

Renaming a user account

1. Open **Active Directory Users and Computers**.

2. Right-click the user name that you need to change, and click **Rename** on the shortcut menu.

3. Type the new user name, and then press **Enter**.

4. In the **Rename User** dialog box, change the appropriate fields.

The renamed user account will maintain the same security descriptors, properties, rights, and permissions that were associated with the old account name.

Properties Associated with Computer Accounts

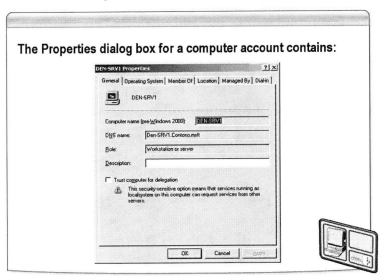

Introduction

The **Properties** dialog box for a computer account contains unique information about each computer account that is stored in Active Directory. The more complete the information in the **Properties** dialog box, the easier it is to search for computers in Active Directory.

Computer account properties

The following table lists the most commonly used properties for computer accounts.

Tab	Properties
General	Computer name, DNS name, description, and role
Operating System	Name and version of the operating system running on the computer and the latest service pack installed
Member Of	The groups in the local domain and any groups to which the computer belongs
Location	The location of the computer
Managed By	Name, office location, street, city, state or province, country or region, telephone number, and fax number of the person who manages the computer
Object	The canonical name of the object, object class, the date the computer account was created, the date it was last modified, and update sequence numbers (USNs)
Security	The users and groups who have permissions for the computer
Dial-in	Remote access permission, callback options, and routing options

Tools used to modify user or computer accounts

You can use Active Directory Users and Computers or the **dsmod** command to modify attributes of existing users or computers in Active Directory.

Note For the complete syntax of the **dsmod** command, at a command prompt, type **dsmod user /?** or **dsmod computer /?**.

Practice: Modifying User and Computer Account Properties

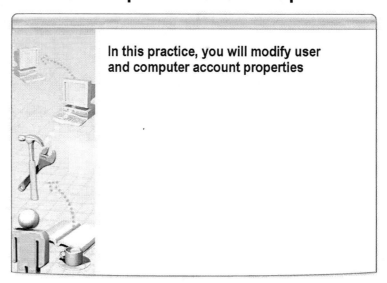

In this practice, you will modify user and computer account properties

Objective

In this practice, you will modify user and computer account properties.

Instructions

Ensure that the DEN-DC1 virtual machine is running.

Practice

▶ **Modify user and computer account properties**

1. Log on to DEN-DC1 as **Administrator**, with a password of **Pa$$w0rd**.

2. Open **Active Directory Users and Computers**.

3. In the **Sales** organizational unit, right-click **Jeff Hay**, and then click
   Properties. Modify the user properties as follows:

   a. On the **General** tab, set

      • **Telephone number: 204-555-0100**

      • **Office: Downtown**

      • **E-mail: Jeff@Contoso.msft**

   b. On the **Dial-in** tab, set **Remote Access Permission** to **Allow access**.

   c. On the **Account** tab, click **Logon Hours**. Configure logon hours to be
      permitted between 8:00 A.M. and 5:00 P.M and then click **OK**.

4. Close **Active Directory Users and Computers**.

5. Open a command prompt window, type the following command and then press ENTER:

    dsmod computer "cn=sales2,ou=sales,dc=contoso,dc=msft" -loc Downtown –desc Workstation

    You should get a "dsmod succeeded" message.

6. Close all windows and log off of DEN-DC1.

Important   Do not shut down the virtual machines.

Lesson: Creating a User Account Template

* What Is a User Account Template?
* What Properties Are in a Template?
* Guidelines for Creating User Account Templates
* Practice: Creating a User Account Template

Introduction

The information in this lesson presents the skills and knowledge that you need to create a user account template.

Lesson objectives

After completing this lesson, you will be able to:

- Explain the purpose of a user account template.

- Describe the properties of a user account template.

- Apply guidelines when creating user account templates.

- Create a user account template.

What Is a User Account Template?

- Employs a user account with properties meeting common user requirements
- Makes creating user accounts with standardized configurations more efficient

User Account Template

Definition

You can simplify the process of creating domain user accounts by creating a user account template. A user account template is an account that has commonly used settings and properties already configured.

Using account templates

For each new user account, you need to add only the information that is unique to that user account. For example, if all sales personnel must be a member of 15 sales groups and have the same manager, you can create a template that includes membership to all the groups and the reporting manager. When the template is copied for a new salesperson, it retains the group memberships and manager that were in the template.

What Properties Are in a Template?

Tab	Properties copied
Address	All properties except **Street Address**
Account	All properties except **Logon Name**
Profile	All properties except **Profile path** and **Home folder** reflect new user's logon name
Organization	All properties except **Title**
Member Of	All properties

Properties

Numerous properties are associated with each account. However, only a limited number of properties can be copied in a template. The following table lists the user properties that can be copied from an existing domain user account to a new domain user account.

Properties tab	Properties copied to new domain user account
Address	All properties except **Street Address** are copied.
Account	All properties except **Logon Name**, which is copied from the **Copy Object – User** dialog box, are copied.
Profile	All properties except the **Profile path** and **Home folder** entries are modified to reflect the new user's logon name.
Organization	All properties except **Title** are copied.
Member Of	All properties are copied.

Additional reading

For more information about profiles, see article 324749, "HOW TO: Create a Roaming User Profile in Windows Server 2003," on the Microsoft Help and Support Web site.

Form more information about home folders, see article 325853, "HOW TO: Use Older Roaming User Profiles with Windows Server 2003," on the Microsoft Help and Support Web site.

Guidelines for Creating User Account Templates

* Create a separate classification for each department

* Create a separate group for short-term and temporary employees

* Set user account expiration dates for short-term and temporary employees

* Disable the account template

* Identify the account template

Guidelines

Consider the following best practices for creating user account templates:

- Create a separate classification for each department in your business group.

- Create a separate group for short-term and temporary employees with logon and workstation restrictions.

- Set user account expiration dates for short-term and temporary employees to prevent them from accessing the network when their contracts expire.

- Disable the account template.

- Identify the account template. For example, place a **T_** before the name of the account to identify the account as an account template or use an underscore at the beginning of the account name to ensure that the template always appears at the top of an alphabetized list.

Practice: Creating a User Account Template

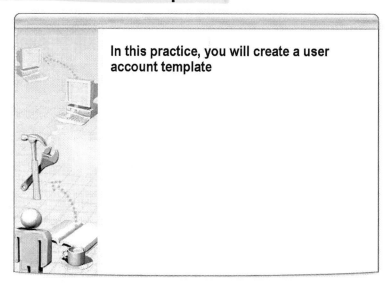

In this practice, you will create a user account template

Objective

In this practice, you will create a user account template.

Practice

► **Create a user account template**

1. Log on to DEN-DC1 as **Administrator**, with a password of **Pa$$w0rd**.

2. Open **Active Directory Users and Computers**.

3. In the **Sales** organizational unit, create a user account with the following property settings:

Property	Value
First name	Sales
Last name	Template
Full name	Sales Template
User logon name	_SalesTemplate
Password	Pa$$w0rd
Description	Salesperson
Office	Downtown
Member Of	G Sales
Department	Sales
Profile path	\\DEN-SRV1\profiles\%username%
Logon Hours	6:00 A.M – 6:00 P.M. Monday to Friday
Disable the account	Enable

4. Click **OK** and then close **Active Directory Users and Computers**.

5. Log off of DEN-DC1.

Lesson: Managing User and Computer Accounts

- Why Enable or Disable User and Computer Accounts?
- What Are Locked-Out User Accounts?
- When to Reset User Passwords
- When to Reset Computer Accounts
- Practice: Resetting and Disabling a User Account

Introduction

The information in this lesson presents the skills and knowledge that you need to enable and disable user and computer accounts.

Lesson objectives

After completing this lesson, you will be able to:

- Explain why you enable and disable user and computer accounts.
- Enable and disable user and computer accounts.
- Explain when to reset user passwords.
- Explain when to reset computer accounts.
- Reset and disable a user account.

Why Enable or Disable User and Computer Accounts?

Scenarios for disabling accounts
- User takes a leave of absence
- Creating accounts that will not be used immediately

Tools available for disabling or enabling accounts
- Active Directory Users and Computers
- Dsmod command

Introduction

After creating user accounts, you perform frequent administrative tasks to ensure that the network continues to meet the organization's needs. These administrative tasks include enabling and disabling user and computer accounts. When you enable or disable an account, you give or restrict access to the account.

Scenarios for enabling and disabling accounts

To provide a secure network environment, a systems administrator must disable user accounts when users do not need their accounts for an extended period but will need to use them later. The following are examples of when you need to enable or disable user accounts:

- If the user takes a two-month leave of absence from work, you disable the account when the user leaves and then enable the account when the user returns.

- When you add accounts in the network that will be used in the future or for security purposes, you disable the accounts until they are needed.

Tools for enabling and disabling accounts

You can use Active Directory Users and Computers to disable or enable an account. When an account is disabled, the user cannot log on. The account appears in the details pane with an **X** on the account icon.

Note To enable and disable user and computer accounts, you must be a member of the Account Operators group, the Domain Admins group, or the Enterprise Admins group in Active Directory, or you must be delegated the appropriate authority. As a security best practice, consider using **runas** to perform this procedure.

Using a command line

You can also enable or disable accounts by using the **dsmod** command. As a security best practice, consider using **runas** to perform this procedure.

To enable or disable accounts by using **dsmod**:

1. Open a command prompt window by using the **runas** command.

2. Type **dsmod user** *UserDN* **-disabled {yes|no}** at the command prompt.

Value	Description
UserDN	Specifies the distinguished name of the user object to be disabled or enabled
{**yes**|**no**}	Specifies whether the user account is disabled for log on (**yes**) or enabled (**no**)

What Are Locked-Out User Accounts?

- **Account lockout thresholds:**
  - Define the number of failed logon attempts
  - Prevent hackers from guessing user passwords
- **Logon failures can occur:**
  - At the logon screen
  - At a screen saver protected by a password
  - When accessing network resources

Introduction

A user account is locked out if the account has exceeded the account lockout threshold for a domain. This might happen if the user has attempted to access the account with an incorrect password too many times or if a computer hacker has attempted to guess users' passwords and invoked the lockout policy on the account.

Account lockout threshold

Authorized users can lock themselves out of an account by mistyping or by typing an incorrect password or by changing their password on a computer while they are logged on to another computer. The computer with the incorrect password continuously tries to authenticate the user. Because the password the computer is using to authenticate the user is incorrect, the user account is eventually locked out.

A security setting in Active Directory specifies the number of failed logon attempts that causes a user to be locked out. A user cannot use a locked-out account until an administrator resets the account or until the lockout duration for the account expires. When a user account is locked out, an error message appears, and the user is not allowed any further logon attempts.

What is a failed logon attempt?

A user can be locked out of an account if there are too many failed password attempts. Failed password attempts happen when:

- A user logs on at the logon screen and supplies a bad password.

- A user logs on with a local account and supplies a domain user account and a bad password while accessing network resources.

- A user logs on with a local account and supplies a domain user account and a bad password while accessing resources by using the **runas** command.

By default, domain account lockout attempts are not recorded when a user unlocks a workstation (by using a password-protected screen saver). You can change this behavior by modifying the **Interactive logon: Require Domain controller authentication to unlock workstation** Group Policy setting.

The built-in administrator cannot be locked out from the console of a domain controller or local machine.

When to Reset User Passwords

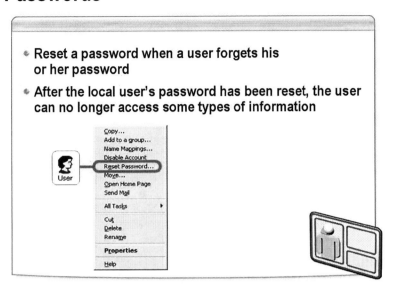

* Reset a password when a user forgets his or her password
* After the local user's password has been reset, the user can no longer access some types of information

Introduction

People occasionally forget their passwords. Without their passwords, these people cannot access their user accounts. Administrators can reset users' passwords so that users can access their accounts again.

Who can reset user account passwords

When you need to reset a user password, you must remember that authorization to reset passwords is restricted.

- Only local administrators are authorized to reset local user passwords.

- Only domain administrators, enterprise administrators, account operators, and other users or groups that have the delegated authority to reset passwords are authorized to reset domain user passwords.

Consequences of resetting local user account passwords

After a local computer user's account password is reset, some types of encrypted information are no longer accessible. This is because the algorithm that generates a local user's encryption key incorporates the user's current password in the calculation. Some examples of information that might not be accessible are:

- E-mail that is encrypted by using the user's public key.

- Internet passwords that are saved on the computer.

- Files that the user has encrypted.

When to Reset Computer Accounts

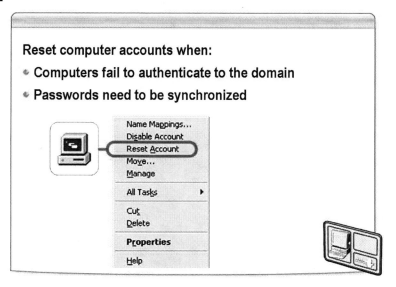

Introduction

As a systems administrator, you occasionally need to reset computer accounts. For example, suppose that your network went through a full backup seven days ago. The computer relayed information to the domain controller that changed the password on the computer account. However, the computer's hard drive crashed, and the computer was restored from tape backup. The computer now has an outdated password, and the user cannot log on because the computer cannot authenticate to the domain. You now need to reset the computer account. Resetting a computer's account allows it to keep the same SID and GUID and the same group memberships.

Considerations

You must consider two issues before resetting the computer account:

- To perform this procedure, you must be a member of the Account Operators group, the Domain Admins group, or the Enterprise Admins group in Active Directory, or you must be delegated the appropriate authority. As a security best practice, consider using **runas** to perform this procedure.

- When you reset a computer account, you break the computer's connection to the domain, and you must rejoin the computer to the domain.

Additional reading

For more information about resetting a domain controller account and resetting a computer account with a script, see article 325850, "HOW TO: Use Netdom.exe to Reset Machine Account Passwords of a Windows Server 2003 Domain Controller," on the Microsoft Help and Support Web site.

For more information about how the data protection API in Windows handles stored passwords, see the article "Windows Data Protection," on the Microsoft MSDN Web site.

Practice: Resetting and Disabling a User Account

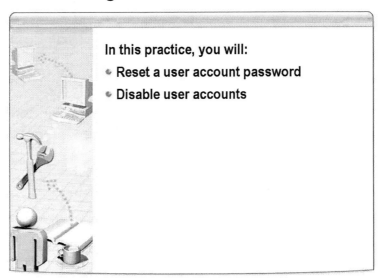

Objective

In this practice, you will

- Reset a user account password.
- Disable user accounts.

Instructions

Ensure that the DEN-DC1 and DEN-CL1 virtual machines are running.

Practice

▶ **Reset a user account password**

1. Log on to DEN-DC1 as **Administrator**, with a password of **Pa$$w0rd**.
2. Open **Active Directory Users and Computers** and then click the **IT Admin** organizational unit.
3. Right-click the **Kerim Hanif** user account, and then click **Reset Password**.
4. In the **Reset Password** dialog box, type **Pa$$w0rd1** in the **New password** and **Confirm password** fields, and then select the **User must change password at next logon** check box.
5. Click **OK**.
6. Click **OK** to confirm that the password has been changed.
7. Switch to DEN-CL1, and then log on as **Kerim@contoso.msft**, with a password of **Pa$$w0rd1**.
8. When prompted to change the password, enter **Pa$$w0rd2** (where 0 is zero) in the **New Password** and **Confirm New Password** fields, and then click **OK**.
9. Click **OK** to confirm that the password has been changed. The logon should be successful.
10. Log off of DEN-CL1.

▶ **Disable user accounts**

1. On DEN-DC1, in **Active Directory Users and Computers**, click the **IT Admin** OU.

2. Right-click the **Luis Bonifaz** user account, and then click **Disable Account**.

3. Click **OK** to confirm that the account has been disabled.

4. Disable the **Kerim Hanif** user account.

5. Close **Active Directory Users and Computers** and then log off of DEN-DC1.

6. Attempt to log on to DEN-CL1 as **luis@contoso.msft**, with a password of **Pa$$w0rd**. The logon should fail, displaying a message that the account has been disabled.

7. Attempt to log on to DEN-CL1 as **Kerim@contoso.msft**, with a password of **Pa$$w0rd2**. The logon attempt will succeed, but any subsequent logon attempt will fail, displaying an account disabled message.

Important   If a user has successfully logged on to the computer and the computer has not been rebooted, the first logon after disabling the account might succeed due to the fast logon features of Windows XP Professional. Subsequent logons will fail.

Lesson: Using Queries to Locate User and Computer Accounts in Active Directory

- Multimedia: Introduction to Locating User and Computer Accounts in Active Directory
- Search Types
- What Is a Saved Query?
- Importing and Exporting Saved Queries
- Practice: Using Saved Queries to Locate Users and Computers in Active Directory

Introduction

The information in this lesson presents the skills and knowledge that you need to use common and custom queries.

Lesson objectives

After completing this lesson, you will be able to:

- Explain the criteria for locating a user or computer account.
- Describe the types of common queries.
- Describe what a saved query is.
- Import and export queries.
- Locate user and computer accounts in Active Directory by using saved queries.

Multimedia: Introduction to Locating User and Computer Accounts in Active Directory

File location

To view the *Introduction to Locating User and Computer Accounts in Active Directory* presentation, open the Web page on the Student Materials compact disc, click **Multimedia**, and then click the title of the presentation. Do not open this presentation unless the instructor tells you to.

Search Types

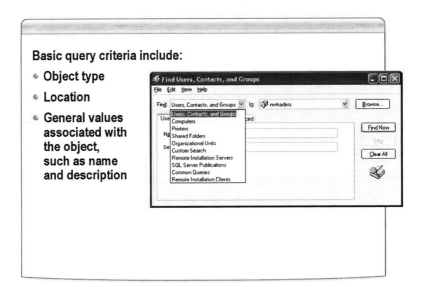

Basic query criteria include:

* Object type

* Location

* General values associated with the object, such as name and description

---

Introduction

Because all user accounts reside in Active Directory, administrators can search for the user accounts that they administer. By searching Active Directory for user accounts, you do not need to browse through hundreds or thousands of user accounts in Active Directory Users and Computers.

In addition to searching for user accounts, you can also search for other Active Directory objects, such as computers, printers, and shared folders. After locating these objects, you can administer them in the **Search Results** box.

Administering objects by using Search Results

After a successful search, the results are displayed, and you can then perform administrative functions on the found objects. The administrative functions that are available depend on the type of object you find. For example, if you search for user accounts, you can rename or delete the user account, disable the user account, reset the password, move the user account to another organizational unit, or modify the user account's properties.

To administer an object in the **Search Results** box, right-click the object, and then click an action on the menu.

Find Users, Contacts, and Groups

Active Directory provides information about all objects on a network, including people, groups, computers, printers, shared folders, and organizational units. It is easy to search for users, contacts, and groups by using the **Find Users, Contacts, and Groups** dialog box.

Find Computers

Use **Find Computers** to search for computers in Active Directory by using criteria such as the name assigned to the computer or the operating system on which the computer runs. After you find the computer you want, you can manage it by right-clicking the computer in the **Search Results** box and then clicking **Manage**.

Find Printers

When a shared printer is published in Active Directory, you can use **Find Printers** to search for the printer by using criteria such as its asset number, the printer language that it uses, or whether it supports double-sided printing. After you find the printer that you want, you can easily connect to it by right-clicking the printer name in the **Search Results** box and then clicking **Connect**, or by double-clicking the printer to connect to the printer.

Find Shared Folders

When a shared folder is published in Active Directory, you can use **Find Shared Folders** to search for the folder by using criteria such as keywords assigned to it, the name of the folder, or the name of the person managing the folder. After you find the folder that you want, open Windows Explorer and display the files located in the folder by right-clicking the folder in the **Search Results** box and then clicking **Explore**.

Find Custom Search

In Active Directory, you can search for familiar objects such as computers, printers, and users. You can also search for other objects, such as a specific organizational unit or certificate template. Use **Find Custom Search** to build custom search queries by using advanced search options or build advanced search queries by using LDAP, which is the primary access protocol for Active Directory.

Find Common Queries

You can use **Find Common Queries** to perform common administrative queries in Active Directory. For example, you can quickly search for user or computer accounts that have been disabled.

Advanced query options

For each search option except **Find Common Queries**, you can use the **Advanced** tab to define a more detailed search. For example, you can search for all users in a city or postal code on the **Advanced** tab.

Using a command line

You can use the **dsquery** command to find users and computers in Active Directory that match the specified search criteria.

For example, to display the user principal names of all users in the Sales organizational unit, at a command prompt, type the following:

dsquery user OU=Sales,DC=contoso,DC=msft -o upn

Note   For the complete syntax of the **dsquery** command, at a command prompt, type **dsquery user /?** or **dsquery computer /?**.

Additional reading

For more information about searching Active Directory, see "Search Companion overview," on the Microsoft Windows Server 2003 Web Site.

What Is a Saved Query?

Introduction

Active Directory Users and Computers has a Saved Queries folder in which you can create, edit, save, and organize saved queries. Before saved queries, administrators were required to create custom Active Directory Services Interfaces (ADSI) scripts that performed a query on common objects. This was an often lengthy process that required knowledge of how ADSI uses LDAP search filters to resolve a query.

Definition

Saved queries use predefined LDAP strings to search only the specified domain partition. You can narrow searches to a single container object. You can also create a customized saved query that contains an LDAP search filter.

All queries are located in the Saved Queries folder named dsa.msc, which is stored in Active Directory Users and Computers. You can create subfolders in the Saved Queries folder to allow you to organize queries. Queries are specific to the domain controller that they were created on. After you successfully create your customized set of queries, you can copy the .msc file to other Windows Server 2003 domain controllers that are in the same domain and reuse the same set of saved queries. You can also export saved queries to an Extensible Markup Language (XML) file. You can then import the queries into other Active Directory Users and Computers consoles located on Windows Server 2003 domain controllers that are in the same domain.

Additional reading

For more information about saved queries, see the article "Using saved queries," on the Microsoft Windows Server 2003 Web site.

Importing and Exporting Saved Queries

Introduction

Queries are valuable tools that assist in finding objects in Active Directory based on many different criteria. But queries are specific to the domain controller that they were created on. Queries can be shared throughout the domain by exporting them to XML files and then importing those files to other domain controllers. In that way, one administrator can write scripts for administrators in other locations to use.

Exporting queries

If you write a complex query that would be useful to other administrators, you can export that query by right-clicking on the query and then clicking **Export Query Definition**. You will be prompted to **Save As an .XML file**. Save the file to a shared folder on the network that only authorized administrators have access to.

Importing queries

You can import a query by right-clicking the Saved Queries folder and then clicking **Import Query Definition**. Navigate to the location of the XML file, and then select it.

Practice: Using Queries to Locate Users and Computers in Active Directory

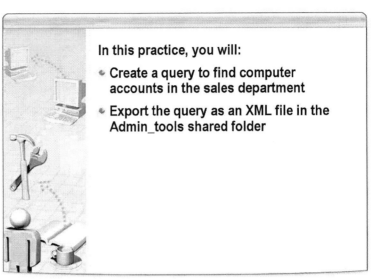

In this practice, you will:

- Create a query to find computer accounts in the sales department
- Export the query as an XML file in the Admin_tools shared folder

Objectives

In this practice, you will:

- Create a query to find computer accounts in the sales department.
- Export the query as an XML file in the Admin_tools shared folder.

Instructions

Ensure that the DEN-DC1 and the DEN-CL1 virtual machines are running.

Practice

▶ **Create a query to find computer accounts in the sales department.**

1. Log on to DEN-DC1 as **Administrator** using a password of **Pa$$w0rd**.

2. Open **Active Directory Users and Computers**, right-click the **Saved Queries** folder, point to **New** and then click **Query**.

3. In the **New Query** dialog box, type **Find Sales Department Computers** in the **Name** field.

4. Click **Define Query**.

5. In the **Find Common Queries** dialog box, click the **Computers** tab. In the **Name** field, click **Starts with**.

6. Type **Sales** in the **Starts with** field.

7. Click **OK** twice.

8. Click the **Find Sales Department Computers** query.

9. The query should find Sales1, Sales2, and Sales3.

▶ **Export the query as an XML file in the Admin_tools shared folder**

1. Right-click the **Find Sales Department Computers** query in the **Saved Queries** folder, and then click **Export Query Definition**.

2. In the **Save As** dialog box, navigate to the **D:\2274\Labfiles\Admin_tools** folder, name the query **Find_Sales_Computers.xml** and then click **Save**.

3. Close **Active Directory Users and Computers** and then Log off of DEN-DC1.

Important Do not shut down the virtual machines.

Lab: Managing User and Computer Accounts

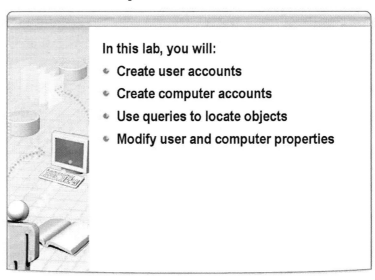

In this lab, you will:
* Create user accounts
* Create computer accounts
* Use queries to locate objects
* Modify user and computer properties

Objectives

After completing this lab, you will be able to:

- Create user accounts.
- Create computer accounts.
- Use queries to locate objects.
- Modify user and computer properties.

Prerequisites

To complete this lab, you must have the following virtual machines:

- DEN-DC1
- DEN-SRV1

Lab setup

Shut down the DEN-CL1 virtual machine without saving changes. Start the DEN-SRV1 virtual machine.

Estimated time to complete this lab: 20 minutes

Exercise 1
Creating User Accounts

In this exercise, you will use a custom MMC to create two new user accounts based on the sales template.

Scenario

Two new salespeople have been hired by Contoso Ltd. You need to create accounts for the new users in the Sales organizational unit in Active Directory.

Tasks	Specific Instructions
1. Create a custom MMC.	a. Log on to DEN-SRV1 as **Judy@contoso.msft** with the password of **Pa$$w0rd**. b. Create a custom MMC, and then add the **Active Directory Users and Computers** snap-in. c. Close the console, and save it as **AD_Admin** in the default location. d. Click **Start**, point to **All Programs**, point to **Administrative Tools**, and then launch **AD_Admin** by using the **Run as** command. Provide the domain administrator's credentials, **contoso\administrator**, with a password of **Pa$$w0rd**.
2. Create user accounts in the Sales organizational unit.	a. In **Active Directory Users and Computers**, click the **Sales** OU. b. Right-click the **Sales Template** user, and then click **Copy**. c. In the **Copy Object – User** dialog box, enter the following: • First Name: **Sunil** • Last Name: **Koduri** • User Logon Name: **Sunil** • Password: **Pa$$w0rd** d. Repeat the preceding steps to create another account with the following information: • First Name: **Jon** • Last Name: **Morris** • User Logon Name: **Jon** • Password: **Pa$$w0rd** e. Enable the accounts.
3. Verify that the template properties were transferred successfully.	a. Open the **Properties** dialog box for one of the accounts that you just created, and verify that the group membership, logon hours, and profile mappings are correct. Review the settings on the **General** tab and the **Organization** tab. b. What values did not transfer from the template?

Exercise 2
Creating Computer Accounts

In this exercise, you will create two new computer accounts.

Scenario

Two new network administrators have been hired by Contoso, Ltd. You added their user accounts earlier. Now you need to create accounts for their computers in the IT Admin organizational unit.

Task	Specific Instructions
1. Create two computer accounts for the new administrators.	a. On DEN-SRV1, in **Active Directory Users and Computers**, click the **IT Admin** organizational unit. b. Create a new computer account with the following parameters: • Name: **Admin2** • Give Kerim Hanif permissions to join the computer to the domain c. Create a second computer with the following parameters: • Name: **Admin3** • Give Luis Bonifaz permissions to join the computer to the domain

Exercise 3
Using Queries to Locate Objects

In this exercise, you will create a query to find users and import a query to find computer accounts.

Scenario

Because new salespeople are frequently hired, you need a query that will easily locate all the current users in the Sales department. You also need a query that will locate all the Sales department computers. Another administrator has built and shared that query. You will import it to you MMC.

Tasks	Specific Instructions
1. Create a saved query to find sales users.	a. Ensure that you are logged on to DEN-SRV1 as Judy Lew. Also make sure that the **AD_Admin** console is open.
	b. In **Active Directory Users and Computers**, create a new query in the **Saved Queries** folder named **Find Sales Users**.
	c. Configure the query to use **Find Users, Contacts and Groups**.
	d. In the **Find Users, Contacts and Groups** dialog box, click the **Advanced** tab.
	e. In the **Field** list, select **User – Department**.
	f. Ensure that **Starts with** is the condition, and type **Sales** in the **Value** field. The query should display all the users in the Sales department.
2. Import a query to locate the computer accounts in the Sales department.	a. Right-click the **Saved Queries** folder, and click **Import Query Definition**.
	b. Navigate to **\\DEN-DC1\admin_tools**.
	c. Select **Find_Sales_Computers.xml**, and click **Open**.
	d. Click **OK**. The query should display the three sales computers.

Exercise 4
Modifying User and Computer Properties

In this exercise, you will modify the properties of multiple users and computer accounts.

Scenario

The location of the Sales department has changed. You need to change the **Office** attribute for the users and the **Description** attribute for the computers in the Sales department.

Tasks	Specific Instructions
1. Use a saved query to locate all the Sales department users and update their **Office** attribute.	a. Ensure that you are logged on to DEN-SRV1 as Judy Lew. Also make sure that the **AD_Admin** console is open. b. In **Active Directory Users and Computers**, expand the **Saved Queries** folder, and then click the **Find Sales Users** query. *Select the first account, and then hold down the SHIFT key and select the last account in the list to select the entire list.* c. Right-click the selected accounts, and then click **Properties**. d. In the **Properties On Multiple Objects** dialog box, select the **Office** check box, and then type **Main Street** in the **Office** field.
2. Use the imported query to locate all the Sales computer accounts and modify their **Description** attribute.	a. In **Active Directory Users and Computers**, expand the **Saved Queries** folder, and then click the **Find Sales Department Computers** query. b. In the Details pane, select all of the computer accounts. c. Right-click the selected accounts, and then click **Properties**. d. On the **General** tab in the **Properties On Multiple Objects** dialog box, change the **Description** setting to **Sales Department**.
3. Complete the lab exercise.	a. Close all programs and shut down all computers. Do not save changes. b. To prepare for the next module, start the DEN-DC1 and DEN-SRV1 virtual computers.

Microsoft

Module 3: Managing Groups

Contents

Overview

- Creating Groups
- Managing Group Membership
- Strategies for Using Groups
- Using Default Groups

Introduction

A *group* is a collection of user accounts. You use groups to efficiently manage access to domain resources, which helps simplify network maintenance and administration. You can use groups separately, or you can place one group within another to further simplify administration.

Before you can effectively use groups, you must understand the function of groups and the types of groups that you can create. The Active Directory® directory service supports different types of groups and also provides options to determine the group's scope, which is how the group can be used in multiple domains.

Objectives

After completing this module, you will be able to:

- Create groups.
- Manage group membership.
- Apply strategies for using groups.
- Manage default groups.

Lesson: Creating Groups

- What Are Groups?
- What Are Domain Functional Levels?
- What Are Global Groups?
- What Are Universal Groups?
- What Are Domain Local Groups?
- What Are Local Groups?
- Guidelines for Creating and Naming Groups
- Who Can Create Groups?
- Practice: Creating Groups

Introduction

The information in this lesson presents the skills and knowledge that you need to create groups.

Lesson objectives

After completing this lesson, you will be able to:

- Explain what groups are and the purpose of groups, group types, and group scopes.
- Identify the domain functional levels.
- Describe global groups.
- Describe universal groups.
- Describe domain local groups.
- Describe local groups.
- Apply best practices for creating and naming groups.
- Explain who can create groups.
- Create groups.

What Are Groups?

Definition

Groups are a collection of user and computer accounts that you can manage as a single unit. Groups:

- Simplify administration by enabling you to grant permissions for resources once to a group rather than to many user accounts individually.
- Can be located in Active Directory or local to an individual computer.
- Are characterized by scope and type.
- Can be nested, which means that you can add a group to another group.

Group scopes

The group scope defines whether the group spans multiple domains or is limited to a single domain. Group scopes enable you to use groups to grant permissions. The group scope defines:

- The domains from which you can add members to the group.
- The domains in which you can use the group to grant permissions.
- The domains in which you can nest the group within other groups.

The group scope also specifies who the members of the group are. Membership rules govern the members that a group can contain and the groups of which a group can be a member. Group members consist of user accounts, computer accounts, and other groups.

To assign the correct members to groups and to use nesting, you must understand the characteristics of the group scope. The group scopes in Active Directory are as follows:

- Global
- Domain local
- Universal

Group types

You use groups to organize user accounts, computer accounts, and other group accounts into manageable units. Working with groups instead of individual users helps simplify network maintenance and administration. The group types in Active Directory are:

- Security groups

   You use security groups to assign user rights and permissions to groups of users and computers. Rights specify what members of a security group can do in a domain or forest, and permissions specify what resources a member of a group can access on the network.

   You can also use security groups to send e-mail messages to multiple users. Sending an e-mail message to the group sends the message to all members of the group. Therefore, security groups have the capabilities of distribution groups.

- Distribution groups

   You use distribution groups with e-mail applications, such as Microsoft® Exchange Server, to send e-mail messages to collections of users. The primary purpose of this type of group is to gather related objects, not to grant permissions.

   Distribution groups are not security-enabled, meaning that they cannot be used to assign permissions. If you need a group for controlling access to shared resources, create a security group.

   Even though security groups have all the capabilities of distribution groups, distribution groups are still required, because some applications can use only distribution groups.

Both distribution and security groups support the three group scopes.

What Are Domain Functional Levels?

	Windows 2000 mixed (default)	Windows 2000 native	Windows Server 2003	Windows Server 2003 interim
Domain controllers supported	Windows NT Server 4.0, Windows 2000, Windows Server 2003	Windows 2000, Windows Server 2003	Windows Server 2003	Windows NT Server 4.0, Windows Server 2003
Group scopes supported	Global, domain local	Global, domain local, universal	Global, domain local, universal	Global, domain local

Group characteristics

The characteristics of groups in Active Directory depend on the domain functional level. Domain functionality enables features that will affect the entire domain and that domain only. Four domain functional levels are available: Microsoft Windows® 2000 mixed, Windows 2000 native, Windows Server™ 2003 interim, and Microsoft Windows Server 2003. By default, domains operate at the Windows 2000 mixed functional level. You can raise the domain functional level to either Windows 2000 native or Windows Server 2003.

The table in the preceding slide lists the domain functional levels and the domain controllers and group scopes that they support.

Note You can convert a group from a security group to a distribution group, and vice versa, at any time, but only if the domain functional level is set to Windows 2000 native or higher.

Additional reading

For more information about raising functional levels, see article 322692, "How to Raise Domain and Functional Levels in Windows Server 2003," on the Microsoft Help and Support Web site.

What Are Global Groups?

	Global group rules
Membership can include	• Mixed functional level: **User and computer accounts from same domain** • Native functional level: **User and computer accounts and global groups from same domain**
Can be a member of	• Mixed functional level: **Domain local groups** • Native functional level: **Universal and domain local groups in any trusting domain and global groups in the same domain**
Scope	**Visible in its own domain and all trusting domains**
Permissions	**All domains in the forest and trusting domains**

Definition

A global group is a security or distribution group that can contain users, groups, and computers that are from the same domain as the global group. You can use global security groups to assign user rights, delegate authority to Active Directory objects, or assign permissions to resources in any domain in the forest or any other trusting domain in another forest.

Characteristics of global groups

The following summarizes the characteristics of global groups:

- **Membership can include:**

  - In Windows 2000 mixed and Windows 2003 interim functional levels, global groups can contain user and computer accounts that are from the same domain as the global group.

  - In Windows 2000 native and Windows Server 2003 functional levels, global groups can contain user accounts, computer accounts, and global groups that are from the same domain as the global group.

- **Global groups can be a member of:**

  - In Windows 2000 mixed and Windows 2003 interim functional levels, a global group can be a member of only domain local or local groups.

  - In Windows 2000 native and Windows Server 2003 functional levels, a global group can be a member of universal, local, and domain local groups in any trusting domain and global groups that are from the same domain as the global group.

- **Scope:**

  A global group is visible within its domain and all trusting domains, which includes all of the domains in the forest.

- **Permissions:**

  You can grant permissions to a global group within its domain and all trusting domains.

When to use global groups

Because global groups have a forest-wide visibility, do not create them for domain-specific resource access. Use a global group to organize users who share the same job tasks and have similar network access requirements. A different group type might be more appropriate for controlling access to resources within a domain.

What Are Universal Groups?

	Universal group rules
Membership can include	• Mixed functional level: **Not applicable** • Native functional level: **User accounts, global groups, and universal groups from any domain in the forest**
Can be a member of	• Mixed functional level: **Not applicable** • Native functional level: **Domain local or universal groups in any domain**
Scope	**Visible in all domains in the forest and all trusting domains**
Permissions	**All domains in the forest and all trusting domains**

Definition

A universal group is a security or distribution group that can contain users, groups, and computers from any domain in its forest. You can use universal security groups to assign user rights and permissions to resources in any domain in the forest.

Characteristics of universal groups

The following list summarizes the characteristics of universal groups:

- **Membership can include:**

  - You cannot create universal security groups in domains at Windows 2000 mixed or Windows 2003 interim functional level.

  - Universal groups can contain user accounts, computer accounts, global groups, and other universal groups from any domain in the forest.

- **Universal groups can be a member of:**

  - The universal security group is not applicable in Windows 2000 mixed and Windows 2003 interim functional levels.

  - Universal groups can be a member of domain local, local, and universal groups in any trusting domain.

- **Scope:**

  Universal groups are visible in all domains in the forest and all trusting domains.

- **Permissions:**

  You can grant permissions to universal groups for all domains in the forest and all trusting domains. The domain must be at the Windows 2000 native or high functional level.

When to use universal groups

Use universal groups to nest global groups so that you can assign permissions to related resources in multiple domains. You can use universal distribution groups to send mail to groups of users. Universal distribution groups can be created in any domain in a Windows 2003 forest in any functional level.

What Are Domain Local Groups?

	Domain local group rules
Membership can include	• Mixed functional level and Windows interim 2003: **User and computer accounts and global groups from any trusted domain** • Native functional level: **User and computer accounts, global and universal groups from any domain in the forest or trusted domains, plus domain local groups from the same domain**
Can be a member of	• Mixed functional level and Windows interim 2003: **None** • Native functional level: **Domain local groups in the same domain**
Scope	**Visible only in its own domain**
Permissions	**Domain to which the domain local group belongs**

Definition

A domain local group is a security or distribution group that can contain other domain local groups that are from its own domain. It can also contain universal groups, global groups, and accounts from any domain in the forest or any trusted domain. You can use domain local security groups to assign user rights and permissions to resources only in the same domain where the domain local group is located.

Characteristics of domain local groups

The following list summarizes the characteristics of domain local groups:

- **Membership can include:**

  - In Windows 2000 mixed and Windows 2003 interim functional levels, domain local groups can contain user accounts, computer accounts, and global groups from any trusted domain. Member servers cannot use domain local groups in Windows 2000 mixed and Windows 2003 interim functional levels.

  - In Windows 2000 native and Windows Server 2000 functional levels, domain local groups can contain user accounts, computer accounts, global groups, and universal groups from any domain in the forest or trusted domains and domain local groups that are from the same domain as the domain local group.

- **Domain local groups can be a member of:**

  - In Windows 2000 mixed and Windows 2003 interim functional levels, a domain local group cannot be a member of any group.

  - In Windows 2000 native and Windows Server 2000 functional levels, a domain local group can be a member of domain local groups that are from the same domain as the domain local group.

- **Scope:**

  A domain local group is visible only in the domain that the domain local group belongs to.

- **Permissions:**

  You can assign permissions to a domain local group for the domain that the domain local group belongs to.

When to use domain local groups

Use a domain local group to assign permissions to resources that are located in the same domain as the domain local group. You can place all global groups that need to share the same resources into the appropriate domain local group.

What Are Local Groups?

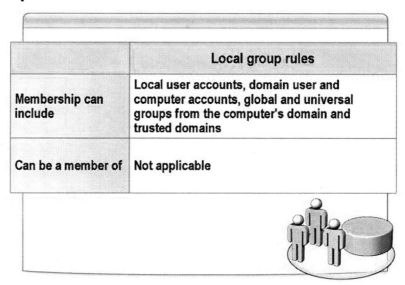

	Local group rules
Membership can include	Local user accounts, domain user and computer accounts, global and universal groups from the computer's domain and trusted domains
Can be a member of	Not applicable

Definition

A local group is a collection of user accounts or domain groups created on a member server or a stand-alone server. You can create local groups to grant permissions for resources residing on the local computer. Windows 2000 and Windows Server 2003 create local groups in the local security database. Local groups can contain users, computers, global groups, and universal groups.

Because groups with a domain local scope are sometimes referred to as local groups, it is important to distinguish between a local group and a group with domain local scope. Local groups are sometimes referred to as machine local groups to distinguish them from domain local groups.

Characteristics of local groups

The following list summarizes the characteristics of local groups:

- In a workgroup environment, local groups can contain only local user accounts from the computer where you create the local group. If the computer is a member of a domain, the local groups can contain domain user and computer accounts, global groups, and universal groups from the computer's domain and trusted domains. Local groups cannot be members of any other group.

When to use local groups

The following are guidelines for using local groups:

- You can use local groups only on the computer where you create the local groups. Local group permissions provide access to resources only on the computer where you created the local group.

- You can use local groups on computers running currently supported Microsoft client operating systems and member servers running Windows Server 2003. You cannot create local groups on domain controllers, because domain controllers cannot have a security database that is independent of the database in Active Directory.

- You can create local groups to limit the ability of local users and groups to access network resources when you do not want to create domain groups.

- Because local groups do not have any built-in redundancy, be sure that the registry of the computer where local groups are used is backed up along with the resources on the computer. In an environment where access to the data is essential, it is better to use domain local groups that are replicated to multiple domain controllers automatically.

Guidelines for Creating and Naming Groups

> • **Create groups in organizational units by using the following naming considerations:**
>   - • Naming conventions for security groups
>   - Incorporate the scope in the group name
>   - Should reflect the group ownership
>   - Use a descriptor to identify the assigned permissions
>   - • Naming conventions for distribution groups
>   - Use short alias names
>   - Do not include a user's alias name in the display name
>   - Allow a maximum of five co-owners of a single distribution group

Introduction

In Active Directory, groups are created in domains. You use Active Directory Users and Computers to create groups in their appropriate containers based on the administrative model.

A standardized naming convention can help you locate and identify groups more easily in a large environment.

Choosing a domain or an organizational unit

Choose the particular domain or organizational unit where you create a group based on the administration requirements for the group.

For example, suppose that your directory has multiple organizational units based on departments. You could create a managers global group in each departmental organizational unit to house the managers accounts and then consolidate them by nesting all those global groups into a Domain_Managers global group.

Important Group Policy assigned to an organizational unit does not affect the members of a group if the user accounts of those members are not located in the same container as the group. For example, if Don Hall is a member of the global group named Domain_Managers, but his user account does not reside in the same container as Domain_Managers, any Group Policy object assigned to the container that contains that global group will not be applied to his user account.

In a multidomain environment, you can nest the groups into universal groups (or other groups with global scope) that can be used elsewhere in the forest. It might be more efficient to nest global groups if the domain functional level is set to Windows 2000 native or higher, the domain contains a hierarchy of organizational units, and administration is delegated to administrators at each organizational unit.

Naming guidelines

A large organization might have many security and distribution groups. The following naming conventions help you manage these groups. Organizations develop their own naming conventions for their security and distribution groups. A group name should identify the scope, the type, who the group was created for, and what permissions the group can have.

Security groups

Consider the following when defining a naming convention for security groups:

- **Scope of security groups:**

  Although the group type and scope are displayed as the group type in Active Directory Users and Computers, organizations can incorporate the scope in the naming convention of the group name.

  For example, Contoso, Ltd., identifies the scope of security groups by adding a first letter to the group name:

  - **G** IT Admins

    G for global groups

  - **U** Enterprise IT Admins

    U for universal groups

  - **DL** IT Resources Full Control

    DL for domain local groups

- **Ownership of the security group:**

  The name for any domain-level security group, whether universal, global, or domain local, should clearly identify function by including the name of the division or team that owns the group.

  The following is an example of a naming convention that Contoso, Ltd., might use to identify group ownership:

  - G **Marketing** Managers

  - DL **IT Admins** Full Control

- **Domain name:**

  In a multidomain environment, the domain name or abbreviation should be placed at the beginning of the group name. For example:

  - G **Contoso** Marketing

- **Purpose of the security group:**

  You can also include the business purpose of the group and maximum permissions the group should have on the network. This naming convention is more applicable to domain local or local groups.

  - DL IT Contoso **OU Admins**

  - DL IT Resources **Full Control**

Distribution groups

Because distribution groups are used only for e-mail purposes, the naming convention must be relevant to an end user.

When defining a naming convention for distribution groups, consider the following:

- **E-mail names:**

  - *Length.* Use a short alias name. To conform to current downstream data standards, the minimum length of this field is three characters and the maximum length is eight characters.

  - *Allowed characters.* You can use all ASCII characters. The only allowed special characters are the hyphen (-) and underscore (_).

  - *Special designations.* Do not use the following character combinations for distributions groups:

    - An underscore (_) as the beginning character of the group name of the alias name

    - A first name or combination of first name and last name that might easily be confused with a user account name

- **Display names:**

  - *User alias names.* For standardization purposes, do not include a user's alias name as part of a display name (for example, Jhay Direct Reports). Include the full name (for example, Jeff Hay's Direct Reports).

  - *Social discussions.* Distribution groups for social discussions should not be allowed, because public folders are a more efficient means of transmitting and storing high-volume communications associated with social discussions. Because a post is visible to multiple users, both network traffic and data storage are minimized if you use public folders instead of corporate distribution groups.

  - *Length.* The maximum length of this field is 40 characters. Abbreviations are acceptable as long as the meaning is clear.

  - *Top of the address book.* Do not use the word *A*, numbers, special characters (especially quotation marks), or a space to begin a description. This makes the name appear at the top of the address book. The address book should begin with individual user names starting with the letter *A*.

  - *Special characters.* Slashes (/) are acceptable in display names, but do not use them in front of server names. Do not use more than one apostrophe (') and do not use the following special characters:
    " * @ # $ % | [ ] ; < > =

- **Ownership:**

  There can be a maximum of five co-owners of a single distribution group.

Local groups

A local group name cannot be identical to any other group or user name on the local computer being administered. A local group name cannot consist solely of periods (.) or spaces. It can contain up to 256 uppercase or lowercase characters, except the following:
" / \ [ ] : ; | = , + * ? < >

Who Can Create Groups?

* In the domain:
  * Account Operators group
  * Domain Admins group
  * Enterprise Admins group
  * Or users with appropriate delegated authority
* On the local computer:
  * Power Users group
  * Administrators group on the local computer
  * Or users with appropriate delegated authority

Introduction

Groups provide administrators with the ability to assign permissions to multiple security principals at one time. The authority to create groups is limited in Active Directory and at the local computer level.

Who can create groups in the domain?

To create groups in Active Directory, you must be a member of the Account Operators group, the Domain Admins group, or the Enterprise Admins group, or you must be delegated the appropriate permissions. As a security best practice, consider logging on with a regular user account and using **Run as** when creating groups.

Who can create local groups?

To create local groups, you must be a member of the Power Users group or the Administrators group on the local computer, or you must be delegated the appropriate authority. If the computer is joined to a domain, members of the Domain Admins group are able to perform this procedure. As a security best practice, consider using **Run as** to perform this procedure.

Tools to create groups

You can use the following tools to create local and domain groups:

* *Local Users and Groups snap-in in Computer Management.* Allows you to create local groups.

* *Active Directory Users and Computers.* Allows you to create groups in any trusted domain where you have authority.

* *Command line.* Allows you to create global, domain local, or universal groups For example, you can use the **dsadd** command to create a global security group named Finance Users. At a command prompt, you would type the following:

  dsadd group "cn=Finance Users,ou=finance,dc=contoso,dc=msft" -samid FinanceUsers -secgrp yes -scope g

The following table lists the most commonly used syntax for the **dsadd** group command.

Value	Description
groupDN	Specifies the distinguished name of the group object that you want to add
samid	Specifies the Security Accounts Manager (SAM) name as the unique SAM account name for this group (for example, operators)
secgrp yes | no	Specifies whether the group you want to add is a security group (**yes**) or a distribution group (**no**)
scope l | g | u	Specifies whether the scope of the group you want to add is domain local (**l**), global (**g**), or universal (**u**)

Note   To view the complete syntax for this command, type **dsadd group /?** at a command prompt.

Practice: Creating Groups

In this practice, you will:

• Create groups by using Active Directory Users and Computers

• Create groups by using the dsadd command-line tool

Objective

In this practice, you will:

■ Create groups by using Active Directory Users and Computers.

■ Create groups by using the **dsadd** command-line tool.

Instructions

Ensure that the DEN-DC1 virtual machine is running.

Practice

▶ **Create groups by using Active Directory Users and Computers**

1. Log on to DEN-DC1 as **Administrator**, with a password of **Pa$$w0rd**.

2. Open **Active Directory Users and Computers**, and select the **Graphics** organizational unit.

3. Right-click the **Graphics** organizational unit, point to **New**, and then click **Group**.

4. In the **New Object – Group** dialog box, ensure that **Global** is selected as the group scope and that **Security** is selected as the group type.

5. Type **G Graphics Managers** in the **Group Name** field.

6. Click **OK**.

7. Repeat steps 3 through 6 to create a second global group named **G Graphics Users**.

8. Create a new domain local group, and then type **DL Graphics Managers** in the **Group Name** field.

9. Change the **Group Scope** to **Domain local**.

10. Click **OK**.

11. Repeat steps 8 through 10 to create the final domain local group, named **DL Graphics Users**.

Practice: Using the command line

▶ **Create groups by using the dsadd command-line tool**

1. Open a command prompt window.

2. Enter the following command and then press ENTER:

   dsadd group "cn=IT Admin,ou=IT Admin,dc=contoso,dc=msft" –samid ITadmin –secgrp yes –scope g

3. Close all windows and log off of DEN-DC1.

Important   Do not shut down the virtual machine.

Lesson: Managing Group Membership

- Determining Group Membership
- Adding and Removing Members from a Group
- Practice: Managing Group Membership

Introduction

Because many users often require access to different resources throughout an organization, administrators might have to grant membership to groups that reside in Active Directory or on local computers.

Lesson objectives

After completing this lesson, you will be able to:

- Determine the membership of a group.
- Add members to and remove members from a group.
- Manage group memberships.

Determining Group Membership

Introduction

All user accounts have a **Member Of** attribute that lists all of the groups that the user is a member of. All groups have a **Members** attribute and a **Member Of** attribute. The **Members** attribute lists all user accounts or other group accounts that are members of the group. The preceding illustration describes the **Members** and **Member Of** attributes.

Members and Member Of tabs

Tom, Jo, and Kim are *members of* the G Denver Admins global group. The global group G Denver Admins is a *member of* the domain local group DL OU Admins.

Sam, Scott, and Amy are *members of* the G Vancouver Admins global group. The global group G Vancouver Admins is a *member of* the domain local group DL OU Admins.

The following table summarizes the information in the slide.

User or group	Members	Member Of
Tom, Jo, Kim	N/A	G Denver Admins
G Denver Admins	Tom, Jo, Kim	DL OU Admins
Sam, Scott, Amy	N/A	G Vancouver Admins
G Vancouver Admins	Sam, Scott, Amy	DL OU Admins
DL OU Admins	G Denver Admins G Vancouver Admins	N/A

By viewing the **Members** and **Member Of** attributes, you can determine which groups a user belongs to or which groups a group belongs to.

Determining group membership	After you add users to groups, Active Directory updates the **Member Of** attribute of their user accounts.

To determine the groups that a user is a member of:

1. In **Active Directory Users and Computers**, in the domain node, click **Users** or click the container that holds the user account.
2. In the Details pane, right-click a user account, and then click **Properties**.
3. In the **Properties** dialog box, click the **Member Of** tab.

Note   You do not need administrative credentials to perform this task. Therefore, as a security best practice, consider performing this task as a user without administrative credentials.

Using a command line	To determine the groups a user is a member of by using **dsget**:

1. Open a command prompt window.
2. Type **dsget user** *UserDN* **-memberof** at the command prompt.

Value	Description
UserDN	Specifies the distinguished name of the user object for which you want to display group membership

Note   To view the complete syntax for this command, type **dsget user /?** at a command prompt.

Adding and Removing Members from a Group

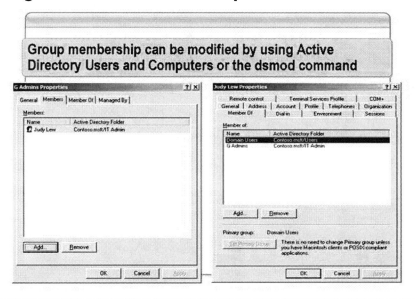

Introduction

After creating a group, you can add members by using Active Directory Users and Computers. Members of groups can include user accounts, computers, or other groups. You can modify membership from the user account or the group account Properties dialog box.

Using Active Directory Users and Computers to modify group membership

To add members to or remove members from a group by configuring the group properties:

1. In Active Directory Users and Computers, in the console tree, click the folder that contains the group to which you want to add a member.

2. In the Details pane, right-click the group, and then click **Properties**.

3. In the **Properties** dialog box, on the **Members** tab, click **Add**.

   If you want to remove a member from the group, click the member, and then click **Remove**.

4. In the **Select Users, Contact, Computers, or Groups** dialog box, in the **Enter the object names to select** box, type the name of the user, group, or computer that you want to add to the group, and then click **OK**.

Tip   You can also add a user account or group by using the **Member Of** tab in the **Properties** dialog box for that user account or group. Use this method to quickly add the same user or group to multiple groups.

To add a user to a group by using the shortcut menu:

1. In **Active Directory Users and Computers**, select the user that you want to add to a group.

2. Right-click the account, and then click **Add to a group**.

3. In the **Select Group** dialog box, in the **Enter the object names to select** box, type the name of the group that you want to add to the user to, and then click **OK**.

Tip   You can also use the shortcut menu for a user that you have located by using the **find** command.

Using dsmod to modify group membership

To modify group membership by using **dsmod**, open a command prompt window, and use the following syntax:

Dsmod group *groupDN* [{**-addmbr** | **-rmmbr** | **-chmbr**} *memberDN ...*] {**-addmbr** | **-rmmbr** | **-chmbr**} **MemberDN** ...

Members specified by **MemberDN ...** are to be added to, removed from, or replaced in the group. Only one of these parameters can be specified in any single command invocation. **MemberDN ...** specifies the distinguished names of one or more members to be added to, deleted from, or replaced in the group specified by **GroupDN**. Each member must be listed using a distinguished name.

Practice: Managing Group Membership

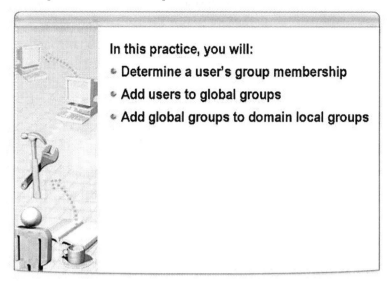

Objectives

In this practice, you will:

- Determine a user's group membership.
- Add users to global groups.
- Add global groups to domain local groups.

Instructions

Ensure that the DEN-DC1 virtual machine is running.

Practice

▶ **Determine a user's group membership**

1. Log on to DEN-DC1 using the **Administrator** account with the password of **Pa$$w0rd**.

2. Open **Active Directory Users and Computers**.

3. Click the **Sales** organizational unit.

4. Open the **Properties** dialog box for **Don Hall**. Click the **Member Of** tab. What groups is **Don Hall** a member of? *Domain Users*

   G Sales , G sales Managers

5. In the **Sales** organizational unit, open the **Properties** dialog box for the **G Sales** group.

   a. Click the **Members** tab. Who is in the G Sales group? *Don Harl*

   Jeff Hay

   Kim Yoshida

   b. Click the **Member Of** tab. What groups does **G Sales** belong to?

   DL Sales Read

► **Add users to global groups**

1. In **Active Directory Users and Computers**, right-click the domain node, and then click **Find**.

2. In the **Find Users, Contacts, and Groups** dialog box, click the **Advanced** tab.

3. In the **Field** list, point to **User** and then click **Department**.

4. Select **Is (exactly)** in the **Condition** list, and then type **Graphics** in the value field.

5. Click **Add** to add the criteria to the condition list.

6. Click **Find Now**.

   The query should return two users, **Graphics User** and **Graphics Manager**.

7. Select both users. Right-click, and then click **Add to a group**.

8. In the **Select Group** dialog box, type **G** in the **Object Name** field, and then click **Check Names**.

   (A list of all global groups will be displayed because your naming convention uses the first letter *G* to distinguish global groups.)

9. Select **G Graphics Users** in the list.

10. Click **OK**.

11. Click **OK** again to add the accounts to the G Graphics Users group.

12. Click **OK** to confirm the group addition.

13. Select just the **Graphics Manager** user account, right-click, and then click **Add to a group**.

14. Repeat steps 8 through 12 to add **Graphics Manager** to the **G Graphics Managers** global group.

15. Close the **Find Users, Contacts, and Groups** dialog box.

► **Add global groups to domain local groups**

1. In Active Directory Users and Computers, click the **Graphics** organizational unit.

2. In the Details pane, double-click **DL Graphics Users**.

3. Click the **Members** tab.

4. Click **Add**.

5. In the **Select Users, Contacts, Computers, or Groups** dialog box, type **G Graphics Users** in the object name field, and then click **Check Names**.

6. Click **OK** twice.

7. Repeat steps 2 through 6 to add the **G Graphics Managers** global group to the **DL Graphics Managers** domain local group.

8. Close Active Directory Users and Computers.

9. Log off of DEN-DC1.

Important   Do not shut down the virtual machines.

Lesson: Strategies for Using Groups

- Multimedia: Strategy for Using Groups in a Single Domain
- What Is Group Nesting?
- Group Strategies
- Class Discussion: Using Groups in a Single-Domain or Multiple-Domain Environment
- Practice: Nesting Groups and Creating Universal Groups
- Modifying the Scope or Type of a Group?
- Why Assign a Manager to a Group?
- Practice: Changing the Scope and Assigning a Manager to a Group

Introduction

To use groups effectively, you need strategies for applying different group scopes. This lesson covers the skills and knowledge that you need to use groups optimally by employing different strategies with groups.

Lesson objectives

After completing this lesson, you will be able to:

- Explain the A G DL P strategy for using groups in a single domain.
- Describe group nesting.
- Describe the following strategies for using groups:
  - A G P
  - A G DL P
  - A G U DL P
  - A G L P
- Implement strategies for using groups.
- Configure group nesting using universal groups.
- Explain what it means to modify the scope or type of a group.
- Explain why you assign a manager to a group.
- Change group scopes and assign group managers.

Multimedia: Strategy for Using Groups in a Single Domain

File location

To view the *Strategy for Using Groups in a Single Domain* presentation, open the Web page on the Student Materials compact disc, click **Multimedia**, and then click the title of the presentation. Do not open this presentation until the instructor tells you to.

Key points

The A G DL P model represents a group strategy where users are placed into global groups, global groups are placed into domain local groups and domain local groups are assigned permission to resources.

User accounts → Global groups → Domain local groups ← Permissions

      (A)   (G)   (DL)   (P)

What Is Group Nesting?

* *Group nesting* means adding a group as a member of another group
* Nest groups to consolidate group management
* Nesting options depend on the domain functional level

Introduction

By using nesting, you can add a group as a member of another group. You can nest groups to consolidate group management. Nesting increases the member accounts that are affected by a single action and reduces replication traffic caused by the replication of changes in group membership.

Nesting options

Your nesting options depend on the domain functional level of your Windows Server 2003 domain. In domains where the domain functional level is set to Windows 2000 native or Windows Server 2003, group membership is determined as follows:

- Universal groups can have as their members: user accounts, computer accounts, universal groups, and global groups from any trusted domain.

- Global groups can have as their members: user accounts, computer accounts, and global groups from the same domain.

- Domain local groups can have as their members: user accounts, computer accounts, universal groups, and global groups, all from any trusted domain. They can also have other domain local groups from within the same domain.

You cannot create security groups with universal scope in domains where the domain functional level is set to Windows 2000 mixed or Windows 2003 interim.

Note Minimize the levels of nesting. A single level of nesting is the most effective method, because tracking permissions is more complex with multiple levels.

Also, troubleshooting becomes difficult if you must trace permissions through multiple levels of nesting. Therefore, document group membership to keep track of permissions.

Group Strategies

Introduction

To use groups effectively, you need strategies for applying the different group scopes. The strategy that you choose depends on the Windows network environment of your organization. In a single domain, the common practice is to use global and domain local groups to grant permissions for network resources. In a network with multiple domains, you can incorporate nested global or universal groups into your strategy.

A G P

With A G P, you place user accounts (A) in global groups (G), and you grant permissions (P) to the global groups. The limitation of this strategy is that it complicates administration when you use multiple domains. If global groups from multiple domains require the same permissions, you must grant permissions to each global group individually.

When to use the A G P strategy

Use A G P for forests with one domain and very few users and to which you will never add other domains.

A G P has the following advantages:

- Groups are not nested and therefore troubleshooting might be easier.

- Accounts belong to a single group scope.

A G P has the following disadvantages:

- Every time a user authenticates with a resource, the server must check the global group membership to determine whether the user is still a member of the group.

- Performance degrades, because a global group is not cached.

Note   Another strategy might be to put users directly into domain local groups and not use global groups. The A DL P strategy has similar characteristics and could be suitable in the same circumstances.

A G DL P

With A G DL P, you place user accounts (A) in global groups (G), place the global groups in domain local groups (DL), and then grant permissions (P) to the domain local groups. This strategy creates flexibility for network growth and reduces the number of times you must set permissions.

When to use the A G DL P strategy

Use A G DL P for a forest consisting of one or more domains and to which you might have to add future domains.

A G DL P has the following advantages:

- Domains are flexible.
- Resource owners require less access to Active Directory to flexibly secure their resources.

A G DL P has the following disadvantage:

- A tiered management structure is more complex to set up initially, but easier to manage over time.

A G U DL P

With A G U DL P, you place user accounts (A) in global groups (G), place the global groups in universal groups (U), place the universal groups in domain local groups (DL), and then grant permissions (P) to the domain local groups.

When to use the A G U DL P strategy

Use A G U DL P for a forest with more than one domain so that administrators can consolidate global groups from multiple domains into one universal group. That universal group could then be placed into any domain local group in any trusting domain and thereby grant rights or permissions to many global groups across multiple domains with one action.

A G U DL P has the following advantages:

- There is flexibility across the forest.
- It enables centralized administration.

Note Domain local groups should not be used to assign permissions to Active Directory objects in a forest with more than one domain because domain local groups cannot be evaluated in other domains. For more information, see article 231273, "Group Type and Scope Usage in Windows," on the Microsoft Help and Support Web site.

A G U DL P has the following disadvantages:

- The membership of universal groups is stored in the global catalog.

  Note The global catalog is a domain controller that stores a copy of all Active Directory objects in a forest. The global catalog stores a full copy of all objects in Active Directory for its host domain and a partial copy of all objects for all other domains in the forest.

- It might be necessary to add more global catalog servers.
- There might be global catalog replication latency. When referring to the global catalog, *latency* is the time it takes to replicate a change to each global catalog server in the forest.

There is a disadvantage to using universal groups only if the universal groups have a very dynamic membership with a lot of global catalog replication traffic as the membership changes in a multidomain forest. With A G U DL P, this is less of an issue, because the membership of universal groups is relatively static (that is, the universal group has global groups, not individual users, as members).

Important Even if you do not use universal groups, in native functional level, a global catalog server must be available to determine whether a universal group membership exists in order for users to have a successful logon. If you are sure you will never use universal groups, you can disable this requirement. For more information, see article 241789, "How to disable the requirement that a global catalog server be available to validate user logons," on the Microsoft Help and Support Web site.

A G L P

Use the A G L P strategy to place user accounts in a global group and grant permissions to the local group. One limitation of this strategy is that you cannot grant permissions for resources outside the local computer.

Therefore, place user accounts in a global group, add the global group to the local group, and then grant permissions to the local group. With this strategy, you can use the same global group on multiple local computers.

Note Use domain local groups whenever possible. Use local groups only when a domain local group has not been created for this purpose.

When to use the A G L P strategy

Use the A G L P strategy when your domain has the following requirements:

- To upgrade from Microsoft Windows NT® 4.0 to Windows Server 2003
- To maintain a Windows NT 4.0 group strategy
- To maintain centralized user management with decentralized resource management

It is recommended that you use A G L P with Windows Server 2003 Active Directory and Windows NT 4.0 member servers.

A G L P has the following advantages:

- It maintains the Windows NT 4.0 group strategy.
- Resource owners own membership to every group that needs access.

A G L P has the following disadvantages:

- Active Directory does not control access.
- You must create redundant groups across member servers.
- It does not enable centralized administration of resources.
- Local group memberships are not replicated.

Class Discussion: Using Groups in a Single-Domain or Multiple-Domain Environment

Examples 1 and 2
Contoso, Ltd., has a single domain that is located in Paris, France. Contoso managers need access to the Inventory database to perform their jobs. What do you do to ensure that the managers have access to the Inventory database?

Example 3
Contoso, Ltd., has expanded to include operations in South America and Asia and now has three domains. You need to grant access to all IT managers from all domains to the IT_Admin tools shared folder in the Contoso domain.

Example 1

Contoso, Ltd., has a single domain that is located in Paris, France. Contoso, Ltd., managers need access to the Inventory database to perform their jobs.

What do you do to ensure that the managers have access to the Inventory database?

_____

_____

_____

_____

Example 2

Contoso, Ltd., has determined that all Accounting division personnel must have full access to the accounting data. Also, Contoso, Ltd., executives must be able to view the data. Contoso, Ltd., wants to create the group structure for the entire Accounting division, which includes the Accounts Payable and Accounts Receivable departments.

What do you do to ensure that the managers have the required access and that there is a minimum of administration?

_____

_____

_____

_____

Example 3

Contoso, Ltd., has expanded to include operations in South America and Asia and now contains three domains: the Contoso.msft domain, the Asia.contoso.msft domain, and the SA.contoso.msft domain. You need to grant access to all IT managers across all domains to the Admin_tools shared folder in the Contoso domain. You will also need to grant those users access to other resources in the future. How can you achieve the desired result with the least amount of administrative effort?

_____

_____

_____

_____

_____

_____

_____

Practice: Nesting Groups and Creating Universal Groups

In this practice, you will:

● Create the Contoso Managers global group

● Nest the departmental Managers global groups into G Contoso Managers

● Create an Enterprise Managers universal group

● Examine the Members and Member Of properties

Objective

In this practice, you will:

■ Create the Contoso Managers global group.

■ Nest the departmental Managers global groups into G Contoso Managers.

■ Create an Enterprise Managers universal group.

■ Examine the Members and Member Of properties.

Instructions

Ensure that the DEN-DC1 virtual machine is running.

Practice

▶ **Create the Contoso Managers global group**

1. Log on to DEN-DC1 by using the **Administrator** account with the password of **Pa$$w0rd**.

2. Open **Active Directory Users and Computers**.

3. Right-click the **Users** container, point to **New**, and then click **Group**.

4. Name the new group **G Contoso Managers**.

5. Ensure that the group scope is set to **Global**, and then click **OK**.

▶ **Nest the departmental Managers global groups into G Contoso Managers**

1. Open the **Properties** dialog box for **G Contoso Managers**.

2. Click the **Members** tab, and then click **Add**.

3. Find the names of objects that start with *G*.

4. Add the **G Graphics Managers**, **G Legal Managers**, and **G Sales Managers** groups to **G Contoso Managers**.

Tip   Hold down the CTRL key and click to select noncontiguous objects in the list.

---

5. Click **OK** three times.

▶ **Create an Enterprise Managers universal group**

1. In the Users container, create a new group, named **U Enterprise Managers**.

2. Change the Group scope setting to **Universal**.

3. Click **OK**.

4. Open the **Properties** dialog box for **U Enterprise Managers**, and then click the **Members** tab.

5. Click **Add**, and then type **G Contoso Managers**.

6. Click **OK** twice.

Note   If there were multiple domains, you would add the global domain managers groups from all domains to the universal managers group.

▶ **Examine the Members and Member Of properties**

1. Open the **Properties** dialog box for the **G Graphics Managers** global group, and then click the **Members** tab. Who are the members?

2. Click the **Member Of** tab. What groups is **G Graphics Managers** a member of?

   _____

   _____

3. Open the **Properties** dialog box for the **G Contoso Managers** global group. Click the **Members** tab. What groups are members?

   _G Graphics Managers_____

   _G Legal Manager_____

   _G Sales Managers_____

4. Now click the **Member Of** tab. What groups is **G Contoso Managers** a member of?

   _U Enterprise Managers_____

   _____

5. Close all windows and log off of DEN-DC1.

Important Do not shut down the virtual machines.

Modifying the Scope or Type of a Group?

* Changing group scope
  * Global to universal
  * Domain local to universal
  * Universal to global
  * Universal to domain local
* Changing group type
  * Security to distribution
  * Distribution to security

Introduction

When you create a new group, by default, the new group is configured as a security group with global scope, regardless of the current domain functional level.

Changing group scope

Although you cannot change group scope in domains with a domain functional level set to Windows 2000 mixed or Windows Server 2003 Interim, you can make the following scope changes in domains with the domain functional level set to Windows 2000 native or Windows Server 2003:

- *Global to universal*. This is allowed only if the group you want to change is not a member of another global group.

  Note You cannot change a group's scope from global to domain local directly. To do that, you must change the group's scope from global to universal and then from universal to domain local.

- *Domain local to universal*. This is allowed only if the group you want to change does not have another domain local group as a member.

- *Universal to global*. This is allowed only if the group you want to change does not have another universal group or a global group from outside of its domain as a member.

- *Universal to domain local*. There are no restrictions for this change.

Changing group type

You can convert a group from a security group to a distribution group, and vice versa, at any time, but only if the domain functional level is set to Windows 2000 native or higher. You cannot convert a group while the domain functional level is set to Windows 2000 mixed or Windows Server 2003 Interim.

You can convert groups from one type to the other in the following scenarios:

- *Security to distribution.* A company splits into two companies. Users migrate from one domain to another domain, but they keep their old e-mail addresses. You want to send them e-mail messages by using old security groups, but you want to remove security context from the group.

- *Distribution to security.* A distribution group gets very large, and the users want to use this group for security-related tasks. However, they still want to use the group for e-mail.

Note Although you can add a contact to a security group and to a distribution group, you cannot grant permissions to contacts. You can send contacts e-mail messages.

Why Assign a Manager to a Group?

Advantages of assigning a manager to a group

Active Directory in Windows Server 2003 allows you to assign a manager to a group as a property of the group. This enables you to:

- Track who is responsible for groups.

- Delegate to the manager of the group the authority to add users to and remove users from the group.

Because people in large organizations are added to and removed from groups so often, some organizations distribute the administrative responsibility of adding users to groups to the people who request the group.

If you document who the manager of the group is, the contact information for that user account is recorded. If the group ever needs to be migrated to another domain or needs to be deleted, the network administrator has a record of who owns the group and that person's contact information. The network administrator can then call or send an e-mail message to the manager to notify the manager about the change that must be made to the group.

Practice: Changing the Scope and Assigning a Manager to a Group

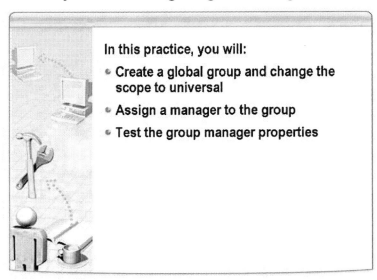

Objective

In this practice, you will:

- Create a global group and change the scope to universal.
- Assign a manager to the group.
- Test the group manager properties.

Instructions

Ensure that the DEN-DC1 and DEN-SRV1 virtual machines are running.

Practice

▶ **Create a global group and change the scope to universal**

1. Log on to DEN-DC1 as the **Administrator** account with the password of **Pa$$w0rd**.
2. Open **Active Directory Users and Computers**.
3. In the **Users** container, create a global group named **G Contoso Helpdesk**.
4. Open the **Properties** dialog box for the group, and then click the **Universal** option in the **Group scope** settings.
5. Click **OK**.

▶ **Assign a manager to the group**

1. Open the **Properties** dialog box for the **G Contoso Helpdesk** group.
2. Click the **Managed By** tab, and then click **Change**.
3. In the **Select User, Contact, or Group** dialog box, enter **Judy Lew**.
4. Click **OK**.
5. On the **Managed By** tab, select the **Manager can update membership list** check box.
6. Click **OK**.
7. Close all windows and log off of DEN-DC1.

► **Test the group manager properties**

1. Log on to DEN-SRV1 as **Judy** with the password of **Pa$$w0rd**.

2. Create a custom Microsoft Management Console (MMC), and then add the Active Directory Users and Computers snap-in.

3. Open **Active Directory Users and Computers**.

4. Click the **Users** container, and then open the **Properties** dialog box for the **G Contoso Managers** global group.

5. Click the **Members** tab, and then click **Add**.

6. Attempt to add **Anne Paper** to this group.

   You should not be able to add any users to this group.

7. Close the **G Contoso Managers Properties** dialog box.

8. Open the **Properties** dialog box for **G Contoso Helpdesk**.

9. Attempt to add **Jeff Hay** to this group.

   This should succeed because Judy Lew was given authority to add users to this group.

10. Close the custom MMC without saving changes.

11. Log off of DEN-SRV1.

Important   Do not shut down the virtual machines.

Lesson: Using Default Groups

- Default Groups on Member Servers
- Default Groups in Active Directory
- When to Use Default Groups
- Security Considerations for Default Groups
- System Groups
- Class Discussion: Using Default Groups vs. Creating New Groups
- Best Practices for Managing Groups

Introduction

This lesson demonstrates how default groups are used.

Lesson objectives

After completing this lesson, you will be able to:

- Explain how default groups are used on member servers.
- Explain how default groups are used in Active Directory.
- Identify when to use default groups.
- Identify the security considerations for default groups.
- Explain how system groups are used.
- Plan a strategy for using default groups or creating new groups.
- Implement best practices for managing groups.

Default Groups on Member Servers

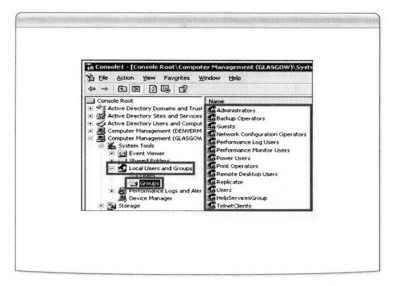

Definition

The Groups folder is located on a member server in the Local Users and Groups console, which displays all built-in default local groups and any local groups you create. The default local groups are created automatically when you install Windows Server 2003. The local groups can contain local user accounts, domain user accounts, computer accounts, global groups, and universal groups.

Default local groups on member servers

The following table describes some of the default local groups on a member or stand-alone server running Windows Server 2003.

Group	Description
Administrators	• Members have full control of the server and can assign user rights and access control permissions to users as necessary.
	• Administrator is a default member account and has full control of the server.
	• Users should be added with caution.
	• When joined to a domain, the Domain Admins group is automatically added to this group.
Guests	• A temporary profile is created for a member when the member logs on.
	• When the guest member logs off, the profile is deleted.
	• The Guest account is disabled by default.
Performance Log Users	• Members can manage performance counters, logs, and alerts on the server locally and from remote clients without being a member of the Administrators group.
Backup Operators	• Members can override security restrictions for the sole purpose of backing up and restoring files on the local machine.

(continued)

Group	Description
Performance Monitor Users	• Members can monitor performance counters on the server locally and from remote clients without being a member of the Administrators or Performance Log Users groups.
Power Users	• Members can create user accounts and then modify and delete the accounts that they have created. • Members can create local groups and then add or remove users from the local groups that they have created. • Members can add or remove users from the Power Users, Users, and Guests groups. • Members can create shared resources and administer the shared resources that they have created. • Members cannot take ownership of files, back up or restore directories, load or unload device drivers, or manage security and auditing logs.
Print Operators	• Members can manage printers and print queues.
Users	• Members can perform common tasks, such as running applications, using local and network printers, and locking the server. • Users cannot share directories or create local printers. • The Domain Users, Authenticated Users, and Interactive groups are members of this group. Therefore, any user account created in the domain becomes a member of this group.

Note   Group memberships can be controlled by configuring restricted group policies in Group Policy. For more information, see Module 7, "Managing the User Environment by Using Group Policy," in Course 2273, *Managing and Maintaining a Microsoft Windows Server 2003 Environment*.

The following additional groups, also default groups on a member server, are not commonly used:

- Network Configuration Operators
- Remote Desktop Users
- Replicator
- HelpServicesGroup
- Terminal Server Users

Note   For more information about default groups on member servers, search for "default local groups" in Windows Server 2003 Help.

Default groups used by network services

The following table describes the default groups used by network services and installed only with the Dynamic Host Configuration Protocol (DHCP) service or the Windows Internet Name Service (WINS).

Group	Membership
DHCP Administrators	• Members have administrative access to the DHCP service. • The DHCP Administrators group provides security to assign limited administrative access to the DHCP server only, while not providing full access to the server. • Members can administer DHCP on a server by using the DHCP console or the **Netsh** command, but they cannot perform other administrative actions on the server.
DHCP Users	• Members have read-only access to the DHCP service. • Members can view information and properties stored on a specified DHCP server. This information is useful to support staff when they need to obtain DHCP status reports.
WINS Users	• Members are permitted read-only access to WINS. • Members can view information and properties stored on a specified WINS server. This information is useful to support staff when they need to obtain WINS status reports.

Default Groups in Active Directory

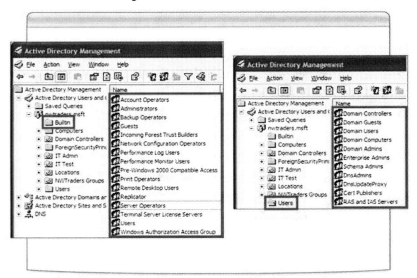

Definition

Default groups are security groups that are automatically created when you install an Active Directory domain. You can use these predefined groups to manage shared resources and delegate specific domain-wide administrative roles.

Default groups and user rights

Many default groups are automatically assigned a set of user rights that determine what each group and their members can do within the scope of a domain or forest. User rights authorize members of a group to perform specific actions, such as log on to a local system or back up files and folders. For example, a member of the Backup Operators group has the right to perform backup operations for all domain controllers in the domain.

Default groups and containers

Several default groups are available in the Users and Builtin containers of Active Directory. The Builtin container contains domain local groups. The Users container contains global groups and domain local groups. You can move groups in the Users and Builtin containers to other group or organizational unit folders in the domain, but you cannot move them to other domains.

Default groups in the Builtin container

The following table describes each default group in the Builtin container in Active Directory. When a member server or stand-alone server becomes a domain controller, all of these default groups are added, along with the user rights that are assigned to each group.

Group	Description
Account Operators	• Members can create, modify, and delete accounts for users, groups, and computers located in the Users or Computers container and organizational units in the domain, except the Domain Controllers organizational unit. • Members do not have permission to modify the Administrators or the Domain Admins group or accounts for members of those groups. • Members can log on locally to domain controllers in the domain and shut them down. • Because this group has significant power in the domain, add users with caution.
Incoming Forest Trust Builders	• Members can create one-way, incoming forest trusts to the forest root domain. • Has no default members.
Pre-Windows 2000 Compatible Access	• Members have read access on all users and groups in the domain. • Provided for backward compatibility for computers running Windows NT 4.0 and earlier. • Add users to this group only if they are using Remote Access Service (RAS) on a computer running Windows NT 4.0 or earlier.
Server Operators	• Members can log on interactively, create and delete shared resources, start and stop some services, back up and restore files, format the hard disk, and shut down the computer. • Has no default members. • Because this group has significant power on domain controllers, add users with caution.

Default groups in the Users container

The following table describes some of the default groups in the Users container and the user rights that are assigned to each group.

Group	Description
Domain Controllers	• Contains all domain controllers in the domain.
Domain Guests	• Contains all domain guests.
Domain Users	• Contains all domain users. • Any user account that is created in the domain is a member of this group automatically.
Domain Computers	• Contains all workstations and servers joined to the domain. • Any computer account that is created becomes a member of this group automatically.
Domain Admins	• Members have full control of the domain. • Is a member of the Administrators group on all domain controllers, all domain workstations, and all domain member servers at the time they are joined to the domain. • The Administrator account is a member of this group. Because the group has full power in the domain, add users with caution.
Enterprise Admins	• Members have full control of all domains in the forest. • Is a member of the Administrators group on all domain controllers in the forest. • The Administrator account is a member of this group. Because this group has full control of all domains in the forest, add users with caution.
Group Policy Creator Owners	• Members can modify Group Policy in the domain. • The Administrator account is a member of this group. Because this group has significant power in the domain, add users with caution.

The following list contains the additional default groups that have special purposes:

■ Schema Admins

■ DnsAdmins

■ DnsUpdateProxy

■ Cert Publishers

■ RAS and IAS Servers

Note For more information about other groups in the Users container, search for "Active Directory default groups" in Windows Server 2003 Help.

When to Use Default Groups

- **Default groups are:**
  - Created during the installation of the operating system or when services are added
  - Automatically assigned a set of user rights
- **Use default groups to:**
  - Control access to shared resources
  - Delegate specific domain-wide administration

Using default groups

Predefined groups help you to control access to shared resources and delegate specific domain-wide administrative roles. Many default groups are automatically assigned a set of user rights that authorize members of the group to perform specific actions in a domain, such as logging on to a local system or backing up files and folders.

When you add a user to a group, the user receives all the user rights assigned to the group and all the permissions assigned to the group for any shared resources.

As a security best practice, it is recommended that members of default groups with broad administrative access use **Run as** to perform administrative tasks.

Security Considerations for Default Groups

> * Place a user in a default group when you are sure that you want to give the user all the user rights and permissions assigned to that group in Active Directory; otherwise, create a new security group
>
> * As a security best practice, members of default groups should use Run as

---

Security considerations for default groups

Only place a user in a default group when you are sure that you want to give the user:

- All the user rights assigned to that group in Active Directory.

- All of the permissions assigned to that group for any shared resources associated with that default group.

Otherwise, create a new security group and assign to the group only those user rights or permissions that the user absolutely requires.

As a security best practice, members of default groups that have broad administrative access should not perform an interactive logon by using administrative credentials. Instead, users with this level of access should use **Run as**.

Warning   Only add members to default groups when members need all rights associated with the group. For example, if you need to add a service account to back up and restore files on a member server, you add the service account to the Backup Operators group. The Backup Operators group has the user rights to back up and restore files on the computer.

However, if your service account only needs to back up files and not restore them, it is better to create a new group. You can then grant the group the user right to back up files and not grant the group the right to restore files.

System Groups

- System groups represent different users at different times
- You can grant user rights and permissions to system groups, but you cannot modify or view the memberships
- Group scopes do not apply to system groups
- Users are automatically assigned to system groups whenever they log on or access a particular resource

Introduction

You cannot change the membership of system groups. The operating system creates them, and you cannot change or manage them. It is important to understand system groups, because you can use them for security purposes.

Definition

Servers running Windows Server 2003 include several special identities in addition to the groups in the Users and Builtin containers. For convenience, these identities are generally referred to as system groups.

System groups represent different users at different times, depending on the circumstances. Although you can grant user rights and permissions to the system groups, you cannot modify or view their memberships.

Group scopes do not apply to system groups. Users are automatically assigned to system groups whenever they log on or access a particular resource.

System groups are often referred to as "special identities."

System groups

The following table describes some of the system groups.

System group	Description
Anonymous Logon	• Represents users and services that access a computer and its resources through the network without using an account name, password, or domain name. • On computers running Windows NT and earlier, the Anonymous Logon group is a member of the Everyone group by default. • On computers running a member of the Windows Server 2003 family, the Anonymous Logon group is not a member of the Everyone group by default. If you want to create a file share for an anonymous user, you grant permissions to the Anonymous Logon group.
Everyone	• Represents all current network users, including guests and users from other domains. Whenever a user logs on to the network, the user is automatically added to the Everyone group. • If security is not a concern for a specific group in your domain, you can grant permissions to the Everyone group. However, because the Anonymous Logon group can become a member of the Everyone group, it is not recommended that you use this group for permissions above read-only.
Network	• Represents users currently accessing a given resource over the network, as opposed to users who access a resource by logging on locally at the computer where the resource is located. Whenever a user accesses a given resource over the network, the user is automatically added to the Network group.
Interactive	• Represents all users currently logged on to a particular computer and accessing a given resource located on that computer, as opposed to users who access the resource over the network. Whenever a user accesses a resource on the computer to which they are currently logged on, the user is automatically added to the Interactive group.
Authenticated Users	• Represents all users within Active Directory. Always use the Authenticated Users group when granting permissions for a resource instead of using the Everyone group, to prevent guests from accessing resources.
Creator Owner	• Includes the user account for the user who created or took ownership of a resource. If a member of the Administrators group creates a resource, the Administrators group is the owner of the resource.

Note These groups have well known Security Identifiers (SIDs). A list of these, along with the well known SIDs of the built-in accounts, is available by searching for "Security Identifiers" on the Microsoft Help and Support Web site.

Class Discussion: Using Default Groups vs. Creating New Groups

> **Contoso, Ltd., has over 100 servers across the world. You must determine:**
>
> * The current tasks that administrators must perform and what minimum level of access users need to perform specific tasks
>
> * Whether you can use default groups or must create groups and assign specific user rights or permissions to the groups

Scenario

Contoso, Ltd., has over 100 servers across the world. You must determine current tasks that administrators must perform and what minimum level of access those users need to perform specific tasks. You also must determine whether you can use default groups or whether you must create groups and assign specific user rights or permissions to the groups to perform the tasks.

Discussion

You must assign default groups or create new groups for the following tasks. List the name of the default group that has the most restrictive user rights for performing the following actions, or determine whether you must create a new group.

1. Backing up and restoring domain controllers

   _____

   _____

   _____

2. Backing up member servers

   _____

   _____

   _____

3. Creating groups in the Contoso, Ltd., Sales organizational unit

_____

_____

_____

4. Logging on to the domain

_____

_____

5. Providing read-only access to the DHCP servers

_____

_____

_____

6. Help desk employees who need access to control the desktop remotely

_____

_____

_____

7. Providing administrative access to all computers in the entire domain

_____

_____

_____

8. Providing access to a shared folder named Data on a server named Den-SRV1

_____

_____

_____

9. Managing the print queue of a specific printer on a print server

    _____

    _____

    _____

10. Configuring network settings on a member server

    _____

    _____

    _____

Best Practices for Managing Groups

* Create groups based on administrative needs

* Add user accounts to the group that is most restrictive

* Use the default group when possible instead of creating a new group

* Use the Authenticated Users group instead of the Everyone group to grant most user rights and permissions

* Limit the number of users in the Administrators group

Best practices

Consider the following best practices for managing groups:

- Create groups based on administrative needs. When you create a group based on a job function and another person takes over that job, you need to change only the group membership. You do not need to change all permissions that are granted to the individual user account. Because of this, it is sometimes advantageous to create a group that has only one member.

- If you have multiple groups to which you can add user accounts, add user accounts to the group that is most restrictive. However, ensure that you grant the appropriate user rights and permissions so that users can accomplish any required task.

- Whenever a default group enables users to accomplish a task, use the default group instead of creating a new group. Create groups only when there are no default groups that provide the required user rights and permissions.

- Use the Authenticated Users group instead of the Everyone group to grant user rights and permissions to most users. Using this group minimizes the risk of unauthorized access, because Windows Server 2003 adds only valid user accounts to members of the Authenticated Users system group.

- Limit the number of users in the Administrators group. Members of the Administrators group on a local computer have Full Control permissions for that computer. Add a user to the Administrators group if the user will perform only administrative tasks.

Lab: Creating and Managing Groups

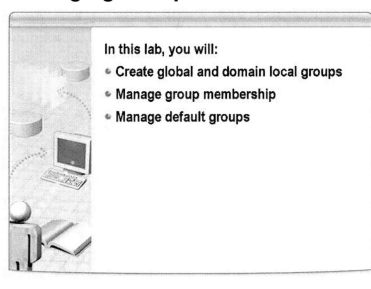

In this lab, you will:
- Create global and domain local groups
- Manage group membership
- Manage default groups

Objectives

After completing this lab, you will be able to:

- Create global and domain local groups.
- Manage group membership.
- Manage default groups.

Prerequisites

To complete this lab, you must have the following virtual machines:

- DEN-DC1
- DEN-SRV1

Estimated time to complete this lab: 30 minutes

Exercise 1
Creating Global and Domain Local Groups

In this exercise, you will create an organizational unit and create two users in that organizational unit. You will also create domain local and global groups.

Scenario

You have to create an organizational unit for the newly created Marketing department. Currently there are only two users. One of them is the marketing manager. You must create accounts and groups according to the approved naming strategy.

Tasks	Specific instructions
1. Create an organizational unit for the Marketing department.	a. Log on to DEN-DC1 as **Administrator** with the password of **Pa$$w0rd**. b. Open **Active Directory Users and Computers**. c. Select the domain node. d. Create a new organizational unit named **Marketing**.
2. Create two users accounts in the Marketing organizational unit.	a. Create a user account called **Marketing Manager** with a logon name of **Mktmgr** and a password of **Pa$$w0rd**. b. Create a user account called **Marketing User** with a logon name of **Mktuser** and a password of **Pa$$w0rd**.
3. Create two global groups, one for Marketing Managers and one for Marketing Users.	a. Create a global group named **G Marketing Managers**. b. Create a global group named **G Marketing Users**.
4. Create domain local groups that will be used to assign permissions to resources for the Marketing team.	a. Create a domain local group named **DL Marketing Full Control**. b. Create a domain local group named **DL Marketing Read-only**.

Exercise 2
Managing Group Membership

In this exercise, you will configure group membership.

Scenario

Now that the organizational unit and the user and group accounts have been created, you must place the proper users in their groups and put the global groups into their appropriate groups.

Tasks	Specific instructions
1. Add users to their global groups.	a. Add the **Marketing Manager** account and the **Marketing User** account to the **G Marketing Users** global group. b. Add the **Marketing Manager** account to the **G Marketing Managers** global group.
2. Nest the Marketing Managers global group into the G Contoso Managers global group.	a. In the Users container, open the **Properties** dialog box for the **G Contoso Managers** group. b. Click the **Members** tab, and then click **Add**. c. Find the **G Marketing Managers** group. d. Click **OK** twice.
3. Add the global groups to the domain local groups.	a. Add the **G Marketing Managers** group to the **DL Marketing Full Control** group. b. Add the **G Marketing Users** group to the **DL Marketing Read-only** group.

Exercise 3
Managing Default Groups

In this exercise, you will add users to the proper groups to allow them to perform their administrative tasks.

Scenario

As domain administrator, you must delegate some of the administrative responsibility to other users. You will give Judy Lew the right to back up and restore information on domain controllers. You will also give her the right to manage printers on domain controllers. You will give Don Hall the right to back up and restore data and configure the network settings on DEN-SRV1.

Tasks	Specific instructions
1. Add Judy Lew to the appropriate default built-in group.	a. In **Active Directory Users and Computers**, locate the user account for **Judy Lew**. b. Open the **Properties** dialog box for **Judy Lew**, and then click the **Member Of** tab. c. Click **Add**, and add the **Print Operators** group. d. Click **Add**, and add **Judy Lew** to the **Backup Operators** group. e. Close **Active Directory Users and Computers**.
2. Add Don Hall to the appropriate default built-in group.	a. Log on to DEN-SRV1 as **Administrator** with the password of **Pa$$w0rd**. b. Open **Computer Management**. c. In **Computer Management**, expand **Local Users and Groups**. d. Click the Groups container, and then open the **Properties** dialog box for the **Backup Operators** group. e. Click **Add**, and then add **Don Hall** to the group. Click **OK**. f. Open the **Properties** dialog box for the **Network Configuration Operators** group. g. Click **Add** and then add **Don Hall** to the group. Click **OK**. h. Close all windows.
3. Complete the lab exercise.	a. Close all programs and shut down all computers. Do not save changes. b. To prepare for the next module, start the DEN-DC1 virtual computer.

Module 4: Managing Access to Resources

Contents

Overview

- Overview of Managing Access to Resources
- Managing Access to Shared Folders
- Managing Access to Files and Folders Using NTFS Permissions
- Determining Effective Permissions
- Managing Access to Shared Files Using Offline Caching

Introduction

This module introduces the job function of managing access to resources. Specifically, the module provides the skills and knowledge that you need to manage access to files and folders by using shared folder permissions, NTFS permissions, or effective permissions and to manage access to shared files by using offline caching.

Objectives

After completing this module, you will be able to:

- Manage access to resources.
- Manage access to shared folders.
- Manage access to files and folders by using NTFS permissions.
- Determine effective permissions.
- Managing access to shared files by using offline caching.

Lesson: Overview of Managing Access to Resources

* Multimedia: Access Control in Microsoft
  Windows Server 2003
* What Are Permissions?
* What Are Standard and Special Permissions?
* Practice: Examining NTFS Permissions
* Multimedia: Permission States

Introduction

The information in this lesson presents the knowledge that you need to manage access to resources.

Lesson objectives

After completing this lesson, you will be able to:

■ Describe the components of access control in Microsoft® Windows Server™ 2003.

■ Define permissions.

■ Explain the differences between standard and special permissions.

■ Determine permissions that are assigned to NTFS folders.

■ Explain the characteristics of implicit and explicit permission states.

Multimedia: Access Control in Microsoft Windows Server 2003

* This presentation explains how Active Directory uses security principals and identifiers to provide access to objects

* Important point to watch for: If you delete a security principle and then create it again with the same name, what is the effect on the permissions?

File location

To view the *Access Control in Microsoft Windows Server 2003* presentation, open the Web page on the Student Materials compact disc, click **Multimedia**, and then click the title of the presentation.

Key points

Key points from the presentation are summarized in the following list:

- Security principal

  A security principal is an account that can be authenticated.

- Security identifier (SID)

  An SID is an alphanumeric structure that is issued when an account is created and that uniquely identifies a security principal.

- Discretionary access control list (DACL)

  Each resource is associated with a DACL, which identifies the users and groups that are allowed or denied access to that resource.

- Access control entry (ACE)

  A DACL contains multiple ACEs. Each ACE specifies a SID, special permissions, inheritance information, and an Allow or a Deny permission.

Additional reading

For more information about access control, see "Access Control Components" on the MSDN Library Web site.

What Are Permissions?

- Permissions define the type of access granted to a user, group, or computer for an object
- You apply permissions to objects such as files, folders, and printers
- You assign permissions to users and groups in Active Directory or on a local computer

Definition

Permissions define the type of access that is granted to a user, group, or computer for an object. For example, you can let one user read the contents of a file, let another user make changes to the file, and prevent all other users from accessing the file. You can set similar permissions on printers so that certain users can configure the printer and other users can only print from it.

Permissions are also applied to any secured objects, such as files, objects in the Active Directory® directory service, and registry objects. Permissions can be granted to any user, group, or computer.

You can grant permissions for objects to:

- Groups, users, and computers and special identities in any trusted domains.
- Local groups and users on the computer where the object resides.

Permission types

There are two levels of permissions. Shared folder permissions allow security principals remote access to shared resources across the network. Shared folder permissions are only in effect when a resource is accessed from the network. NTFS permissions, on the other hand, are always in effect, whether connecting across the network or logged on to the local machine where the resource is located. NTFS permissions are built in to the NTFS file system and cannot be disabled on an NTFS volume.

Note This lesson discusses NTFS permissions. Additional information about NTFS permissions is covered later in this module. Shared folder permissions are discussed in the next lesson.

When you set permissions, you specify the level of access for groups and users. The permissions attached to an object depend on the type of object. For example, the permissions that are attached to a file are different from those that are attached to a registry key. Some permissions, however, are common to most types of objects.

The following permissions are common permissions:

- Read permissions
- Write permissions
- Delete permissions

What Are Standard and Special Permissions?

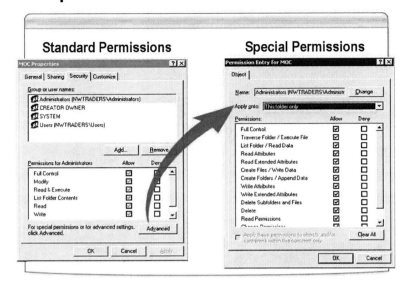

Standard Permissions	**Special Permissions**

Introduction

You can grant standard and special permissions for objects. Standard permissions are the most frequently assigned permissions. Special permissions provide you with a finer degree of control for assigning access to objects.

Standard permissions

The system has a default level of security settings for a specific object. These are the most common set of permissions that a systems administrator uses on a daily basis. The list of standard permissions that are available varies depending on what type of object you are modifying the security for.

Special permissions

Special permissions are a more detailed list of permissions. A standard NFTS permission of Read is related to the following special permissions:

- List Folder/Read Data
- Read Attributes
- Read Extended Attributed
- Read Permissions

If the systems administrator removes a special permission that relates to a standard permission, the check box for the standard permission is no longer selected. The check box for the special permission in the standard permission list is selected.

Practice: Examining NTFS Permissions

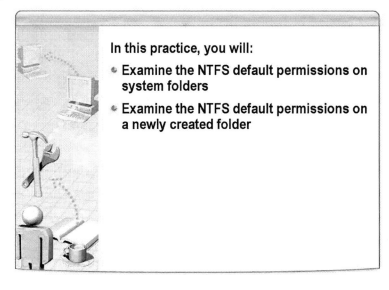

In this practice, you will:
* Examine the NTFS default permissions on system folders
* Examine the NTFS default permissions on a newly created folder

Objectives

In this practice, you will:

- Examine the NTFS default permissions on the system folders.
- Examine the NTFS default permissions on a newly created folder.

Instructions

Ensure that the DEN-DC1 virtual machine is running.

Practice

▶ **Examine the NTFS default permissions on the system folders**

1. Log on to DEN-DC1 as **Administrator** with a password of **Pa$$w0rd**.
2. Open **My Computer** (or Windows Explorer).
3. Expand the **C:** drive.
4. Right-click **Windows**, and then click **Sharing and Security**.
5. Click the **Security** tab.

   What are the default permissions of **Authenticated Users**?

   _____

   _____

   What are the default permissions of **Server Operators**?

   _____

   _____

What are the default permissions of **Creator Owner**?

_____

_____

6. Click **Cancel**.

▶ **Examine the NTFS default permissions on a newly created folder**

1. Create a new folder named **Test** at the root of the **C:** drive.

2. Right-click the **Test** folder and then click **Sharing and Security**.

3. Click the **Security** tab.

    How are these permissions different from those in the Windows folder?

    _____

    _____

    _____

    _____

4. Close all open windows and log off of DEN-DC1.

▶ **To prepare for the next practice**

1. Start the DEN-CL1 virtual machine.

2. Start the DEN-SRV1 virtual machine.

Multimedia: Permission States

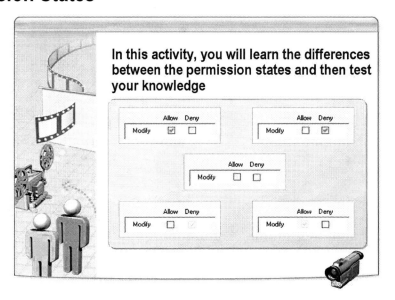

File location

To start the *Permission States* activity, open the Web page on the Student Materials compact disc, click **Multimedia**, and then click the title of the activity.

Lesson: Managing Access to Shared Folders

* What Are Shared Folders?
* What Are Administrative Shared Folders?
* Tools to Create and Manage Shared Folders
* Shared Folder Permissions
* Methods to Connect to Shared Folders
* What Are Published Shared Folders?
* How Published Shared Folders Are Used
* Best Practices For Using Shared Folders
* Practice: Managing Access to Shared Folders

Introduction

The Windows Server 2003 family organizes files into directories that are graphically represented as folders. These folders contain all types of files and can contain subfolders. Some of these folders are reserved for operating system files and program files. Users should never place any data into the operating system folders or program file folders.

Shared folders give users access to files and folders over a network. Users can connect to the shared folder over the network to access the folders and files that they contain. Shared folders can contain applications, public data, or a user's personal data. Using shared application folders centralizes administration by enabling you to install and maintain applications on a server instead of client computers. Using shared data folders provides a central location for users to access common files and makes it easier to back up data contained in those files.

Lesson objectives

After completing this lesson, you will be able to:

- Explain what shared folders are.
- Explain what administrative shared folders are.
- Use tools to create and manage shared folders.
- Explain what shared folder permissions are.
- Describe the various methods to connect to a shared folder.
- Explain what published shared folders are.
- Explain how published shared folders are used.
- Describe the best practices for using shared folders.
- Manage access to shared folders.

What Are Shared Folders?

* Shared folders show an icon of a hand holding the folder
* You can share only folders, not files
* Default permission on shared folders is Everyone, Read
* When you copy or move a shared folder, the folder is no longer shared
* To hide a shared folder, include a $ after the name of the shared folder
* Users access hidden shares by typing the UNC path

Introduction

When you share a folder, the folder is made accessible to multiple users simultaneously over the network. After a folder is shared, users can access all of the files and subfolders in the shared folder if they are granted permission.

You can place shared folders on a file server and also place them on any computer on the network. You can store files in shared folders according to categories or functions. For example, you can place shared data files in one shared folder and shared application files in another.

Characteristics of shared folders

Some of the most common characteristics of shared folders are as follows:

- A shared folder appears in Microsoft Windows® Explorer with an icon of a hand holding the folder.

- You can share only folders, not individual files. If multiple users need access to the same file, you must place the file in a folder and then share the folder.

- When a folder is shared, Read permission is granted to the Everyone group as the default permission. Remove the default permission and grant Change permission or Read permission to groups as needed.

- When users or groups are granted permissions to a shared folder, the default permission is Read.

- When you copy a shared folder, the original shared folder is still shared, but the copy is not shared. When a shared folder is moved to another location, the folder is no longer shared.

- You can hide a shared folder if you append a dollar sign ($) to the name of the shared folder. The user cannot see the shared folder in the user interface, but the user can access the shared folder by typing the Universal Naming Convention (UNC) name—for example, **\\server\secrets$**.

What Are Administrative Shared Folders?

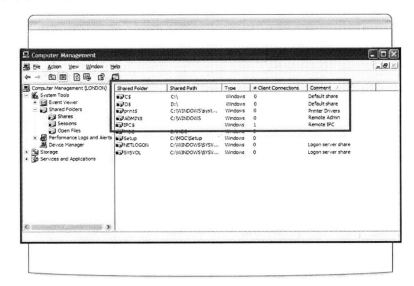

Introduction

Windows Server 2003 automatically shares folders that enable you to perform administrative tasks. These default administrative shares have a dollar sign ($) at the end of the share name. The dollar sign hides the shared folder from users who browse to the computer in My Network Places. Administrators can quickly administer files and folders on remote servers by using these hidden shared folders.

Types of administrative shared folders

By default, members of the Administrators group have the Full Control permission for administrative shared folders. You cannot modify the permissions for administrative shared folders. The following table describes the purpose of the default administrative shared folders in Windows Server 2003.

Shared folders	Purpose
C$, D$, E$	Use these shared folders to remotely connect to a computer and perform administrative tasks. The root of each partition (that has a drive letter assigned to it) on a hard disk is automatically shared. When you connect to this folder, you have access to the entire partition.
Admin$	This is the systemroot folder, which is C:\Windows by default. Administrators can access this shared folder to administer Windows Server 2003 without knowing the name of the actual folder in which the operating system is installed.
Print$	This folder provides access to printer driver files for client computers. When you install the first shared printer, the *systemroot*\system32\ spool\drivers folder is shared as Print$. Only members of the Administrators, Server Operators, and Print Operators groups have Full Control permission for this folder. The Everyone group has Read permission for this folder.

| (*continued*) | |
Shared folders	**Purpose**
IPC$	This interprocess communications share is used during remote administration of a computer and when viewing a computer's shared resources.
FAX$	This shared folder is used to temporarily cache files and access cover pages on the server.

Additional reading   For more information about IPC$, see article 101150, "Operating Characteristics and Restrictions of Named Pipes," on the Microsoft Help and Support Web site.

Tools to Create and Manage Shared Folders

Who can create shared folders?

* On Windows Server 2003 domain controllers
  * Administrators group
  * Server Operators group
* On Windows Server 2003 member or stand-alone servers
  * Administrators group
  * Power Users group

Tools used to create and manage shared folders

* Computer Management
* Window Explorer or My Computer
* The Net Share command

Introduction

In Windows Server 2003, the only groups that can create shared folders are the Administrators, Server Operators, and Power Users groups. These groups are built-in groups that are placed in the Groups folder in Computer Management or the Built-In container in Active Directory Users and Groups.

When you create a shared folder, you assign a shared folder name and can provide a comment that describes the folder and its contents. You can also limit the number of users who can access the folder, grant permissions, and share the same folder multiple times under different network share names.

Groups that can create shared folders

The following table describes who can share folders.

To share folders:	You must be a member of:
On a Windows Server 2003 domain controller	The Administrators or Server Operators group
On a stand-alone or member server running Windows Server 2003	The Administrators or Power Users group

Using Computer Management to create shared folders

You can use the Computer Management Microsoft Management Console (MMC) to create and manage shared folders. You can start the Computer Management MMC by using the **runas** command, which allows you, as an administrator, power user, or server operator to share folders without logging onto the system. Computer Management can also be used remotely. Computer Management has three subfolders:

■ *The Shares folder.* Displays a listing of the share names of all the shared folders on the machine. This folder also displays the actual path in the file system to the shared folder. You can create new shared folders by using the shortcut menu for the Shares folder. You can also stop sharing existing shared folders.

- *The Sessions folder*. Displays information about the current remote sessions in place and allows you to forcefully disconnect users.

- *The Open Files folder*. Displays information about the files that are in use by the current sessions and allows you to forcefully close open files.

You can also send console messages to currently connected machines from Computer Management.

Using My Computer or Windows Explorer

Both My Computer and Windows Explorer provide views of the file system. By accessing the **Properties** dialog box for a folder, you can share, or stop sharing, folders.

Using the net share command

The **net share** command creates, deletes, or displays shared folders. For example, to share a folder named C:\data on the network with the share name Data, type:

net share data=C:\data

The **net share** command uses the following syntax:

net share *SharedFolderName*=*Drive*:*Path*

Value	Description
SharedFolderName=*Drive*:*Path*	This is the network name of the shared folder and the absolute path of its location.

For a complete listing of the **net share** syntax, type **net share /?** at a command prompt.

Shared Folder Permissions

Permission	Description
Read (Default, applied to the Everyone group)	• Allows you to view data in files and attributes • Allows you to view file names and subfolder names • Allows you to run program files
Change (Includes all Read permissions)	• Allows you to add files and subfolders • Allows you to change data in files • Allows you to delete subfolders and files
Full Control (Includes all Read and Change permissions)	• Allows you to change NTFS file and folder permissions

Introduction

Shared folder permissions apply only to users who connect to the folder over the network. They do not restrict access to users who access the folder at the computer where the folder is stored. You can grant shared folder permissions to user accounts, groups, and computer accounts.

Important By default, users will have the same level of access to subfolders under a shared folder as they have on the parent folder.

Permissions

Shared folder permissions include the following:

- **Read**

  Read is the default shared folder permission and is applied to the Everyone group. Read permission enables you to:
  - View file names and subfolder names.
  - View data in files and attributes.
  - Run program files.

- **Change**

  Change permission includes all Read permissions and also enables you to:
  - Add files and subfolders.
  - Change data in files.
  - Delete subfolders and files.

- **Full Control**

  Full Control includes all Read and Change permissions and also enables you to change permissions for NTFS files and folders.

Methods to Connect to Shared Folders

Introduction

After you create a shared folder, users can access the folder across the network by using multiple methods. Users can access a shared folder on another computer by using **My Network Places**, by using the Map Network Drive feature, by searching Active Directory, or by using the **Run** command on the **Start** menu.

Using My Network Places

The **My Network Places** dialog box can be launched from the **Network and Internet Connections** section of Control Panel. You can also configure the **Start** menu to display the **My Network Places** shortcut. From **My Network Places**, any user can launch the Add A Network Place wizard. The wizard allows a user to browse to, or type in the address of a network location, such as a UNC path or an FTP site, and provide a friendly name for the network location. For example, a user could use the wizard to map to the UNC path of *\\server\data*, but give it a friendly name of My Reports.

Note   When you open a shared folder over the network, Windows Server 2003 automatically adds it to **My Network Places**.

Using Map Network Drive

When you want to associate a drive letter and icon with a specific shared folder, you must map to a network drive. This makes it easier to refer to the location of a file in a shared folder. You can also use drive letters to access shared folders for which you cannot use a UNC path, such as a folder for an older application. The **Map Network Drive** dialog box can be accessed on the shortcut menu of My Computer or on the **Tools** menu in Windows Explorer or My Computer. The **Map Network Drive** dialog box allows users to select a drive letter to assign to the mapping and either type in the UNC path or browse for the network path. It also allows users to connect using alternative credentials.

Using the Run command

When you use the **Run** command on the **Start** menu to connect to a network resource, a drive letter is not required. This enables you to connect to the shared folder an unlimited number of times, independent of available drive letters.

When you enter the server name in the format *servername*, a list of available shared folders appears. Windows Server 2003 gives you the option to choose one of the entries based on the shared folders that are available to you.

What Are Published Shared Folders?

* **A published shared folder:**
  * Is a shared folder object in Active Directory
  * Can maintain static friendly names
* **Clients:**
  * Can search Active Directory for published shared folders
  * Do not need to know the name of the server to connect to a shared folder
  * Can search by using keywords if they do not know the exact name of the share

---

Definition

Publishing resources and shared folders in Active Directory enables users to search Active Directory and locate resources on the network even if the physical location of the resources changes.

For example, if you move a shared folder to another computer, all shortcuts that users have on their desktops pointing to the Active Directory object that represents the published shared folder continue to work, as long as you update the reference to the physical location. Users do not have to update their shortcuts.

Publishing the folder

You can publish any shared folder in Active Directory that can be accessed by using a UNC name. You publish shared folders by creating a shared folder object in Active Directory that points to the UNC path of the shared folder. After a shared folder is published, a user at a computer running Microsoft Windows Server 2003 or a domain client running Microsoft Windows XP Professional can use Active Directory to locate the object representing the shared folder and then connect to the shared folder.

You can publish information about printers and shared folders by using Computer Management or Active Directory Users and Computers.

Viewing the published shared folder

When you publish the shared folder by using Computer Management, the shared folder becomes a child object of the computer account. To view shared folders as an object, in **Active Directory Users and Computers**, on the **View** menu, click **Users, Group, and Computers as containers**. Then, in the console tree, click the computer account. In the Details pane, you will see all the published shared folders that are associated with the computer account.

When a shared folder is published using Active Directory Users and Computers, it appears as an object in the container in which it was created.

> **Important**   You cannot use publishing to create new shared folders. You can only advertise existing shared folders by publishing them in the Active Directory.

Using keywords

Administrators who publish shared folders can create a list of keywords to assist users in searching for shared folders. For example, sales personnel might need to find a shared customer list but might not know the exact name of the share or the server where the shared folder is located. The administrator can configure a list of keywords such as customers, contacts, or clients and associate them with the share. This list of keywords should be developed in collaboration with the users who will be accessing the shared folders.

Static friendly names

The published name of a shared folder in Active Directory will remain static because it is merely a pointer to a UNC path. If a set of shared folders is moved to a new file server, the administrator need only change the properties of the shared folder object in Active Directory to reflect the new UNC path. End users' shortcuts to the published object will continue to function.

> **Important**   The permissions that you need to create or modify shared folder objects in the Active Directory have no direct correlation to the permissions that you need to access the contents of the shared folder. Administrators do not need any permission on the actual shared folder to create and modify its associated shared folder object in Active Directory.

How Published Shared Folders Are Used

Introduction

In a large enterprise that has many shared folders available on many different network servers in multiple domains; users might have difficulty locating the shared folders they need to do their jobs. Clients can use **My Network Places** to search Active Directory for published shared folders.

Administrators might also have to locate shared folders to perform maintenance on them. For example, an administrator might have to change the root path when a set of folders is moved to a new server. Administrators can use the **Find** command in Active Directory Users and Computers to search for shared folders.

Using My Network Places

Client computers that have Windows XP Professional installed and have accounts in the domain can search Active Directory for shared folders by using the link in the **Network Tasks** section of **My Network Places**. To view the **Search Active Directory** link, the Windows XP client must have the **Show Common Tasks in Folders** feature turned on in **Folder Options**. This is the default setting. The link brings up the Active Directory search box. In the **Find** drop-down list, users can select **Shared Folders** as the type of object to search for. Users have the option to search in a particular domain or search all domains by selecting **Entire Directory** in the **Look In** box.

After users find the shared folders they are looking for, they can open the folders directly or map a drive letter to them from the search results list.

Important   Any user can map a drive letter to connect to a shared folder. Shared folder permissions specify whether that user can open the folder and access the contents.

Best Practices for Using Shared Folders

* Use the Authenticated Users group instead of Everyone
* Share folders with the appropriate level of permission
* Use groups to grant access rather than individual users
* Publish shared folders in larger environments

Introduction

Shared folders provide access to network resources. Administrators must keep security and ease of management in mind when setting permissions on shared folders.

Using Authenticated Users instead of Everyone

Use the Authenticated Users group to grant permissions because on computers running Windows Server 2003, Everyone includes Authenticated Users and Guest. On computers running earlier versions of Windows, Everyone includes Authenticated Users and Guest plus Anonymous Logon.

The Authenticated Users group includes all users and computers whose identities have been authenticated, but it does not include Guest even if the Guest account has a password.

Sharing with appropriate permissions

Assign the least level of permissions to shared folders that users and groups need to perform their duties.

Granting access to groups rather than users

Groups simplify administration. Individual users might come and go from the organization, but groups can remain constant. It is easier to change group memberships than to reassign permissions for individual users as job functions change.

Publishing shared folders in larger environments

If many shared folders are spread across multiple servers, you can publish the shared folders in Active Directory to facilitate users locating and accessing the shares without having to know the exact location of the data.

Practice: Managing Access to Shared Folders

In this practice, you will:

● Connect to an administrative share

● Create a shared folder and grant permissions

● Publish a shared folder and create keywords

● Map a drive letter to the shared folder and test permissions

Objectives

In this practice, you will:

- Connect to an administrative share.
- Create a shared folder and grant permissions.
- Publish a shared folder and create keywords.
- Map a drive letter to the shared folder and test permissions.

Instructions

Ensure that the DEN-DC1 and DEN-CL1 virtual machines are started.

Practice

▶ **Connect to an administrative share**

1. Log on to DEN-CL1 as **Judy@contoso.msft** with the password of **Pa$$w0rd**.

2. Click **Start**, click **Run**, and then type **\\DEN-DC1\Admin$**. Click **OK**.

3. In the **Connect to den-dc1.contoso.msft** dialog box, enter the domain administrators credentials.

   The contents of the **Admin$** share will be displayed.

4. Open the **Properties** dialog box for any folder. Notice that you can use the Security tab to modify NTFS permissions but that you cannot create a new shared folder.

5. Close the **Admin$** share, and then log off DEN-CL1.

▶ **Create a shared folder and grant permissions**

1. Log on to DEN-DC1 as **Administrator** with the password of **Pa$$w0rd**.

2. Open Windows Explorer, and navigate to **C:\Sales**.

3. Right-click the **Sales** folder and then click **Sharing and Security**.

4. Click **Share this folder**.

5. Ensure that the **Share** name is **Sales**.

6. Click **Permissions**.

7. In the **Permissions for Sales** dialog box, remove the **Everyone** group.

8. Click **Add**.

9. In the **Select Users, Computers, or Groups** dialog box, type **DL Sales Read**.

10. Click **OK**.

11. Leave the default permission of **Read** for the **DL Sales Read** group.

12. Click **Add**.

13. In the **Select Users, Computers or Groups** dialog box, type **DL Sales Modify**.

14. Click **OK**.

15. Assign **Change** permission to the **DL Sales Modify** group.

16. Click **OK** twice.

▶ **Publish a shared folder and create keywords**

1. Open **Active Directory Users and Computers**.

2. Right-click the **Sales** organizational unit, point to **New**, and then click **Shared Folder**.

3. In the **New Object - Shared Folder** dialog box, type **Sales Data** in the **Name** field.

4. In the **Network Path** field, type **\\DEN-DC1\Sales**.

5. Click **OK**.

6. Right-click **Sales Data** and then click **Properties**.

7. Click the **Keywords** button.

8. In the **Keywords** dialog box, enter the following keywords, clicking **Add** after each one: **Contacts, Clients, Customers**.

9. Click **OK** twice.

10. Close all windows and then log off of DEN-DC1.

▶ **Map a drive letter to the shared folder and test permissions**

1. Log on to DEN-CL1 as **Don@contoso.msft** with a password of **Pa$$w0rd**.

2. Click **Start**, click **My Computer**, and then click **My Network Places** in **Other Places** on the taskbar.

3. In **My Network Places**, under **Network Tasks**, click **Search Active Directory**.

4. In the **Find** box, select **Shared Folders**.

5. In the **Keywords** field, type **clients**. (Keywords are not case-sensitive.)

6. Click **Find Now**.

   The **Sales Data** folder should appear in the list of results.

7. Right-click the **Sales Data** folder and then click **Map Network Drive**.

8. Click **Finish**.

9. Close the **Find Shared Folders** dialog box.

10. Close all open windows.

11. Open **My Computer**. In the **Network Drives** section, you should see an icon for **Sales on Den-dc1**.

12. Double-click the **Sales** drive. You should see the contents of the shared folder displayed.

13. Close **My Computer**, and log off.

14. Log on to DEN-CL1 as **Judy@contoso.msft** with a password of **Pa$$w0rd**.

15. Repeat steps 2 through 8 to map to the **Sales Data** folder.

16. Open **My Computer**, and attempt to access the Sales Data folder.

    You should see an "Access Denied" message. Although the user was able to map a drive letter to the shared folder, the user was not able to access the content of the share because the share permissions prevented it.

17. Log off.

Important   Do not shut down the virtual machines.

Lesson: Managing Access to Files and Folders Using NTFS Permissions

* What Is NTFS?
* NTFS File and Folder Permissions
* What Is NTFS Permissions Inheritance?
* Effects on NTFS Permissions When Copying and Moving Files and Folders
* Best Practices for Managing Access to Files and Folders Using NTFS Permissions
* Practice: Managing Access to Files and Folders Using NTFS Permissions

Introduction

The information in this lesson presents the skills and knowledge that you need to manage access to files and folders by using NTFS permissions.

Lesson objectives

After completing this lesson, you will be able to:

- Explain what NTFS is.
- Explain what NTFS file and folder permissions are.
- Explain what NTFS permissions inheritance is.
- Explain the effects on NTFS permissions of copying and moving files and folders.
- Explain best practices for managing access to files and folders by using NTFS permissions.
- Manage access to files and folders using NTFS permissions.

What Is NTFS?

NTFS is a file system that provides:

* Reliability

* Security at the file level and folder level

* Improved management of storage growth

* Multiple user permissions

Introduction

NTFS is a file system that is available on Windows Server 2003. NTFS provides performance and features that are not found in either FAT (file allocation table) or FAT32.

Benefits of NTFS

NTFS provides the following benefits:

■ *Reliability*. NTFS uses log file and checkpoint information to restore the integrity of the file system when the computer is restarted. If there is a bad-sector error, NTFS dynamically remaps the cluster containing the bad sector and allocates a new cluster for the data. NTFS also marks the cluster as unusable.

■ *Greater security*. NTFS files use the Encrypting File System (EFS) to secure files and folders. If EFS is enabled, files and folders can be encrypted for use by single or multiple users. The benefits of encryption are data confidentiality and data integrity, which means that data is protected against malicious or accidental modification.

NTFS also stores a DACL with every file and folder on an NTFS partition. The DACL contains a list of all user accounts, groups, and computers that are granted access for the file or folder and the type of access that they are granted. For a user to access a file or folder, the DACL must contain an entry, called an ACE, for the user account, group, or computer that the user is associated with. The ACE must specifically allow the type of access that the user is requesting for the user to access the file or folder. If no ACE exists in the DACL, Windows Server 2003 denies the user access to the resource.

■ *Improved management of storage growth*. NTFS supports disk quotas, which enable you to specify the amount of disk space that is available to a user. By using disk quotas, you can track and control disk space usage and configure whether users are allowed to exceed a warning level or storage quota limit.

NTFS supports larger files and a larger number of files per volume than FAT or FAT32. NTFS also manages disk space efficiently by using smaller cluster sizes. For example, a 30-gigabyte (GB) NTFS volume uses 4-kilobyte (KB) clusters. The same volume formatted with FAT32 uses 16-KB clusters. Using smaller clusters reduces wasted space on hard disks.

■ *Multiple user permissions*. If you grant NTFS permissions to an individual user account and to a group to which the user belongs, you grant multiple permissions to the user. NTFS combines these multiple permissions to produce the user's effective permissions.

Additional reading   For more information about NTFS, see "NTFS" on the Microsoft TechNet Web site.

For more information about FAT and NTFS, see "Choosing Between FAT and NTFS" on the Microsoft Windows 2000 Advanced Server Documentation Web site.

NTFS File and Folder Permissions

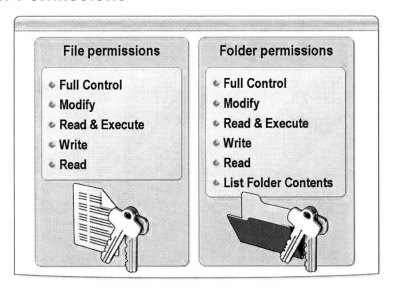

Introduction

NTFS permissions are used to specify which users, groups, and computers can access files and folders. NTFS permissions also dictate what users, groups, and computers can do with the contents of the file or folder.

NTFS file permissions

The following table lists the standard NTFS file permissions that you can grant and the type of access that each permission provides.

NTFS file permission	Allows the user to:
Full Control	Change permissions, take ownership, and perform the actions permitted by all other NTFS file permissions
Modify	Modify and delete the file and perform the actions permitted by Write permission and Read & Execute permission
Read & Execute	Run applications and perform the actions permitted by Read permission
Write	Overwrite the file, change file attributes, and view file ownership and permissions
Read	Read the file and view file attributes, ownership, and permissions

NTFS folder permissions

Permissions control access to folders and the files and subfolders that are contained in those folders. The following table lists the standard NTFS folder permissions that you can grant and the type of access that each permission provides.

NTFS folder permission	Allows the user to:
Full Control	Change permissions, take ownership, delete subfolders and files, and perform actions permitted by all other NTFS folder permissions
Modify	Delete the folder and perform actions permitted by Write permission and Read & Execute permission
Read & Execute	Traverse folders and perform actions permitted by Read permission and List Folder Contents permission
Write	Create new files and subfolders in the folder, change folder attributes, and view folder ownership and permissions
Read	View files and subfolders in the folder, folder attributes, ownership, and permissions
List Folder Contents	View the names of files and subfolders in the folder

Implicit and explicit Deny permission

Permissions can also be implicitly or explicitly denied. If a user does not have permissions assigned to his or her user account and does not belong to any groups that have been assigned permission, that user is implicitly denied access to the resource.

A user or a group can also be explicitly denied access to a resource. In that case, it does not matter what other permissions that user might have on the resource. An explicit Deny permission always overrides all other permissions. Explicit Deny permission should be used only in special cases. For example, suppose that all users in the Human Resources department have access to the employee records of all personnel but that only the Human Resources manager has access to the records of senior management. All other users are explicitly denied access.

Important   An explicit Allow permission will override an inherited Deny permission.

What Is NTFS Permissions Inheritance?

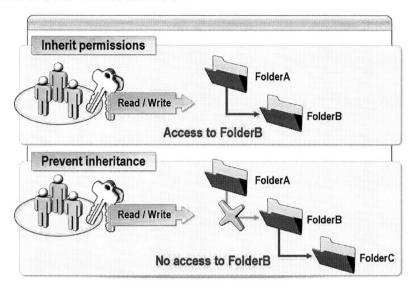

Definition

By default, permissions that you grant to a parent folder are inherited by the subfolders and files that are contained in the parent folder. When you create files and folders, and when you format a partition with NTFS, Windows Server 2003 automatically assigns default NTFS permissions. Inherited permissions are indicated by shaded permission check boxes on the **Security** tab.

Controlling permissions inheritance

A security principal that is inheriting permissions can have additional NTFS permissions assigned, but the inherited permissions cannot be removed until inheritance is blocked. You can prevent subfolders and files from inheriting permissions that are assigned to the parent folder. When you prevent permissions inheritance, you can either:

- Copy inherited permissions from the parent folder.

  - or -

- Remove the inherited permissions and retain only the permissions that were explicitly assigned.

The folder on which you prevent permissions inheritance becomes the new parent folder, and the subfolders and files that are contained in it inherit the permissions assigned to it. Permissions can be inherited only from a direct parent.

Why prevent propagating permissions?

Permissions inheritance simplifies how permissions for parent folders, subfolders, and resources are assigned. However, you might want to prevent inheritance so that permissions do not propagate from a parent folder to subfolders and files.

For example, you might need to keep all Sales department files in one Sales folder for which everyone in the Sales department has Write permission. However, for a few files in the folder, you might need to limit the permissions to Read. To do so, prevent inheritance on each file so that the Write permission does not propagate to the files contained in the folder.

Effects on NTFS Permissions When Copying and Moving Files and Folders

* **When you copy files and folders, they inherit the permissions of the destination folder**
* **When you move files and folders within the same partition, they retain their permissions**
* **When you move files and folders to a different partition, they inherit the permissions of the destination folder**

Introduction

When you copy or move a file or folder, the permissions might change, depending on where you move the file or folder. It is important to understand the changes that the permissions undergo when being copied or moved.

Effects of copying files and folders

When you copy a file or folder from one folder to another folder, or from one partition to another partition, permissions for the files or folders might change. Copying a file or folder has the following effects on NTFS permissions:

- When you copy a file or folder within a single NTFS partition, the copy of the folder or file inherits the permissions of the destination folder.

- When you copy a file or folder to a different NTFS partition, the copy of the folder or file inherits the permissions of the destination folder.

- When you copy a file or folder to a non-NTFS partition, such as a FAT partition, the copy of the folder or file loses its NTFS permissions, because non-NTFS partitions do not support NTFS permissions.

- When you copy a file or folder within a single NTFS partition or between NTFS partitions, you must have Read permission for the source folder and Write permission for the destination folder.

Effects of moving files and folders

When you move a file or folder, permissions might change, depending on the permissions of the destination folder. Moving a file or folder has the following effects on NTFS permissions:

- When you move a file or folder within an NTFS partition, the folder or file retains its original permissions. If the permissions of the new parent folder are changed at a later time, the file or folder will inherit the new permissions. Permissions explicitly applied to the folder will be retained. Permissions previously inherited will be lost.

- When you move a file or folder to a different NTFS partition, the folder or file inherits the permissions of the destination folder. When you move a folder or file between partitions, Windows Server 2003 copies the folder or file to the new location and then deletes it from the old location.

- When you move a file or folder to a non-NTFS partition, the folder or file loses its NTFS permissions, because non-NTFS partitions do not support NTFS permissions.

- When you move a file or folder within an NTFS partition or between NTFS partitions, you must have both Write permission for the destination folder and Modify permission for the source file or folder. Modify permission is required to move a folder or file, because Windows Server 2003 removes the folder or file from the source folder after it copies it to the destination folder.

Effects of copying and moving within volumes

The following table lists the possible copy and move actions and describes how Windows Server 2003 handles the permission state of a file or folder.

Action	Result
Copy a file or folder within a volume	Inherits permission state of the destination folder
Move a file or folder within a volume	Retains original permission state of the source
Copy a file or folder between volumes	Inherits permission state of the destination folder
Move a file or folder between volumes	Inherits permission state of source file or folder

Best Practices for Managing Access to Files and Folders Using NTFS Permissions

* Grant permissions to domain local groups instead of to users

* Group resources to simplify administration

* Allow users only the level of access that they require

* Grant Read & Execute permission for application folders

Best practices

When managing access to files and folders, consider the following best practices when granting NTFS permissions:

- Grant permissions to groups instead of users. Because it is inefficient to maintain user accounts directly, avoid granting permissions to individual users.

- Use Deny permissions in the following situations:

  - To exclude a subset of a group that has Allow permissions.

  - To exclude one permission when you have already granted Full Control permissions to a user or group.

- If possible, do not change the default permission entries for file system objects, particularly on system folders and root folders. Changing default permissions can cause unexpected access problems or reduce security.

- Never deny the Everyone group access to an object. If you deny everyone access to an object, you deny administrators access. Instead, it is recommended that you remove the Everyone group, as long as you grant permissions for the object to other users, groups, or computers.

- Grant permissions to an object that is as high on the tree as possible so that the security settings are propagated throughout the tree. You can quickly and effectively grant permissions to all children or a subtree of a parent object. By doing this, you affect the most objects with the least effort. Grant permissions that are adequate for the majority of users, groups, and computers.

- To simplify administration, group files according to function. For example:
  - Group program files into folders where commonly used applications are kept.
  - Group data folders containing home folders into one folder.
  - Group data files that are shared by multiple users into one folder.
- Grant Read & Execute permission to the Users and Administrators groups for application folders. This prevents users or viruses from accidentally deleting or damaging data and application files.
- Only allow users the level of access that they require. For example, if a user only needs to read a file, grant Read permission for the file to the user or group to which the user belongs.

Practice: Managing Access to Files and Folders Using NTFS Permissions

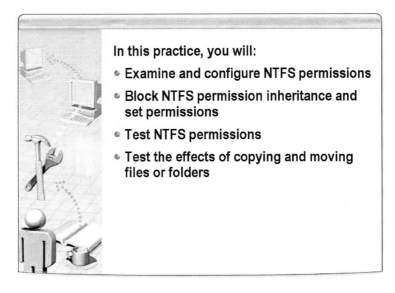

In this practice, you will:
- Examine and configure NTFS permissions
- Block NTFS permission inheritance and set permissions
- Test NTFS permissions
- Test the effects of copying and moving files or folders

Objectives

In this practice, you will:

- Examine and configure NTFS permissions.
- Block NTFS permission inheritance and set permissions.
- Test NTFS permissions.
- Test the effects of copying and moving files or folders.

Instructions

Ensure that the DEN-DC1 and DEN-SRV1 virtual machines are started.

Practice

▶ **Examine and configure NTFS permissions**

1. Log on to DEN-SRV1 as **Administrator** with the password of **Pa$$w0rd**.

2. Open Windows Explorer, and then expand the **C:\Legal** folder.

3. Right-click the **Legal** folder, and then click **Sharing and Security**.

4. Click the **Security** tab, examine the default permissions.

   Notice that all the NTFS permissions that have been granted have shaded check boxes, indicating that they are inherited permissions. They are being inherited from the direct parent—in this case, C:\.

5. Select the **Users** group, and then click **Remove**. Read the message in the Security message box, and then click **OK**.

► **Block NTFS permission inheritance and set permissions**

1. Click the **Advanced** button.

2. Clear the check box **Allow inheritable permissions from the parent to propagate to this object and all child objects. Include these with entries explicitly defined here.**

3. Read the message in the **Security** message box, and then click **Remove**.

4. Click **OK**.

5. Click **Add**.

6. In the **Select Users, Computers, or Groups** dialog box, type **DL Legal Write** and then click **OK**.

7. Grant the **DL Legal Write** group **Read** and **Write** permissions.

8. Click **Add**.

9. Type **DL Legal Modify** and then click **OK**.

10. Assign the **DL Legal Modify** group **Modify** permission.

11. Click the **Administrators** account, and then assign it **Full Control**. Click **OK**.

12. Close Windows Explorer, and then log off.

► **Test NTFS permissions**

1. Log on to DEN-SRV1 as **LegalManager**, with a password of **Pa$$w0rd**.

2. Open Windows Explorer, and then click the **C:\Legal** folder.

3. Create a text file named **Legal.txt**.

   This should succeed, because the Legal Manager group is a member of G Legal Managers, which in turn is a member of DL Legal Modify.

4. Close Windows Explorer, and then log off.

5. Log on as **LegalUser**, with a password of **Pa$$w0rd**.

6. Open Windows Explorer.

7. Click the **Legal** folder, and then open **Legal.txt**.

8. Enter some text, and then save and close the file.

   This should succeed, because LegalUser is a member of G Legal, which in turn is a member of DL Legal Write.

9. Attempt to delete the **Legal.txt** file.

   You should receive an "Access Denied" error message because users must at least modify permission in order to delete files that they do not own.

10. Close all open windows, and then log off.

▶ **Test the effects of copying and moving files or folders**

1. Log on to DEN-SRV1 as **Administrator** with the password of **Pa$$w0rd**.

2. Open Windows Explorer and then click the **C:\Legal** folder.

3. Open the **Properties** dialog box for the **C:\Legal\Briefs** folder.

4. Click the **Security** tab. Note the current NTFS permissions. Click **Cancel**.

5. Connect to the administrative share **\\DEN-DC1\c$**.

6. Cut and paste the Briefs folder **C:\Legal\Briefs** to **\\den-dc1\c$**.

7. Open the **Properties** dialog box for the **C:\Briefs** folder on DEN-DC1, and examine the NTFS permissions.

   How are they different from the original location?

   _____

   _____

   _____

8. Close the administrative share window.

9. On DEN-SRV1, move the Documents folder **C:\Legal\Documents** to **C:**, and then examine the NTFS permissions.

   Have they changed from the original location?

   _____

   _____

10. Close all open windows and log off of DEN-SRV1.

Important Do not shut down the virtual machines.

Lesson: Determining Effective Permissions

* What Are Effective Permissions on NTFS Files and Folders?
* Class Discussion: Applying NTFS Permissions
* Effects of Combined Shared Folder and NTFS Permissions
* Class Discussion: Determining Effective NTFS and Shared Folder Permissions
* Practice: Determining Effective NTFS and Shared Folder Permissions

Introduction

If you grant NTFS permissions to an individual user account and a group to which the user belongs, you grant multiple permissions to the user. NTFS combines these multiple permissions to produce the user's effective permissions.

Lesson objectives

After completing this lesson, you will be able to:

■ Explain what effective NTFS permissions are and how to determine them for files and folders.

■ Explain the effects of combined shared folder and NTFS permissions.

■ Determine the effective NTFS and shared folder permissions.

What Are Effective Permissions on NTFS Files and Folders?

* NTFS permissions are cumulative
* File permissions override folder permissions
* Deny overrides all permissions
* Creators of files and folders are their owners

Introduction

Windows Server 2003 provides a tool that shows effective permissions, which are cumulative permissions based on group membership. The information is calculated from the existing permissions entries and is displayed in a read-only format.

Characteristics of effective permissions

Effective permissions have the following characteristics:

- *Cumulative permissions are the combination of the highest NTFS permissions granted to the user and all the groups that the user is a member of.* For example, if a user is a member of a group that has Read permission and a member of a group that has Modify permission, the user has Modify permission.

- *NTFS file permissions take priority over folder permissions.* For example, if a user has Modify permission to a folder but only has Read permission to certain files in that folder. The effective permission for those files will be Read.

- *Explicit Deny permissions override equivalent Allow permissions.* However, an explicit Allow permission can override an inherited deny permission. For example, if a user is explicitly denied write access to a folder but be explicitly allowed write access to a subfolder or a particular file, the explicit Allow would override the inherited Deny.

- *Every object is owned in an NTFS volume or in Active Directory.* The owner controls how permissions are set on the object and to whom permissions are granted. For example, a user can create a file in a folder where the user normally has Modify permission, but because that user created the file, the user will have the ability to change the permissions. The user could then grant himself or herself Full Control over the file.

Important   An administrator who needs to repair or change permissions on a file but does not have Change Permission permission must take ownership of the file.

Ownership

By default, in the Windows Server 2003 family, the owner of an object is the user who creates the object. Objects created during installation and any object created by a member of the local Administrators group will be owned by the Administrators group. The owner can always change permissions on an object, even when the owner is denied all access to the object.

Ownership can be taken by the following individuals:

- An administrator. By default, the Administrators group is given the **Take ownership of files or other objects** user right.

- Anyone or any group that has **Take ownership** permission for the object in question.

- A user who has the **Restore files and directories** privilege.

Ownership can be transferred in the following ways:

- The current owner can grant **Take ownership** permission to another user. The user must actually take ownership to complete the transfer.

- An administrator can take ownership.

- A user who has the **Restore files and directories** privilege can double-click **Other users and groups** and specify any user or group to assign ownership to while performing a restore operation.

Important   Permissions on a shared folder are not part of the effective permissions calculation. Access to shared folders can be denied through shared folder permissions even when access is allowed through NTFS permissions.

Class Discussion: Applying NTFS Permissions

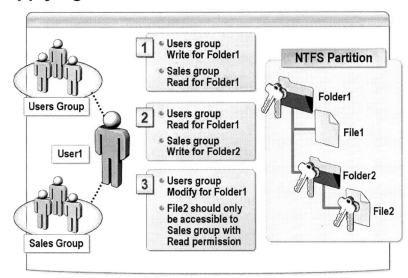

Introduction	In this exercise, you are presented with a scenario in which you are asked to apply NTFS permissions. You and your classmates will discuss possible solutions to the scenario.
Discussion	User1 is a member of the Users group and the Sales group.

1. The Users group has Write permission, and the Sales group has Read permission for Folder1. What permissions does User1 have for Folder1?

_____

_____

_____

_____

2. The Users group has Read permission for Folder1. The Sales group has Write permission for Folder2. What permissions does User1 have for File2?

_____

_____

_____

_____

3. The Users group has Modify permission for Folder1. File2 should be accessible only to the Sales group, and they should only be able to read File2. What do you do to ensure that the Sales group has only Read permission for File2?

_____

_____

_____

_____

Effects of Combined Shared Folder and NTFS Permissions

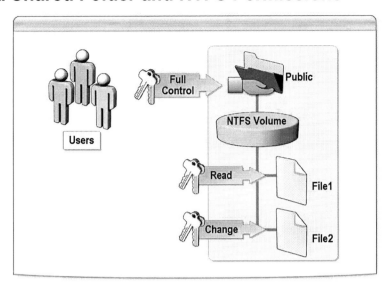

Introduction

When allowing access to network resources on an NTFS volume, it is recommended that you use the most restrictive NTFS permissions to control access to folders and files, combined with the most restrictive shared folder permissions that control network access.

What are combined permissions?

When you create a shared folder on a partition formatted with NTFS, both the shared folder permissions and the NTFS permissions combine to secure file resources. NTFS permissions apply whether the resource is accessed locally or over a network.

When you grant shared folder permissions on an NTFS volume, the following rules apply:

■ By default, the Everyone group is granted the shared folder permission Read.

■ Users must have the appropriate NTFS permissions for each file and subfolder in a shared folder, in addition to the appropriate shared folder permissions, to access those resources.

■ When you combine NTFS permissions and shared folder permissions, the resulting permission is the most restrictive permission of the effective shared folder permissions or the effective NTFS permissions.

Class Discussion: Determining Effective NTFS and Shared Folder Permissions

Objective

In this discussion, you will determine the effective NTFS and shared folder permissions.

Class discussion

The graphic on this page illustrates two shared folders that contain folders or files that have been assigned NTFS permissions. Look at each example and determine a user's *effective* permissions.

1. In the first example, the Users folder has been shared, and the Users group has the shared folder permission Full Control. User1, User2, and User3 have been granted the NTFS permission Full Control to *only* their folder. These users are all members of the Users group.

   Do members of the Users group have Full Control to *all* home folders in the Users folder once they connect to the Users shared folder?

   _____

   _____

   _____

2. In the second example, the Data folder has been shared. The Sales group has been granted the shared folder permission Read for the Data shared folder and the NTFS permission Full Control for the Sales folder.

    What are the Sales group's effective permissions when they access the Sales folder by connecting to the Data shared folder?

    _____

    _____

    _____

Practice: Determining Effective NTFS and Shared Folder Permissions

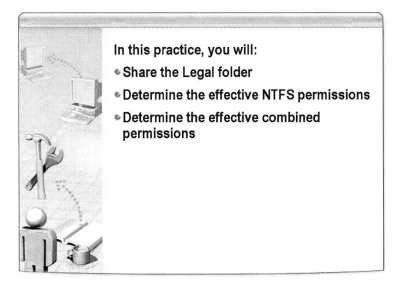

In this practice, you will:
- Share the Legal folder
- Determine the effective NTFS permissions
- Determine the effective combined permissions

Objectives

In this practice, you will:

- Share the Legal folder.
- Determine the effective NTFS permissions.
- Determine the effective combined permissions.

Instructions

Ensure that the DEN-DC1, DEN-CL1 and DEN-SRV1 virtual machines are started.

Practice

▶ **Share the Legal folder**

1. Log on to DEN-SRV1 as **Administrator** with the password of **Pa$$w0rd**.

2. In Windows Explorer, locate the **C:\Legal** folder.

3. Right-click **C:\Legal** and then click **Sharing and Security**.

4. Click the **Sharing** tab and then share the folder using a share name of **Legal**.

5. Click **Permissions**. Remove the **Everyone** group, and then add the **Authenticated Users** group and assign **Read** permission.

6. Click **OK** twice. An icon of a hand should appear under the Legal folder to indicate that it is shared.

▶ **Determine the effective NTFS permissions**

1. Open the **Properties** dialog box for the Legal folder, and then click the **Security** tab.

2. Click **Advanced**.

3. Click the **Effective Permissions** tab.

4. Click **Select** to locate the user or group that you want to test.

5. Type **LegalManager**, and then click **OK**.

   What NTFS permissions does the LegalManager account have?

   Traverse Folder / Execute File
   (List Folder / Read Data

6. Test the LegalUser account.

   What NTFS permissions does the LegalUser account have?

   Read Attributes
   Read Extented Attributes

7. Test the Authenticated Users group.

   What NTFS permissions does the Authenticated Users group have?

   None

8. Close all open windows and log off.

▶ **Determine the effective combined permissions**

1. Log on to DEN-CL1 as **Legalmanager**, with a password of **Pa$$w0rd**.

2. Click **Start**, click **Run**, and then type **\\DEN-SRV1\Legal**. Attempt to create a new text document in the Legal shared folder.

   Did it succeed? Why or why not?

   Unable to create the file 'New Text Document.txt'

   Access is denied

3. Log off.

4. Log on as **Judy** with the password of **Pa$$w0rd**.

5. Click **Start**, click **Run**, and then type **\\DEN-SRV1\Legal** Attempt to create a new document in the Legal folder.

   What are the results?

6. Close all windows, and then log off.

Important Do not shut down the virtual machines.

Lesson: Managing Access to Shared Files Using Offline Caching

* What Is Offline Files?
* How Offline Files Are Synchronized
* Offline File Caching Options
* Practice: Using Offline Caching

Introduction

The information in this lesson presents the skills and knowledge that you need to manage access to shared files by using offline caching.

Lesson objectives

After completing this lesson, you will be able to:

■ Explain what Offline Files is.

■ Explain how offline files are synchronized.

■ Explain the offline file caching modes.

■ Configure offline caching.

What Is Offline Files?

* Offline Files is a document-management feature that provides the user with consistent online and offline access to files

* Advantages of using Offline Files:
  * Support for mobile users
  * Automatic synchronization
  * Performance advantages
  * Backup advantages

Definition

Offline Files is an important document-management feature that provides the user with consistent online and offline access to files. When the client disconnects from the network, anything that has been downloaded to the local cache remains available. Users can continue working as though they were still connected to the network. They can continue editing, copying, deleting, and so forth. The files are cached in a folder named CSC (Client Side Caching) in the %systemroot% directory.

From the user's perspective, the workspaces appear identical, whether they are on or off the network. Visual cues, such as icons, menus, and Active Directory, remain the same, including the view of the mapped network drives. Network files appear in the same network drive directory and can be accessed, copied, edited, printed, or deleted precisely as they are when they are online. When you reconnect to the network, client and server files are automatically resynchronized.

Advantages of using Offline Files

Using Offline Files has the following advantages:

■ Support for mobile users

When a mobile user views the shared folder while disconnected, the user can still browse, read, and edit files, because they have been cached on the client computer. When the user later connects to the server, the system reconciles the changes with the server.

■ Automatic synchronization

You can configure synchronization policy and behavior based on the time of day and network connection type by using Synchronization Manager. For example, you can configure synchronization so that it occurs automatically when the user logs on to a direct local area network (LAN) connection, but only at a user's request when he or she uses a dial-up connection.

- Performance advantages

  Offline Files provides performance advantages for networks. While connected to the network, clients can still read program files from the local cache, reducing the amount of data transferred over the network. Programs will generally start and run faster.

- Backup advantages

  Offline Files solves a dilemma facing most enterprise organizations today. Many organizations implement a backup policy that requires all user data to be stored on managed servers. The organization's IT department often does not back up data stored on local disks. This becomes a problem for mobile users of portable computers.

  If you want to access data when offline, a mechanism is needed to replicate data between the portable computer and the servers. Some organizations use the Briefcase tool. Others use batch files or replicate data manually. With clients running Windows Server 2003, Windows XP, or Windows 2000, replication between client and server is managed automatically. Files can be accessed while you are offline and are automatically synchronized with the managed server.

Additional reading   For more information about offline file security, see "Securing Offline Files" on the Microsoft TechNet Web site.

How Offline Files Are Synchronized

* **Disconnected from the network**
    * Files are synchronized at logoff. The user works with the locally cached copy
* **Logged on to the network**
    * Files are synchronized at logon. The user works with the network version of the files
* **If a file has been modified in both locations**
    * The user must choose which version of the file to keep or to rename one file and keep both versions

Introduction

A user can configure a file on a network to be available offline, provided that Offline Files is enabled for the folder in which the file resides and Offline Files are enabled on the client. By default, the Offline Files feature is disabled on all Microsoft servers and enabled on Windows 2000 Professional and Windows XP Professional. When users configure files to be available offline, the users work with the network version of the files while they are connected to the network and then with a locally cached version of the files when they are not connected to the network.

Synchronization events

When a user configures a file to be available offline, depending on the settings, the following synchronization events might occur when the user disconnects from the network:

- When the user logs off the network, the Windows client operating system synchronizes the network files with a locally cached copy of the file.

- While the computer is disconnected from the network, the user works with the locally cached copy of the file.

- When the user again logs on to the network, the Windows client operating system synchronizes any offline file that the user has modified with the network version of the file. If the file has been modified on both the network and the user's computer, the Windows client operating system prompts the user to choose which version of the file to keep, or the user can rename one file and keep both versions.

Important Using offline files is not a substitute for document version control. If two users work with the same offline file at the same time and then synchronize the file with the network version, one of the versions might be lost.

Additional reading

For more information about how clients synchronize offline files, see "Offline Files overview" on the Microsoft TechNet Web site.

Offline File Caching Options

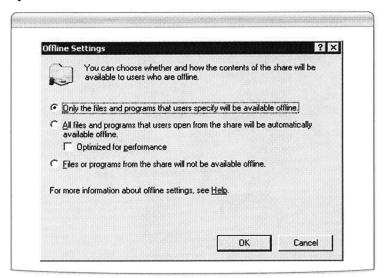

Introduction	When you create shared folders on the network, you can specify the caching option for the files and programs in that folder. There are three different caching options.
Manual caching of documents	Manual caching of documents provides offline access for only the files and programs that the user specifies will be available. This caching option is ideal for a shared network folder containing files that several people will access and modify. This is the default option when you configure a shared folder to be available offline.
Automatic caching of documents	With automatic caching of documents, all files and programs that users open from the shared folder are automatically available offline. Files that the user does not open are not available offline. Older copies are automatically overwritten by newer versions of files.
Automatic caching of programs	The **Optimized for performance** option provides automatic caching of programs, which provides offline access to shared folders containing files that are not to be changed. Automatic caching of programs reduces network traffic, because offline files are opened directly. The network versions are not accessed in any way, and the offline files start and run faster than the network versions.
	When you use automatic caching of programs, be sure to restrict permissions for the files contained in the shared folders to Read access.

Practice: Using Offline Caching

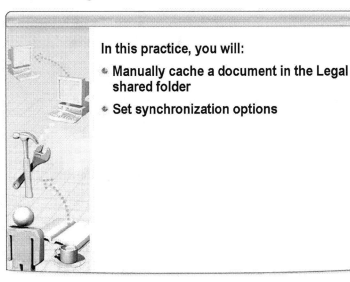

Objectives

In this practice, you will:

- Manually cache a document in the Legal shared folder.
- Set synchronization options.

Instructions

Ensure that the DEN-DC1, DEN-CL1 and DEN-SRV1 virtual machines are started.

Practice

▶ **Manually cache a document in the Legal shared folder**

1. Log on to DEN-SRV1 as **Administrator** with the password of **Pa$$w0rd**.
2. Open **Windows Explorer** and then click the **C:\Legal** folder.
3. Right-click **C:\Legal** and then click **Sharing and Security**.
4. On the **Sharing** tab, click **Permissions**.
5. Increase the permissions for the **Authenticated Users** group to **Change**. Click **OK** twice.

Important   This setting is configured for the purposes of the exercise and is not a recommended security best practice.

---

6. Create a text file named **cached.txt** and a file named **admin.txt** in the Legal folder.
7. Close all windows and log off of DEN-SRV1.
8. Log on to DEN-CL1 as **Legalmanager** with a password of **Pa$$w0rd**.
9. Click **Start**, click **Run**, and then type **DEN-SRV1**. Click **OK**.

10. In the DEN-SRV1 window, right-click the **Legal** shared folder, and then click **Map Network Drive**.

11. Click **Finish**, and then close all open windows.

12. Open **My Computer**, and then double-click the **Legal on den-srv1(Z)** drive.

13. Right-click the **Cached.txt** file, and then click **Make Available Offline**.

14. In the **Offline Files Wizard**, click **Next**.

15. Click the check box to accept synchronization at logon and logoff. Click **Next**.

16. Clear the **Enable Reminders** check box, and select the **Create a shortcut to the Offline Files folder on my desktop** check box.

17. Click **Finish**.

18. Close all open windows, and then log off.

▶ **Set synchronization options**

1. Log on to DEN-CL1 as **Administrator**.

2. Open **Control Panel**.

3. Click **Network Connections**, right-click **Local Area Connection**, and then click **Disable**.

4. Log off.

5. Log on to DEN-CL1 as **LegalManager**.

6. Open **My Computer** and then double-click the **Legal** mapped drive.

7. Only the **Cached.txt** file should appear in the list of files. It will have a double blue arrow to indicate that it is cached locally.

8. Open the **Cached.txt** file, enter some text, and then click **Save** and **Exit**.

9. Log off.

10. Log on as **Administrator**, and enable **Local Area Connection**.

11. Log off.

12. Log on to DEN-CL1 as **LegalManager**.

    Synchronization should occur.

13. Open the **Legal** mapped drive.

    You should see all files in the Legal folder now. The Cached.txt file should contain the changes you made while offline.

14. Close all open windows.

15. Click **Start**, point to **All Programs**, point to **Accessories**, and then click **Synchronize**.

16. In the **Items to Synchronize** dialog box, select the **\\den-srv1\Legal on Den-srv1** folder, and then click **Setup**.

17. In the **Synchronization Settings** dialog box, clear the **When I log on to my computer** check box.

18. Click **OK**.

19. Click **Close**.

20. Log off.

Important   Do not shut down the virtual machines.

Lab: Managing Access to Resources

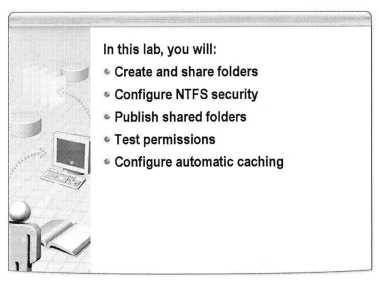

Objectives

After completing this lab, you will be able to:

- Create and share folders.
- Configure NTFS security.
- Publish shared folders.
- Test permissions.
- Configure automatic caching.

Prerequisites

To complete this lab, you must have the following virtual machines:

- DEN-DC1
- DEN-SRV1
- DEN-CL1

Estimated time to complete this lab: 30 minutes

Exercise 1
Creating and Sharing Folders

In this exercise, you will create and share two folders on DEN-SRV1.

Scenario

You are the Network Administrator for Contoso, Ltd. You have been asked to create two shared network folders to contain product information for Contoso, Ltd. The two folders will be named Research and Price List. The Administrators group should have Full Control permission for all folders. All Authenticated Users should have Read access. The Sales department managers should have Change permission for the Price List folder. The Legal department managers should have Change permission for the Research folder.

Tasks	Specific instructions
1. Create and share two folders.	a. Log on to DEN-SRV1 as **Administrator** with the password of **Pa$$w0rd**. b. Create two folders on C:\, one named **Research** and one named **Price List**.
2. Share the folders and set permissions.	a. Share the **Research** folder with the share name **Research**. b. Set the following share permissions for the **Research** folder: **Administrators:** **Full Control** **Authenticated Users:** **Read** **DL Research Change:** **Change** c. Share the **Price List** folder with the share name **Price List**. d. Set the following share permissions on the **Price List** folder: **Administrators:** **Full Control** **Authenticated Users:** **Read** **DL Sales Modify:** **Change**

Exercise 2
Configuring NTFS Security

In this exercise you will set the NTFS permissions on shared folders

Scenario

In this exercise, you will set the NTFS permissions on the shared folders to give the Administrators group Full Control permission for all folders. All Authenticated Users should have Read and Execute access. The Sales Managers group should have Modify permission for the Price List folder. The Legal Managers group should have Modify permission for the Research folder.

Task	Specific instructions
1. Configure NTFS permissions.	a. Right-click the **Research** folder and then click **Sharing and Security**. b. On the **Security** tab, click **Advanced**. c. Clear the check box to prevent permission inheritance, and then remove all permissions. Click **OK**. d. Configure the new NTFS permissions for the Research folder as follows: **Administrators:** **Full Control** **Authenticated Users:** **Read and Execute** **DL Research Change:** **Modify** e. Right-click the **Price List** folder and then click **Sharing and Security**. f. On the **Security** tab, click **Advanced**. g. Clear the check box to prevent permission inheritance, and then remove all permissions. Click **OK**. h. Configure the new NTFS permissions for the Price List folder as follows: **Administrators:** **Full Control** **Authenticated Users:** **Read and Execute** **DL Sales Modify:** **Modify**

Exercise 3
Publishing Shared Folders

In this exercise, you will publish the shared folders.

Scenario

Users in all domains must be able to find and access the Price List and Research folders. You will publish these folders in Active Directory with keywords to make it easy for users to find them.

Task	Specific instructions
1. Publish the folders in Active Directory by using Computer Management.	a. On DEN-SRV1, open **Computer Management**. b. Expand the **Shared Folders** node, and then click the **Shares** folder. c. Right-click the **Research** share, and then click **Properties**. d. On the **Publish** tab, select the **Publish this share in Active Directory** check box. e. Click the **Edit** box next to **Keywords**, and enter the keywords **Development** and **Products**, clicking **Add** after each one. f. Click **OK** twice. g. Publish the **Price List** shared folder with the keyword **Prices**. h. Close all open windows.

Exercise 4
Testing Permissions

In this exercise, you will test the network access by logging on as two different users and testing permissions.

Scenario

You must make sure that the right people have the right access. You will perform testing.

Task	Specific instructions
1. Test access as Don Hall and Judy Lew.	a. Log on to DEN-CL1 as the sales manager **Don** with the password of **Pa$$w0rd**.
	b. Connect to the **\\DEN-SRV1\Price List** shared folder.
	c. Create a new text document named **Prices.txt**.
	This will succeed because the domain local group DL Sales Managers has the proper access.
	d. Close all open windows, and then log off.
	e. Log on to DEN-CL1 as **Judy** with the password of **Pa$$w0rd**.
	f. Connect to the **\\DEN-SRV1\Price List** folder.
	g. Open the **Prices.txt** file.
	The file should open because the Authenticated Users group has Read access.
	h. Attempt to modify and save the file.
	This attempt should fail because the Authenticated Users group has Read access.
	i. Close all open windows, and then log off.

Exercise 5
Configuring Automatic Caching

In this exercise, you will configure a shared folder to provide automatic caching of documents.

Scenario

Many sales personnel use laptops and travel to client sites. You want to ensure that they automatically have the most recent versions of the price list on their laptops. You will configure the Price List folder to provide automatic caching.

Task	Specific instructions
1. Configure automatic caching for the Price List shared folder	a. Ensure that you are logged on to DEN-SRV1 as Administrator. b. Open **Windows Explorer** and then click the **Price List** folder. c. Right-click the **Price List** folder and then click **Sharing and Security**. d. On the **Sharing** tab, click **Caching**. e. Select **All files and programs that users open from the share will be automatically available offline**. f. Click **OK** twice. g. Close all open windows, and then log off.
2. Complete the lab exercise.	a. Close all programs and shut down all computers. Do not save changes. b. To prepare for the next module, start the DEN-DC1 and DEN-SRV1 virtual computers.

Module 5: Managing Access to Objects in Organizational Units

Contents

Overview

- Modifying Permissions for Active Directory Objects
- Delegating Control of Organizational Units

Introduction

The information in this module introduces the job function of managing access to objects in organizational units. Specifically, the module provides the skills and knowledge that you need to explain the permissions available for managing access to objects in the Active Directory® directory service and delegate control of an organizational unit.

Objectives

After completing this module, you will be able to:

- Modify permissions for Active Directory objects.
- Delegate control of organizational units.

Lesson: Modifying Permissions for Active Directory Objects

* What Are Active Directory Object Permissions?
* Characteristics of Active Directory Object Permissions
* Permissions Inheritance for Active Directory Object Permissions
* Effects of Moving Objects on Permissions Inheritance
* What Are Effective Permissions for Active Directory Objects?
* Practice: Modifying Permissions for Active Directory Objects

Introduction

Every object in Active Directory has a security descriptor that defines which accounts have permission to access the object and what type of access is allowed. The Microsoft® Windows Server™ 2003 family uses these security descriptors to control access to objects.

Lesson objectives

After completing this lesson, you will be able to:

- Explain what Active Directory object permissions are.
- Describe the characteristics of Active Directory object permissions.
- Describe permissions inheritance for Active Directory object permissions.
- Describe the effects of moving objects on permission inheritance.
- Explain what effective permissions are for Active Directory objects.
- Modify permissions for Active Directory objects.

What Are Active Directory Object Permissions?

Permission	Allows the user to:
Full Control	Change permissions, take ownership, and perform the tasks that are allowed by all other standard permissions
Write	Change object attributes
Read	View objects, object attributes, the object owner, and Active Directory permissions
Create All Child Objects	Add any type of object to an organizational unit
Delete All Child Objects	Remove any type of child object from an organizational unit

Introduction

Active Directory object permissions secure resources by enabling you to control which administrators or users can access individual objects or object attributes and the type of access allowed. You use permissions to assign administrative privileges for an organizational unit or a hierarchy of organizational units to manage Active Directory objects. You can also use permissions to assign administrative privileges for a single object class to a specific user or group.

Standard and special permissions

Standard permissions are the most frequently granted permissions and consist of a collection of special permissions. Special permissions give you a higher degree of control over the type of access that you can grant for objects. The standard permissions are as follows:

- Full Control
- Write
- Read
- Create All Child Objects
- Delete All Child Objects

Access authorized by permissions

An administrator or the owner of the object must grant permissions for the object before users can access it. The Windows Server 2003 family stores a list of user access permissions, called the discretionary access control list (DACL), for every object in Active Directory. The DACL for an object lists who can access the object and the specific actions that each user can perform on the object.

Additional reading

For more information about Active Directory permissions, see "Best practices for assigning permissions on Active Directory objects" on the Microsoft Web site.

Characteristics of Active Directory Object Permissions

Active Directory object permissions can be:

* Allowed or denied

* Implicitly or explicitly denied

* Set as standard or special permissions

    * Standard permissions are the most frequently assigned permissions

    * Special permissions provide a finer degree of control for assigning access to objects

* Set at the object level or inherited from its parent object

---

Introduction

NTFS permissions and Active Directory object permissions are similar. Active Directory object permissions can be allowed or denied, implicitly or explicitly denied, set as standard or special permissions, and set at the object level or inherited from the parent object.

Note To view the **Security** tab in the properties dialog box for Active Directory objects, you must enable **Advanced Features** on the **View** menu in the Active Directory administration tool.

Allowing and denying permissions

You can allow or deny permissions. Denied permissions take precedence over any permission that you otherwise allow to user accounts and groups. You should use Deny permissions only when it is necessary to remove a permission that a user is granted by being a member of a group.

Implicit or explicit permissions

You can implicitly or explicitly deny permissions as follows:

* *When permission to perform an operation is not allowed, it is implicitly denied.* For example, if the Marketing group is granted Read permission for a user object, and no other security principal is listed in the DACL for that object, users who are not members of the Marketing group are implicitly denied access. The operating system does not allow users who are not members of the Marketing group to read the properties of the user object.

* *You explicitly deny a permission when you want to exclude a subset within a larger group from performing a task that the larger group has permissions to perform.* For example, it might be necessary to prevent a user named Don from viewing the properties of a user object. However, Don is a member of the Marketing group, which has permissions to view the properties of the user object. You can prevent Don from viewing the properties of the user object by explicitly denying Read permission to him.

Standard and special permissions

You can configure most Active Directory object permissions tasks by using standard permissions. Standard permissions are the most commonly used; however, if you need to grant a finer level of permissions, you will use special permissions. Special permissions allow you to set permissions on a particular class of object or individual attributes of a class of object. For example, you could grant a user Full Control over the group object class in a container or just grant the user the ability to modify group memberships in a container. Or you can grant users just the permissions needed to change a single attribute, such as the phone number, on all user accounts.

Inherited permissions

In general, when permissions are set on a parent object, new objects inherit the permissions of the parent. You can remove inherited permissions, but you can also reenable them if needed.

The way that you assign permissions on the parent object affects permission inheritance. If you manually assign a standard permission on an organizational unit, the permission applies only to the organizational unit, not to the objects in the organizational unit. The two exceptions to this rule are the Create All Child Objects and Delete All Child Objects permissions, which will allow you to perform those actions in the organizational unit.

The reason for these exceptions is that permissions are applied to **This Object Only** by default when you assign permissions manually. For example, if a user named Greg has been manually assigned Full Control on an organizational unit, Greg can create an object, such as a user account, in that organizational unit because he has the Create All Child Objects permission. However, Greg will not be able to set the password or any other attributes for the new user account because he does not have permission on the **User** object class.

To modify this, use the **Advanced Security** settings at the organizational unit level to modify the permissions granted to **This object and all child objects**. The default selection is **This object and all child objects** when you assign permission by using the Delegation of Control Wizard.

Note   The Delegation of Control Wizard will be discussed in the next lesson.

Permissions Inheritance for Active Directory Object Permissions

- Child containers inherit permissions set on a parent container
- Inheritable permissions propagate from parent to child when:
  - A child object is created
  - The permissions on the parent object are modified
- Inheritance can be blocked

Benefits of permissions inheritance

A parent object passes permissions down to an object, called a child, through inheritance. A child object can inherit permissions only from its parent object. Permissions inheritance in Active Directory minimizes the number of times that you need to grant permissions for objects.

Permissions inheritance in Windows Server 2003 simplifies the task of managing permissions in the following ways:

- You do not need to apply permissions manually to child objects when they are created.
- The permissions that are applied to a parent object are applied consistently to all child objects.
- To modify permissions for all objects in a container, you need to modify only the permissions for the parent object. The child objects automatically inherit those changes.

Preventing permissions inheritance

You can prevent permissions inheritance so that a child object does not inherit permissions from its parent object. When you prevent inheritance, only the permissions that you set explicitly apply.

When you prevent permissions inheritance, the Windows Server 2003 family enables you to:

- *Copy inherited permissions to the object.* The new permissions are explicit permissions for the object. They are a copy of the permissions that the object previously inherited from its parent object. After the inherited permissions are copied, you can make any necessary changes to the permissions.
- *Remove inherited permissions from the object.* By removing these permissions, you eliminate all inherited permissions for the object. You can then grant any new permission that you want for the object.

Effects of Moving Objects on Permissions Inheritance

* Explicit permissions set on an object remain the same if an object is moved
* Moved objects inherit permissions from the new parent organizational unit
* Moved objects no longer inherit permissions from the previous parent organizational unit

Introduction

Modifying Active Directory objects affects permissions inheritance. As a systems administrator, you will be asked to move objects between organizational units in Active Directory when organizational or administrative functions change. When you do this, the inherited permissions will change. It is imperative that you are aware of these consequences prior to modifying Active Directory objects.

Effects of moving objects

When you move objects between organizational units, the following conditions apply:

- Permissions that are set explicitly remain the same.

- An object inherits permissions from the organizational unit that it is moved to.

- An object no longer inherits permissions from the organizational unit that it is moved from.

Note   When modifying Active Directory objects, you can move multiple objects at the same time.

The following types of items can be moved within the Active Directory structure:

- User account
- Contact account
- Printer
- Group
- Shared folder
- Computer
- Domain controller
- Organizational unit

Tip   You can use the click and drag method to move objects in Active Directory if you enable Users, Computers and Groups as Containers view.

What Are Effective Permissions for Active Directory Objects?

* Permissions are cumulative
* Deny permissions override all other permissions
* Object owners can always change permissions
* Retrieving effective permissions

Introduction

You can use the Effective Permissions tool to determine what the permissions for an Active Directory object are. This tool calculates the permissions that are granted to the specified user or group and takes into account the permissions that are in effect from group memberships and any permissions inherited from parent objects.

Characteristics

Effective permissions for Active Directory objects have the following characteristics:

- Cumulative permissions are the combination of Active Directory permissions that are granted to the user and group accounts.

- Deny permissions override the same level of inherited permissions. Permissions explicitly assigned take priority.

Important An explicit Allow permission set on an object class or attribute will override an inherited Deny permission.

- Every object has an owner, whether in an NTFS volume or Active Directory. The owner controls how permissions are set on the object and to whom permissions are granted.

  The person who creates an Active Directory object is its owner. Objects that are created during Active Directory installation or by any member of the built-in Administrators group are owned by the Administrators group. The owner can always change permissions for an object, even when the owner is denied all access to the object.

  The current owner can grant **Take Ownership** permission to another user, which enables that user to take ownership of that object at any time. The user must actually take ownership to complete the transfer of ownership.

Retrieving effective permissions

To retrieve information about effective permissions in Active Directory, you must have permission to read membership information. If the specified user or group is a domain object, you must have permission to read the object's membership information on the domain. The following users have these default domain permissions:

- Domain administrators have permission to read membership information on all objects.

- Local accounts, including local administrators, on a workstation or stand-alone server do not have read membership permission and cannot read membership information for a domain user.

- Authenticated domain users can read membership information only when the domain is in pre-Windows 2000 functional level.

Practice: Modifying Permissions for Active Directory Objects

In this practice, you will:

* Create a new organizational unit and document the permissions

* Remove the inherited permissions and document the new permissions

* Manually assign Full Control to a user account and create a new object

* Test the permissions

* Examine effective permissions

Objectives

In this practice, you will:

- Create a new organizational unit and document the permissions.
- Remove the inherited permissions and document the new permissions.
- Manually assign Full Control to a user account and create a new object.
- Test the permissions.
- Examine effective permissions.

Instructions

Ensure that the DEN-DC1 and the DEN-CL1 virtual machines are running.

Practice

▶ **Create a new organizational unit and document the permissions**

1. Log on to DEN-DC1 as **Administrator** with the password of **Pa$$w0rd**.

2. Open **Active Directory Users and Computers**.

3. At the domain level, create a new organizational unit named **Test**.

4. On the **View** menu of **Active Directory Users and Computers**, click **Advanced Features**.

5. Right-click the **Test** OU and then click **Properties**.

6. Click the **Security** tab. Examine the list of security entries. An explicit permission has a selected check box under **Allow** or **Deny**. Special and inherited permissions have a shaded selected check box under **Allow** or **Deny**. Document the following default permissions:

Group or user names	Inherited	Explicit
Account Operators		X
Administrators	X	
Authenticated Users		X
Domain Admins		X
Enterprise Admins	X	
Enterprise Domain Controllers	X	X
Pre-Windows 2000 Compatible Access	X	
Print Operators		X
System		X

Tip To determine whether a permission is explicit or inherited, look in the **Inherited From** column on the **Permissions** tab in the **Advanced Security Settings** dialog box.

▶ **Remove the inherited permissions and document the new permissions**

1. On the **Security** tab of the **Test Properties** dialog box, click **Advanced**.

2. In the **Advanced Security Settings for Test** dialog box, on the **Permissions** tab, clear the **Allow inheritable permissions from the parent to propagate to this object and all child objects. Include these with entries explicitly defined here** check box.

3. In the **Security** dialog box, click **Remove**.

4. In the **Advanced Security Settings for Test** dialog box, click **OK**.

5. Examine the new security settings for the **Test** organizational unit.

6. Document the new security settings.

Group or user names	Inherited	Explicit
Account Operators		X
Administrators		
Authenticated Users		X
Domain Admins		X
Enterprise Admins		
Enterprise Domain Controllers		X
Pre-Windows 2000 Compatible Access		
Print Operators		X
System		X

What groups are no longer on the list?

_____

_____

▶ **Manually assign Full Control to a user account and create a new object**

1. On the **Security** tab, click **Add**, and then type **Judy Lew**. Click **OK**.

2. Grant the Judy Lew account **Full Control**, and then click **Apply**.

3. Click **Advanced**, select **Judy Lew** in the **Permission entries** list, and then click **Edit**. Notice that Full Control permission applies to **This object only**. Click **Cancel**.

4. Click **OK** twice.

5. Create another organizational unit inside **Test** named **Test1**.

6. Examine the security properties of **Test1**. Notice that **Judy Lew** does not appear in the security list.

7. Click **Cancel**.

8. Close **Active Directory Users and Computers**.

▶ **Test the permissions**

1. Log on to DEN-CL1 as **Administrator** with the password of **Pa$$w0rd**.

2. Connect to **\\DEN-DC1\Admin_Tools**, and install the **adminpak** administrative tools.

3. Log off, and then log on to DEN-CL1 as **Judy** with the password of **Pa$$w0rd**.

4. At the **Run** command prompt, type **dsa.msc** to launch Active Directory Users and Computers, and then attempt to create a new user called **Test User** in the **Test** organizational unit. When you click **Finish**, you should receive an error message. Read the message, and then click **OK**.

5. Attempt to modify any of the properties of the user that you just created. You will not be able to.

6. Attempt to create an object in the **Test1** organizational unit. You will not be able to.

7. Attempt to modify the properties of the **Test1** organizational unit. You will not be able to.

▶ **Examine effective permissions**

1. On DEN-DC1, open **Active Directory Users and Computers"** click the **Test** organizational unit.

    Notice that the user account that Judy Lew created is disabled. Why?

    _____

    _____

    _____

    _____

2. Right-click the **Test** OU and then click **Properties**.

3. Click the **Security** tab, and then click **Advanced** to open the **Advanced Security Settings for Test** dialog box.

4. Click the **Effective Permissions** tab, and then click **Select**.

5. Enter **Judy Lew** and then click **OK**.

    What are her effective permissions?

    List contents,   Read All properties, Read permissions

    What are her effective permissions on the user account she created?

    Full Control, List contents —

    What are her effective permissions on the Test1 organizational unit? Why does she have these permissions?

    _____

    _____

6. Close all open windows and log off of DEN-DC1 and DEN-CL1.

Important Do not shut down the virtual machines.

Lesson: Delegating Control of Organizational Units

- What Is Delegation of Control of an Organizational Unit?
- The Delegation of Control Wizard
- Modifying the Delegation of Control Wizard
- Custom Management Consoles and Taskpads
- Practice: Delegating Control of an Organizational Unit

Introduction

Active Directory enables you to efficiently manage objects by delegating administrative control of the objects. You can use the Delegation of Control Wizard and customized consoles in Microsoft Management Console (MMC) to grant specific users the permissions to perform various administrative and management tasks.

Lesson objectives

After completing this lesson, you will be able to:

- Describe what it means to delegate control of an organizational unit.
- Describe the purpose and function of the Delegation of Control Wizard.
- Modify the Delegation of Control Wizard.
- Create custom management consoles and taskpads.
- Delegate control of an organizational unit by using the Delegation of Control Wizard.

What Is Delegation of Control of an Organizational Unit?

* Assigning management of an organizational unit to another user or group
* Delegated administration:
  * Eases administration by distributing routine administrative tasks
  * Provides users or groups more control over local network resources
  * Eliminates the need for multiple administrative accounts

OU1   Admin1

Admin2   Domain   Admin3

OU2   OU3

Definition

Delegation of control is the ability to assign the responsibility of managing Active Directory objects to another user or group. By delegating control, you can eliminate the need for multiple administrative accounts that have broad authority.

Why delegate administrative control?

Delegated administration in Active Directory helps to ease the administrative burden of managing your network by distributing routine administrative tasks to multiple users. With delegated administration, you can assign basic administrative tasks to regular users or groups. For example, you could give a supervisor the right to modify the membership of a group in his or her department.

By delegating administration, you give groups in your organization more control of their local network resources. You also help secure your network from accidental or malicious damage by limiting the membership of administrator groups.

Ways to define the delegation of administrative control

You define the delegation of administrative control in the following four ways:

- Grant permissions to create or modify all objects in a specific organizational unit or in the domain.

- Grant permissions to create or modify some types of objects in a specific organizational unit or at the domain level.

- Grant permissions to create or modify a specific object in a specific organizational unit or at the domain level.

- Grant permissions to modify specific attributes of an object, such as granting the permission to reset passwords on a user account, in a specific organizational unit or at the domain level.

The Delegation of Control Wizard

* Use the Delegation of Control Wizard to specify:
   * The user or group to which you want to delegate control
   * The organizational units and objects that you want to grant the user or group the permission to control
   * The tasks that you want the user or group to be able to perform
* The Delegation of Control Wizard automatically assigns to users the appropriate permissions

Introduction

You use the Delegation of Control Wizard to select the user or group to which you want to delegate control. You also use the wizard to grant users permissions to control organizational units and objects and to access and modify objects.

Delegating permissions

You can use the Delegation of Control Wizard to grant permissions at the organizational unit level. You must manually grant additional specialized permissions at the object level.

In **Active Directory Users and Computers**, right-click the organizational units that you want to delegate control for, and then click **Delegate control** to start the wizard. You can also select the organizational unit and then click **Delegate control** on the **Action** menu.

Options

The following table describes the options in the Delegation of Control Wizard.

Option	Description
Users or Groups	The user accounts or groups to which you want to delegate control.
Tasks to Delegate	A list of common tasks, or the option to customize a task. When you select a common task, the wizard summarizes your selections to complete the delegation process. When you choose to customize a task, the wizard presents Active Directory object types and permissions for you to choose from.
Active Directory Object Type	Either all objects or only specific types of objects in the specified organizational unit.
Permissions	The permissions to grant for the object or objects.

Note The Delegation of Control Wizard can append permissions to an organizational unit if the wizard is run more than once. However, you cannot use the wizard to remove permissions.

Modifying the Delegation of Control Wizard

> * The list of common tasks in the Delegation Wizard is controlled by templates in the delegwiz.ini file
> * You can modify the list of common tasks by modifying the delegwiz.ini file to include other templates

Introduction

The Delegation of Control Wizard provides a quick way to assign the permissions that are required to perform many common tasks. To suit their needs, some organizations might want to modify the list of common tasks that the wizard provides. You can modify the list of common tasks by creating templates and configuring the delegwiz.ini file to include the template in the common tasks list.

The delegwiz.ini file

The delegwiz.ini file is a text file that resides in the %systemroot%\inf folder—usually C:\Windows\Inf. The file consists of three sections. The first section contains the version signature. The next section lists the templates in the order in which they appear in the file. The last section contains the templates.

Modifying the delegwiz.ini file

You can modify the delegwiz.ini file by using any text editor. You can write your own templates, or you can use one of the templates available through the Microsoft Web site.

Note   The Active_Directory_Delegation_Appendices.doc contains 70 templates that you can use to modify the delegwiz.ini file. The Active_Directory_Delegation_Appendices.doc is on the Student CD and can be downloaded from the Microsoft Web site.

To modify the delegwiz.ini file, create or copy a template into the delegwiz.ini file, and then modify the Templates line of the file to include your custom template in the correct position. You will need to copy the delegwiz.ini file into the %systemroot%\inf folder on all domain controllers on which you want the file to be available. You should make a backup copy of your custom delegwiz.ini file because the installation of service packs could overwrite the custom delegwiz.ini file with a default version.

Note   For more information about Active Directory delegation, download the "Best Practices for Delegating Active Directory Administration" document from the Microsoft Download Center Web site.

Custom Management Consoles and Taskpads

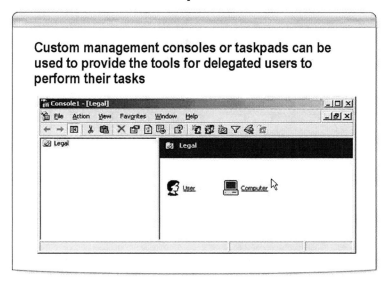

Custom management consoles or taskpads can be used to provide the tools for delegated users to perform their tasks

Introduction

After users have been delegated administrative tasks, they will need tools to perform the tasks that they have been authorized to do.

Custom management consoles

You can customize management consoles to display only the sections of Active Directory that you want the user to see. The view can be restricted such that users see only the portion of the directory where they have permissions. In that way, you can hide the complexities of the directory service. For example, if a user is responsible for managing user accounts in only one organizational unit, you can customize the view in Active Directory Users and Computers so that the user can view only the required organizational unit.

Taskpads

Taskpads can further simplify management tasks by providing a task-based management console that allows a user to perform a task by clicking a button in the management console. If you have users who need to perform simple Active Directory tasks such as reset passwords for all users in a specific organizational unit, you can create a taskpad that provides a very simple interface for performing that task.

The domain administrator can create a custom management console for Active Directory administration by launching a new MMC and adding the Active Directory Users and Computers snap-in. To restrict the view, right-click the section of the domain tree that you want to expose, and then click **New window from here**.

You can create taskpads by right-clicking an organizational unit and then selecting the option to create a **New taskpad view**. The New Taskpad Wizard will launch, allowing you to create the taskpad view. The administrator can then run the New Task Wizard to create icons that the user can click to perform tasks.

Important   The Active Directory administrative tools must be installed on the workstation of the delegated user for custom consoles or taskpads to function.

Practice: Delegating Control of an Organizational Unit

In this practice, you will:

- Delegate control of the sales users to Don Hall and the sales computers to Judy Lew

- Examine the permissions assigned by the Delegation of Control Wizard

- Test the delegated permissions for the Sales organizational unit

Objectives

In this practice, you will:

- Delegate control of the Sales users to Don Hall and the Sales computers to Judy Lew.

- Examine the permissions assigned by the Delegation of Control Wizard.

- Test the delegated permissions for the Sales organizational unit.

Instructions

Ensure that the DEN-DC1 and the DEN-CL1 virtual machines are running.

Practice

▶ **Delegate control of the sales users to Don Hall and the sales computers to Judy Lew**

1. Log on to DEN-DC1 as **Administrator** with the password of **Pa$$w0rd**.

2. Open **Active Directory Users and Computers**, right-click **Sales**, and then click **Delegate Control**.

3. In the **Delegation of Control Wizard**, on the **Welcome** page, click **Next**.

4. On the **Users or Groups** page, add **Don Hall**, and then click **Next**.

5. In the **Tasks to Delegate** page select the **Create, delete and manage user accounts** check box.

6. Click **Next**, click **Finish**.

7. Run the **Delegation of Control Wizard** again.

8. On the **Users or Groups** page, add **Judy Lew**, and then click **Next**.

9. On the **Tasks to Delegate** page, click **Create a custom task to delegate**, and then click **Next**.

10. On the **Active Directory Object Type** page, click **Only the following objects in the folder**, and then select the **Computer objects** check box.

11. Select the **Create selected objects in this folder** and **Delete selected objects in this folder** check boxes, and then click **Next**.

12. On the **Permissions** page, select the **General** check box.

13. Under **Permissions**, select the **Read** and **Write** check boxes, and then click **Next**.

14. On the **Completing the Delegation of Control Wizard** page, click **Finish**.

▶ **Examine the permissions assigned by the Delegation of Control Wizard**

1. Right-click the **Sales** OU and then click **Properties**.

2. Click the **Security** tab.

3. Click **Advanced**, and view **Don Hall** in the **Permission entries** list.

   What permissions are assigned to Don Hall?

   _____ Full control _____

   _____ Create/Delete User Objects _____

   _____

4. Locate **Judy Lew**.

   What permissions are assigned to Judy Lew?

   _____ · Create/Delete Computer Objects _____

   _____ · Special _____

   _____

5. Close all open windows.

▶ **Test the delegated permissions for the Sales organizational unit**

1. Log on to DEN-CL1 as **Don** with the password of **Pa$$w0rd**.

2. Open the **Run** command, and then type **dsa.msc** to launch **Active Directory Users and Computers**.

3. Right-click the **Sales** organizational unit, and then create a new user with the following:

   a. First name: **Test**

   b. Last name: **2**

   c. User name: **Test2**

   d. Password: **Pa$$w0rd**

   This task will succeed because Don Hall was delegated the authority to perform that task.

4. Right-click the **Legal** organizational unit.

    What permission does Don Hall have on the Legal organizational unit?

    _____

    _____

5. Log off.

6. Log on to DEN-CL1 as **Judy** with the password of **Pa$$w0rd**.

7. Click **Start, Run**, and then type **Dsa.msc** in the text box.

8. Create a new computer account named **Computer1** in the **Sales** organizational unit.

    This will succeed because Judy Lew was granted authority to perform that custom task.

9. Try to perform tasks on user objects.

    What other permission does Judy Lew have in the Sales organizational unit?

    _____

    _____

10. Close all windows and then log off of DEN-CL1 and DEN-DC1.

Important   Do not shut down the virtual machines.

Lab: Managing Access to Objects in Organizational Units

In this lab, you will:

● Modify the Delegation of Control Wizard and delegate permissions

● Test the delegated permissions

● Delegate permissions in the Legal organizational unit and create a taskpad

● Test the delegated permissions

Objectives

After completing this lab, you will be able to:

■ Modify the Delegation of Control Wizard and delegate permissions.

■ Test the delegated permissions.

■ Delegate permissions in the Legal organizational unit and create a taskpad.

■ Test the delegated permissions.

Prerequisites

To complete this lab, you must have the following virtual machines:

■ DEN-DC1

■ DEN-CL1

Estimated time to complete this lab: 30 minutes

Exercise 1
Modifying the Delegation of Control Wizard and Delegating Permissions

In this exercise, you will delegate administrative control of objects in an organizational unit.

Scenario

Contoso, Ltd., has a password policy that allows three failed logon attempts before a user is locked out of their account. Since Contoso, Ltd. has enforced strong passwords, the occurrence of locked-out accounts has increased. You will delegate to the local department managers the authority to unlock a locked-out user account. To ease administration of this task, you will modify the Delegation of Control Wizard's list of common tasks to include the authority to unlock locked-out user accounts. You will use a preconfigured delegwiz.ini file to replace the default file.

Tasks	Specific instructions
1. Examine the default delegwiz.ini file.	a. Log on to DEN-DC1 as **Administrator**.
	b. Open the **C:\Windows\Inf\delegwiz.ini** file in Notepad.
	c. Examine the current **delgwiz.ini** file.
	d. Close Notepad.
	e. Open **Active Directory Users and Computers**, and run the **Delegation of Control Wizard** for the **Legal** organizational unit.
	f. Add the **Legalmanager** user account, and then click **Next**.
	g. On the **Tasks to Delegate** page, notice how the list of common tasks relates to the delegwiz.ini file. What is the first common task in the list?
	h. Cancel the Delegation of Control Wizard.
	i. Open the **D:\2274\Labfiles\Admin_Tools \delegwiz.ini** file in Notepad.
	j. Compare the modified file with the original.
	What new task has been added to the list of templates?
	What permission is being granted by the template?
	k. Close Notepad without saving the files.
2. Replace the delegwiz.ini file with the delegwiz.ini file located in the **D:\2274\ Labfiles\Admin_Tools** folder.	a. Copy the **delegwiz.ini** file from the **D:\2274\Labfiles\Admin_Tools** folder to the **C:\Windows\Inf** folder.
	b. Click **Yes** in the **Confirm File Replace** dialog box.

(continued)

Tasks	Specific instructions
3. Grant the Legal department manager the authority to unlock locked-out user accounts.	a. Switch to **Active Directory Users and Computers**, and run the **Delegation of Control Wizard** on the **Legal** organizational unit. b. Add the **Legalmanager** user account, and then click **Next**. c. On the **Tasks to Delegate** page, what is the last common task in the list now? d. Select the **Unlock locked User accounts** check box. Click **Next**. e. Click **Finish**.

Exercise 2
Testing the Delegated Permissions

In this exercise, you will unlock a locked-out user account as the Legal department manager.

Scenario

Now that the Legal department manager has been granted the authority to unlock locked-out user accounts, you need to ensure that the delegation is working properly.

Task	Specific instructions
1. Lock out the **Legaluser** account by attempting to log on with an incorrect password.	**a.** Attempt to log on to DEN-CL1 as **Legaluser** four times with the wrong password. On the fourth attempt, you will receive a message informing you that the account has been locked out. **b.** Log on to DEN-CL1 as **legalmanager** with a password of **Pa$$w0rd**. **c.** At the **Run** command prompt, type **dsa.msc**. **d.** In **Active Directory Users and Computers**, click the **Legal** organizational unit, and then open the **Properties** dialog box for the **Legal User** account. **e.** Click the **Account** tab, and then clear the **Account is locked out** check box. Can the Legal department manager modify any other properties of the user account? **f.** Close all windows and log off of DEN-CL1.

Exercise 3

Granting Permissions in the Legal Organizational Unit and Creating a Taskpad

In this exercise, you will delegate to Judy Lew the authority to create, delete, and manage user and computer accounts in the Legal organizational unit and then create a taskpad to allow her to perform those tasks.

Scenario

Judy Lew will be in control of creating new user and computer accounts for the Legal organizational unit. Delegate that authority, and then create a taskpad to facilitate those tasks.

Tasks	Specific instructions
1. Delegate control to Judy Lew.	**a.** Switch to DEN-DC1. **b.** Run the Delegation of Control Wizard for the **Legal** organizational unit. **c.** Add **Judy Lew**, and then delegate to her the authority to **Create, delete, and manage user accounts**. **d.** Run the **Delegation of Control Wizard** for the **Legal** organizational unit a second time. **e.** Add **Judy Lew**, and then delegate to her the authority to have **Full Control** over computer objects.
2. Create a taskpad for Judy Lew.	**a.** On DEN-DC1, at the **Run** command prompt, type **MMC**, and then add the **Active Directory Users and Computers** snap-in. **b.** Right-click the **Legal** organizational unit and then click **New Window from here**. **c.** On the **Window** menu of **Console 1 [Legal]**, switch to **Console Root** to display the entire forest again. **d.** Close **Console Root** view by clicking the X in the top-right corner of the window. **e.** Right-click the **Legal** organizational unit, and then select **New Taskpad View**. **f.** In the **New Taskpad View Wizard**, click **Next** on the **Welcome** page. **g.** On the **Taskpad Display** page, click **Next** to accept the defaults. **h.** On the **Taskpad Target** page, click **Next** to accept the defaults. **i.** Click **Next** to accept the name and description. **j.** Ensure that the **Start New Task Wizard** check box is selected, and then click **Finish**. **k.** On the **Welcome to the New Task Wizard** page, click **Next**. **l.** On the **Command Type** page, click **Next** to accept the default **Menu Command** selection. **m.** On the **Shortcut Menu Command** page, select **Tree Item Task** in the **Command Source** drop-down list.

(continued)

Tasks	Specific instructions
2. *(continued)*	**n.** In the **Available commands** list, select **New->Computer**, and then click **Next**.
	o. On the **Name and Description** page, type **Create a Computer Account** in the **Task name** field, and then click **Next**.
	p. On the **Task Icon** page, click a computer icon and then click **Next**.
	q. On the **Completing the New Task Wizard** page, select the **Run this wizard again** check box, and then click **Finish**.
	r. Repeat the steps to create the shortcut menu command **New->User**.
	s. Click **Finish**.
	t. On the console **File** menu, click **Options**.
	u. In the **Options** dialog box, in the **Console mode** drop-down list, select **User mode, limited access, single window**.
	v. Clear the **Allow the user to customize views** check box. Click **OK**.
	w. Save the custom taskpad in the **D:\2274\Labfiles\Admin_Tools** folder as **Legal.msc**.

Exercise 4

Testing the Delegated Permissions

In this exercise, you will log on as Judy Lew and use the taskpad to perform administrative tasks.

Scenario

Judy Lew will copy the taskpad to the client running Microsoft Windows® XP Professional and then use the taskpad to perform administrative tasks.

Tasks	Specific instructions
1. Copy the taskpad from Den-DC1 to DEN-CL1.	a. Log on to DEN-CL1 as **Judy** with the password of **Pa$$w0rd**. b. Connect to **\\DEN-DC1\admin_tools**. c. Copy the **Legal.msc** taskpad to the desktop of DEN-CL1.
2. Test the permissions.	a. Double-click **Legal.msc**. b. Click the **Create a User Account** icon. c. The **New Object – User** dialog box will appear. d. Create a test user account called **Test User 3**. It will succeed. Can you add a snap-in to the management console from the **File** menu?
3. Complete the lab exercise.	a. Close all programs and shut down all computers. Do not save changes. b. To prepare for the next module, start the DEN-DC1 and DEN-CL1 virtual computers.

Module 6: Implementing Group Policy

Contents

Overview

- Implementing Group Policy Objects
- Implementing GPOs in a Domain
- Managing the Deployment of Group Policy

Introduction

The information in this module introduces the job function of implementing Group Policy. Specifically, the module provides the skills and knowledge that you need to explain the purpose and function of Group Policy in a Microsoft® Windows Server™ 2003 environment, implement Group Policy objects (GPOs), and manage GPOs.

Objectives

After completing this module, you will be able to:

- Implement GPOs.
- Implement GPOs in a domain.
- Manage the deployment of Group Policy.

Lesson: Implementing Group Policy Objects

- What Is Group Policy?
- Processing Group Policy Objects
- What Are User and Computer Configuration Settings?
- Local Computer Group Policy
- Practice: Set Local Computer Group Policy

Introduction

Group Policy gives administrators the ability to control the user and computer environment. This lesson describes how to implement Group Policy.

Lesson objectives

After completing this lesson, you will be able to:

- Explain what Group Policy is.
- Describe how Group Policies are processed.
- Describe user and computer configuration settings.
- Describe local computer policies.
- Set local computer policy settings.

What Is Group Policy?

Definition

All computers with Microsoft Windows® 2000, Windows XP, or Windows Server 2003 operating systems are capable of accepting Group Policy settings. The local Group Policy settings can be used to manage the local computer in a standalone or domain environment. The Active Directory® directory service can use Group Policy to manage users and computers in a domain. For example, you can define Group Policy settings that affect the entire domain or define settings that affect specific organizational units (OUs) or use local Group Policy settings to affect a single computer.

When using Group Policy, you can define the state of a user's work environment, and then rely on the local operating system or Active Directory to enforce these Group Policy settings. You can apply Group Policy settings across an entire organization, or you can apply Group Policy settings to specific groups of users and computers.

Note You cannot apply Group Policy settings to computers that have legacy operating systems, such as Windows NT 4.0 or Windows 98.

Active Directory Group Policy settings are stored in GPOs. GPOs are stored in Sysvol in Active Directory. Local computer Group Policy settings are stored on the local hard drive in the %windir%/system32/GroupPolicy hidden folder.

Administrative Templates

There are several template files with an .adm extension that are included with Windows. These files, called Administrative Templates, provide policy information for the items that are under the Administrative Templates folder in the console tree of Group Policy Object Editor. Administrative Templates include registry-based settings, which are available under Computer Configuration and User Configuration in the Group Policy Object Editor.

An .adm file consists of a hierarchy of categories and subcategories that define how the policy settings appear. It also contains the following information:

- Registry locations that correspond to each policy setting
- Options or restrictions in values that are associated with each policy setting
- For many policy settings, a default value
- Explanation of each policy setting's function
- The versions of Windows that support each setting

Additional reading

For more information about Group Policy, see:

- "Introduction to IntelliMirror® Configuration Management Technologies" on the Microsoft Web site.
- "Group Policy settings overview" on the Microsoft Web site.

Processing Group Policy Objects

Group Policies are processed in the following order:
- Local computer Group Policy
- Group Policy objects linked to the site
- Group Policy objects linked to the domain
- Group Policy objects linked to the OU

Introduction

GPOs are processed in a particular order. Because the last policy applied determines the user and computer environment, the order of processing is an important consideration when designing a Group Policy strategy.

Local computer Group Policy

The Group Policy of the local computer is always applied first. Local policies are stored on the hard drive of the local computer and are applied to all users who log on to the local machine. Local policies are usually implemented in a workgroup or standalone environment.

Site Group Policy

If the computer is a member of an Active Directory forest, then any GPOs linked to the site will be applied after the local computer policy. Sites and domains do not have a physical relationship. One site may contain multiple domains or one domain may span multiple sites. Because a GPO resides in the Sysvol folder of a domain controller, a GPO linked to a site may force a GPO to be applied across domain boundaries if there are multiple domains in the site. This may result in Group Policy not being applied consistently across a single domain that spans multiple sites. Careful consideration should be given to linking a GPO to a site.

Domain Group Policy

After site GPOs have been applied, any GPOs linked to the domain will be applied. The domain GPO is unique because this is the only container where domain account policies can be applied.

Organizational Unit Group Policy

GPOs can be linked to any parent or child organizational unit. All GPOs that are linked to parent OUs and child OUs are applied to user and computer accounts. The GPOs linked to the parent OU are applied first, followed by GPOs linked to the child OUs. The GPOs linked to the immediate container object are applied last.

Additional reading

For more information about how clients apply Group Policy, see "Order of processing settings" on the Microsoft Web site.

What Are User and Computer Configuration Settings?

Group Policy settings for users control:
- Software settings
- Windows settings
- Security settings
- Desktop settings

Group Policy settings for computers control:
- Software settings
- Windows settings
- Security settings
- Operating system

Introduction

You can enforce Group Policy settings for computers and users by using the Computer Configuration and User Configuration settings in Group Policy.

User configuration

The User Configuration setting modifies the HKEY_CURRENT_USER hive of the registry. Group Policy settings for users include software settings, Windows settings, desktop settings, security settings, application settings, folder redirection options, and user logon and logoff scripts. User-related Group Policy settings are requested when users log on to the computer and settings that have changed are applied during the periodic refresh cycle. Security settings are refreshed at least every 16 hours, whether they have changed or not.

Group Policy settings that customize the user's desktop environment or enforce lockdown policies on users are contained under User Configuration in Group Policy Object Editor.

Software settings for user configuration

The Software Settings folder under User Configuration contains software settings that apply to users regardless of which computer they log on to. This folder also contains software installation settings.

Windows settings for user configuration

The Windows Settings folder under User Configuration contains Windows settings that apply to users regardless of which computer they log on to. The Windows Settings folder also contains the following folders:

- Folder Redirection
- Security Settings
- Scripts

Desktop Settings

The Administrative Templates folder contains the following folders:

- Windows Components
- Start Menu and Taskbar
- Desktop
- Control Panel
- Shared Folders
- Network
- System

These Administrative Templates folders contain the Group Policy settings that control the user's environment. You can create your own .adm files or add existing ones to allow any aspect of the user environment to be controlled by Group Policy. For example, you can add the Microsoft Office 2003 templates from the Office 2003 resource kit and use Group Policy to control application settings.

Computer configuration

The computer configuration modifies the HKEY_LOCAL_MACHINE hive of the registry. Group Policy settings for computers control how the operating system behaves, security settings, computer startup and shutdown scripts, configuration of Windows components, computer-assigned application options, and application settings. Computer-related Group Policy settings are requested by the client computer when the operating system initializes, and only settings that have changed are applied during the periodic refresh cycle. Security settings are refreshed at least every 16 hours whether they have changed or not. In general, computer-related Group Policy settings take precedence over conflicting user-related Group Policy settings. However, this is not consistent, so we recommended that you read the information supplied with each policy setting.

Group Policy settings that customize the desktop environment for all users of a computer or enforce security policies on a network's computers are contained under Computer Configuration in the Group Policy Object Editor.

Software settings for computer configuration

The Software Settings folder under Computer Configuration contains software settings. Software assigned to a computer will be installed the next time the computer reboots and will be available to all users who log on to the computer. This folder also contains software installation settings.

Windows settings for computer configuration

The Windows Settings folder under Computer Configuration contains Windows settings that apply to all users who log on to the computer. This folder also contains the following items:

- Security Settings
- Security settings for computer configuration
- Scripts

Security settings are available in the Windows Settings folder under Computer Configuration and User Configuration in Group Policy Object Editor. Security settings are rules that you configure on a computer or multiple computers that protect resources on a computer or network. With security settings, you can define the security policy of an organizational unit, domain, or site.

Administrative Templates

The Administrative Templates folder contains the following folders:

- Windows Components
- System
- Network
- Printer

These folders contain settings to allow you to control operating system behavior for all computers affected by the policy. For example, you can configure how Terminal Services will function or pre-populate printer search locations.

Additional reading

For more information about extending Group Policy, see "Advanced methods of extending Group Policy" on the Microsoft Web site.

Local Computer Group Policy

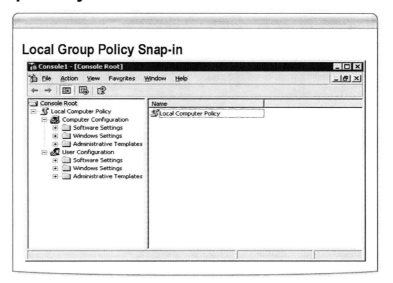

Introduction	All computers with Windows 2000, Windows XP, or Windows Server 2003 operating systems can have local Group Policy settings applied to the local computer's registry. The local Group Policy snap-in is similar, but it is not identical to the Group Policy Object Editor in Active Directory. Settings that deal with domain configurations are not included in the local Group Policy snap-in.
When to use local Group Policy	In a workgroup or a standalone situation, the only method available to control the user and computer environment so that users cannot modify the settings is by using local Group Policy settings or by directly accessing the registry. Direct modification of the registry is not recommended.
	Local policies can also be used in the domain environment but are usually not used because it is more efficient to centralize the configuration of Group Policy through Active Directory rather than configure each individual computer.
How to set local Group Policy	To set local Group Policy, you must create a custom MMC and add the Group Policy snap-in and configure the snap-in to modify the local computer settings. Only administrators can set local Group Policy.
How to modify local Group Policy behavior	Any settings you configure in the local Group Policy will apply to all local or domain users who log on the computer. You can change this behavior by modifying NTFS permissions on the %systemroot%\system32\GroupPolicy hidden folder. You can deny permission to the Group Policy folder to users and groups that you do not want to be affected by local policy. For example, you may have a restrictive policy that you want to affect all users of the computer except administrators. You would deny access to administrators to the Group Policy folder to accomplish this. If an administrator needs to modify the policy later, the administrator would have to give permission back to the administrator account to allow the modification.
Local Security Policy snap-in	The Administration Tools folder includes a shortcut to the Local Security Policy snap-in. This snap-in is a link to the Security Settings folder of the local Group Policy. This snap-in allows Administrators quick access to the security settings of the local machine without having to create a custom MMC.

Practice: Set Local Computer Group Policy

In this practice, you will:

* Create a custom MMC and add the Group Policy snap-in for the local computer

* Configure a Group Policy setting to remove the user name from the Start menu

* Configure a Group Policy setting to prevent Windows Messenger from automatically running at logon

Objective

In this practice, you will:

- Create a custom MMC and add the Group Policy snap-in for the local computer.

- Configure a Group Policy setting to remove the user name from the Start menu.

- Configure a Group Policy setting to prevent Windows Messenger from automatically running at logon.

Instructions

Ensure that the DEN-DC1 and DEN-CL1 virtual machines are running.

Practice

▶ **Create a custom MMC and add the Group Policy snap-in for the local computer**

1. Log on to DEN-CL1 as **Administrator** with the password of **Pa$$w0rd**.

2. Click **Start**, click **Run** and type **MMC**. Click **OK**.

3. In the Console1 window, click the **File** menu, and then click **Add/Remove Snap-in**.

4. From the **Add/Remove Snap-in** dialog box, click **Add**.

5. Add the **Group Policy** snap-in.

6. On the **Select Group Policy Object** dialog box, ensure that **Local Computer** is entered in the field, and click **Finish**.

7. Click **Close**, and click **OK**.

▶ **Configure a Group Policy setting to remove the user name from the Start menu**

1. Expand **Local Computer Policy, User Configuration, Administrative Templates**, and then click the **Start Menu and Taskbar** folder.

2. Double-click the **Remove user name from start menu** setting.

Tip The **Remove user name from start menu** setting is the fourth setting from the bottom of the list.

---

3. Select **Enabled**, and click **OK**.

4. Open a command prompt and type **gpupdate /force** to force the refresh of Group Policy.

5. Click the **Start** menu. The name of the logged-on user should no longer be displayed.

6. Switch back to the custom MMC and double-click **Remove user name from start menu**.

7. Select **Not Configured**, and click **OK**.

8. Refresh the Group Policy application by using **gpupdate /force**.

9. Close the command prompt window.

10. Click the **Start** menu. The name of the logged-on user should be displayed again.

▶ **Configure a Group Policy setting to prevent Windows Messenger from automatically running at logon**

1. Switch back to the custom MMC and expand **Computer Configuration, Administrative Templates, Windows Components,** and then click **Windows Messenger**.

2. Select the **Do not automatically start Windows Messenger initially** setting and read the information associated with it.

3. Double-click the **Do not automatically start Windows Messenger initially** setting, click **Enabled**, and click **OK**.

4. Close the custom MMC without saving it.

5. Log off of DEN-CL1.

Lesson: Implementing GPOs in a Domain

- Tools Used to Manage GPOs
- What Is a GPO Link?
- How Group Policy Settings Are Inherited in Active Directory
- Backup, Restore, and Import GPOs
- Practice: Implementing GPOs in a Domain

Introduction

Implementing Group Policy in a domain provides the network administrator with greater control over computer configurations throughout the network. Also, by using Group Policy in Windows Server 2003, you can create a managed desktop environment that is tailored to the user's job responsibilities and experience level, which can decrease demand for network support.

Lesson objectives

After completing this lesson, you will be able to:

- Understand the tools used to create GPOs.
- Explain what a GPO link is.
- Explain how Group Policy permission is inherited in Active Directory.
- Backup, Restore, and Import GPOs.
- Implement GPOs in a domain.

Tools Used to Manage GPOs

- **Default Group Policy tools**
  - Active Directory Users and Computers
  - Active Directory Sites and Services
  - Local Group Policy Custom Management Console
- **Add-in tools**
  - Group Policy Management Console (GPMC)

Introduction

The Group Policy Object Editor can be opened through various management consoles.

Active Directory Users and Computers

You can open the Group Policy Object Editor from Active Directory Users and Computers to manage GPOs for domains and organizational units. In the **Properties** dialog box for a domain or an organizational unit, there is a **Group Policy** tab. On this tab, you can manage GPOs for the domain or organizational units.

Active Directory Sites and Services

You can open Group Policy Object Editor from Active Directory Sites and Services to manage GPOs for sites. In the **Properties** dialog box for a site, there is a **Group Policy** tab. On this tab, you can manage GPOs for the site.

Note If the Group Policy Management Console (GPMC) is installed, the Active Directory Users and Computers and Active Directory Sites and Services Group Policy controls are replaced by a button to launch the Group Policy Management console.

Local Group Policy Custom Management Console

You can edit the local computer settings on all computers with Windows 2000, Windows XP, or Windows Server 2003 operating systems installed by creating a custom management console and adding the Group Policy snap-in.

**Group Policy
Management Console**

The Group Policy Management Console is an add-on tool for managing Group Policy. The GPMC consolidates the management of Group Policy across the enterprise.

The Group Policy Management Console combines the functionality of multiple components in a single user interface (UI). The UI is structured to match the way you use and manage Group Policy. It incorporates functionality related to Group Policy from the following tools into a single MMC snap-in:

- Active Directory Users and Computers
- Active Directory Sites and Services
- Resultant Set of Policy (RSoP)

The GPMC also provides the following extended capabilities that were not available in previous Group Policy tools. With the GPMC, you can:

- Back up and restore GPOs.
- Copy and import GPOs.
- Use Windows Management Instrumentation (WMI) filters.
- Report GPO and Resultant Set of Polices (RSoP) data.
- Search for GPOs.

**Group Policy
Management vs. default
Group Policy tools**

Prior to Group Policy Management, you managed Group Policy by using a variety of Windows-based tools, including Active Directory Users and Computers, Active Directory Sites and Services, and RSoP. Group Policy Management consolidates management of all core Group Policy tasks into a single tool. Because of this consolidated management, Group Policy functionality is no longer required in these other tools.

After installing the GPMC, you still use each of the Active Directory tools for its intended directory management purpose, such as creating user, computer, and group objects. However, you must use the GPMC to perform all tasks related to Group Policy. Group Policy functionality is no longer available through the Active Directory tools when the GPMC is installed.

The GPMC does not replace Group Policy Object Editor. You still must edit GPOs by using Group Policy Object Editor. The GPMC integrates editing functionality by providing direct access to Group Policy Object Editor.

Note   The Group Policy Management Console does not come with Windows Server 2003. It is a free download from the Microsoft Web site.

The GPMC can be used to manage Group Policy in a Windows 2000 domain, but it cannot be installed on a Windows 2000 server or Windows 2000 Professional operating system. It can be installed on a computer with the Windows XP Professional operating system if the .NET Framework 1.1 has been installed.

Note   The dotnetfx.exe can be downloaded from the Microsoft Web site to install the .NET Framework 1.1.

What Is a GPO Link?

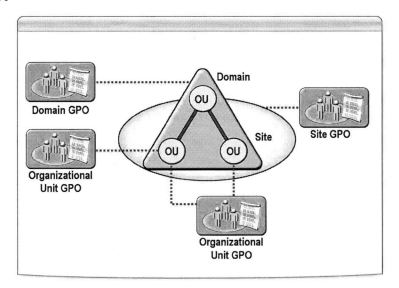

Introduction

All GPOs are stored in a container in Active Directory called Group Policy Objects. When a GPO is linked to a site, domain, or organizational unit, the GPO is also listed in the Group Policy Objects container. As a result, you can centrally administer and deploy the GPOs to many domains or organizational units.

Creating an unlinked GPO

When you create a GPO in the Group Policy Objects container, the GPO is not deployed to any users or computers until a GPO link is created. You can create an unlinked GPO by using the Group Policy Management Console. You might create unlinked GPOs in a large organization where one group creates GPOs and another group links the GPOs to the required site, domain, or organizational unit. Members of the Group Policy Creator Owners group can create GPOs, but they cannot link them.

Creating a linked GPO

When you create a GPO linked to a site, domain, or organizational unit, you actually perform two separate operations: creating the new GPO, and then linking it to the site, domain, or organizational unit. When delegating permissions to link a GPO to a domain, organizational unit, or site, you must have Modify permission for the domain, organizational unit, or site that you want to delegate.

By default, only members of the Domain Admins and Enterprise Admins groups have the necessary permissions to link GPOs to domains and organizational units. Only members of the Enterprise Admins group have the permissions to link GPOs to sites.

Important You cannot link a GPO to default containers in Active Directory. For example, the Users or Computers containers cannot be directly linked to GPOs. However, any GPO linked to the domain applies to users and computers in these containers.

How Group Policy Settings Are Inherited in Active Directory

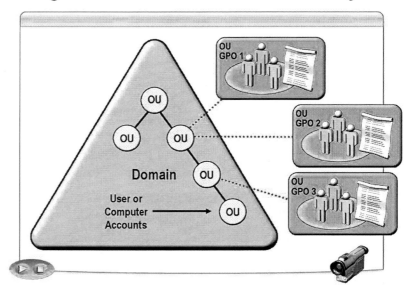

Introduction

The order in which Windows Server 2003 applies GPOs depends on the Active Directory container to which the GPOs are linked. The GPOs are applied first to the site, then to domains, and then to organizational units in the domains.

Flow of inheritance

A child container inherits GPOs from the parent container. This means that the child container can have many Group Policy settings applied to its users and computers without having a GPO directly linked to it. However, there is no inheritance of policies between parent and child domains like there is between parent and child organizational units.

Order of inheritance

GPOs are cumulative, meaning that they are inherited. Group Policy inheritance is the order in which Windows Server 2003 applies GPOs. The order in which GPOs are applied and how GPOs are inherited determines which settings affect users and computers. If there are multiple GPOs that have conflicting values, the GPO applied last takes precedence.

You can also have multiple GPOs linked to the same containers. For example, you can have three GPOs linked to a single domain. Because the order in which the GPOs are applied may affect the resultant Group Policy settings, there is a priority of Group Policy settings for each container.

To view the GPOs that will be applied to members of a site, domain or OU, view the inheritance tab in GPMC. The items listed with the lowest priority number are applied last and, therefore, take precedence.

Multimedia activity

The "Implementing Group Policy" activity includes multiple choice and drag-and-drop exercises that test your knowledge. To start the activity, open the Web page on the Student Materials CD, click **Multimedia**, and then click **Implementing Group Policy**. Read the instructions, and then click the **Effects of Group Policy Settings** tab to begin the activity.

Back Up, Restore, and Import GPOs

The GPMC allows you to
* Back up GPOs
* Restore GPOs
* Import settings from backed-up GPOs

Introduction

The GPMC supports backing up and restoring GPOs. This allows you to recover GPOs in case of loss or corruption. Once GPOs have been backed up, it is possible to import the settings into a new GPO to simplify the creation of policies that need similar, but not identical, settings.

Backing up GPOs

The GPMC allows you to back up individual GPOs or to back up all GPOs in a single operation. You only need to provide a storage location for the backup. Any local or network folder can be used as the backup location. To back up an individual GPO, right-click and select **Backup** and provide a location. To back up all policies, right-click the **Group Policy Objects** folder, select **Back Up All**, and provide a location.

Important   WMI filters and IPSec policies are external to the GPO and will not be backed up by a backup operation of GPOs.

Restoring GPOs

Backed-up GPOs can be restored from the backup location in case of disaster recovery or a corrupted GPO. To restore a GPO, right-click the **Group Policy Objects** container and select **Manage Backups**. Then select the GPO you need and restore it. You can edit the view to see only the most recent version of the backups, and you can view the settings prior to restoring the GPO.

Importing GPOs

If you have a backup of a GPO, you can import those settings into a new or existing GPO. This can be a useful feature if you have organizational units with similar requirements. For example, one GPO could be created to hold both the user and computer settings that are common to all containers. Those settings could be imported into many other GPOs and then customized as required. The **Import Settings Wizard** will scan the settings during the import operation to check for references such as UNC paths or Windows security groups that may need to be adjusted in the destination GPO. If the wizard finds such references, it will prompt the user to create or locate a Migration Table. A Migration Table allows you to adjust any references that need to be changed in the GPO.

Important   Importing settings into an existing GPO will overwrite all current settings.

Practice: Implementing GPOs in a Domain

In this practice, you will:

- Install the Group Policy Management Console on DEN-CL1
- Create an unlinked GPO
- Create a linked GPO
- Back up and restore a GPO

Objective

In this practice, you will:

- Install the Group Policy Management Console on DEN-CL1.
- Create an unlinked GPO.
- Create a linked GPO.
- Back up and restore a GPO.

Instructions

Ensure that the DEN-DC1 and DEN-CL1 virtual machines are running.

Practice

▶ **Install the Group Policy Management Console on DEN-CL1**

1. Log on to DEN-CL1 as **Administrator**.
2. Connect to **DEN-DC1\Admin_tools**, double-click the **dotnetfx.exe** file and click **Yes** to install the Microsoft .NET Framework 1.1.
3. Accept the license agreement, and click **Install**.
4. Click **OK** when the installation completes.
5. Double-click the **gpmc.msi** in the **Admin_Tools** folder to install the Group Policy Management Console.
6. On the Welcome screen, click **Next**.
7. Accept the license agreement, and click **Next**.
8. When installation completes, click **Finish**.
9. Close the Admin_Tools window.

▶ **Create an unlinked GPO**

1. Right-click the **Start menu**, and then click **Open All Users**.

2. Double-click the **Programs** folder.

3. Double-click **Administrative Tools**,

4. Double-click **Group Policy Management**.

5. Expand Forest:contoso.msft, expand Domains, expand the Contoso.msft, and expand the **Group Policy Objects** container.

    What GPOs are in the container?

     Group policy Modeling

    ,, Result

6. Right-click the **Group Policy Objects** container, and click **New**.

7. In the **New GPO** dialog box, type **Remove Search** and click **OK**.

▶ **Create a linked GPO**

1. Right-click the **Graphics** OU, and click **Create and Link a GPO Here**.

2. In the **New GPO** dialog box, type **Graphics Lockdown** and click **OK**.

3. Expand the **Graphics** OU. Notice an icon with a black arrow appears for the Graphics Lockdown GPO indicating that it is linked to the Graphics OU.

4. Expand the **Group Policy Objects** container. Notice that the Graphics Lockdown GPO resides in this container.

▶ **Back up and restore a GPO**

1. Right-click the **Graphics Lockdown** GPO, and click **Back up**.

2. In the **Backup Group Policy Object** dialog box, Browse to **C:** drive and create a **New Folder** called **GPO Backup**. Click **OK**.

3. Click **Back Up** and click **OK**.

4. Delete the **Graphics Lockdown** GPO from the Group Policy Objects folder.

5. Right-click the **Group Policy Objects** folder, and click **Manage Backups**.

6. Select the **Graphics Lockdown** GPO, and click **Restore**.

7. Click **OK** twice and click **Close**. Notice that the **Graphics Lockdown** GPO has been restored.

8. Close all open windows and log off.

Important Do not shut down the virtual machines.

Lesson: Managing the Deployment of Group Policy

- Attributes of a GPO Link
- Blocking the Inheritance of a GPO
- What Happens When GPOs Conflict
- Filtering the Deployment of a GPO
- Discussion: Modifying Group Policy Inheritance
- Practice: Managing the Deployment of Group Policy

Introduction

The deployment of Group Policy can be managed through a number of different methods. The effects of Group Policy can be modified by using the techniques described in this lesson.

Lesson objectives

After completing this lesson, you will be able to:

- Describe attributes of a GPO link.
- Block the inheritance of a GPO.
- Explain what happens when GPOs conflict.
- Explain what it means to filter the deployment of a GPO.
- Modify Group Policy inheritance.
- Manage the deployment of Group Policy.

Attributes of a GPO Link

> - **Enforced**
>   - Take precedence over other GPO settings
> - **Link Enabled or Disabled**
>   - Links can be disabled for troubleshooting
> - **Deleted**
>   - Links can be deleted without deleting the GPO
> - **Multiple Links**
>   - When there are multiple GPOs linked to a container there is an order of precedence

Introduction

You can enable, disable, enforce, and group GPO links. These options significantly affect the user and computer accounts in the organizational unit that the GPO is linked to.

The Enforced option

The **Enforced** option is an attribute of the GPO link, *not* the GPO itself. If you have a GPO that is linked to multiple containers, you configure the **Enforced** option on each individual container. Furthermore, if the same GPO is linked elsewhere, the **Enforced** option does not apply to that link unless you also modify that link.

All Group Policy settings contained in the GPO whose link is configured with **Enforced** apply, even if they conflict with Group Policy settings processed after them or if inheritance is blocked lower in the Active Directory tree. You should enable the **Enforced** option only for the links to the GPO that represents critical organization-wide rules. Link the GPO high in the Active Directory tree so that it affects multiple organizational units. For example, you will want to link a GPO with network security settings to a domain or site.

Important   Before Group Policy Management is installed, the **Enforced** option is called **No Override** in Active Directory Users and Computers.

Enabling and disabling a link

Link Enabled is another attribute that you may use when you are troubleshooting a GPO. You can disable the GPO link by clearing the **Link Enabled** option, instead of deleting the GPO link. By disabling the link, you only change the effect on the user and computer accounts in the organizational unit and all child organizational units. You do not affect other links to the GPO. For example, you can temporarily disable a link to test if it was causing a conflict for one OU while still having the settings apply to other OUs.

Deleted

When a GPO link is deleted, the policy is not physically deleted. Just the link is deleted. In order to delete the GPO from the domain, you must delete it from the Group Policy Object container.

Multiple links

When multiple GPOs are linked to an organizational unit, GPOs are applied in priority. The policy with the lowest order number in the Group Policy list is applied last. Conflicting settings will be overwritten by policies with a higher priority (a lower number). If Group Policy settings in the GPO conflict, the last one applied takes precedence.

Blocking the Inheritance of a GPO

Introduction

You can prevent a child container from inheriting any GPOs from parent containers by enabling **Block Policy inheritance** on the child container.

Why use Block Policy inheritance?

Enabling **Block Policy inheritance** on a child container prevents the container from inheriting all Group Policy settings from all GPOs. This is useful when an Active Directory container requires unique Group Policy settings and you want to ensure that Group Policy settings are not inherited. For example, you can use **Block Policy inheritance** when the administrator of an organizational unit must control all GPOs for that container.

Considerations

Consider the following when using **Block Policy inheritance**:

- You cannot selectively choose which GPOs are blocked. **Block Policy inheritance** affects all GPOs from all parent containers, except GPOs configured with the **Enforced** option.

- **Block Policy inheritance** does not block the inheritance of a GPO linked to a parent container if the link is configured with the **Enforced** option.

Multimedia activity

The "Implementing Group Policy" activity includes multiple choice and drag-and-drop exercises that test your knowledge. To access the activity, open the Web page on the Student Materials CD, click **Multimedia**, and then click **Implementing Group Policy**. Read the instructions, and then click the **Managing the Deployment of Group Policy** tab to begin the activity.

What Happens When GPOs Conflict

How conflicts are resolved:

When Group Policy settings in the Active Directory hierarchy conflict, the settings for the child container GPO apply

Introduction

Complex combinations of GPOs sometimes create conflicts; these conflicts could require modification to default inheritance behavior. When a Group Policy setting is configured for a parent organizational unit, and the same Group Policy setting is not configured for a child organizational unit, the objects in the child organizational unit inherit the Group Policy setting from the parent organizational unit.

How conflicts are resolved

When Group Policy settings are configured for both the parent organizational unit and the child organizational units, the settings for both organizational units apply. If the Group Policy settings conflict, the child organizational unit's settings will have priority. For example, a Group Policy setting for a parent organizational unit prohibits access to the Control Panel while a Group Policy setting applied to its child organizational unit specifically allows access to the Control Panel. Users in the child organizational unit will have access to the Control Panel because the policy linked to the child organizational unit was applied last.

Filtering the Deployment of a GPO

Introduction

By default, all Group Policy settings in GPOs that affect the container are applied to all users and computers in that container, which may not produce the results that you desire. By using the filtering feature, you can determine which settings are applied to the users and computers in the specific container.

Permissions for GPOs

You can filter the deployment of a GPO by setting permissions on the GPO link to determine the access of the read or deny permission on the GPO. Before Group Policy settings can apply to a user or computer account, an account must have both Read and Apply Group Policy permissions for the GPO. The default permissions for a new GPO have the following access control entries (ACEs):

- Authenticated Users—Allow Read and Allow Apply Group Policy

- Domain Admins, Enterprise Admins and SYSTEM—Allow Read, Allow Write, Allow Create All Child objects, Allow Delete All Child objects

- Creator Owner—Special permission to create and edit, but not apply, child objects

- Enterprise Domain Controllers—Allow Read

Filtering methods

Use the following methods to filter access:

- Explicitly deny

  Use this method to deny access to the Group Policy. For example, you could explicitly deny permission to the Administrators security group, which would prevent administrators in the organizational unit from receiving the GPO settings.

- Remove Authenticated Users

  You can remove the Authenticated Users group and add the specific users, groups, or computers to whom the GPO settings will be applied.

Discussion: Modifying Group Policy Inheritance

Requirements

• **Set up GPOs with the following requirements**
  • Antivirus protection
  • Office suite
  • An accounting application

How do you set up your GPOs?

Contoso.msft
  Sales
  Payroll
  Training

Class discussion

You have determined that the following conditions must exist in your network:

- An antivirus application must be installed on all computers in the domain.

- The Microsoft Office suite must be installed on computers in the domain, except those in the Payroll department.

- A line-of-business accounting application must be installed on all computers in the Payroll department, except those that are used by administrators of the Payroll organizational unit.

How do you set up GPOs so that the above conditions are met?

_____

_____

_____

_____

_____

Practice: Managing the Deployment of Group Policy

In this practice, you will

- Link a GPO to the domain to remove the Search option from the Start menu
- Test the results
- Create a conflicting GPO for the Graphics OU and block inheritance at the Sales OU
- Test the results
- Enforce the Remove Search GPO
- Test the results

Objective

In this practice, you will:

- Link a GPO to the domain to remove the Search option from the Start menu.
- Test the results.
- Create a conflicting GPO for the Graphics OU and block inheritance at the Sales OU.
- Test the results.
- Enforce the Remove Search GPO.
- Test the results.

Instructions

Ensure that the DEN-DC1 and DEN-CL1 virtual machines are running.

Practice

▶ **Link a GPO to the domain to remove the Search option from the Start menu**

1. Log on to DEN-CL1 as **Administrator**.
2. Right-click the **Start** menu, and then click **Open All Users**.
3. Double-click the **Programs** folder.
4. Double-click **Administrative** Tools.
5. Create a shortcut on the desktop linked to **Group Policy Management**.
6. Double-click **Group Policy Management**.
7. Right-click the **Contoso.msft** domain. Click **Link an Existing GPO**.
8. In the **Select GPO** dialog box, click **Remove Search**, and click **OK**.
9. Right-click the **Remove Search** GPO, and click **Edit**
10. In the **Group Policy** dialog box, expand **User Configuration**.

11. Expand **Administrative Templates** and then click **Start Menu and Taskbar**. **Enable** the **Remove Search menu from Start Menu** setting.

12. Click **OK**.

13. Close all open windows and log off.

▶ **Test the results**

1. Log on to DEN-CL1 as **Don** with a password of **Pa$$w0rd**.

2. Click the **Start** menu. Ensure there is no Search folder.

3. Log off.

4. Log on as **GraphicsUser** with a password of **Pa$$w0rd**.

5. Click the **Start** menu. Ensure there is no Search folder. The Search folder has been removed for all users because the GPO was linked to the domain.

6. Log off.

▶ **Create a conflicting GPO for the Graphics OU and block inheritance at the Sales OU**

1. Log on to DEN-CL1 as **Administrator**. Notice there is no Search folder on the **Start** menu for Administrator.

2. Open the **GPMC** and create and link a GPO called **Enable Search** to the **Graphics** OU.

3. Edit the **Enable Search** policy and locate the **Remove Search menu from Start Menu**, set it to be **Disabled**, and click **OK**.

4. In the **GPMC**, right-click the **Sales** OU, and click **Block Inheritance**.

5. Close all windows and log off.

▶ **Test the results**

1. Log on to DEN-CL1 as **Don**.

2. Click the **Start** menu. Ensure that the Search folder is back on the **Start** menu.

3. Log off and log on as **GraphicsUser**.

4. Click the **Start** menu. Ensure that the Search folder is on the **Start** menu.

5. Log off and log on as **Administrator**.

    Does Administrator have a Search folder on the **Start** menu?

_____

_____

▶ **Enforce the Remove Search GPO**

1. Open the GPMC and expand the domain.

2. Right-click the **Remove Search** GPO linked to the domain, and click **Enforced**.

3. Click **Run**, and type **GPupdate /force** to force **Group Policy** to refresh.

4. Log off of DEN-CL1.

▶ **Test the results**

1. Log on to DEN-CL1 as **Don** and then as **GraphicsUser**.

    Is the Search folder available on the Start menu for either user? Why or why not?

    _____

    _____

2. Close all open windows and log off.

Important   Do not shut down the virtual machines.

Lab: Implementing Group Policy

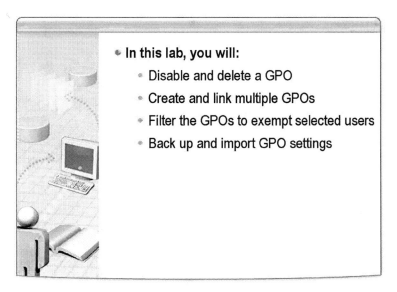

In this lab, you will:
- Disable and delete a GPO
- Create and link multiple GPOs
- Filter the GPOs to exempt selected users
- Back up and import GPO settings

Objectives

After completing this lab, you will be able to:

- Disable and delete a GPO.
- Create and link multiple GPOs.
- Filter the GPOs to exempt selected users.
- Back up and import GPO settings.

Prerequisites

To complete this lab, you must have the following virtual machines:

- DEN-DC1
- DEN-CL1

Estimated time to complete this lab: 30 minutes

Exercise 1
Disabling and Deleting a GPO

In this exercise, you disable and delete a GPO link.

Scenario

Contoso Ltd. has determined that users need access to the Search utility to perform their jobs. You will disable the GPO and then delete the link.

Tasks	Detailed Steps
1. Disable the GPO link.	a. Log on to DEN-CL1 as **Administrator**. b. Open the **Group Policy Management** console and expand the domain. c. Right-click the **Remove Search** GPO and click **Link Enabled** to remove the checkmark. Notice the arrow on the link icon becomes dimmed.
2. Delete the GPO link.	a. Right-click the **Remove Search** GPO and click **Delete**. b. Read the warning message in the **Group Policy Management** dialog box and click **OK**. c. Open **Run** and type **GPupdate /force** to refresh the policy. d. Open the **Group Policy Objects** container. Has the Remove Search policy been deleted?

Exercise 2
Creating and Linking Multiple GPOs

Scenario

To limit the number of calls to the help desk, Contoso, Ltd., has decided to remove the Run command from the Start menu for all domain users and to remove access to Control Panel to users in the Sales OU and the Graphics OU. You will create and link the GPOs to accomplish this.

Tasks	Detailed Steps
1. Create and link a GPO to the domain.	a. In Group Policy Management, right-click the domain.
	b. Create and link a GPO called **Remove Run Command**.
	c. **Edit** the policy.
	d. Expand **User Configuration, Administrative Templates, Start Menu and Taskbar** folder, **Enable** the **Remove Run menu from the Start Menu** setting.
	e. Close the Group Policy window.
2. Create and link a GPO to the Sales OU and the Graphics OU that prohibits access to Control Panel.	a. Right click the **Sales** OU.
	b. Click **Block Inheritance** to remove the check mark. This will disable inheritance blocking for the **Sales** OU.
	c. Create and link a GPO to the **Sales** OU called **Remove Control Panel**.
	d. **Edit** the policy.
	e. Expand **User Configuration, Administrative Templates, Control Panel** folder, locate and **Enable** the **Prohibit access to the Control Panel** setting.
	f. Right-click the **Graphics** OU and click **Link an Existing GPO**.
	g. In the **Select GPO** dialog box, click the **Remove Control Panel** GPO and click **OK**.
3. Determine which OUs the Remove Control Panel GPO is linked to.	a. Expand the **Group Policy Objects** folder and click the **Remove Control Panel** GPO.
	b. In the right pane, on the **Scope** tab, look under the **Location** heading.
	c. What containers are listed under the **Location** heading?
	d. If necessary, log off of DEN-CL1.
4. Test the setting as the sales manager.	a. Log on to DEN-CL1 as **Don** with the password of **Pa$$w0rd**.
	b. Click the **Start** menu. Ensure that the **Run** command has been removed from the **Start** menu. Ensure that **Control Panel** does not appear on the **Start** menu.
	c. Log off.

Exercise 3
Filtering the GPOs to Exempt Selected Users

In this exercise, you will filter the GPO permissions to exempt selected users.

Scenario

It has been determined that the domain administrators need access to the Run command. You will filter permissions to exempt the domain administrators from the Remove Run Command GPO. It has also been determined that the sales managers need access to Control Panel. You will filter permissions to exempt the sales managers from the Remove Control Panel GPO.

Tasks	Detailed Steps
1. Filter permissions on the Remove Run Command GPO to exempt domain administrators.	a. Log on to DEN-CL1 as **Administrator**. b. Open **Group Policy Management** and expand the domain. c. Click the **Remove Run Command** GPO. d. In the right pane, click the **Delegation** tab. e. Click **Advanced**. f. In the **Remove Run Command Security Settings** dialog box, select **Domain Admins** and check the box to **Deny** the **Apply Group Policy** permission. g. Click **OK** and click **Yes** after reading the **Security** warning message. h. Log off and then log on again to DEN-CL1 as **Administrator**. i. Click the **Start** menu. The **Run** command should be on the **Start** menu.
2. Filter permissions on the Remove Control Panel GPO to exempt the sales managers.	a. Switch to the **Group Policy Management** console and expand the **Sales** OU. b. Click the **Remove Control Panel** GPO. c. In the right pane, click the **Delegation** tab. d. Click **Advanced**. e. In the **Remove Control Panel Security Settings** dialog box, click **Add**. f. Type **G Sales Managers** and click **OK**. g. **Deny** the **Apply Group Policy** permission to **G Sales Managers**. Click **OK** and click **Yes** at the security message. h. Close all windows and log off. i. Log on as **Don** with the password of **Pa$$w0rd**. j. Click the **Start** menu. Ensure that **Control Panel** appears and that the **Run** command does not appear on the Start menu. k. Close all windows and log off.

Exercise 4
Backing Up and Importing GPO Settings

In this exercise, you will back up and import GPO settings.

Scenario

Another organizational unit needs a similar GPO configuration as the Remove Control Panel GPO. You will back up the Remove Control Panel GPO and then import the settings into a new GPO.

Tasks	Detailed Steps
1. Back up the Remove Control Panel GPO.	a. Log on to DEN-CL1 as **Administrator**. b. Open the **Group Policy Management** console and expand the domain. c. Click the **Group Policy Objects** folder. d. Right-click the **Remove Control Panel** GPO and click **Backup**. e. In the **Backup Group Policy Object** dialog box, ensure that **C:\GPO Backup** is the location. f. Click **Back Up** and then click **OK**.
2. Import the settings into a new GPO named **Imported**.	a. Right-click the **Group Policy Objects** container, create a new policy called **Imported** and click **OK**. b. Right-click the **Imported** GPO and click **Import Settings**. c. In the **Import Settings Wizard**, click **Next**. d. On the **Backup GPO** page, click **Next**. e. On the **Backup Location** page, ensure that the location is set to **C:\GPO backup** and click **Next**. f. On the **Source GPO** page, select the **Remove Control Panel** GPO and click **Next**. g. On the **Scanning Backup** page, click **Next**. h. Read the summary and click **Finish**. Click **OK** after the import is complete. i. **Edit** the **Imported** GPO to see that the settings were imported correctly.
3. Complete the lab exercise.	a. Close all programs and shut down all computers. Do not save changes. b. To prepare for the next module, start the DEN-DC1 and DEN-CL1 virtual computers.

Module 7: Managing the User Environment by Using Group Policy

Contents

Overview

- Configuring Group Policy Settings
- Assigning Scripts with Group Policy
- Restricting Group Membership and Access to Software
- Configuring Folder Redirection
- Determining Applied GPOs

Introduction

This module introduces the job function of managing the user environment by using Group Policy. Specifically, the module provides the skills and knowledge that you need to configure Group Policy to assign scripts, restrict group membership, and restrict access to software and to configure Folder Redirection.

Objectives

After completing this module, you will be able to:

- Configure Group Policy settings.
- Assign scripts with Group Policy.
- Restrict group membership and access to software.
- Configure Folder Redirection.
- Determine Applied Group Policy objects (GPOs).

Lesson: Configuring Group Policy Settings

* Why Use Group Policy?
* What Are Enabled and Disabled Group Policy Settings?
* Practice: Configuring Group Policy Settings

Introduction

After completing this lesson, you will be able to configure Group Policy settings.

Lesson objectives

After completing this lesson, you will be able to:

- Explain why you use Group Policy.
- Explain disabled and enabled Group Policy settings.
- Configure Group Policy settings.

Why Use Group Policy?

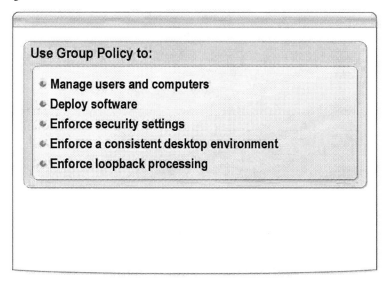

Use Group Policy to:

- Manage users and computers
- Deploy software
- Enforce security settings
- Enforce a consistent desktop environment
- Enforce loopback processing

Introduction

Managing user environments means controlling what users can do when logged on to the network. You can control their desktops, network connections, and interface through Group Policy. You manage user environments to ensure that users have only enough access to the operating system and applications to perform their jobs. This can help reduce the number of support calls to the help desk.

Tasks you can perform with Group Policy

When you centrally configure and manage user environments, you can perform the following tasks:

- Manage users and computers

    By managing user desktop settings with registry-based policies, you ensure that users have the same computing environments even if they log on from different computers. You can control how Microsoft® Windows Server™ 2003 manages user profiles, which includes how a user's personal data is made available. You can control Windows® group memberships and restrict access to software. By redirecting user folders from the user's local hard disks to a central location on a server, you can ensure that the user's data is available to the user regardless of the computer he or she logs on to.

- Deploy software

    Software is deployed to computers or users through the Active Directory® directory service. With software deployment, you can ensure that users have their required programs, service packs, and hotfixes.

■ Enforce security settings

By using Group Policy in Active Directory, the systems administrator can centrally apply the security settings required to protect the user environment. In Windows Server 2003, you can use the Security Settings extension in Group Policy to define the security settings for local and domain security policies.

■ Enforce a consistent desktop environment

Group Policy settings provide an efficient way to enforce standards, such as logon scripts and password settings. For example, you can prevent users from making changes to their desktops.

■ Enforce loopback processing

In some situations, you may want the user configuration to be consistent for any user who logs on to the computer. For example, your company may provide access to a computer in a public space that allows access to the Internet. You want all users who log on to have the same user environment, regardless of whom the user is. By enabling the loopback setting in the computer configuration, you can configure a user environment that will be enforced for all users who log on to the computer.

Additional reading

For more information about desktop management, see:

■ "Customizing the Desktop" at the Windows XP Resource Kit page on the Microsoft Web site.

What Are Enabled and Disabled Group Policy Settings?

Enable a policy setting	If you enable a policy setting, you are enabling the action of the policy setting. For example, to revoke someone's access to Control Panel, you enable the policy setting **Prohibit access to the Control Panel**.
Disable a policy setting	If you disable a policy setting, you are reversing the action of the policy setting. For example, if a policy setting has enabled the **Prohibit access to the Control Panel** setting on a parent container and you need to reverse that setting for a child container, then you would use a specific policy that disables the **Prohibit access to the Control Panel at the child container level**.
	This is helpful when you have one GPO that delivers many settings, and you want one group to be exempt from some, but not all, of the settings. You can apply a GPO that enables many policy settings on the parent organizational unit and another GPO that disables certain settings on a child organizational unit.
Not Configured	By default, a Group Policy has no enabled settings. When you enable settings, you are configuring the Group Policy setting. If you want to remove all enabled settings, you would click **Not Configured**.
	For example, if a GPO setting is enabled in order to restrict access to a function and it is later determined that access to that function is required, then selecting the **Not Configured** option reverts the setting back to the default.

Multivalued policy settings

Some GPOs require you to provide additional information after you enable an object. Sometimes you may need to select a group or computer if the policy setting needs to redirect the user to information. Other times, as the slide shows, to enable proxy settings, you must provide the name or Internet Protocol (IP) address of the proxy server and the port number.

Note The **Settings** tab in the Administrative Templates folder indicates the operating systems that support the policy setting. The **Explain** tab has information about the effects of the **Enabled** and **Disabled** options on a user and computer account.

Practice: Configuring Group Policy Settings

In this practice, you will:

- Create a GPO to configure a standard user desktop

- Create a GPO to reverse a setting in the standard desktop GPO for the Legal department

Objective

In this practice, you will:

- Create a GPO to configure a standard user desktop that:
    - Prohibits user configuration of Offline Files.
    - Hides the screen saver tab in display properties.
    - Prevents users from adding printers.
    - Configure Web proxy settings.
- Create a GPO to reverse a setting in the standard desktop GPO for the legal department.

Instructions

Ensure that the DEN-CL1 and the DEN-DC1 virtual machines are running.

Practice

▶ **Create a GPO to configure a standard user desktop**

1. Log on to DEN-DC1 as **Administrator** with the password of **Pa$$w0rd**.
2. Click **Start**, point to **Administrative Tools**, and then click **Group Policy Management**.
3. Expand **Forest: contoso.msft/ Domains**.
4. Right-click **contoso.msft** and then click **Create and Link a GPO Here**.
5. In the **New GPO** dialog box, type **Standard Desktop**. Click **OK**.
6. Right-click the **Standard Desktop** GPO and then click **Edit**.
7. Expand **User Configuration**, **Administrative Templates**, **Network**, and click **Offline Files**.
8. Double-click **Prohibit user configuration of Offline Files**, and then click **Enabled**.
9. Click **OK**.

10. Expand **User Configuration, Administrative Templates, Control Panel**, and then click **Display**.

11. Double-click **Hide Screen Saver tab**, and then click **Enabled**.

12. Click **OK**.

13. Click the **Printers** folder, double-click **Prevent addition of printers**, and then click **Enabled**.

14. Click **OK**.

15. Expand **Windows Settings, Internet Explorer Maintenance**, and click **Connection**.

16. Double-click **Proxy Settings**, and then click **Enable proxy settings**.

17. In the **HTTP** field, type **10.10.0.2**. In the **Port** field, type **8080**.

18. Click **OK** and then close the **Group Policy Object Editor**.

19. Click **Start**, click **Run**, and then type **gpupdate /force**. Click **OK**.

20. Click **Start**, point to **Control Panel**, and then click **Display**. Notice that the **Screen Saver** tab is not displayed.

21. Click **OK**.

22. Log on to DEN-CL1 as **Legalmanager** with a password of **Pa$$w0rd**.

23. In **My Computer**, click the **Tools** menu, and then click **Folder Options**. Notice that there is no **Offline Files** tab.

24. Close the **Folder Options** dialog box and close **My Computer**.

▶ **Create a GPO to reverse a setting in the standard desktop GPO for the legal department**

1. Switch to DEN-DC1 and in the **Group Policy Management** console expand **contoso.msft**. Click the **Legal** OU.

2. Create and link a GPO called **Reverse Offline Files Setting**.

3. Right-click the **Reverse Offline Files Setting** GPO and click **Edit**.

4. Expand **User Configuration, Administrative Templates, Network**, and click **Offline Files**.

5. Double-click **Prohibit user configuration of Offline Files**, and then click **Disabled**. Click **OK**. Close the **Group Policy Object Editor**.

6. Close **Group Policy Management** and then log off of DEN-DC1.

7. Switch back to DEN-CL1 and, from **Run**, type **gpupdate /force**.

8. In **My Computer**, click the **Tools** menu, and then click **Folder Options**. Notice there is an **Offline Files** tab now. **Cancel** and close **My Computer**.

9. Click **Start** and then click **Printers and Faxes**. Notice the **Add Printer** icon is not available. Check the **Screen Saver** tab and the **Internet Settings, Proxy Settings** to see they are still being enforced.

10. Close all windows and log off.

Important   Do not shut down the virtual machines.

Lesson: Assigning Scripts with Group Policy

- What Are Group Policy Script Settings?
- Why Use Group Policy Scripts?
- Practice: Assigning Scripts with Group Policy

Introduction

You can use Group Policy to deploy scripts to users and computers. A script is a batch file or a Microsoft Visual Basic® script that can execute code or perform management tasks. You can use Group Policy script settings to automate the process of running scripts.

As with all Group Policy settings, you configure a Group Policy script setting once, and Windows Server 2003 continually implements and enforces it throughout your network.

Lesson objectives

After completing this lesson, you will be able to:

- Explain what Group Policy script settings are.
- Describe the benefits of using Group Policy scripts.
- Assign scripts with Group Policy.

What Are Group Policy Script Settings?

Group Policy script settings can be used to assign:
- For computers
  - Startup scripts
  - Shutdown scripts
- For users
  - Logon scripts
  - Logoff scripts

Introduction	There are script settings under both Computer Configuration and User Configuration in Group Policy. You can use Group Policy to run scripts when a computer starts and shuts down and when a user logs on and logs off. You can specify any script that runs in Windows Server 2003, including batch files, executable programs, JavaScript, Visual Basic, Scripting Edition (VBScript), and any scripts supported by Windows Script Host (WSH).
Computer startup and shutdown scripts	At startup, the computer policy is applied and the startup scripts run. The scripts run synchronously by default and in the following order: local, site, domain, organizational unit, child organizational unit, and so on. Each script must complete or time out before the next one starts. The default time-out is 600 seconds. No user interface appears while computer policies are processed. You can use several policy settings to modify this behavior. Computer startup and shutdown scripts execute under the local system account.
User logon and logoff scripts	At logon, user policy is applied. User logon scripts are processed. Unlike Microsoft Windows NT® 4.0 scripts, Group Policy–based logon scripts are hidden and asynchronous by default. If you run multiple scripts where one script depends on other scripts completing, you will have to change the processing to be synchronous.

Location of scripts

Scripts can be located anywhere on the network, as long as the user or computer receiving the script has network access and Read permission to the location. The preferred location for scripts is in the Sysvol folder. In that way, scripts will be replicated to all domain controllers through the replication of the Sysvol folder. You can add your script to the Scripts folder of the GPO in Sysvol by using the GPMC.

Note In Active Directory Users and Computers, you can assign logon scripts individually to user accounts in the **Properties** dialog box for each user account. However, Group Policy is the preferred method for running scripts, because you can manage these scripts centrally, along with startup, shutdown, and logoff scripts.

Additional reading

For more information about scripting tools, see the TechNet Script Center on the Microsoft TechNet page of the Microsoft Web site.

Why Use Group Policy Scripts?

Group Policy scripts can:

* Perform tasks that cannot be done through other Group Policy settings

* Clean desktops and return computers to their original state

* Provide a secure environment by clearing temp folders and page files

Benefits of Group Policy scripts

To help you manage and configure user environments, you can:

- Run scripts that perform tasks that you cannot perform through other Group Policy settings. For example, you can populate user environments with network connections, printer connections, shortcuts to applications, and corporate documents.

- Clean up desktops when users log off and shut down computers. You can remove connections that you added with logon or startup scripts so that the computer is in the same state as when the user started the computer.

- Shutdown scripts and logoff scripts can be used to delete the contents of temp directories or clear the pagefile to make the environment more secure.

Many predefined scripts are available in the Portable Script Center. The Portable Script Center is a free download from the Microsoft Web site.

Note The Portable Script Center is included on the Student compact disc. Visit the Microsoft Web site to get the most current version.

Practice: Assigning Scripts with Group Policy

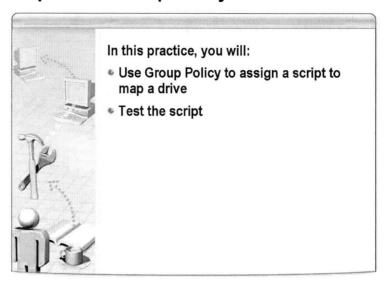

In this practice, you will:
- Use Group Policy to assign a script to map a drive
- Test the script

Objective

In this practice, you will:

- Use Group Policy to assign a script to map a drive.
- Test the script.

Instructions

Ensure that the DEN-CL1 and the DEN-DC1 virtual machines are running.

Practice

▶ **Use Group Policy to assign a script to map a drive**

1. Log on to DEN-DC1 as **Administrator** with the password of **Pa$$w0rd**.
2. Click **Start**, point to **Administrative Tools**, and then click **Group Policy Management**.
3. Create and link a GPO called **Drive Mapping** to the **IT Admin** OU.
4. Right-click and edit the **Drive Mapping** GPO.
5. Expand **User Configuration**, **Windows Settings**, and then click **Scripts (Logon/Logoff)**.
6. Double-click the **Logon** policy.
7. In the **Logon Properties** dialog box, click **Show Files** to display the contents of the **Logon** folder. Notice the path in the **Address** bar.
8. Open **My Computer** and copy the **D:\2274\Labfiles\Admin_Tools\ map.bat** file into the **Logon** folder.
9. Close **My Computer** and then close the **Logon** folder.
10. In the **Logon Properties** dialog box, click **Add**.
11. In the **Add a Script** dialog box, click **Browse**.
12. In the **Browse** dialog box, click **map.bat** and click **Open**.
13. Click **OK** twice.
14. Close all open windows and log off.

▶ **Test the script**

1. Log on to DEN-CL1 as **Judy** with the password of **Pa$$w0rd**.

2. Open **My Computer**. Ensure that you have a J drive that maps to **DEN-DC1\Admin_Tools**.

3. Close all windows and log off of DEN-CL1.

Important   Do not shut down the virtual machines.

Lesson: Restricting Group Membership and Access to Software

* Restricting Group Membership
* What Is a Software Restriction Policy?
* Software Restriction Rules
* Practice: Restricting Group Membership and Access to Software

Introduction

In a large network environment, one of the challenges of network security is controlling the membership of built-in groups on workstations and member servers. Another concern is preventing access to unauthorized software on workstations.

Lesson objectives

After completing this lesson, you will be able to:

■ Configure Group Policy to restrict group membership.

■ Explain what Software Restriction policies are.

■ Explain the function of Software Restriction rules.

■ Restrict group membership and software using group policies.

Restricting Group Membership

> **Group Policy can control group membership:**
> * For any group on a local computer
> * For any group in Active Directory

Introduction

Built-in groups on workstations and member servers have inherent rights to perform system tasks. Controlling the membership of these groups can be difficult. Group Policy provides settings that allow you to control group membership.

Restricting group membership

You can use the Restricted Groups policy to control group membership. Use the policy to specify what members are placed in a group. If a Restricted Groups policy is defined and Group Policy is refreshed, any current member not on the Restricted Groups policy members list is removed. This can include default members, such as administrators. Although any domain groups can be controlled by assigning Restricted Groups policies to domain controllers, this setting should be used primarily to configure membership of critical groups like Enterprise Admins and Schema Admins. This setting can also be used to control the membership of built-in local groups on workstations and member servers. For example, you can place the Helpdesk group into the local Administrators group on all workstations.

Local users cannot be specified in a domain GPO. Any local users who are currently in the local group that the policy controls will be removed. The only exception is that the local Administrators account will always be in the local Administrators group.

Important   The Restricted Groups policy setting does not add to the list of users who have been manually placed in a group. Once a Restricted Groups policy exists, it removes any users who are not specified in the policy.

You can configure the membership of a group by listing the names of the members on the **Members of this group** list. You can also control what groups the group is nested into by adding those groups to the **This group is a member of** list.

What Is a Software Restriction Policy?

* A policy-driven mechanism that identifies and controls software on a client computer
* A mechanism restricting software installation and viruses
* A component with two parts:
    * A default rule with two options:
        Unrestricted
        Disallowed
    * Exceptions to the default rule

Introduction

Software restriction policy provides administrators with a policy-driven mechanism for identifying software and controlling its ability to run on a client computer. Software restriction policies are a part of the Microsoft security and management strategy to assist enterprises in increasing the reliability, integrity, and manageability of their computers.

Restricting access to software

When you assign Group Policy to restrict access to software for a specific computer, it will affect any user who logs on to that computer. When you assign a Group Policy setting to restrict access to software for a specific user, the setting will affect that user regardless of what computer the user logs on to. The setting is configured using the same method for users or computers.

Software Restriction policy is one of many new management features in Windows XP and Windows Server 2003. Software restriction policy can be used to:

- Fight viruses.
- Regulate which ActiveX® controls can be downloaded.
- Run only digitally signed scripts.
- Ensure that only approved software is installed on system computers.
- Lock down the computer.

A Software Restriction policy must be created first. A Software Restriction policy consists of security levels, rules, and settings. There are two rules available, Unrestricted and Disallowed. The default security level is Unrestricted.

- *Unrestricted.* This rule allows all software to be run except for software that is specifically identified as an exception to the rule. The identified software packages are not able to run.

  This policy allows users to install new software programs but still allows an administrator the ability to lock down undesirable software and prevent it from running on client computers. When a new virus or other undesirable software package is identified, the administrator can immediately update the policy to include the new software and prevent it from running on client computers. Users must reboot the computer if the setting is a computer configuration setting, or log off and back on again if the policy is a user configuration setting, before the new software policy will be implemented.

- *Disallowed.* This rule does not allow any software to run on the client computer except for software that has been specifically identified as an exception to the rule. The identified software packages are the only ones that can be run on the client computers affected by the policy. This policy is recommended for use only in very high-security environments or locked-down environments. It can be difficult to manage because each allowed application must be individually identified and because the policy might need to be updated each time a service pack is applied to a software package.

Important   Software Restriction policies will only apply when users log on to Windows XP operating systems or later.

Software Restriction Rules

Hash Rule
* Use to employ MD5 or SHA1 hash of a file to confirm identity
* Use to allow or prohibit a certain version of a file from being run

Certificate Rule
* Checks for digital signature on application
* Use when you want to restrict Win32 applications and ActiveX content

Path Rule
* Use when restricting the path of a file
* Use when multiple files exist for the same application
* Essential when SRPs are strict

Internet Zone Rule
* Controls how Internet Zones can be accessed
* Use in high-security environments to control access to Web applications

Introduction

Software Restriction policy rules identify whether an application is allowed to run.

When you create a rule, you first identify the application. Then you identify it as an exception to the Unrestricted or Disallowed default setting. Each rule can include comments to describe its purpose. The enforcement engine included in Windows XP queries the rules in the software restriction policy before allowing a program to run.

Software restriction rules

A software restriction policy uses one or more of the following four rules to identify software.

You can designate which applications are allowed or disallowed by creating rules. There are four types of rules that can be created.

* *Hash rule.* A *hash* is a fingerprint that uniquely identifies a software program or executable file, even if the program or executable file is moved or renamed. In this way, administrators can use a hash to track a particular version of an executable file or program that they do not want users to run. This might be the case if a program has security or privacy vulnerabilities or could compromise the stability of the system.

  With a hash rule, software programs remain uniquely identifiable because the hash rule match is based on a cryptographic calculation involving the contents of the file. The hash rule compares the Message Digest 5 (MD5) algorithm or SHA1 hash of a file with the one attempting to run.

  The only file types that are affected by hash rules are those that are listed in the Designated File Types section of the details pane for Software Restriction Policies.

- *Certificate rule.* A certificate rule specifies a signed software publisher's certificate. For example, an administrator can require signed certificates for all scripts and ActiveX controls.

  - When a certificate rule is applied, it checks for a digital signature on the application (for example, Authenticode®). A certificate rule is a strong way to identify software because it uses signed hashes contained in the signature of the signed file to match files regardless of name or location.

  - A certificate rule can be used when you want to restrict both Microsoft Win32® applications and ActiveX content.

  - You can use a hash rule to configure exceptions to a certificate rule, configure the hash rule to identify the executable, and then either allow or restrict the application with the hash rule.

- *Path rule.* A path rule specifies either a folder or a fully qualified program path. When a path rule specifies a folder, the comparison also extends to all subfolders of the folder specified.

  - Path rules support both local and Uniform Naming Convention (UNC) paths.

  - The administrator must define all directories for launching a specific application in the path rule. For example, if the administrator has created a shortcut on the desktop to start an application, in the path rule, the user must have access to both the executable file and the shortcut paths to run the application. Attempting to run the application by using only one part of the path will trigger the Software Restricted warning. Many applications use the %ProgramFiles% variable to install files. If this variable is set to another directory on a different drive, some applications will still copy files to the original C:\Program Files subdirectory. Therefore, it is a best practice to leave path rules defined to the default directory location.

  - Path rules are an essential ingredient of software restriction policy enforcement.

- *Internet zone rule.* Internet zone rules are based on Internet Explorer security zones. You can allow or disallow an application based on the Internet zone from which the application is downloaded. A rule can be created for any of the five zones: Internet, local computer, local intranet, restricted sites, and trusted sites. These rules only apply to software that uses the Windows installer.

Four path rules are configured by default. They are designed to preserve access to the operating system.

Software Restriction settings

There are three settings that can be configured for the Software Restriction policy. They are as follows:

Enforcement Properties determine whether software library files are excluded from the software policy restrictions. Also, you can use this option to prevent software policy restrictions from applying to local administrators.

Designated File Types allow you to add or delete file types from the list of what is considered to be executable code.

Trusted Publishers allow you to define whether end users, local administrators, or enterprise administrators can select trusted publishers. In addition, you can use this option to specify revocation-checking options.

Practice: Restricting Group Membership and Access to Software

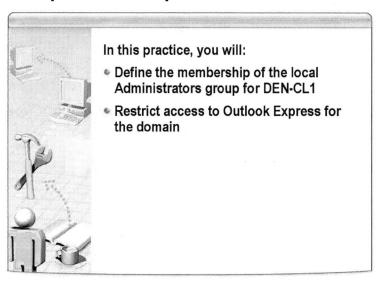

In this practice, you will:

● Define the membership of the local Administrators group for DEN-CL1

● Restrict access to Outlook Express for the domain

Objectives

In this practice, you will:

■ Define the membership of the local Administrators group for DEN-CL1.

■ Restrict access to Microsoft Outlook® Express for the domain.

Instructions

Ensure that the DEN-CL1 and the DEN-DC1 virtual machines are running.

Practice

▶ **Define the membership of the local Administrators group for DEN-CL1**

1. Log on to DEN-DC1 as **Administrator**.

2. Open **Active Directory Users and Computers**.

3. Click the **Computers** container and move the DEN-CL1 computer account into the **IT Admin** organizational unit. Click **Yes** at the Active Directory prompt.

4. Click **Start**, point to **Administrative Tools**, and then click **Group Policy Management**.

5. Create and link a GPO named **Admin Membership** to the **IT Admin** organizational unit.

6. Edit the **Admin Membership** GPO.

7. Expand **Computer Configuration, Windows Settings, Security Settings** and then click **Restricted Groups**.

8. Right-click **Restricted Groups** and then click **Add Group**.

9. In the **Add Group** dialog box, type **Administrators** and then click **OK**.

10. In the **Administrators Properties** dialog box, in the **Members of this group** section click **Add**.

11. In the **Add Member** dialog box, type **Contoso\G Admins** and then click **OK**.

12. Click **Add** again and locate and add the **Domain Admins** group.

13. Click **OK** twice.

14. Close the **Group Policy Object Editor**.

15. Log on to DEN-CL1 as **Judy** with the password of **Pa$$w0rd**.

16. Click **Start**, click **Run**, and then type **gpupdate /force**. Click **OK**.

17. Right-click **My Computer** and click **Manage** to open **Computer Management** and expand **Local Users and Groups**.

18. Click **Groups** and then open the **Administrators** group.

    Who is in the **Administrators** group?

    _____

    _____

19. Close all open windows.

▶ **Restrict access to Microsoft Outlook® Express for the domain**

1. Switch back to DEN-DC1.

2. Edit the **Default Domain Policy**.

3. Expand **User Configuration**, **Windows Settings**, **Security Settings**, and then click **Software Restriction Policies**.

4. Right-click **Software Restriction Policies** and then click **New Software Restriction Policies**.

5. Open the **Security Levels** folder and notice the default setting.

6. Open the **Additional Rules** folder and notice the default rules to allow access to the operating system.

7. Right-click the **Additional Rules** folder and then click **New Path Rule**.

8. In the **New Path Rule** dialog box, click **Browse**.

9. Browse to **C:\Program Files\Outlook Express\msimn.exe** and then click **OK**.

10. Click **OK**.

11. Switch back to DEN-CL1 and, from **Run**, type **gpupdate /force**. Click **OK**.

12. Attempt to open **Outlook Express**. Read the Error message and click **OK**.

13. Close all open windows and log off of both DEN-DC1 and DEN-CL1.

Important   Do not shut down the virtual machines.

▶ **To prepare for the next practice**

• Start the DEN-SRV1 virtual machine.

Lesson: Configuring Folder Redirection

* What Is Folder Redirection?
* Folders That Can Be Redirected
* Settings That Configure Folder Redirection
* Security Considerations for Configuring Folder Redirection
* Practice: Configuring Folder Redirection

Introduction

Windows Server 2003 enables you to redirect folders that are included in the user profile from the users' local hard disks to a central server. By redirecting these folders, you can ensure user access to data regardless of the computers to which they log on.

Folder Redirection makes it easier for you to manage and back up data. The folders that you can redirect are My Documents, Application Data, Desktop, and Start Menu. Windows Server 2003 automatically creates these folders and makes them part of the user profile for each user account.

Lesson objectives

After completing this lesson, you will be able to:

■ Explain Folder Redirection.

■ Explain which folders can be redirected.

■ Determine which settings configure Folder Redirection.

■ Explain security considerations for configuring Folder Redirection.

■ Configure Folder Redirection.

What Is Folder Redirection?

Folder Redirection allows:

- Redirection to folders on the local computer or on a network drive
- Folders on a server appear as if they are located on the local drive

---

Introduction

When you redirect folders, you change the storage location of folders from the local hard disk on the user's computer to a shared folder on a network file server. After you redirect a folder to a file server, it still appears to the user as if it is stored on the local hard disk. You can redirect four folders that are part of the user profile: My Documents, Application Data, Desktop, and Start Menu.

Benefits of Folder Redirection

By storing data on the network, users benefit from increased availability and frequent backup of their data. Redirecting folders has the following benefits:

- The folder data is accessible from any network access point.

- The data in the folders is centrally stored so that the files that they contain are easier to manage and back up.

- Files that are located in redirected folders, unlike files that are part of a roaming user profile, are not copied and saved on the computer that the user logs on to. This means that when a user logs on to a client computer, no storage space is used for these files and that data that might be confidential does not remain on a client computer.

- Data that is stored in a shared network folder can be backed up as part of routine system administration. This is safer because it requires no action on the part of the user.

- As an administrator, you can use Group Policy to set disk quotas that limit the size of special folders.

- Data specific to a user can be redirected to a different hard disk on the user's local computer rather than to the hard disk holding the operating system files. This protects the user's data if the operating system must be reinstalled.

Folders That Can Be Redirected

- My Documents
- Application Data
- Desktop
- Start Menu

Introduction

You can redirect the My Documents, Application Data, Desktop, and Start Menu folders. An organization should redirect these folders to preserve important user data and settings. There are several advantages to redirecting each of these folders. The advantages vary according to your organization's needs.

Redirected folders

You can use Folder Redirection to redirect any of the following folders in a user profile:

- My Documents

  Redirecting My Documents is particularly advantageous because the folder tends to become large over time.

  Offline Files technology gives users access to My Documents even when the users are not connected to the network. This is particularly useful for people who use portable computers.

- Application Data

  A Group Policy setting controls the behavior of Application Data when client-side caching is enabled. This setting synchronizes application data that is centralized on a server with the local computer. As a result, the user can work online or offline. If any changes are made to the application data, synchronization updates the application data on the client and server.

- Desktop

  You can redirect Desktop and all of its files, shortcuts, and folders to a centralized server.

- Start Menu

  When you redirect Start Menu, its subfolders are also redirected.

Settings That Configure Folder Redirection

- Use basic Folder Redirection for common files and limited-access files

- With advanced Folder Redirection, the server hosting the folder location is based on group membership

Introduction

There are three available settings for Folder Redirection: none, basic, and advanced. Basic folder redirection is for users who must redirect their folders to a common area or users who need their data to be private. Advanced redirection allows you to specify different network locations for different Windows user groups.

Basic Folder Redirection

You have the following basic options for Folder Redirection:

- *Redirect folder to the following location* All users who redirect their folders to a common area can see or use each other's data in the redirected folder. To do this, choose a **Basic** setting and set **Target folder location** to **Redirect folder to the following location**. Use this option for all redirected folders that contain data that is not private. An example of this is redirecting My Documents for a team of Accounts Receivable personnel who all share the same data. The Root Path field allows you to specify the UNC path that the folder will be redirected to.

- *Create a folder for each user under the root path* For users who need their redirected folders to be private, choose a **Basic** setting and set **Target folder location** to **Create a folder for each user under the root path**. Use this option for users who need their data to be private, like managers who keep personal data about employees. The Root Path field allows you to specify the UNC path that the folder will be redirected to. You only need to put in the server name and the share name and Group Policy will append the %username% variable to automatically create a subfolder named for the user and move the redirected folder into it.

- *Redirect to the local userprofile location* This setting will redirect the folder back into the default location of the user's profile on the local hard drive.

- *Redirect to the user's home directory* This setting is only available for the My Documents folder. Use this option only if you have already deployed home folders.

Advanced Folder Redirection

When you select **Advanced – specify locations for various user groups**, folders are redirected to different locations based on the security group membership of the users. After you specify the group whose folders you want to have redirected, you will see the same options that are provided for basic redirection.

Settings

The Settings tab allows you to specify whether the user will be granted exclusive rights to the redirected folder and whether the current contents of the folder will be moved to the new location. You can also specify whether the folder should remain in the network location or be moved back to the local user's profile if the Group Policy is removed.

Security Considerations for Configuring Folder Redirection

* NTFS permissions for Folder Redirection root folder
* Shared folder permissions for Folder Redirection root folder
* NTFS permissions for each user's redirected folder

Introduction

Folder Redirection can create folders for you; this is the recommended option. When you use this option, the correct permissions are set automatically. If you manually create folders, you will need to know the correct permissions. The following tables show which permissions to set for Folder Redirection.

Note Although it is not recommended, administrators can create the redirected folders before Folder Redirection creates them.

NTFS permissions required for the root folder

Set the following NTFS permissions for the root folder.

User account	Folder Redirection defaults	Minimum permissions needed
Creator/owner	Full Control, this folder, subfolders, and files	Full Control, this folder, subfolders, and files
Administrators	No permissions	No permissions
Everyone	No permissions	No permissions
Local System	Full Control, this folder, subfolders, and files	Full Control, this folder, subfolders, and files
Security group of users who need to put data on the shared network server	N/A	List Folder/Read Data, Create Folders/Append Data—This folder only

Shared folder permissions required for the root folder

Set the following shared folder permissions for the root folder.

User account	Folder Redirection defaults	Minimum permissions needed
Authenticated Users	Full Control	Change
Security group of users who need to put data on the shared network server	N/A	Change

NTFS permissions required for each user's redirected folder

Set the following NTFS permissions for each user's redirected folder.

User account	Folder Redirection defaults	Minimum permissions needed
UserName	Full Control, owner of folder	Full Control, owner of folder
Local System	Full Control	Full Control
Administrators	No permissions	No permissions
Everyone	No permissions	No permissions

Note   When offline folders are synchronized over the network, the data is transmitted in plain text format. The data is then susceptible to interception by network monitoring tools.

Additional reading

For more information about Folder Redirection, see "Best practices for Folder Redirection," on the Microsoft Web site.

Practice: Configuring Folder Redirection

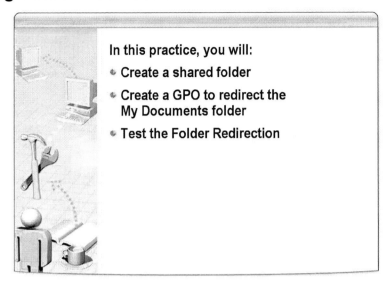

In this practice, you will:
* Create a shared folder
* Create a GPO to redirect the My Documents folder
* Test the Folder Redirection

Objective

In this practice, you will:

- Create a shared folder.
- Create a GPO to redirect the My Documents folder.
- Test the Folder Redirection.

Instructions

Ensure that the DEN-CL1, DEN-SRV1 and the DEN-DC1 virtual machines are running.

Practice

▶ **Create a shared folder**

1. Log on to DEN-DC1 as **Administrator**.
2. Open Windows Explorer and create a folder named **C:\Redirect**.
3. Share the folder to **Authenticated Users** with **Full Control** permission.
4. Close Windows Explorer.

▶ **Create a GPO to redirect the My Documents folder**

1. Open the **Group Policy Management** console and create and link a GPO named **Folder Redirection** to the **Legal** organizational unit.
2. Edit the **Folder Redirection** GPO.
3. Expand **User Configuration**, **Windows Settings**, and then expand **Folder Redirection**.
4. Right-click the **My Documents** folder and then click **Properties**.
5. In the **My Documents Properties** dialog box, select the setting **Basic-Redirect everyone's folder to the same location**.
6. Ensure that the **Target folder location** is set to **Create a folder for each user under the root path**.

7. In the **Root Path** field, type **\\DEN-DC1\Redirect**.

8. Click the **Settings** tab. Note the default settings for the **My Documents** folder.

9. Click **OK**.

10. Close all open windows and log off of DEN-DC1.

▶ **Test the Folder Redirection**

1. Log on to the DEN-CL1 as **Legaluser** with the password of **Pa$$w0rd**.

2. Click **Start**, right-click the **My Documents** folder and click **Properties**. What is the path in the Target folder location field?

_____

Note It may require two logons to see the results of the GPO.

3. Click **OK**

4. Open the **My Documents** folder. Create a new document named **legal.txt**. Enter some text and save the document.

5. Close all open windows and log off.

6. Log on to DEN-SRV1 as **Legaluser**.

7. Open the **My Documents** folder and open the **legal.txt** document. You should see the text you entered.

8. Close all open windows and log off.

Important Do not shut down the virtual machines.

Lesson: Determining Applied GPOs

* What Are gpupdate and gpresult?
* What Is Group Policy Reporting?
* What Is Group Policy Modeling?
* What Are Group Policy Results?
* Practice: Determining Applied GPOs

Introduction

Group Policy is the primary administrative tool for defining and controlling the operation of programs, network resources, and the operating system for users and computers in an organization. In an Active Directory environment, Group Policy is applied to users or computers on the basis of their membership in sites, domains, or organizational units. Group Policy is refreshed at regular intervals but can also be refreshed manually. Group Policy also has many reporting features to help you document, test, and troubleshoot Group Policy.

Lesson objectives

After completing this lesson, you will be able to:

- Explain what **gpupdate** and **gpresult** are.
- Explain what Group Policy reporting is.
- Explain what Group Policy modeling is.
- Explain what Group Policy results are.
- Determine applied GPOs.

What Are gpupdate and gpresult?

Use gpupdate to:

* Manually refresh updated Group Policy settings
* Force the refresh of all Group Policy settings
* Force a reboot or logoff if required to refresh the settings

Use gpresult to:

* Display the resulting set of policies for a user or computer
* Redirect the resulting set of policies information to a file

Introduction

The **gpupdate** command-line tool can refresh Group Policy settings, including security settings. By default, Group Policy settings are refreshed every 90 minutes on a workstation or server and every five minutes on a domain controller. You can run **gpupdate** to force Group Policy settings to be refreshed.

Because Group Policies can be applied at multiple levels to any computer or user, Group Policy generates a resulting set of policies at logon. The **gpresult** command displays Group Policy settings and Resultant Set of Policy (RSoP) data for a user or a computer. You can use **gpresult** to see what policy setting is in effect and to troubleshoot problems.

Examples of gpupdate

The following examples show how you can use the **gpupdate** command:

- C:\gpupdate
- C:\gpupdate /force
- C:\gpupdate /boot

Parameters of gpupdate

Gpupdate has the following parameters.

Value	Description
/Target:{**Computer** | **User**}	Specifies that only user or only computer policy settings are refreshed. By default, both user and computer policy settings are refreshed.
/Force	Reapplies all policy settings. By default, only policy settings that have changed are reapplied.
/Wait:{*Value*}	Sets the number of seconds to wait for policy processing to finish. The default is 600 seconds. The value '0' means not to wait. The value '-1' means to wait indefinitely.
/Logoff	Causes a logoff after the Group Policy settings are refreshed. This is required for those Group Policy client-side extensions that do not process policy settings during a background refresh cycle but do process policy settings when a user logs on. Examples include user-targeted Software Installation and Folder Redirection. This option has no effect if there are no extensions called that require a logoff.
/Boot	Causes the computer to restart after the Group Policy settings are refreshed. This is required for those Group Policy client-side extensions that do not process policy during a background refresh cycle but do process policy when the computer starts. Examples include computer-targeted Software Installation. This option has no effect if there are no extensions called that require the computer to restart.
/Sync	Causes the next foreground policy setting to be applied synchronously. Foreground policy settings are applied when the computer starts and when the user logs on. You can specify this for the user, computer, or both by using the **/Target** parameter. The **/Force** and **/Wait** parameters are ignored.

The following examples show how you can use the **gpresult** command:

Examples of gpresult

- C:\gpresult /user *targetusername* /scope computer

- C:\gpresult /s *computer* /u *domain/user* /p *password* /user *targetusername* /scope USER

- C:\gpresult /z >policy.txt

Parameters of gpresult

Gpresult has the following parameters.

Value	Description
/s *computer*	Specifies the name or IP address of a remote computer. Do not use backslashes. The default is the local computer.
/u *domain/user*	Runs the command with the account permissions of the user that is specified by *User* or *Domain/User*. The default is the permissions of the user who is currently logged on to the computer that issues the command.
/p *password*	Specifies the password of the user account that is specified in the /u parameter.
/user *targetusername*	Specifies the user name of the user whose RSoP data is to be displayed.
/scope {user|computer}	Displays either user or computer policy settings. Valid values for the /scope parameter are **user** or **computer**. If you omit the /scope parameter, **gpresult** displays both user and computer policy settings.
/v	Specifies that the output will display verbose policy information. Use this switch when you want to see the settings applied.
/z	Specifies that the output will display all available information about Group Policy. Because this parameter produces more information than the /v parameter, redirect output to a text file when you use this parameter (for example, you can type **gpresult /z >policy.txt**).
/?	Displays help in the command prompt window.

What Is Group Policy Reporting?

Definition

A systems administrator can make hundreds of changes to a GPO. Group Policy reporting allows you to verify changes made to a GPO without actually opening the GPO and expanding every folder. You can generate a Hypertext Markup Language (HTML) report that lists the items in the GPO that are configured. This report can be printed or saved for documentation purposes.

Settings tab

The **Settings** tab of the details pane for a GPO or GPO link in Group Policy Management shows an HTML report that displays all the defined settings in the GPO. Any user with read access to the GPO can generate this report. If you click **show all** at the top of the report, the report is fully expanded, and all settings are shown. Also, using a context menu, you can print the reports or save them to a file as either HTML or Extensible Markup Language (XML).

Note   The new Internet Explorer Enhanced Configuration prompts the user to add the Web site to the list of trusted sites. You should add the site to the list to avoid having the prompt come up every time you view the settings. To add the site you must clear the **Require server verification (https:) for all sites in this zone** and click **Add**.

What Is Group Policy Modeling?

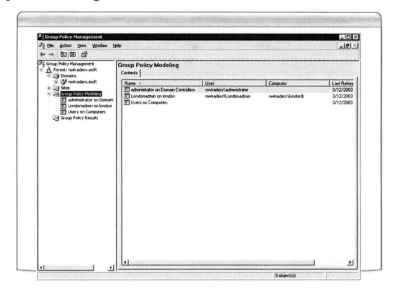

Introduction

Group Policy Modeling enables you to simulate a GPO deployment that is applied to users and computers before you actually deploy the GPO. The simulation creates a report that takes into account the user's organizational unit, the computer's organizational unit, and any group membership and can include Windows Management Instrumentation (WMI) filtering. It also takes into account any Group Policy inheritance issues or conflicts.

Requirements

If you want to use Group Policy Modeling, there must be a Windows Server 2003 domain controller in the forest. This is because the simulation is performed by a service that is only present on Windows Server 2003 domain controllers.

Results of Group Policy Modeling

To perform a Group Policy Modeling query, the user uses the Group Policy Modeling Wizard. After the user completes the Group Policy Modeling Wizard, a new node in the console tree of Group Policy Management appears under **Group Policy Modeling** to display the results. The **Contents** tab in the details pane for Group Policy Modeling displays a summary of all Group Policy Modeling queries that the user has performed.

For each query, Group Policy Management shows the following data:

- **Name**. This is the user-supplied name of the modeling results.
- **User**. This is the user object (or the organizational unit where the user object is located) that the modeling query is based on.
- **Computer**. This is the computer object (or the organizational unit where the computer object is located) that is the subject of the modeling query.
- **Last refresh time**. This is the last time the modeling query was refreshed.

For each query, the details pane for the node contains the following three tabs:

- **Summary**. This contains an HTML report of the summary information, including the list of GPOs, security group membership, and WMI filters.
- **Settings**. This contains an HTML report of the policy settings that were applied in this simulation.
- **Query**. This lists the parameters that were used to generate the query.

What Are Group Policy Results?

Introduction

The data that is presented in Group Policy Results is similar to Group Policy Modeling data. However, unlike Group Policy Modeling data, this data is not a simulation. It is the actual RSoP data obtained from the target computer.

Requirements

Unlike Group Policy Modeling, the data in Group Policy Results is obtained from the client and is not simulated on the domain controller. Technically, a Windows Server 2003 domain controller is not required to be in the forest if you want to access Group Policy Results. However, the client must be running Windows XP or Windows Server 2003. It is not possible to get Group Policy Results data for a client running Microsoft Windows 2000.

Note By default, only users with local administrator privileges on the target computer can remotely access Group Policy Results data. To gather this data, the user performing the query must have access to remotely view the event log.

Results of Group Policy Results

Each Group Policy Results query is represented by a node under the Group Policy Results container in the console tree of Group Policy Management. The details pane for each node has the following three tabs:

- **Summary**. This contains an HTML report of the summary information including the list of GPOs, security group membership, and WMI filters.

- **Settings**. This contains an HTML report of the policy settings that were applied.

- **Events**. This shows all policy-related events from the target computer.

Windows Firewall settings

The Windows Firewall is enabled by default in Windows XP with SP2 installed. It is designed to block all unsolicited connection attempts. This default setting impacts how RSoP is used across the network. If the Windows Firewall is enabled, then Group Policy should be configured to allow remote administrative tasks in order for RSoP information to be generated. The **Computer Configuration, Administrative Templates, Network Connections, Windows Firewall, Domain Profile** section of Group Policy contains a firewall setting to allow remote administration exceptions. This setting should be enabled to generate RSoP reporting.

Important   In order to generate RSoP information for a specific user on a specific computer, the user you are querying on must have a profile on that computer.

Practice: Determining Applied GPOs

In this practice, you will:
* Refresh GPO settings with gpupdate
* Use Group Policy reporting to view the settings in a GPO and save the report
* Create a Group Policy Results report

Objectives

In this practice, you will:

■ Refresh GPO settings with **gpupdate**.

■ Use Group Policy reporting to view the settings in a GPO and save the report.

■ Create a Group Policy Results report.

Instructions

Ensure that the DEN-CL1, DEN-SRV1 and the DEN-DC1 virtual machines are running.

Practice

▶ **Refresh GPO settings with gpupdate**

1. Log on to DEN-DC1 as **Administrator**.

2. Open the **Group Policy Management** console, click the **Group Policy Objects** folder, and edit the **Default Domain Policy**.

3. Expand **User Configuration**, **Administrative Templates**, and then click **Start Menu and Taskbar**.

4. Enable the **Remove Help menu from the Start Menu** setting.

5. Expand **Computer Configuration**, **Administrative Templates**, **Network**, **Network Connections**, **Windows Firewall**, and then click **Domain Profile**.

6. Double-click the **Windows Firewall: Allow remote administration exception** setting.

7. On the **Settings** tab, click **Enabled**, type **localsubnet** in the **Allow unsolicited incoming messages from** field, and click **OK**.

8. Close the **Group Policy Object Editor**.

9. Click the **Start** menu. Notice that **Help and Support** still appears.

10. From **Run**, type **gpupdate /force**.

11. **Help and Support** should no longer appear on the **Start** menu.

► **Use Group Policy reporting to view the settings in a GPO and save the report**

1. Expand the **Group Policy Objects** folder.

2. In the left console pane, click the **Standard Desktop** GPO.

3. In the right pane, click the **Settings** tab.

4. In the **Internet Explorer** dialog box, click **Add**.

5. In the **Trusted Sites** dialog box, clear the **Require server verification (https:) for all sites in this zone** check box, click **Add**, and then click **Close**.

6. View the settings of the GPO.

7. Right-click anywhere on the report and select **Save Report** from the shortcut menu.

8. Save the report as an HTML file in C:\.

9. Close **Group Policy Management**.

10. Browse to C:\ and open the **Standard Desktop.htm** file. Click **OK** at the **Information Bar** prompt.

11. View the report.

12. Close all open windows.

► **Create a Group Policy Results report**

1. Open **Group Policy Management**.

2. Right-click the **Group Policy Results** folder and then click **Group Policy Results Wizard**.

3. In the **Group Policy Results Wizard**, click **Next**.

4. In the **Computer Selection** page, select **Another computer**, type **DEN-SRV1**, and then click **Next**.

5. In the **User Selection** page, select **Contoso\Legaluser** and then click **Next**.

6. In the **Summary of Selections** page, click **Next**.

7. Click **Finish**.

8. Browse through the report information.

9. Close all windows and log off.

Important   Do not shut down the virtual machines.

Lab: Managing the User Environment by Using Group Policy

After completing this lab, you will be able to:

* Create and apply a GPO to the Graphics organizational unit

* Assign a logon script to connect to the Graphics1 printer

* Use a GPO to configure the membership of the Backup Operators group

* Use the Group Policy Results Wizard to verify the policy settings

Objectives

After completing this lab, you will be able to:

- Create and apply a GPO to the Graphics organizational unit.

- Assign a logon script to connect to the Graphics1 printer.

- Use a GPO to configure the membership of the Backup Operators group.

- Use the Group Policy Results Wizard to verify the policy settings.

Prerequisites

To complete this lab, you must have the following virtual machines:

- DEN-DC1

- DEN-CL1

Estimated time to complete this lab: 40 minutes

Exercise 1
Creating and Applying a GPO to the Graphics Organizational Unit

In this exercise, you will create a GPO to configure the desktop for the Graphics department.

Scenario

Contoso Ltd. has determined the Graphics department needs a more detailed configuration than the Standard Desktop GPO provides. You will create and link a GPO named Graphics Desktop to further configure the users in the Graphics department. You will create a GPO that removes the Run command and populates the home page of Internet Explorer.

Properties	Special Instructions
1. Create and link a GPO.	**a.** Log on to DEN-DC1 as **Administrator** with the password of **Pa$$w0rd**. **b.** Open **Group Policy Management** and create and link a GPO named **Graphics Desktop** to the **Graphics** organizational unit.

2. Edit the policy.	**a.** Right-click and edit **Graphics Desktop**.
	
	 b. Expand **User Configuration, Administrative Templates** and configure as follows:
	
	   • In **Start Menu and Taskbar**, enable the **Remove Run menu from Start Menu** setting.
	
	   • In **Windows Components**, in **Windows Messenger**, enable the **Do not allow Windows Messenger to be run** setting.
	
	   • In **Control Panel**, in **Display**, enable the **Prevent changing wallpaper** setting.
	
	   • In **Desktop**, enable the **Hide and disable all items on the desktop** setting.
	
	 c. Close the **Group Policy Object Editor**.

3. Test the policy.	**a.** Log on to DEN-CL1 as **GraphicsUser** with the password of **Pa$$w0rd**. **b.** Ensure that the desktop has nothing displayed. **c.** Ensure that the **Run** command does not appear on the **Start** menu. **d.** In **Control Panel**, switch to **Classic View**, double-click **Display** and attempt to change the desktop wallpaper. **e.** Attempt to launch Windows Messenger. **f.** Close all open windows and log off.

Exercise 2
Assigning a Logon Script to Connect to the Graphics1 Printer

In this exercise, you will create and assign a logon script that connects users in the Graphics organizational unit to the Graphics1 printer.

Scenario

Contoso Ltd. employees are not allowed to add printers. You must create a GPO that connects the Graphics users to the Graphics1 printer. You will use the Printers.vbs script provided in the Admin_Tools folder.

Tasks	Special instructions
1. Create a GPO.	a. Switch to DEN-DC1 and create and link a GPO named **Map Printer** to the **Graphics** organizational unit. b. Edit the **Map Printer** GPO.
2. Edit the GPO.	a. Expand **User Configuration**, **Windows Settings**, **Scripts**, and then double-click **Logon**. b. In the **Logon Properties** box, click **Show Files** to display the Logon folder window. c. Start Windows Explorer and copy **D:\2274\Labfiles\Admin_Tools\ printer.vbs** to the **Logon** folder. d. Close the **Logon** folder, and then click **Add**. e. In the **Add a Script** dialog box, click **Browse**, and then select **printer.vbs**. f. Click **OK** twice. g. Click **OK** to close the **Logon Properties** window. h. Close the **Group Policy Object Editor**.
3. Test the setting.	a. Log on to DEN-CL1 as **GraphicsUser** with the password of **Pa$$w0rd**. b. Open the **Printers and Faxes** folder. c. Ensure that the **Graphics1** printer appears. d. Close all open windows and log off of DEN-CL1.

Exercise 3
Using a GPO to Configure the Members of the Backup Operators Group

In this exercise, you will configure a GPO to place the G Admins global group in the Backup Operators group on all workstations and servers in the domain.

Scenario

Judy Lew has been assigned to back up data on all workstations and servers in the domain. You will create a GPO to ensure that Judy Lew is placed in the Backup Operators group on all workstations and servers. Judy Lew is a member of the G Admins global group.

Tasks	Special instructions
1. Create a GPO.	a. Switch to DEN-DC1 and create and link a GPO named **Backup Operators** to the **contoso.msft** domain. b. Edit the **Backup Operators** GPO.
2. Edit the GPO.	a. Expand **Computer Configuration**, expand **Windows Settings**, and then expand **Security Settings**. Click the **Restricted Groups** folder. b. Right-click the **Restricted Groups** folder and then click **Add Group**. c. In the **Add Group** dialog box, type **Backup Operators**, and then click **OK**. d. In the **Backup Operators Properties** dialog box, click **Add** in the **Members of this group** section, and then type **Contoso\G Admins**. e. Click **OK** twice. f. Close the **Group Policy Object Editor**.
3. Test the setting.	a. Log on to DEN-CL1 as **Administrator**. b. From **Run**, type **gpupdate /force**. c. Open **Computer Management**, and then expand **Local Users and Groups**, and **Groups** and then open the **Backup Operators** group. d. Ensure that the **G Admins** group is a member.

Exercise 4
Using the Group Policy Results Wizard to Verify the Policy Settings

In this exercise, you will use the Group Policy Results Wizard to verify the policy settings for the GraphicsUser user account.

Scenario

You need to document which GPO settings are applied to Graphics department users. You will use the Group Policy Results Wizard to verify the policy settings for the GraphicsUser user account.

Tasks	Special instructions
1. Run the Group Policy Results Wizard.	a. Switch to DEN-DC1. b. In **Group Policy Management**, right-click **Group Policy Results** and click **Group Policy Results Wizard**. c. On the **Group Policy Results Wizard Welcome** screen, click **Next**. d. On the **Computer Selection** screen, click **Another computer**, type **DEN-CL1** in the field, and then click **Next**. e. On the **User Selection** screen, notice that only users who have logged on to DEN-CL1 are listed. f. Select **GraphicsUser**, and then click **Next**. g. On the **Summary of Selections** screen, click **Next**. h. Click **Finish**.
2. View and save the report.	a. Click the **Summary** tab of the report. b. In the **Computer Configuration Summary** section, expand **Group Policy Objects** and **Applied GPOs**. What GPOs are being applied to the computer? c. In the **User Configuration Summary** section, expand **Group Policy Objects** and **Applied GPOs**. What GPOs are being applied to the user? d. Click the **Settings** tab. What GPO is applying the setting that hides the screen saver? What GPO is applying the setting that removes the **Run** command from the **Start** menu? e. Right-click the report and then click **Save Report**. Save the report as an HTML file in the **My Documents** folder.
3. Complete the lab exercise.	a. Close all programs and shut down all computers. Do not save changes. b. To prepare for the next module, start the DEN-DC1 and DEN-CL1 virtual computers.

Module 8: Implementing Administrative Templates and Audit Policy

Contents

Overview

* Managing User Rights in Windows Server 2003
* Using Security Templates to Secure Computers
* Testing Computer Security Policy
* Configuring Auditing
* Managing Security Logs

Introduction

This module will provide a broad overview of security in Microsoft® Windows Server™ 2003. You will learn how to use security templates and test computer security policy. You will also learn how to configure auditing and manage security logs.

Objectives

After completing this module, you will be able to:

- Manage user rights in Windows Server 2003.
- Use security templates to secure computers.
- Test computer security policy.
- Configure auditing.
- Manage security logs.

Lesson: Managing User Rights in Windows Server 2003

* What Are User Rights?
* User Rights vs. Permissions
* User Rights Assigned to Built-In Groups
* Practice: Assigning User Rights

Introduction

In this lesson, you will learn about user rights, permissions, and user rights assigned to built-in groups. You will also learn how to assign user rights.

Lesson objectives

After completing this lesson, you will be able to:

- Describe user rights.
- Distinguish between rights and permissions.
- Describe the user rights that are assigned to built-in groups.
- Assign user rights.

What Are User Rights?

Examples of User Rights

Definition

When a user logs on to a computer or accesses a computer over the network, the user receives an access token on that computer that includes their user rights. A user right authorizes a user who is accessing a computer to perform certain actions on the system. Users who do not have the appropriate rights to perform an action are blocked from performing that action.

Who do user rights apply to?

User rights can apply both to individual users and to groups. However, user rights are best administered when they are assigned to groups. Assigning user rights to groups ensures that a user who logs on as a member of a group automatically receives the rights that are associated with that group. Windows Server 2003 enables an administrator to assign rights to users and groups.

User rights that are assigned to a group are applied to all members of the group while they are members. If a user is a member of multiple groups, the user's rights are cumulative, which means that the user has more than one set of rights. In general, user rights assigned to one group do not conflict with the rights assigned to another group. The only time that rights assigned to one group might conflict with those assigned to another is in the case of certain logon rights. To remove rights from a user, the administrator simply removes the user from the group. The user no longer has the rights assigned to that group.

Common user rights

Common user rights include the following:

- *Allow log on locally.* Enables a user to log on to the local computer or to the domain from a local computer.

- *Change the system time.* Enables a user to set the time of the internal clock of a computer.

- *Shut down the system.* Enables a user to shut down a local computer.

- *Access this computer from a network.* Enables a user to access a computer running Windows Server 2003 from any other computer on the network.

User Rights vs. Permissions

Introduction

Administrators can assign specific user rights to group accounts or to individual user accounts. These rights authorize users to perform specific actions, such as log on to a system interactively or back up files and directories. User rights are different from permissions—user rights are attached to user accounts, and permissions are attached to objects.

What are user rights?

User rights determine which users can perform a specific task on a computer or in a domain. Rights apply to the entire system, rather than to a specific resource, and affect the overall operation of the computer or domain. All users accessing network resources must have certain common rights on the computers they use, such as the right to log on to the computer. Administrators can assign specific common user rights to groups or to individual users. Additionally, Windows Server 2003 assigns certain rights to built-in groups by default.

What are permissions?

Permissions define the type of access granted to a user or group for an object or object property. For example, you can grant Read and Write permissions to the Finance group for a file named Payroll.xls.

You can grant permissions for any secured objects such as files, objects in the Active Directory® directory service, or registry objects. You can grant permissions to any user, group, or computer. It is a good practice to grant permissions to groups.

You can grant permissions for objects to:

- Groups, users, and special identities in the domain.

- Groups and users in any trusted domains.

- Local groups and users on the computer where the object resides.

When you provide access to file resources on a computer running Windows Server 2003, you can control who has access to resources and the nature of their access by granting the appropriate permissions. Permissions define the type of access assigned to a user or group for any resource.

For example, users in the Human Resources department of an organization might need to modify the organization's document describing Human Resources policies. To facilitate this, the administrator must grant the appropriate permission to the members of the Human Resources department.

To grant permissions for individual files and folders, Windows Server 2003 uses the NTFS file system. You can also control the permissions for accessing shared folder resources and network printers.

User Rights Assigned to Built-In Groups

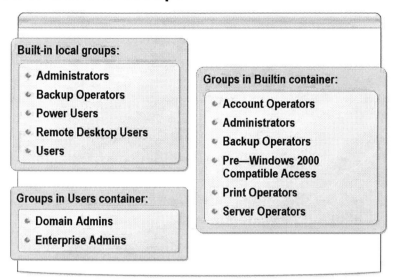

Built-in local groups:

* Administrators
* Backup Operators
* Power Users
* Remote Desktop Users
* Users

Groups in Builtin container:

* Account Operators
* Administrators
* Backup Operators
* Pre—Windows 2000 Compatible Access
* Print Operators
* Server Operators

Groups in Users container:

* Domain Admins
* Enterprise Admins

Introduction

By default, Windows Server 2003 assigns certain rights to built-in groups. The built-in groups include local groups, groups in the Builtin container, and groups in the Users container.

Built-in groups and user rights

Use built-in groups to assign rights to users when possible. However, if the built-in group assigns too many rights, you should create a security group for the task and directly assign user rights to that group. For example, if you want to allow users only to back up files and directories, but not to be able to restore them, create a security group and assign it the right to back up files and directories rather than use the Backup Operators built-in group. The Backup Operators group has the right to back up and restore files and directories.

User rights assigned to local groups

Specific user rights are assigned to the following local groups:

- *Administrators*. This group has full rights to the computers in the domain, including the following rights:

  - Access this computer from the network; Adjust memory quotas for a process; Allow log on locally; Allow log on through Terminal Services; Back up files and directories; Bypass traverse checking; Change the system time; Create a pagefile; Debug programs; Force shutdown from a remote system; Increase scheduling priority; Load and unload device drivers; Manage auditing and security log.

- *Backup Operators*. This group has the following rights:

  - Access this computer from the network; Allow log on locally; Back up files and directories; Bypass traverse checking; Restore files and directories; Shut down the system.

- *Power Users*. This group has the following rights:
  - Access this computer from the network; Allow log on locally; Bypass traverse checking; Change the system time; Profile single process; Remove computer from docking station; Shut down the system.
- *Remote Desktop Users*. This group has the following right:
  - Allow log on through Terminal Services.
- *Users*. This group has the following rights:
  - Access this computer from the network; Allow log on locally; Bypass traverse checking.

User rights assigned to groups in the Builtin container

Specific user rights are assigned to groups in the Builtin container:

- *Account Operators*. This group has the following rights:
  - Allow log on locally; Shut down the system.
- *Administrators*. This group has full rights to the computers in the domain, including the following rights:
  - Access this computer from the network; Adjust memory quotas for a process; Allow log on locally; Back up files and directories; Bypass traverse checking; Change the system time; Create a pagefile; Debug programs; Enable computer and user accounts to be trusted for delegation; Force a shutdown from a remote system; Increase scheduling priority; Load and unload device drivers; Manage auditing and security log.
- *Backup Operators*. This group has the following rights:
  - Allow log on locally; Back up files and directories; Restore files and directories; Shut down the system.
- *Pre-Windows 2000 Compatible Access*. This group has the following rights:
  - Access this computer from the network; Bypass traverse checking.
- *Print Operators*. This group has the following rights:

  Allow log on locally; Shut down the system.
- *Server Operators*. This group has the following rights:
  - Allow log on locally; Back up files and directories; Change the system time; Force shutdown from a remote system; Restore files and directories; Shut down the system.

User rights assigned to groups in the Users container

Specific user rights are assigned to groups in the Users container:

- *Domain Admins*. This group has full rights to the computers and other objects in the domain, including the following rights:

  - Access this computer from the network; Adjust memory quotas for a process; Allow log on locally; Back up files and directories; Bypass traverse checking; Change the system time; Create a pagefile; Debug programs; Enable computer and user accounts to be trusted for delegation; Force a shutdown from a remote system; Increase scheduling priority; Load and unload device drivers; Manage auditing and security log.

- *Enterprise Admins*. (Appears only in the forest root domain.) This group has full rights to the computers and other objects in the domain, including the following rights:

  - Access this computer from the network; Adjust memory quotas for a process; Allow log on locally; Back up files and directories; Bypass traverse checking; Change the system time; Create a pagefile; Debug programs; Enable computer and user accounts to be trusted for delegation; Force shutdown from a remote system; Increase scheduling priority; Load and unload device drivers; Manage auditing and security log.

Note The **Properties** dialog box of the user right does not display the users or groups who are assigned the user right by default. You can view this information and an explanation of the function of the user right by clicking Help on the user right shortcut menu.

Additional reading

For more information about user rights and upgrading operating systems, see article 323042, "Required User Rights for the Upgrade from Windows 2000 to Windows Server 2003," in the Microsoft Knowledge Base at the Microsoft Help and Support Web site.

For more information about user rights and service accounts, see article 325349, "HOW TO: Grant Users Rights to Manage Services in Windows Server 2003," in the Microsoft Knowledge Base at the Microsoft Help and Support Web site.

Practice: Assigning User Rights

In this practice, you will:

● Assign the Authenticated Users group the right to change the system time

● Assign Judy Lew the right to log on locally to the domain controller

---

Objectives

In this practice, you will:

- Assign the Authenticated Users group the right to change the system time.
- Assign Judy Lew the right to log on locally to the domain controller.

Instructions

Ensure that the DEN-DC1 and the DEN-CL1 virtual machines are running.

Practice

▶ **Assign the Authenticated Users group the right to change the system time**

1. Log on to DEN-CL1 as **Don** with the password of **Pa$$w0rd**.

2. Double-click the clock on the taskbar to attempt to change the system time.

3. Read the error message, and then click **OK**.

4. Log on to DEN-DC1 as **Administrator** with the password of **Pa$$w0rd**.

5. Click **Start**, point to **Administrative Tools**, and click **Domain Security Policy**.

6. Navigate to **Security Settings/Local Policies/User Rights Assignment/ Change the system time**, and then right-click and click **Properties**.

7. In the **Change the system time Properties** dialog box, select the **Define these policy settings** check box.

8. Click **Add User or Group**, and then type **Authenticated Users** in the **User and group names** field.

9. Click **OK** twice, and then close the **Default Domain Security Settings** console.

10. Log off of DEN-DC1.

11. Switch to DEN-CL1, and at the **Run** command, type **gpupdate /force**. Click **OK** and then log off DEN-CL1.

12. Log on to DEN-CL1 as **Don**.

13. Double-click the clock on the taskbar to attempt to change the system time. Verify that the **Date and Time Properties** dialog box appears.

Note It may take two logons for the new setting to take effect.

---

14. Close all programs, and then log off from DEN-CL1.

▶ **Assign Judy Lew the right to log on locally to the domain controller**

1. Attempt to log on to DEN-DC1 as **Judy** with the password of **Pa$$w0rd**.

2. Read the logon message, and then click **OK**.

3. Log on to DEN-DC1 as **Administrator**.

4. Click **Start**, point to **Administrative Tools**, and then click **Domain Controller Security Policy**.

5. Navigate to **Security Settings/Local Policies/User Rights Assignment/ Allow log on locally**, and then right-click and click **Properties**.

6. Notice the default list of groups that have the right to log on to the domain controller.

7. Click **Add User or Group**, and then type **Contoso\Judy** in the **User and group names** field.

8. Click **OK** twice.

9. To refresh the security settings click **Start**, click **Run**, type **gpupdate /force** and then click **OK**,

10. Log off from DEN-DC1.

11. Attempt to log on to DEN-DC1 as **Judy** with the password of **Pa$$w0rd**. The logon should succeed.

12. Log off DEN-DC1.

Lesson: Using Security Templates to Secure Computers

- What Is a Security Policy?
- What Are Security Templates?
- What Are Security Template Settings?
- Windows Server 2003 Security Guide Templates
- Windows XP Security Guide Templates
- Ways to Deploy Security Templates
- Practice: Using Security Templates to Secure Computers

Introduction

You create security templates to create a security policy and alter a security policy to meet the security needs of your company. You can implement security policies in several different ways. The method you use depends on your organization's size and security needs. Smaller organizations, or those not using Active Directory, can configure security manually on an individual basis. If your organization is large or requires a high level of security, consider using Group Policy objects (GPOs) to deploy security policy.

Lesson objectives

After completing this lesson, you will be able to:

- Describe a security policy.
- Describe security templates.
- Describe security template settings.
- Describe the security templates that are included in the Windows Server 2003 Security Guide.
- Describe the security templates that are included in the Microsoft Windows® XP Security Guide.
- Explain ways to deploy security templates.
- Use security template to secure computers.

What Is a Security Policy?

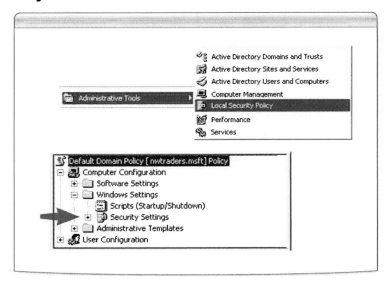

Definition

A security policy is a combination of security settings that affect the security on a computer. You can use a security policy to establish account policies and local policies on your local computer and in Active Directory.

Security policy on a local computer

With a local security policy, you can control:

- Account policies.
- Local policies.
- Public Key policy.
- Software Restriction policy.
- IP Security policies.

If your network does not use Active Directory, you can configure a security policy by using Local Security Policy, which is found on the **Administrative Tools** menu on computers running Windows Server 2003.

Security policies in Active Directory

Security policies in Active Directory have the same security settings as a security policy on local computers plus a number of extra settings to deal with domain configurations. However, administrators of Active Directory–based networks can save considerable administrative time by using Group Policy to deploy the security policy. You can edit or import security settings in a GPO for any site, domain, or organizational unit, and the security settings are automatically deployed to the computers when the computers start. When editing a GPO, expand **Computer Configuration** or **User Configuration** and then expand **Windows Settings** to find the security policy settings.

Additional reading

For more information about default domain user rights, see article 324800, "HOW TO: Reset User Rights in the Default Domain Group Policy in Windows Server 2003," in the Microsoft Knowledge Base at the Microsoft Help and Support Web site.

What Are Security Templates?

Template	Description
Setup security.inf	Default security settings
DC security.inf	Default security settings for a domain controller
Compatws.inf	Modifies permissions and registry settings for application compatibility
Securedc.inf and Securews.inf	Enhances security settings
Hisecdc.inf and Hisecws.inf	Increases the restrictions on security settings
Rootsec.inf	Specifies permissions for the root of the system drive
IESacls.inf	Configures auditing and permissions on registry keys of Internet Explorer

Definition

A security template is a collection of configured security settings. Windows Server 2003 provides predefined security templates that contain the recommended security settings for different situations.

You can use predefined security templates as a base to create security policies that are customized to meet different organizational requirements. You customize the templates with the Security Templates snap-in. After you customize the predefined security templates, you can use them to configure security on an individual computer or thousands of computers.

How security templates are applied

You can configure individual computers with the Security Configuration and Analysis snap-in or the **secedit** command-line tool or by importing the template into Local Security Policy. You can configure multiple computers by importing a template into Security Settings, which is an extension of Group Policy.

You can also use a security template as a baseline for analyzing a system for potential security holes or policy violations by using the Security Configuration and Analysis snap-in. By default, the predefined security templates are stored in *systemroot*/Security/Templates.

Predefined templates

Windows Server 2003 provides the following predefined templates:

- Default security (Setup security.inf)

  The Setup security.inf template is created during installation of the operating system for each computer and represents the default security settings that are applied during installation, including the file permissions for the root of the system drive. It can vary from computer to computer, based on whether the installation was a clean installation or an upgrade. You can use this template on servers and client computers, but not on domain controllers. You can apply portions of this template for disaster recovery.

  Default security settings are applied only to clean installations of Windows Server 2003 on an NTFS partition. When computers are upgraded from Microsoft Windows NT® version 4.0, security is not modified. Also, when you install Windows Server 2003 on a FAT (file allocation table) file system, security is not applied to the file system.

- Domain controller default security (DC security.inf)

  The DC security.inf template is created when a server is promoted to a domain controller. It reflects default security settings on files, registry keys, and system services. Reapplying the template resets these settings to the default values, but doing so might overwrite permissions on new files, registry keys, and system services created by other applications. You can apply the template by using the Security Configuration and Analysis snap-in or the **secedit** command-line tool.

- Compatible (Compatws.inf)

  Default permissions for workstations and servers are primarily granted to three local groups: Administrators, Power Users, and Users. Administrators have the most privileges, and Users have the least.

  Members of the Users group can successfully run applications that take part in the Windows Logo Program for Software. However, they might not be able to run applications that do not meet the requirements of the program. If other applications are to be supported, the Compatws.inf template changes the default file and registry permissions that are granted to the Users group. The new permissions are consistent with the requirements of most applications that do not belong to the Windows Logo Program for Software.

- Secure (Secure*.inf)

  The Secure templates define enhanced security settings that are least likely to affect application compatibility. For example, the Secure templates define stronger password, lockout, and audit settings.

- Highly Secure (hisec*.inf)

  The Highly Secure templates are supersets of the Secure templates. They impose further restrictions on the levels of encryption and signing that are required for authentication and for the data that flows over secure channels and between server message block (SMB) clients and servers.

- System root security (Rootsec.inf)

  By default, Rootsec.inf defines the permissions for the root of the system drive. You can use this template to reapply the root directory permissions if they are inadvertently changed, or you can modify the template to apply the same root permissions to other volumes. As specified, the template does not overwrite explicit permissions that are defined on child objects. It propagates only the permissions that are inherited by child objects.

- Internet Explorer Security (Iesacls.inf)

  Iesacls.inf is designed to establish auditing for registry keys that are associated with Microsoft Internet Explorer. The permissions are set on these keys to allow the Everyone group Full Control access to the keys. Auditing is configured to track when anyone attempts to modify the values of those keys.

Additional reading

For more information about applying security policies, see article 325351, "HOW TO: Apply Local Policies to All Users Except Administrators on Windows Server 2003 in a Workgroup Setting," in the Microsoft Knowledge Base at the Microsoft Help and Support Web site.

For more information about **secedit**, see "Secedit" at the Microsoft TechNet Web site.

What Are Security Template Settings?

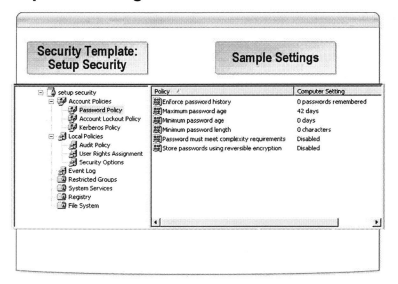

Introduction

Security templates contain security settings for all security areas. You can apply templates to individual computers or deploy them to groups of computers by using Group Policy. When you apply a template to existing security settings, the settings in the template are merged into the computer's security settings.

You can configure and analyze security settings for computers by using the Security Settings Group Policy extension or Security Configuration and Analysis.

Types of security template settings

The following list describes each of the security template settings:

- Account Policies

  You can use account policy settings to configure password policies, account lockout policies, and Kerberos version 5 (V5) protocol policies for the domain. A domain's account policy defines the password history, the lifetime of the Kerberos V5 tickets, account lockouts, and more.

- Local Policies

  Local policy settings, by definition, are local to computers. Local policies include audit policies, the assignment of user rights and permissions, and various security options that can be configured locally.

  It is important not to confuse local policy settings with setting policies locally. As with all of these security settings, you can configure these settings by using Local Security Policy and Group Policy.

- Event Log

  You use event log settings to configure the size, access, and retention parameters for application logs, system logs, and security logs.

■ Restricted Groups

You use restricted group settings to manage the membership of built-in groups that have certain predefined capabilities, such as Administrators and Power Users, in addition to domain groups, such as Domain Admins. You can add other groups to the restricted group, along with their membership information. This enables you to track and manage these groups as part of security policy.

You can also use restricted group settings to track and control the reverse membership of each restricted group. Reverse membership is listed in the **Members Of** column, which displays other groups to which the restricted group must belong.

■ System Services

You use system services settings to configure security and startup settings for services running on a computer. System services settings include critical functionality, such as network services, file and print services, telephony and fax services, and Internet or intranet services. The general settings include the service startup mode (automatic, manual, or disabled) and security on the service.

■ Registry

You use registry settings to configure security on registry keys.

■ File System

You use file system settings to configure security on specific file paths.

Important   When you use the Local Security Policy tool to edit the policies of a member server, only the Account Policies, Local Policies, Public Key Policies, Software Restriction Policies, and IP Security Policies on Active Directory areas are available.

Also, you can assign password settings, account lockout settings, and Kerberos settings at the domain or organizational unit level. However, if you configure the policy at the organizational unit level, the settings affect only the local Security Accounts Manager (SAM) databases of computer objects in the organizational unit, not the domain password policies. Windows Server 2003 does not process any changes that you make to these three settings in a GPO at the site level.

Additional reading   For more information about security template best practices, see the TechNet article "Best practices for Security Templates" at the Microsoft TechNet Web site.

Windows Server 2003 Security Guide Templates

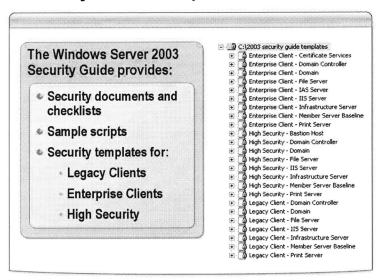

Introduction

The Windows Server 2003 Security Guide provides a set of documents, tools, and templates to help secure Windows Server 2003 in many environments. While Windows Server 2003 is secure after a default installation, there are a number of security options that you can configure based on specific requirements. The material in the Windows Server 2003 Security Guide explains the different requirements to secure three distinct environments. The three environments considered are named Legacy Client, Enterprise Client, and High Security.

Legacy Client settings

The Legacy Client settings are designed to work in an Active Directory domain running on Windows Server 2003 domain controllers with client computers and member servers running Microsoft Windows 98, Windows NT 4.0, and later.

Enterprise Client settings

The Enterprise Client settings are designed to work in an Active Directory domain running on Windows Server 2003 domain controllers with client computers and member servers running Microsoft Windows 2000, Windows XP, and later.

High Security environment

The High Security settings are also designed to work in an Active Directory domain running on Windows Server 2003 domain controllers with client computers and member servers running Windows 2000, Windows XP, and later. However, the High Security settings are so restrictive that many applications might not function, performance of the servers might be noticeably slower, and managing the servers will be more challenging.

Note   The Windows Server 2003 Security Guide is included on the Student Materials compact disc and is also available at the Microsoft Download Center Web site.

Windows XP Security Guide Templates

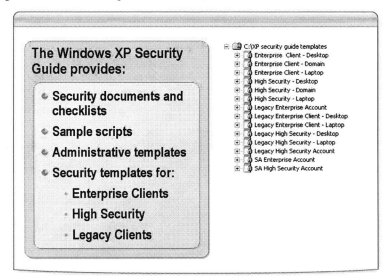

Introduction

The Windows XP Security Guide v2.0 describes the features and recommended settings for Microsoft Windows XP Service Pack 2 (SP2).

New templates

The guide includes tested templates for security settings on these elements and much more:

- Windows Firewall, which replaces Internet Connection Firewall (ICF)
- Remote procedure call (RPC) communications
- Memory protection
- E-mail handling
- Web download controls
- Spyware controls

Administrative templates

The Windows XP Security Guide version 2.0 includes administrative templates that control the settings of Microsoft Office 2003 products. You can configure all options of the Tools menu of any of the Microsoft Office 2003 products through Group Policy by importing the administrative templates into a GPO and modifying the settings. For example, the macro security settings or default file locations can be enforced by adding these administrative templates to a Group Policy. The templates need to be added to each GPO where they need to be applied.

Types of security templates

Enterprise Clients. The enterprise environment consists of a Windows 2000 or Windows Server 2003 Microsoft Active Directory domain. The clients in this environment will be managed using Group Policy that is applied to containers, sites, domains, and organizational units. Group Policy provides a centralized method to manage security policy across the environment.

High Security. The high-security environment consists of elevated security settings for the client. When applying high-security settings, user functionality is limited to specific functions that are required only for the necessary tasks. Access is limited to approved applications, services, and infrastructure environments.

Caution   The High Security templates were designed for high-security environments. The High Security templates provide maximum security without regard for functionality of applications. These templates should be fully tested before being deployed.

Legacy Clients. The stand-alone environment consists of those organizations that have some computers that cannot be joined to a domain or computers that are members of a Windows NT 4.0 domain. These clients have to be configured using Local Policy settings. The management of stand-alone machines can be considerably more challenging than using an Active Directory–based domain for management of user accounts and policies.

Note   The Windows XP Security Guide is included on the Student Materials compact disc and is also available at the Microsoft Download Center Web site.

Ways to Deploy Security Templates

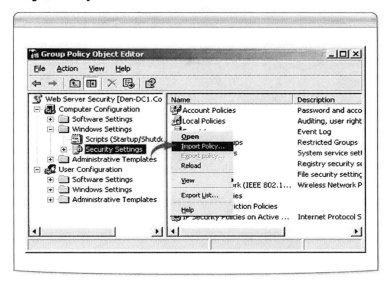

Introduction

In a domain environment, the most efficient way to provide consistent security settings to large numbers of computers is to use a GPO. You can configure templates based on the roles of computers in the organization and import them into GPOs. For example, you can develop a custom template and import it into the GPO used to configure all the organization's Web servers.

In a stand-alone environment, there is no central authority to deliver security settings. You must configure security on an individual basis. Templates become even more valuable in this situation. By configuring a group of templates for computers based on their role, you can provide consistent security settings to those computers. As security needs change, you only need to change the template and reapply it to the computers to get the desired results.

Deploying security templates to GPOs

You can import custom security templates into the security settings section of any GPO. Then you can configure security settings for all the computer accounts in the organizational unit by linking it to the GPO. This requires that your organizational unit structure places computer accounts in organizational units based on their role in the organization. For example, you might have an organizational unit that contains all of your computers running Microsoft SQL Server™. When a new computer running SQL Server is brought on to the network and its computer account is placed in the SQL organizational unit, the security will be automatically configured based on the GPO that is linked to the organizational unit.

Deploying security templates to stand-alone computers

You can import a custom template directly into a stand-alone computer's security settings. By developing custom templates for different computer roles, you can provide consistent security for computers that are not members of your domain. For example, you can create a custom template that will configure identical security settings for all your Microsoft Internet Security and Acceleration (ISA) servers that are stand-alone computers on your perimeter network.

The Security Configuration Wizard

The Security Configuration Wizard (SCW) is an attack-surface reduction tool for members of the Microsoft Windows Server 2003 family with Service Pack 1 (SP1). SCW determines the minimum functionality that is required for a server's role or roles and disables functionality that is not required. SCW guides you through the process of creating, editing, applying, or rolling back a security policy based on the selected roles of the server. The security policies that you create by using SCW are XML files that, when applied, configure services, network security, specific registry values, audit policy, and if applicable, Internet Information Services (IIS). SCW is an optional component included with Windows Server 2003 SP1. You can install and run SCW only on computers running a member of the Windows Server 2003 family with SP1. The computers that you target with SCW must run a member of the Windows Server 2003 family with SP1. SCW is not used with Microsoft Windows Small Business Server 2003.

Practice: Using Security Templates to Secure Computers

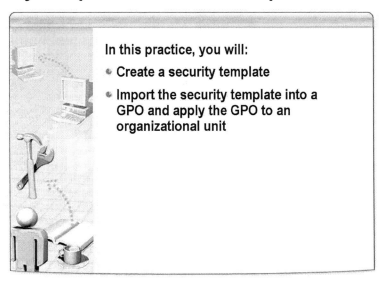

In this practice, you will:
- Create a security template
- Import the security template into a GPO and apply the GPO to an organizational unit

Objectives

In this practice, you will:

- Create a security template.
- Import the security template into a GPO and apply the GPO to an organizational unit.

Instructions

Ensure that the DEN-DC1 and the DEN-CL1 virtual machines are running.

Practice

▶ **Create a security template**

1. Log on to DEN-DC1 as **Administrator**.
2. Create a custom Microsoft Management Console (MMC), and then add the Security Templates snap-in.
3. Expand Security Templates, in the console tree, right-click **C:\WINDOWS\security\templates**, and then click **New Template**.
4. In the **C:\WINDOWS\security\templates** dialog box, in the **Template Name** box, type **SecureXP**, and then click **OK**.
5. In the Security Templates MMC, expand **SecureXP**, **Local Policies**, and **Security Options**, and then double-click **Accounts: Rename administrator account**.
6. Select the **Define this policy setting in the template** check box, type **XPAdmin** in the field, and then click **OK**.
7. Double-click **Interactive logon: Do not display last user name**.
8. Select the **Define this policy setting in the template** check box, click **Enabled**, and then click **OK**.
9. Right-click **File System**, and then click **Add File**.
10. Select **C:\Program Files** in the **Add a file or folder** dialog box, and then click **OK**.

11. Click **Add** in the **Database Security for %ProgramFiles%** dialog box, add the **DL Sales Modify** group, and then click **OK**.

12. Assign **Modify** permission to the **DL Sales Modify** group, and then click **OK**.

13. In the **Add Object** dialog box, take note of the settings, and then click **OK** to accept the defaults.

14. Close and save the Security Templates MMC as **Security Templates**.

15. Click **Yes** in the **Save Security Templates** dialog box to save the SecureXP template to the default location.

▶ **Import the security template into a GPO and apply the GPO to an organizational unit**

1. Open **Group Policy Management** and then create and link a GPO named **XP Security** to the **Sales** organizational unit.

2. Right-click and edit the **XP Security** policy.

3. In the **Group Policy Object Editor**, expand **Computer Configuration**, **Windows Settings**, and **Security Settings**.

4. Right-click **Security Settings**, and then click **Import Policy**.

5. In the **Import Policy From** dialog box, click **Secure XP.inf**, and then click **Open**.

6. Close the **Group Policy Object Editor** and **Group Policy Management**.

7. Open **Active Directory Users and Computers**, and move **DEN-CL1** from the **Computers** container to the **Sales** organizational unit.

8. Close **Active Directory User and Computers** and then log off of DEN-DC1.

9. Log on to DEN-CL1 as **Administrator**.

10. Click **Start**, click **Shutdown**, and then click **Restart**. Do not shut down the virtual machine.

11. Log on to DEN-CL1 as **Administrator**.

12. Open **Computer Management**, expand **Local Users and Groups** and then click **Users**.

    What is the name of the built-in administrator account?

    _____

13. Close all open windows, and then log off.

Important   Do not shut down the virtual machines.

Lesson: Testing Computer Security Policy

- What Is the Security Configuration and Analysis Tool?
- Practice: Testing a Computer Security Policy

Introduction

Before you deploy a security template to large groups of computers, it is important to analyze the results of applying a configuration to ensure that there are no adverse effects on applications, connectivity, or security. A thorough analysis also helps you to identify security holes and deviations from standard configurations. You can use the Security Configuration and Analysis snap-in to create and review possible scenarios and adjust a configuration.

Lesson objectives

After completing this lesson, you will be able to:

- Describe the Security Configuration and Analysis tool.
- Test computer security by using the Security Configuration and Analysis tool.

What Is the Security Configuration and Analysis Tool?

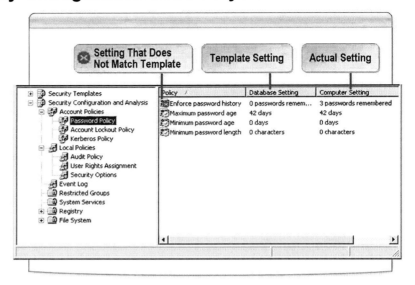

Introduction	The most common tool that you can use to analyze computer security is the Security Configuration and Analysis tool.
Security Configuration and Analysis tool	The Security Configuration and Analysis tool compares the security configuration of the local computer to an alternative configuration that is imported from a template (an .inf file) and stored in a separate database (an .sdb file). When analysis is complete, you can browse the security settings in the console tree to see the results. Discrepancies are marked with a red flag. Consistencies are marked with a green check mark. Settings that are not marked with either a red flag or a green check mark are not configured in the database.
Why use the Security Configuration and Analysis tool?	After analyzing the results by using the Security Configuration and Analysis tool, you can perform various tasks, including:

- Eliminating discrepancies by configuring the settings in the database to match the current computer settings. To configure database settings, double-click the setting in the Details pane.

- Importing another template file, merging its settings, and overwriting settings where there is a conflict. To import another template file, right-click **Security Configuration and Analysis**, and then click **Import Template**.

- Exporting the current database settings to a template file. To export another template file, right-click **Security Configuration and Analysis**, and then click **Export Template**.

■ Configuring a computer's security settings with the settings in the template. To configure the computer to match the template settings, right-click **Security Configuration and Analysis**, and then click **Configure Computer Now**. You should use **Configure Computer Now** only to modify security areas *not* affected by Group Policy settings, such as security on local files and folders, registry keys, and system services. Otherwise, when the Group Policy settings are applied, the Group Policy settings from the domain controller will take precedence over local settings. In general, do not use **Configure Computer Now** when you are analyzing security for domain-based clients, since you will have to configure each client individually. In this case, you should return to **Security Templates**, modify the template, and reapply it to the appropriate GPO.

Note You can also use the **secedit** command-line utility to analyze computer security settings. By using the **secedit** tool in a batch file or an automatic task scheduler, you can automatically create and apply templates and analyze system security. You can also run the **secedit** tool dynamically from a command prompt window. The **secedit** tool is useful when you have multiple computers on which you must analyze or configure security and must perform these tasks during off-hours.

Additional reading

For more information about the security tools, see "Security Configuration Manager" and "Best Practices for Security Configuration and Analysis" on the Microsoft TechNet Web site.

Practice: Testing a Computer Security Policy

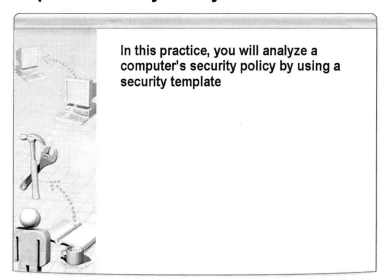

In this practice, you will analyze a computer's security policy by using a security template

Objective

In this practice, you will analyze a computer's security policy by using a security template.

Instructions

Ensure that the DEN-DC1 and the DEN-CL1 virtual machines are running.

Practice

▶ **Analyze a computer's security policy by using a security template**

1. Log on to DEN-CL1 as **Administrator**.

2. Create an MMC, and then add the **Security Configuration and Analysis** snap-in.

3. In the console tree, right-click **Security Configuration and Analysis**, and then click **Open Database**.

4. In the **Open Database** dialog box, type **Enterprise Client** in the **File name** field, and then click **Open**.

5. In the **Import Template** dialog box, in the **Look in** field, browse the network to **\\Den-DC1\Admin_Tools\XP security templates**, select **Enterprise Client – Desktop.inf**, and then click **Open**.

6. In the console tree, right-click **Security Configuration and Analysis**, and then click **Analyze Computer Now**.

7. In the **Perform Analysis** dialog box, click **OK** to accept the default path for the log file.

8. When the analysis is complete, expand **Local Polices** and click **Security Options**.

   What are the **Database** and **Computer** settings for **Renaming the administrator account**?

   _____

   _____

   Do the Database and Computer settings for **Interactive logon: Do not display last user name** agree?

   _____

   _____

9. Click **File System, C:**.

   What are the **Database** and **Computer** settings for the **Program Files** directory?

   _____

   _____

10. Close all open windows and log off of **DEN-CL1**.

▶ **To prepare for the next practice**

● Start DEN-SRV1 to prepare for the next practice.

Note   Do not shut down the virtual machines.

Lesson: Configuring Auditing

* What Is Auditing?
* What Is an Audit Policy?
* Types of Events to Audit
* Guidelines for Planning an Audit Policy
* Practice: Configuring Auditing
* Best Practices for Configuring Auditing

Introduction

No security strategy is complete without a comprehensive auditing strategy. More often than not, organizations learn this only after they experience a security incident. Without an audit trail of actions, it is almost impossible to successfully investigate a security incident. You must determine as part of your overall security strategy what events you need to audit, the level of auditing appropriate for your environment, how the audited events are collected, and how they are reviewed.

Lesson objectives

After completing this lesson, you will be able to:

- Describe auditing.
- Describe what an audit policy is.
- Describe types of events to audit.
- Identify the guidelines for planning an audit policy.
- Configure auditing.
- Apply best practices while configuring auditing.

What Is Auditing?

- **Auditing tracks user and operating system activities and records selected events in security logs**

  | What occurred? | Who did it? | When? |

  | What was the result? |

- **Enable auditing to:**

  - Create a baseline
  - Determine damages
  - Detect threats and attacks
  - Prevent further damage

- **Audit access to objects, management of accounts, and users logging on and logging off**

Definition

Auditing is the process that tracks user and operating system activities by recording selected types of events in the security log of a server or a workstation. Security logs contain various audit entries, which contain the following information:

- The action that was performed
- The user who performed the action
- The success or failure of the event and when the event occurred
- Additional information, such as the computer where the event occurred

Why perform auditing?

Enable auditing and monitor audit logs to:

- Create a baseline of normal network and computer operations.
- Detect attempts to penetrate the network or computer.
- Determine what systems and data have been compromised during or after a security incident.
- Prevent further damage to networks or computers after an attacker has penetrated the network.

The security needs of an organization help determine the amount of auditing that is used. For example, a minimum-security network might choose to audit failed logon attempts to monitor against potential brute-force attacks. A high-security network might choose to audit both successful and failed logon attempts to track any unauthorized users who successfully gain access to the network.

Although auditing might provide valuable information, excessive auditing fills the audit log with unnecessary information. This can potentially affect the performance of your system and make it extremely difficult to find relevant information.

Types of events to audit   The most common types of events to audit are when:

- Objects, such as files and folders, are accessed.

- Managing user accounts and group accounts.

- Users log on to and log off the system.

Additional reading   For more information about auditing, see the TechNet article "Auditing overview" at the Microsoft TechNet Web site.

What Is an Audit Policy?

* An audit policy determines the security events that will be reported to the network administrator

* Set up an audit policy to:

    * Track success or failure of events

    * Minimize unauthorized use of resources

    * Maintain a record of activity

* Security events are stored in security logs

Introduction

Establishing an audit policy is an important part of security. Monitoring the creation or modification of objects gives you a way to track potential security problems, helps to ensure user accountability, and provides evidence in the event of a security breach.

Definition

An audit policy defines the types of security events that computers running Windows Server 2003 record in the security log on each computer. Windows Server 2003 writes events to the security log on the specific computer where the event occurs.

Why set up an audit policy?

Set up an audit policy for a computer to:

- Track the success and failure of events, such as attempts to log on, attempts by a particular user to read a specific file, changes to a user account or group membership, and changes to security settings.

- Minimize the risk of unauthorized use of resources.

- Maintain a record of user and administrator activity.

Use Event Viewer to view events that Windows Server 2003 records in the security log. You can also archive log files to track trends over time. This is useful to determine trends in the use of printers, access to files, and attempts at unauthorized use of resources.

How can you implement an audit policy?

You can set up an audit policy on any single computer, either directly by using the Local Policy snap-in or indirectly by using Group Policy, which is more commonly used in large organizations. After an audit policy is designed and implemented, information begins to appear in the security logs. Each computer in the organization has a separate security log that records local events.

When you implement an audit policy:

- Specify the categories of events that you want to audit. Examples of event categories are user logon, user logoff, and account management. The event categories that you specify constitute your audit policy.

- Set the size and settings of the security log. You can view the security log by using Event Viewer.

- Determine which objects you want to monitor access to and what type of access you want to monitor and whether you want to audit directory service access or object access. For example, if you want to audit attempts by users to open a particular file, you can configure audit policy settings in the object access event category so that successful and failed attempts to read a file are recorded.

Default audit policies

The default auditing settings for servers are configured by administrative templates. The following security templates configure default auditing settings:

- Setup security.inf
- Hisecdc.inf
- Hisecws.inf
- Securedc.inf
- Securews.inf

To view the policy settings that each security template configures, in the Security Templates snap-in, navigate to **Local Policies\Audit Policy** for each administrative template.

Additional reading

For more information about audit policies, see the TechNet article "Auditing policy" at the Microsoft TechNet Web site.

Types of Events to Audit

- Account Logon
- Account Management
- Directory Service Access
- Logon
- Object Access
- Policy Change
- Privilege Use
- Process Tracking
- System

Introduction

The first step in creating a strategy for auditing the operating system is to determine what type of actions or operations that you need to record.

Determining what events to audit

What operating system events should you audit? You do not want to audit every event, because auditing all operating system events requires enormous system resources and might negatively affect system performance. You should work with other security specialists to determine what operating system events to audit. Only audit events that you believe will be useful for later reference.

An effective way to begin determining what events to audit is to gather the relevant group of people and discuss the following issues:

- What actions or operations you want to track
- On what systems you want to track these events

For example, you might decide to track:

- All domain and local logon events on all computers.
- The use of all files in the Payroll folder on the HR server.

The success and failure events

In Windows Server 2003, audit events can be split into two categories:

- Success events

  A success event indicates that the operating system has successfully completed the action or operation. Success events are indicated by a key icon.

- Failure events

  A failure event indicates that an action or operation was attempted but did not succeed. Failure events are indicated by a padlock icon.

Failure events are very useful for tracking attempted attacks on your environment, but success events are much more difficult to interpret. The vast majority of success events are indications of normal activity, and an attacker who accesses a system also generates a success event.

Often, a pattern of events is as important as the events themselves. For example, a series of failures followed by a success might indicate an attempted attack that was eventually successful.

Similarly, the deviation from a pattern might also indicate suspicious activity. For example, suppose that the security logs show that a user at your organization logs on every workday between 8 A.M. and 10 A.M., but suddenly the user is logging on to the network at 3 A.M. Although this behavior might be innocent, it should be investigated.

Events that Windows Server 2003 can audit

The first step in implementing an audit policy is to select the types of events that you want Windows Server 2003 to audit. The following table describes the events that Windows Server 2003 can audit.

Event	Example
Account Logon	An account is authenticated by a security database. When a user logs on to the local computer, the computer records the Account Logon event. When a user logs on to a domain, the authenticating domain controller records the Account Logon event.
Account Management	An administrator creates, changes, or deletes a user account or group; a user account is renamed, disabled, or enabled; or a password is set or changed.
Directory Service Access	A user accesses an Active Directory object. To log this type of access, you must configure specific Active Directory objects for auditing.
Logon	A user logs on to or off a local computer, or a user makes or cancels a network connection to the computer. The event is recorded on the computer that the user accesses, regardless of whether a local account or a domain account is used.
Object Access	A user accesses a file, folder, or printer. The administrator must configure specific files, folders, or printers to be audited, the users or groups that are being audited, and the actions that they will be audited for.
Policy Change	A change is made to the user security options (for example, password options or account logon settings), user rights, or audit policies.
Privilege Use	A user exercises a user right, such as changing the system time (this does not include rights that are related to logging on and logging off) or taking ownership of a file.
Process Tracking	An application performs an action. This information is generally useful only for programmers who want to track details about application execution.
System	A user restarts or shuts down the computer, or an event occurs that affects Windows Server 2003 security or the security log.

Events edited by default

The Setup security.inf template includes default settings that enable auditing of successful account logon events and successful logon events. No other events are audited by default.

Guidelines for Planning an Audit Policy

* Determine the computers to set up auditing on

* Determine which events to audit

* Determine whether to audit success or failure events

* Determine whether to track trends

* Review security logs frequently

Introduction

Auditing too many types of events can create excess overhead, which might result in diminished system performance.

Guidelines

Use the following guidelines when planning an audit policy:

- Determine the computers to set up auditing on. Plan what to audit for each computer, because Windows Server 2003 audits events on each computer separately. For example, you might frequently audit computers used to store sensitive or critical data, but you might infrequently audit client computers that are used solely for running productivity applications.

- Determine the types of events to audit, such as the following:

  - Access to files and folders

  - Users logging on and off

  - Shutting down and restarting a computer running Windows Server 2003

  - Changes to user accounts and groups

- Determine whether to audit success or failure events, or both. Tracking success events can tell you how often Windows Server 2003 or users access specific files or printers. You can use this information for resource planning. Tracking failure events can alert you to possible security breaches.

- Determine whether you need to track trends of system usage. If so, plan to archive event logs. Some organizations are required to maintain a record of resource and data access. For example, a legal firm might need to track who accesses documents.

- Review security logs frequently and regularly according to a schedule. Configuring auditing alone does not alert you to security breaches.

Practice: Configuring Auditing

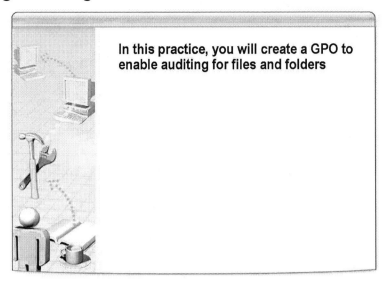

In this practice, you will create a GPO to enable auditing for files and folders

Objective

In this practice, you will create a GPO to enable auditing for files and folders.

Instructions

Ensure that the DEN-DC1, DEN-SRV1 and the DEN-CL1 virtual machines are running.

Practice

▶ **Create a GPO to enable auditing for files and folders**

1. Log on to DEN-DC1 as **Administrator**.

2. Open **Active Directory Users and Computers**, and move the **DEN-SRV1** computer account from the **Computers** container into the **Legal** organizational unit.

3. Close **Active Directory Users and Computers**.

4. Open **Group Policy Management**, and create and link a GPO named **Legal Auditing** to the **Legal** organizational unit.

5. Right-click and edit the **Legal Auditing** policy.

6. Expand **Computer Configuration, Windows Settings, Security Settings, Local Polices, Audit Policy**, and double-click **Audit object access**.

7. In the **Audit object access Properties** dialog box, select the **Define these policy settings** check box, select **Success** and **Failure**, and then click **OK**.

8. Close the **Group Policy Object Editor**.

9. Log on to DEN-SRV1 as **Administrator**.

10. Open Windows Explorer, right-click **C:\Legal**, and then click **Sharing and Security**.

11. Share the **Legal** folder with the share name **Legal**, and then assign the Everyone group **Change** permission to the share.

12. Click the **Security** tab, and then assign the **DL Legal Write** group **Write** permission.

13. Click **Advanced**, and then select the **Auditing** tab in the **Advanced Security Settings for Legal** dialog box.

14. Add the **Everyone** group, audit them for **Full Control** of **Successful** and **Failed**, and then click **OK** three times.

15. At the **Run** command prompt, type **gpupdate /force** to refresh the policy. Click **OK**

16. Log on to DEN-CL1 as **Don**, and then connect to **DEN-SRV1\Legal**.

17. Attempt to delete the **Briefs** folder. Click **Yes** to confirm the deletion. You will receive an *Error Deleting file or Folder* message. Click **OK** to acknowledge the message.

18. Close all open windows on DEN-CL1 and log off.

19. Return to DEN-SRV1, and then open the **Security** log in Event Viewer. You will see a padlock icon, indicating the failure event. Double-click the entry and examine it.

20. Close all open windows, and then log off all computers.

Important   Do not shut down the virtual machines.

Best Practices for Configuring Auditing

Best practices

Apply the following best practices while performing auditing:

- Audit success events in the directory service access category.

  By auditing success events in the directory service access category, you can find out who accessed an object in Active Directory and what operations were performed.

- Audit success events in the object access category.

  By auditing success events in the object access category, you can ensure that users are not misusing their access to secured objects.

- Audit success and failure events in the system category.

  By auditing success and failure events in the system category, you can detect unusual activity that indicates that an attacker is attempting to gain access to your computer or network.

- Audit success and failure events in the policy change category on domain controllers.

  If an event is logged in the policy change category, someone has changed the Local Security Authority (LSA) security policy configuration. If you use Group Policy to edit your audit policy settings, you do not need to audit events in the policy change category on member servers.

- Audit success and failure events in the account management category.

  By auditing success events in the account management category, you can verify changes that are made to account properties and group properties. By auditing failure events in the account management category, you can see whether unauthorized users or attackers are trying to change account properties or group properties.

- Audit success events in the logon category.

  By auditing success events in the logon category, you have a record of when each user logs on to or logs off a computer. If an unauthorized person steals a user's password and logs on, you can find out when the security breach occurred.

- Audit success events in the account logon category on domain controllers.

  By auditing success events in the account logon category, you can see when users log on to or log off the domain. You do not need to audit events in the account logon category on member servers.

- Set an appropriate size for the security log.

  It is important to configure the size of the security log appropriately, based on the number of events that your audit policy settings generate.

Additional reading   For more information about managing audit logs, see article 325898, "HOW TO: Set Up and Manage Operation-Based Auditing for Windows Server 2003, Enterprise Edition," in the Microsoft Knowledge Base at the Microsoft Help and Support Web site.

Lesson: Managing Security Logs

* Types of Log Files
* Common Security Events
* Tasks Associated with Managing the Security Log Files
* Practice: Managing Security Logs

Introduction

You can configure the security logs to record information about Active Directory and server events. These events are recorded in the Windows security log. The security log can record security events, such as valid and invalid logon attempts, as well as events that are related to resource use, such as creating, opening, or deleting files. You must log on as an administrator to control what events are audited and displayed in the security log.

Lesson objectives

After completing this lesson, you will be able to:

- Describe the types of security log files and the information contained in each log file.

- Identify common security events.

- Describe tasks that are associated with managing the security log files.

- Manage security log files.

Types of Log Files

The following logs are available in Event Viewer:
- Application
- Security
- System
- Directory service
- File Replication service

Introduction

The security log records events, such as valid and invalid logon attempts, and events related to resource use, such as creating, opening, or deleting files or other objects. For example, if logon auditing is enabled, attempts to log on to the system are recorded in the security log. After an audit policy is designed and implemented, information begins to appear in the security log.

Each computer in the organization has a separate security log that records local events. Domain controllers hold the security log information about Active Directory.

Logs available in Event Viewer

You can view the following logs in Event Viewer, depending on the type of computer that you are using and the services that are installed on that computer:

- *Application*. Contains events generated by applications installed on the computer, including server applications, such as Microsoft Exchange Server or Microsoft SQL Server, and desktop applications, such as Microsoft Office.

- *Security*. Contains events generated by auditing. These events include logons and logoffs, access to resources, and changes in policy.

- *System*. Contains events generated by components and services in Windows Server 2003.

- *Directory service*. Appears only on domain controllers. The directory service event log contains, for example, Active Directory replication.

- *File Replication service*. Appears only on domain controllers. The file replication service event log contains, for example, events that are related to the replication of Group Policy.

Tip If you decide to use auditing extensively, increase the size of the security log in the Event Log section of the security policy for the Default Domain Controllers GPO.

Security log files format

Security log files are also stored in the *systemroot*/system32/config directory. Security logs can be exported and archived in the following file formats:

- Event log files (.evt; the default)
- Comma-delimited files (.csv)
- Text files (.txt)

Common Security Events

Logon	Event description
Event ID 528	Successful logon
Event ID 529	Unsuccessful logon attempt
Event ID 539	Attempts to log on to a locked out account
Security Log	**Event description**
Event ID 517	Security log cleared
Shutdown	**Event description**
Event ID 513	System is shut down

Introduction

Many events appear in the security log. The following are some common scenarios that might be cause for concern and suggestions for diagnosing problems by using the event log.

Invalid logon attempts and account lockout

A successful logon generates an Event ID 528. When a user attempts to guess another user's password, he or she will likely make several incorrect guesses. Each incorrect guess generates an Event ID 529, which is also generated by a misspelled user name. If an account becomes locked out, subsequent attempts generate an Event ID 539.

Intermittent instances of these events might occur when a user types incorrectly or forgets a password. Repeated instances in a short time period might indicate a password attack.

Change of file ownership

The owner of a file in the NTFS file system can modify the file's permissions to read and modify the file. A user who has the user right to take ownership can access any file by first taking ownership of that file. This change of ownership constitutes the use of a user right and generates an Event ID 578.

Clearing the security log

An unscrupulous administrator with the user right to clear the security log from Event Viewer can clear the log to hide his or her security-sensitive activities.

The security log must always be cleared according to a well-planned schedule and only immediately after a full copy of the log is archived. If the log is cleared under any other circumstances, the administrator must justify his or her actions. Clearing the security log generates an Event ID 517, which is the first event generated in the new log.

System shutdown

Ordinarily, mission-critical servers must be shut down only by administrators. You can prevent others from shutting down a server by assigning or denying the **Shut down the system** user right in the local security policy or by using Group Policy.

To determine whether the **Shut down the system** right was mistakenly assigned, audit the system Event ID 513, which identifies who shut down the computer.

Additional reading

For more information about security events, see article 299475, "Windows 2000 Security Event Description (Part 1 of 2)" and article 301677, "Windows 2000 Security Event Description (Part 2 of 2)" on the Microsoft TechNet Web site.

Tasks Associated with Managing the Security Log Files

Introduction

All audited events in Windows NT, Windows Server 2003, and Windows XP are recorded in the security log in Event Viewer. Security-related events might also be recorded in the application and system logs.

Evaluate the configuration of the log file

Before you enable audit policies, you must evaluate whether the default configuration of the log files in Event Viewer is appropriate for your organization.

To view the log files settings in Event Viewer:

1. On the **Administrative Tools** menu, click **Event Viewer**.

2. Right-click the Security event log, and then click **Properties**.

Log file location

By default, the security log is stored in the *systemroot*/System32/config directory in a file named SecEvent.evt. In Windows Server 2003, you can change the log file location in the security log **Properties** dialog box. In Windows NT 4.0 and Windows Server 2000, you must edit the registry to change the location of each log file.

By default, only the System account and the Administrators group have access to the security log. This ensures that nonadministrators cannot read, write, or delete security events. If you move the log to a new location, ensure that the new file has the correct NTFS permissions. Because the Event Viewer service cannot be stopped, changes to this setting are not applied until the server is restarted.

Maximum log file size

By default, the maximum size that the security log can grow to before the overwrite settings is initiated is 16,384 KB. Because hard disk space is much more readily available now than it was in the past, you will likely want to increase this setting. The amount by which you increase this setting depends on the overwrite settings configured for the log file, but a good general guideline is to set the maximum size to at least 50 MB. You can change the maximum size of the log file on individual computers in the security log **Properties** dialog box or on many computers by using security templates or editing the registry.

The maximum size that you should set for the combined total size of all event logs is 300 MB. Each security event is 350 to 500 bytes, so a 10 MB event log contains approximately 20,000 to 25,000 security events.

Log file overwrite settings

When you configure the security log settings, you must define the overwrite settings when the maximum log file size is reached. The following list describes the overwrite event options.

- *Overwrite events as needed.* New events continue to be written when the log is full. Each new event replaces the oldest event in the log.

- *Overwrite events older than [x] days.* Events are retained in the log for the number of days you specify before they are overwritten. The default is seven days.

- *Do not overwrite events.* New events are not recorded, and the event log must be cleared manually.

Delegate the right to manage the file

To delegate the rights to manage the security log file, configure the Group Policy setting **Manage auditing and security log**. This setting is found in Computer Configuration/Windows Settings/Security Settings/Local Policies/User Rights Assignment.

Practice: Managing Security Logs

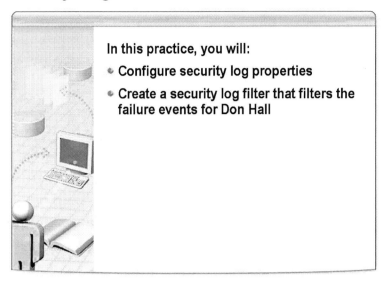

In this practice, you will:
* Configure security log properties
* Create a security log filter that filters the failure events for Don Hall

Objectives

In this practice, you will:

■ Configure security log properties.

■ Create a security log filter that filters the failure events for Don Hall.

Instructions

Ensure that the DEN-DC1, DEN-SRV1 and the DEN-CL1 virtual machines are running.

Practice

▶ **Configure security log properties**

1. Log on to DEN-SRV1 as **Administrator**.

2. In **Administrative Tools**, open **Event Viewer**.

3. Right-click the **Security** log, and click **Properties**.

4. On the **General** tab, type **30016** in the **Maximum log size** field.

5. Change the overwrite settings to **Do not overwrite events (clear log manually)**, and then click **Apply**.

▶ **Create a security log filter that filters the failure events for Don Hall**

1. In the **Security Properties** dialog box, click the **Filter** tab.

2. In the **Event types** section, clear all check boxes except **Failure audit**.

3. In the **User** field, type **Don**, and then click **OK**.

4. View the results in the security log. There will be only **Failure Audit events** for **Don**.

5. Close all open windows, and then log off.

Important   Do not shut down the virtual machines.

Lab: Managing Security Settings

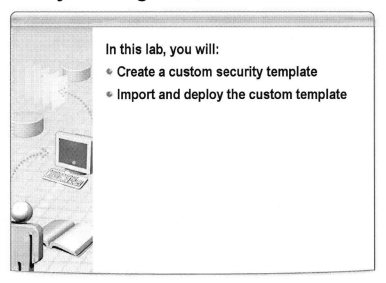

In this lab, you will:

● Create a custom security template

● Import and deploy the custom template

Objectives

After completing this lab, you will be able to:

- Create a custom security template.
- Import and deploy the custom template.

Prerequisites

To complete this lab, you must have the following virtual machines:

- DEN-DC1
- DEN-SRV1

Estimated time to complete this lab: 20 minutes

Exercise 1
Creating a Custom Security Template

In this exercise, you will create a custom security template.

Scenario

The security team has finished testing the security requirements for Contoso, Ltd. They have given you security requirements that you must use to create a custom security template named Graphics Security Policy.

Tasks	Special instructions
1. Create a new custom security template based on the securews template.	a. Log on to DEN-DC1 as **Administrator**. b. Open the **Security Templates** MMC. c. In the Security Templates snap-in, right-click the **securews** template, and then click **Save As**. d. In the **Save As** dialog box, type **Graphics Security Policy** in the **File name** field, and then click **Save**.
2. Enable audit, security policies, and event log properties.	a. Expand the **Graphics Security Policy** template. b. Expand **Local Policies**, and click **Audit Policy**. Notice that some auditing policies are enabled because this template was copied from the securews template. c. Enable **Audit object Access** for **Success** and **Failure**, and then click **OK**. d. Click **Security Options**. Notice that many security policies are enabled because this template was copied from the securews template. e. Configure the **Accounts: Rename administrator account** to set **Graphics Admin** as the name of the built-in administrator account. f. Change the **Interactive logon: Do not display last user name** from **Disabled** to **Enabled**, and then click **OK**. g. In the **Security Templates** tree, click **Event Log**. h. Double-click **Maximum security log size**, configure the log to be **99,840 KB**, and then click **OK**. i. Double-click the **Retain security log** setting, configure the period to be **7 days**, and then click **OK**. j. Click **OK** to accept the suggested value for the retention method.
3. Save the Graphics Security Policy template.	a. Right-click the **Graphics Security Policy** template, and then click **Save**. b. Close the Security Templates MMC. Click **No** to save console settings.

Exercise 2
Importing and Deploying the Custom Template

In this exercise, you will import the Graphics Security Policy template to a GPO that is linked to the Graphics organizational unit.

Tasks	Special instructions
1. Import the Graphics Security Policy template into a GPO.	a. On DEN-DC1, open **Group Policy Management**, and create and link a GPO named **Graphics Security** to the **Graphics** organizational unit.
	b. Right-click and edit the **Graphics Security Policy**.
	c. Expand **Computer Configuration**, **Windows Settings**, and then click **Security Settings**.
	d. Right-click **Security Settings**, and then click **Import Policy** to import the **Graphics Security Policy** template.
	e. Close the **Group Policy Object Editor**, and close **Group Policy Management**.
	f. Open **Active Directory Users and Computers**, and move **the DEN-SRV1** computer account from the Legal OU into the **Graphics** OU.
2. Test the settings.	a. Log on to DEN-SRV1 as **Administrator**.
	b. At the **Run** command prompt, type **gpupdate /force**. Click **OK**.
	c. In **Computer Management**, expand **Local Users and Groups**, and then click the **Users** folder. What is the name of the built-in administrators account?
3. Complete the lab exercise.	▪ Close all programs and shut down all computers. Do not save changes.

Module 9: Preparing to Administer a Server

Contents

Overview

- Introduction to Administering a Server
- Configuring Remote Desktop to Administer a Server
- Managing Remote Desktop Connections

Introduction

A major responsibility of a systems administrator is to administer the servers in an organization. Because most systems administrators are not located in the same room as the servers they manage, it is important to understand how to manage servers remotely, as well as from the server console.

This module describes how to use Microsoft® Windows Server™ 2003 to administer servers, what tools to use, and what permissions are required to administer a server. It also discusses how to administer remote connections and why that is an important aspect of system administration.

Objectives

After completing this module, you will be able to:

- Explain the tasks, tools, and rights that are required to administer a server.
- Configure Remote Desktop for Administration and client preferences.
- Manage remote desktop connections.

Lesson: Introduction to Administering a Server

* Group Memberships Used to Administer a Server
* What Is the Run as Feature?
* What Is Computer Management?
* Role of MMC in Remote Administration
* Practice: Introduction to Administering a Server

Introduction

This lesson introduces the tasks, tools, and rights that are required to administer a server. This information is the foundation that you need to perform your job as a systems administrator. This lesson describes the proper use and function of the server administration tools and explains the concepts of remote and local server administration.

Lesson objectives

After completing this lesson, you will be able to:

- Describe the group memberships that are used to administer a server.

- Describe the purpose and function of the **Run as** feature.

- Describe the role of the Computer Management tool in remote administration.

- Describe the role of the Microsoft Management Console (MMC) in remote administration.

- Configure MMC to manage a server remotely.

Group Memberships Used to Administer a Server

Built-in domain local group	Description
Administrators	Performs all administrative tasks on clients and servers
Backup Operators	Backs up, restores servers by using Backup
Account Operators	Creates, deletes, modifies user accounts and groups
Server Operators	Shares disk resources, backs up and restores files
Print Operators	Sets up, manages network printers

Introduction

To administer a server, you need appropriate permissions. You will need to understand these permissions to assign them appropriately and to perform your own administrative duties. The easiest way to assign administrative permissions is through domain local groups.

Built-in domain local groups

In a domain, built-in groups are created in the Active Directory® directory service. These groups have preset permissions that limit group member access to system tasks. These groups cannot be deleted.

The following list describes the most commonly used built-in domain local groups and their predetermined level of permissions.

- *Administrators*. Members of the Administrators domain local group can perform all functions that the operating system supports. Administrators can assign themselves any user rights that they do not have by default. The membership of the Administrators domain local group should be restricted to only users who require full system access and are highly trusted. Log on as an administrator only when necessary.

  Be cautious when adding other users to the Administrators group. For example, if a help desk technician is responsible for the printers in your organization, add the technician to the Print Operators group instead of the Administrators group.

- *Backup Operators*. Members of the Backup Operators domain local group can back up and restore files by using the Backup tool.

- *Account Operators.* Members of the Account Operators domain local group can manage user accounts, groups, computer accounts, and InetOrgPerson accounts. The exception is that only a member of the Administrators domain local group can modify the Administrators domain local group or any operator domain local group.

- *Server Operators.* Members of the Server Operators domain local group can share disk resources, log on to a server interactively, create and delete network shares, start and stop services, format the hard disk of the server, and shut down the computer. They can also back up and restore files by using the Backup tool.

- *Print Operators.* Member of the Print Operators domain local group can set up local and network printers to ensure that users can easily connect to and use printer resources.

Note The Administrators, Server Operators, and Backup Operators groups can also be found on member servers and stand-alone servers as built-in local groups.

Domain local groups can protect resources

Using a variety of built-in domain local groups and their associated permission levels can protect resources from security breaches. A systems administrator should always be assigned to the most restricted group that provides the appropriate rights and the permissions that are necessary to accomplish the task. For example, a systems administrator who manages only printers and backup server data should be a member of the printer operators group and should have authority to back up server data.

Domain local group permissions

Members of the built-in domain local groups are assigned permissions to perform system tasks, such as backing up files, restoring files, and changing the system time. You can use these groups for administering resources, such as file systems or printers that are located on any computer in the domain where common access permissions are required.

When you run your computer as a member of the Administrators domain local group, the system is vulnerable to Trojan horse attacks and other security risks. The simple act of visiting an Internet site or opening an e-mail attachment can lead to system damage, because an unfamiliar Internet site or e-mail attachment may contain Trojan horse code that can be downloaded to the system and executed.

Note In a domain environment, members of the Domain Admins global group are automatically added to the Administrators domain local group and to the Administrators local group on each computer. All other built-in groups do not have any members by default.

What Is the Run as Feature?

> * **The Run as feature allows secondary logon.**
>   **Use Run as to:**
>
>   * Log on with a nonadministrative account and still perform administrative tasks
>   * Limit system vulnerability
>   * Open MMC custom consoles
> * **You can access Run as from several locations**

Introduction

By using the **Run as** feature, also known as a secondary logon, administrators can log on with a nonadministrative account and still perform administrative tasks. Each time an administrative task is performed, the required administrative tool is run using the credentials of a user account with administrative permissions.

Requires two user accounts

To use **Run as** to perform administrative tasks requires two user accounts: a regular account with basic privileges and an administrative account. Each administrator should use an exclusive administrative account.

Login with your non-administrative account and use the **runas** command for system administration tasks. This practice preserves network security, limiting system exposure while you perform nonadministrative tasks. Some items, such as Windows Explorer, the Printers folder, and desktop items, are launched indirectly by Windows. These items cannot be started with **Run as**.

For tasks that cannot be performed by using the **runas** command, such as upgrading the operating system or configuring system parameters, log off your user account and then log on with your administrator account.

Use Run as to open MMC-created custom consoles

To administer local or remote computers, you can use the **Run as** command to open custom consoles you have created in the Microsoft Management Console (MMC). Using the **Run as** command offers you access to the services and administrative tools that are included in the console, while providing you with the appropriate permissions on the system for the components that are administered by the console.

Any user can use Run as

Although the **Run as** command is primarily intended for systems administrators, any user with multiple accounts can use **Run as** to start programs under different account contexts without logging off.

Three ways to use Run as

There are three ways to use the **Run as** command:

- You can right-click a program located on the **Start** menu, and then click **Run as**.

- You can right-click a program in Windows Explorer, and then click **Run as**.

- You can also use the **runas** command from a command prompt. This method is typically used for scripting administrative tasks or to start a command shell in the local administrative context. To use **Run as** from a command prompt, type **runas /user:***domain_name\user_name program_name*

For example, to run the Computer Management tool from the command line as an administrator, open a command prompt and then type **runas /user:contoso\admininistrator "mmc %windir%\system32 \compmgmt.msc"**

Set up runas shortcuts

You can also set up **runas** shortcuts to the services and administrative tools that you use most often, including Performance, Computer Management, Device Manager, and Disk Manager.

See the following table for commands.

Tool	Command line
Computer Management	**runas /user:contoso\administrator "mmc %windir%\system32\ compmgmt.msc"**
Device Manager	**runas /user:contoso\administrator "mmc %windir%\system32\ devmgmt.msc"**
Disk Manager	**runas /user:contoso\administrator "mmc %windir%\system32\ diskmgmt.msc"**
Active Directory	**runas /user:contoso\administrator "mmc %windir%\system32\dsa.msc"**
MMC	**runas /user:contoso\administrator mmc**
Command Prompt	**runas /user:contoso\administrator cmd**
Performance Monitor	**runas /user:Contoso\administrator "mmc %windir%\system32\perfmon.msc"**

Note Windows Server 2003 SP1 includes a new version of the Administration Tools. These tools can be installed on computers running Windows Server 2003 and Windows XP. Previous versions of the Administration Tools must be uninstalled before installing the SP1 version.

What Is Computer Management?

* A collection of administrative tools
* Use to manage remote and local computers

Tool	Description
System tools	* Monitor system events * Create and manage shared resources * View a list of connected users * View device configurations
Storage tools	* Set properties for storage devices * Update disk information
Services and applications tools	* Manage applications and services * Start and stop system services

Definition

Computer Management is a collection of administrative tools that you can use to administer a local computer or remote computers.

Use Computer Management to manage computers

You can use Computer Management to:

- Monitor system events, such as logon times and application errors.

- Create and manage shared resources.

- View the list of users who are connected to a local or remote computer.

- Start and stop system services, such as Task Scheduler and Indexing Service.

- Set properties for storage devices.

- View device configurations and add new device drivers.

- Manage applications and services.

Computer Management console

The Computer Management console organizes the administrative tools into the following three categories:

- System Tools

- Storage

- Services and Applications

The following sections describe the tools in these categories and explain how to use them to perform administrative tasks.

System Tools

These System Tools manage system events and system performance:

- *Event Viewer.* Use Event Viewer to manage and view events that are recorded in the application, security, and system logs. You can monitor the logs to track security events and to identify possible software, hardware, and system problems.

- *Shared Folders.* Use Shared Folders to view connections and resources that are in use on the computer. You can create, view, and manage shared resources; view open files and sessions; and close files and disconnect sessions.

- *Local Users and Groups.* Use Local Users and Groups to create and manage your local user accounts and groups.

- *Performance Logs and Alerts.* Use Performance Logs and Alerts to monitor and collect data about your computer's performance.

- *Device Manager.* Use Device Manager to view the hardware devices that are installed in your computer, update device drivers, modify hardware settings, and troubleshoot device conflicts.

Storage

You use the tools in Storage to manage the properties of storage devices.

- *Removable Storage.* Use Removable Storage to track your removable storage media and to manage the libraries or data-storage systems that contain them.

- *Disk Defragmenter.* Use Disk Defragmenter to analyze and defragment volumes on your hard disks.

- *Disk Management.* Use Disk Management to perform disk-related tasks, such as converting disks or creating and formatting volumes. Disk Management helps you manage your hard disks and the partitions or volumes they contain.

Services and Applications

The tools in Services and Applications help you manage services and applications on the specified computer.

- *Services.* Use Services to manage services on local and remote computers. You can start, stop, pause, resume, or disable a service. For example, you can use Services to stop a service on a remote computer.

- *WMI Control.* Use WMI Control to configure and manage the Windows Management Service.

- *Indexing Service.* Use Indexing Service to manage the Indexing service and to create and configure additional catalogs to store index information.

Role of MMC in Remote Administration

* **Microsoft Management Console**
  * Provides an interface to snap-ins that manage hardware, software, and network services
* **Use MMC in remote administration to:**
  * Perform tasks that are frequently accomplished on remote computers
  * Manage similar tasks on many remote computers

Introduction

Microsoft Management Console (MMC) provides an interface that you can use to create, save, and open administrative tools, called snap-ins, that manage the hardware, software, and network components of Windows Server 2003. When you open an administrative tool in MMC, you can specify whether to apply the tool on the local computer or on a remote computer.

Use MMC for remote and local administration

To perform similar tasks on many servers, use MMC snap-ins. Most of the administrative tools that are provided with Windows Server 2003 family operating systems are MMC snap-ins that you can use to administer remote servers as well as your local computer.

Advantages of MMC snap-ins

The advantages of using MMC snap-ins are that you can:

- Create a console that contains the tools you use for the tasks you perform most often. For example, you use Computer Management to administer a remote server.

- Set the focus for a tool to any of the servers that you administer, and switch between servers and tools within a single MMC console. For example, you can use the Computer Management snap-in to view the performance of multiple remote servers.

Note If Windows Firewall is enabled on a remote server, port 445 must be opened to allow the administrative tools to work as expected for remote computer administration.

Practice: Introduction to Administering a Server

In this practice, you will:
* Create a custom MMC console to manage and monitor shared folders on multiple servers
* Use the runas command to open the MMC

Objective

In this practice, you will:

- Create a custom MMC console to manage and monitor shared folders on multiple servers.
- Use the **runas** command to open the MMC.

Instructions

Ensure that the DEN-DC1 and DEN-CL1 virtual machines are running.

Practice

▶ **Create a custom MMC console to manage and monitor shared folders on multiple servers**

1. Start the DEN-DC1 virtual machine. (Wait for the machine to be fully started before proceeding to step 2.)

2. Start the DEN-CL1 virtual machine.

3. With the active window being DEN-CL1 virtual machine, press <RIGHT> ALT+DELETE.

4. Log on to the domain as Paul West.

   a. In the **Log on to Windows** box, in the **User name** text box, type **Paul**.

   b. In the **Password** box, type **Pa$$w0rd**. (The 0 is a zero.)

   c. In the **Log on to** box, ensure that **Contoso** is displayed and then click **OK**.

5. On the **Start** menu, click **Run**.

6. In the **Run** dialog box, type **mmc** and then click **OK**.

7. In the **Console1** window, click the **File** menu and then click **Add/Remove Snap-in**.

8. In the **Add/Remove Snap-in** dialog box, click **Add**.

9. In the **Add Standalone Snap-in** dialog box, double-click the items to add as follows.

10. Add a Computer Management snap-in for the local machine.

    a. In the **Computer Management** dialog box, ensure that **Local computer** is selected.

    b. Click **Finish**.

11. Add a **Computer Management** snap-in for DEN-DC1.

    a. In the **Computer Management** dialog box select **Another computer** and type **DEN-DC1**.

    b. Click **Finish**.

12. In the **Add Standalone Snap-in** dialog box, click **Close**.

13. In the **Add/Remove Snap-in** dialog box, click **OK**.

14. In the Computer Management (Local) tree, expand **System Tools**, expand **Shared Folders**, and then click **Shares**. Notice that you are unable to view the shares.

15. In the Computer Management (DEN-DC1) tree, expand **System Tools**, expand **Shared Folders**, and then click **Shares**. Notice that you are unable to view the shares.

16. Save the console on the desktop as **MMC1**.

    a. Click the **File** menu and then click **Save As**.

    b. Click **Desktop**.

    c. In the **File name** box, type **MMC1**, and then click **Save**.

17. Close **MMC1**.

Practice

▶ **Use the runas command to open the MMC**

1. Right-click **MMC1** and then click **Run as**.

2. Click the option button next to **The following user** and, in the **User name** box, type **Contoso\Administrator** and, in the **Password box**, type **Pa$$w0rd**, and then click **OK**.

3. Verify that you can monitor shares on DEN-CL1 and DEN-DC1.

4. Close all open windows and log off of DEN-CL1.

Important Do not shut down the virtual machines.

Lesson: Configuring Remote Desktop to Administer a Server

* What Is Remote Desktop for Administration?
* Why Use Remote Desktop for Administration?
* What Are the Requirements for Remote Desktop Service?
* What Are Client Preferences for Remote Desktop Connection?
* Remote Desktop Connection vs. Remote Desktops
* Guidelines for Using Remote Administration Tools
* Practice: Configuring Remote Desktop to Administer a Server

Introduction

This lesson explains how to configure Remote Desktop for Administration and how to configure the client to allow access to the servers by using Remote Desktop for Administration. This lesson also describes how to establish the connection between the administrator's computer and the server.

Lesson objectives

After completing this lesson, you will be able to:

- Describe Remote Desktop for Administration and explain how it works.
- List the uses for Remote Desktop for Administration.
- List the requirements for Remote Desktop Service.
- Explain client preferences for Remote Desktop.
- Explain the differences between Remote Desktops and Remote Desktop Connections.
- Apply guidelines for using Remote Administration tools.
- Enable and use Remote Desktop.

What Is Remote Desktop for Administration?

| Introduction | By using Remote Desktop for Administration, you can manage one or more remote computers from a single location. In a large organization, you can use remote administration to centrally manage many computers that are located in other buildings or even in other cities. In a small organization, you can use remote administration to manage a single server that is located in an adjacent office. |

Introduction

By using Remote Desktop for Administration, you can manage one or more remote computers from a single location. In a large organization, you can use remote administration to centrally manage many computers that are located in other buildings or even in other cities. In a small organization, you can use remote administration to manage a single server that is located in an adjacent office.

Remote access to servers

Remote Desktop for Administration provides access to a server from a computer at another location by using Remote Desktop Protocol (RDP). RDP transmits the user interface to the client session, and it also transmits the keyboard and mouse clicks from the client to the server.

You can create up to two simultaneous remote connections. Each session to which you log on is independent of other client sessions and the server console session. When you use Remote Desktop for Administration to log on to the remote server, it is as if you are logged on to the server locally.

Remote Desktop Connection and Remote Desktops snap-in

Remote Desktop for Administration provides two tools that you can use to administer a remote server: Remote Desktop Connection and the Remote Desktops snap-in.

Each instance of the Remote Desktop Connection tool creates its own window and allows you to administer one remote server per window.

The Remote Desktops snap-in is useful for administrators who remotely administer multiple servers or for administrators who must connect to the console session remotely. The Remote Desktops snap-in displays a split window with a console tree on the left and remote connection information in the details pane on the right.

Remote Desktops allows no more than two desktop connections to the server at one time.

Note   To allow more than two Remote Desktop connections, you must install Terminal Services. For more information about Terminal Services, see the white paper, *Technical Overview of Terminal Services*, under **Additional Reading** on the Student Materials compact disc.

Remote Desktop Service

Remote Desktop Service provides server access. It is installed with Windows Server 2003 and must be enabled before you can configure Remote Desktop Administration.

Note   If Windows Firewall is enabled on the remote server, port 3389 must be open for Remote Desktop clients to be able to connect to the server.

Why Use Remote Desktop for Administration?

- ✦ **Provide remote access to most configuration settings**
- ✦ **Diagnose a problem and test multiple solutions quickly**
- ✦ **Allow access to servers from anywhere in the world**
- ✦ **Perform time-consuming batch administrative jobs, such as tape backups**
- ✦ **Upgrade server applications and operating systems remotely**

Introduction

Remote Desktop for Administration is a convenient and efficient service that can greatly reduce the overhead that is associated with remote administration. For example, Remote Desktop for Administration allows multiple systems administrators to manage remote servers.

Remote sessions

Remote Desktop for Administration allows you either to start a new remote session on a server or to remotely take over the console session on a server. However, there can be only one console session running on a server at one time. If you log on to the console remotely while another administrator is logged on to the console session, the first administrator is locked out.

Note System messages that are sent to the console are displayed at the console session and not at the other remote sessions.

Run earlier versions of Windows

By using Remote Desktop Connection, systems administrators can also fully manage computers that are running Windows Server 2003 family operating systems from computers that are running earlier versions of Windows.

Access to configuration settings

Remote Desktop for Administration is useful because it provides remote access to most configuration settings, including Control Panel, which usually cannot be configured remotely.

By using a Remote Desktop session, you can access MMC, Active Directory, Microsoft Systems Management Server, network configuration tools, and most other administrative tools.

Multiple uses

Using Remote Desktop for Administration can help you diagnose a problem and test multiple solutions quickly.

You can access the servers from anywhere in the world by using a wide-area network (WAN), a virtual private network (VPN), or a dial-up connection. When you run a time-consuming batch administrative job, such as a tape backup, you can start the job, disconnect from the corporate network, and later reconnect to check progress.

You can use Remote Desktop for Administration to upgrade server applications remotely and to perform tasks that are not usually possible unless you are working at the console.

Administrative tasks are quicker and more intuitive than using command-line utilities, although it is still possible to open a command prompt.

What Are the Requirements for Remote Desktop Service?

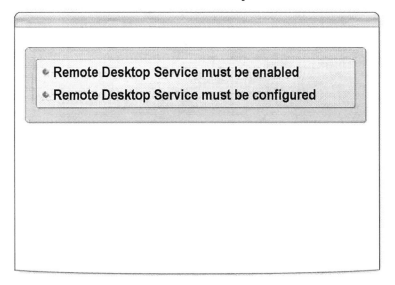

• Remote Desktop Service must be enabled
• Remote Desktop Service must be configured

Introduction

Clients running Remote Desktop Connection or Remote Desktops connect to the Remote Desktop Service on the remote server. Understanding how to enable and configure Remote Desktop Service is essential for remote administration.

Remote Desktop Service configuration

Remote Desktop Service must be enabled locally on the remote server by a systems administrator who is working at the console. The systems administrator must have the appropriate permissions to administer the computer. By default, members of the local Administrators group have remote connection privileges to the remote server.

The built-in domain local group Remote Desktop Users is assigned the right to log on to servers in the domain remotely through Remote Desktop. By default, this group has no members. If any user that is not a member of the Administrators group needs to use Remote Desktop for Administration then add them to this group.

Remote Desktop Service is enabled on the **Remote** tab of System Properties by selecting the **Allow users to connect remotely to this computer** check box.

What Are Client Preferences for Remote Desktop Connection?

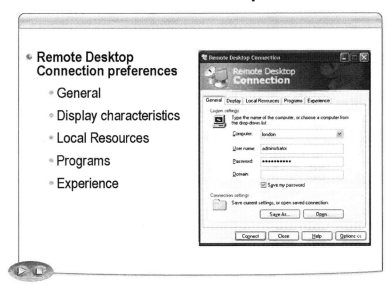

Introduction

To configure your remote desktop connection, you must set up client preferences. To do this, use the Remote Desktop Connection interface to configure the information about the connection and the client computer.

General

Use the **General** tab to provide information that is required for automatic logon to the remote server. This information includes the name of the server, the user name and password, and the domain name. If you save your password and connection settings, on later visits you can save time by opening a saved connection.

Display

Use the **Display** tab to change the screen size and color settings of the remote desktop and to hide or display the connection bar in full-screen mode.

Local Resources

Use the **Local Resources** tab to allow or restrict remote desktop access to the disk drives, serial ports, printers, sound, or Windows key combinations on your local computer. Allowing access from the remote desktop is called *resource redirection*. When you allow the remote desktop to have access to these resources, the remote desktop can use the resources for the duration of the session.

If you choose to make your local disk drive available to the remote desktop, easy access to files to or from the remote is the benefit. Conversely, the remote desktop has access to the contents of your local disk drive. If this access is not appropriate, you can clear the **Disk drives** check box to keep your local disk drive from being redirected to the remote desktop.

Programs

Use the **Programs** tab to specify that a program starts upon connection to the remote server.

Experience

Use the **Experience** tab to improve the performance of your remote server connection by allowing certain characteristics of the remote Windows session, such as the Desktop background, to appear as if they are enabled on the remote computer. You can also improve the performance of your connection by selecting a faster connection speed. The default connection speed, 56 kilobits per second (Kbps), offers good performance for most networks. Use the faster speed settings to enable richer graphical features, such as desktop wallpaper or menu sliding and fading.

Remote Desktop Connection vs. Remote Desktops

Service	Functions
Remote Desktop Connection	• Connects to one server per instance • Displays connections full screen or in a window • Opens a remote server session by default
Remote Desktops	• Connects to multiple servers simultaneously • Displays connections in the MMC console • Opens a console session by default

Introduction

Windows Server 2003 comes with two clients that allow administrators to connect to the remote desktop:

- Remote Desktop Connection
- Remote Desktops snap-in

Remote Desktop Connection

Using Remote Desktop Connection, you can connect to one server. You can run multiple copies of Remote Desktop Connection to connect to multiple servers, but you must switch between Remote Desktop Connection sessions to manage each server. Each connection can be displayed full screen or in a window.

When you connect to a server using Remote Desktop Connection, you will open a remote session by default.

Remote Desktops snap-in

You can use the Remote Desktops snap-in to connect to multiple servers simultaneously. Each connection is displayed in an MMC console. The console tree displays the name of the server and the details pane displays the remote session.

When you connect to a server by using Remote Desktops, the console session opens by default.

Use the command line tool

You can also connect to the console session on a remote server by using the **Run** command and the **mstsc** command-line tool with the **/console** option. Command-line options for **mstsc** can be included as part of the target in a shortcut.

For example, you can use the command **Mstsc /console /v:DEN-DC1 /w:800 /h:600** to open a remote console connection to DEN-DC1 using a window size of 800 by 600.

See the following table for common **mstsc** command-line options.

Switch	Description
ConnectionFile	**Specifies the name of an .rdp file for the connection.**
/v:*server*	**Specifies the remote computer to which you want to connect.**
/console	**Connects to the console session of the specified Windows Server 2003 server.**
/f	**Starts Remote Desktop connection in full-screen mode.**
/w:*width* /h:*height*	**Specifies the dimensions of the Remote Desktop Screen.**
/?	**Displays help for mstsc.**

Guidelines for Using Remote Administration Tools

Tool	Use to:
Computer Management	Manage and monitor server: •Events •Shared folders •Data storage •Start and stop services
Remote Desktop for Administration	Perform any administrative task that is possible at the server console

Introduction

Windows Server 2003 operating systems provide several tools that support remote location server management. These tools expand your flexibility because you can work as though you are physically present at each server in your organization. By understanding the functions of each tool, you can choose the most appropriate one for your remote administration tasks.

Computer Management tool tasks

The tasks that you can perform by using the Computer Management tool in remote administration are described in the following table.

Application	Task
Server configuration	Manage and monitor shared folders
Accounts	Modify users and groups
Network connectivity	Monitor events
	Manage and monitor performance logs and alerts
	Start and stop services
Data storage	Manage data storage

Important   With the Computer Management MMC, you do not need to be a local administrator on the server you are administering. You only need to have permissions to perform the specific tasks that you need to perform. To use Remote Desktop for Administration, you must have access to connect to the remote desktop on each server. By default, only members of the Administrators group and the Remote Desktop Users groups have the required permissions.

Remote Desktop for Administration tasks

The following table describes the use of each Remote Desktop for Administration tool.

Application	Task
Software applications	Install software applications
Server configuration	Defragment a disk
	Domain controller promotion/demotion
	Modify Microsoft .NET Framework configuration
	Modify folder options
Device drivers	Modify device drivers
Update software	Install service packs
	Install hotfixes
	Update system management properties
Desktop options	Modify date and time
	Modify display settings
	Modify fonts
	Modify regional and language settings
	Modify Distributed File System (DFS) services
Hardware configurations	Modify keyboard options
	Modify mouse options
	Modify modem options
	Modify power options
	Modify printer options
	Add and remove printers
Network connectivity	Modify Internet options
	Modify network connection configuration
	Monitor network connections
	Modify accessibility options
	Modify Internet Information Services (IIS) settings
Schedule tasks	Modify scheduled tasks
Accounts	Modify system options
	Modify user and group accounts
Licensing and certificate	Modify licensing
	Modify certificates
Remote services	Modify Component Services
	Modify Data Sources Open Database Connectivity (ODBC)
	Configure and enable Routing and Remote Access
	Modify Terminal Services
Data storage	Manage data storage

Practice: Configuring Remote Desktop to Administer a Server

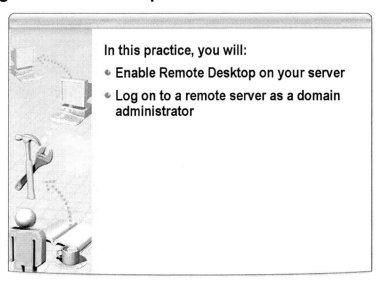

In this practice, you will:
- Enable Remote Desktop on your server
- Log on to a remote server as a domain administrator

Objective

In this practice, you will:

- Enable Remote Desktop on your server.
- Log on to a remote server as a domain administrator.

Instructions

Ensure that the DEN-DC1 and DEN-CL1 virtual machines are running.

Practice

▶ **Enable Remote Desktop on your server**

1. Make sure that the DEN-DC1 virtual machine is the active Window. Press <RIGHT>ALT+DELETE.

2. Log on to the domain as **Administrator** with the password of **Pa$$w0rd**.

3. Click **Start**, right-click **My Computer**, and then click **Properties**.

4. On the **Remote** tab, in the **Remote Desktop** box, select the **Enable Remote Desktop on this computer** check box. Click **OK** at the Remote Sessions dialog box.

5. Click **OK** to close all dialog boxes.

Practice

▶ **Log on to a remote server as a domain administrator**

1. Make sure that the DEN-CL1 virtual machine is the active window.

2. Log on as **Paul** with a password of **Pa$$w0rd**.

3. Click the **Start** menu, point to **All Programs**, point to **Accessories**, point to **Communications**, and then click **Remote Desktop Connection**.

   Alternately, you can open a command prompt and use the **mstsc** command to connect to DEN-DC1:

   mstsc /v:DEN-DC1 /f

4. Connect to the DEN-DC1 computer using the following parameters:

User name	Administrator
Password	Pa$$w0rd
Domain	Contoso

5. Verify that DEN-DC1 appears at the top of the screen.

6. Log off the remote computer.

7. Close all windows and log off of DEN-CL1 and DEN-DC1.

Important   Do not shut down the virtual machines.

Lesson: Managing Remote Desktop Connections

- What Are Timeout Settings for Remote Desktop Connections?
- What Is Terminal Services Manager?
- Best Practices for Remote Administration
- Practice: Managing Remote Desktop Connections

Introduction

As a systems administrator, you must monitor users, sessions, and applications on the remote server and perform various tasks to manage the server connection. In this lesson, you will learn the importance of managing Remote Desktop Connection and learn how to terminate sessions that are no longer in use.

Lesson objectives

After completing this lesson, you will be able to:

- Explain timeout settings in Terminal Services Configuration.
- Explain Terminal Services Manager and when it is used.
- Describe best practices for remote administration.
- Manage and monitor remote desktop connections.

What Are Timeout Settings for Remote Desktop Connections?

* Remote connections consume valuable server resources
* Use timeout settings to preserve server resources

Timeout Settings	Description
End a disconnected session	Forces a user to log off after disconnecting
Active session limit	Disconnects the user after the time limit is exceeded
Idle session limit	Disconnects the user after the amount of idle time is exceeded

Introduction

Each Remote Desktop connection consumes valuable server resources. To ensure that resources are properly used, administrators should configure timeout settings for Remote Desktop connections.

Establish timeout sessions

You must establish timeout sessions for these connections because as long as a session is active, it continues to consume valuable server resources. When a session is disconnected but not logged off, that session is using one of two available connections to the server.

Log off a session

Logging off from a session ends the session that is running on the server. Any applications that are running in the session are closed, and unsaved data is lost.

Disconnect a session

After you establish a connection with a remote server, the connection remains open until you log off. When you disconnect from a session, the session continues to run on the server. The user can log on to the server and resume the session. The session remains open until the user logs off, until an administrator closes it, or until the timeout setting is reached.

Timeout options

Use Terminal Services Configuration to set the appropriate timeouts. The following timeout options are available when viewing the **Sessions** tab in the properties of **RDP-Tcp**:

- *End a disconnected session.* Allows you to set the maximum amount of time that a disconnected session remains open on a server.

- *Active session limit.* Allows you to set the maximum amount of time that a user's session can remain active on the server.

- *Idle session limit.* Allows you to set the length of time that a session can be idle before it is logged off.

By default the timeout options are configured per user in the Properties of each user. To override the user settings and use server based timeout options select the **Override user settings** check box. Group Policy can also be used to configure the timeout options for users or servers.

What Is Terminal Services Manager?

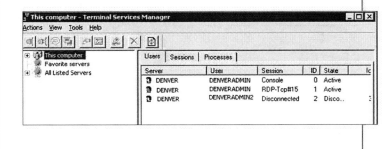

- Monitors user sessions
- Manually forces user logoff or session disconnect
- You can oversee all users and sessions on a server from one location

Introduction	You can use Terminal Services Manager to view information about Remote Desktop sessions on your server. Use this tool to monitor users and sessions on each server and to manage disconnected sessions from the remote server.
Obtain administrative information	Use Terminal Services Manager to obtain administrative information about the established Remote Desktop sessions. You can oversee all users and sessions on a terminal server from one location.
Monitor disconnected sessions	Using Terminal Services Manager, you can view the disconnected sessions on the server. Disconnected sessions display the word "Disconnected" under the Session and the State columns.

Important A disconnected session must be logged off in order to terminate it. It is important to log off all sessions when they are no longer in use, so that the limited number of remote connections can be used most efficiently.

Log off disconnected sessions	The **Log Off** command enables you to log off a user from a session on the server. Be aware that logging off a user without warning can result in loss of data at the user's session. When you log off a user, all processes end, and the session is deleted from the server.

Best Practices for Remote Administration

Coordinate remote administration tasks with other administrators

Use Terminal Services for application sharing

Configure the Remote Desktop session to disconnect when connection is broken

Configure disconnect and reset timeouts

Avoid tasks that require reboots

Avoid relying on server console messages

Introduction

Use the following best practices for Remote Administration.

Coordinate remote administration tasks with other administrators

The Remote Desktop feature of Windows Server 2003 is not meant to provide a managed multi-user experience. Using the two remote connections plus the console can implement a collaborative operation, but it is not designed to support general access by multiple simultaneous administrators. In particular, ensure that administrators do not run potentially destructive applications at the same time. For example, two administrators trying to reconfigure the disk subsystem can undermine each other's work, or even worse, destroy data. Use the Terminal Services Manager tool or the query user command line utility to check for the presence of other administrators.

Use Terminal Services for application sharing

Many general office applications require special installation, install scripts, or environment management to perform well in a remote session. Terminal Services provides these when you install Terminal Server, but they are not available for Remote Desktop for Administration. For general desktop and application remote access requirements, use a dedicated server with Terminal Server installed.

Configure the Remote Desktop session to disconnect when connection is broken

This is the default setting, and is especially important if you perform system updates over unreliable network connections. If a session is interrupted due to a network problem, the session goes into a disconnected state and continues executing the processes that were running before the interruption occurred. If the session is configured to reset when the connection breaks, all processes running in that session will stop, this is similar to stopping an application by using End Task.

Configure disconnect and reset timeouts

Because it is not possible to have more than two remote sessions, remote administrators might be locked out of a server if two remote sessions (using different user accounts) are in either an active or disconnected state. When configuring disconnect timeouts, it is critical that sessions that are disconnected do not get reset prematurely. If disconnected sessions are reset too quickly then minor network interruptions may stop lengthy tasks that are in progress, such as disk defragmentation or batch scripts.

Avoid tasks that require reboots

Some tasks, for example system upgrades and domain controller promotion, require reboots at their completion. These tasks work correctly from within a Remote Desktop session, but you should be aware that something as simple as a floppy disk in the drive or a bad boot sector on the disk could prevent the server from restarting. Therefore, it is advisable not to remotely reboot mission-critical servers unless you have the ability to physically intervene at the server if a problem occurs.

Avoid relying on server console messages

It is not possible to see server console messages when logging on using Terminal Services unless you are connected to the console session. Therefore, it is good practice to check the Server event logs, rather than rely on a system pop-up.

Practice: Managing Remote Desktop Connections

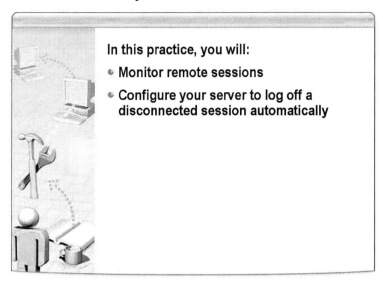

In this practice, you will:

● Monitor remote sessions

● Configure your server to log off a disconnected session automatically

Objective

In this practice, you will:

■ Monitor remote sessions.

■ Configure your server to log off a disconnected session automatically.

Instructions

Ensure that the DEN-DC1 and DEN-CL1 virtual machines are running.

Practice

▶ **Monitor remote sessions**

1. On DEN-CL1, log on as **Paul** with a password of **Pa$$w0rd**.

2. On the **Start** menu, point to **All Programs**, point to **Accessories**, point to **Communications**, and then click **Remote Desktop Connection**.

3. Connect to the DEN-DC1 computer using the following parameters:

User name	Administrator
Password	Pa$$w0rd
Domain	Contoso

4. Verify that DEN-DC1 appears at the top of the screen.

5. Close the Remote Desktop window without logging off. Click **OK** in the **Disconnect Windows session** dialog box.

6. Switch to the DEN-DC1 virtual machine.

7. Log on as **Administrator** with a password of **Pa$$w0rd**.

8. Click **Start**, point to **Administrative Tools**, and then click **Terminal Services Manager**.

9. If a **Terminal Services Manager** message box appears, click **In the future, do not show this message**, and then click **OK**.

10. Right-click the disconnected session, and then click **Log Off**. Click **OK**.

11. Close Terminal Services Manager.

▶ **Configure your server to log off a disconnected session automatically**

1. Click **Start**, point to **Administrative Tools** and then click **Terminal Services Configuration**.

2. Right-click **RDP-Tcp** and then click **Properties**.

3. On the **Sessions** tab, click the **Override user settngs** check box, next to **End a disconnected session**, select **1 minute**, and then click **OK**.

4. Close Terminal Services Configuration.

5. Switch to the DEN-CL1 virtual machine.

6. On the **Start** menu, point to **All Programs**, point to **Accessories**, point to **Communications**, and then click **Remote Desktop Connection**.

7. Connect to the DEN-DC1 computer using the following parameters:

User name	Administrator
Password	Pa$$w0rd
Domain	Contoso

8. Verify that DEN-DC1 appears at the top of the screen.

9. Close the Remote Desktop window without logging off. Click **OK** in the **Disconnect Windows session** dialog box.

10. Switch to the DEN-DC1 virtual machine.

11. Click **Start**, point to **Administrative Tools**, and then click **Terminal Services Manager**.

12. View the disconnected session until it is removed in one minute.

13. Close Terminal Services Manager.

14. Log off of DEN-DC1 and DEN-CL1.

▶ **To prepare for the next lab**

• Start the DEN-SRV1 virtual machine.

Important Do not shut down the virtual machines.

Lab: Preparing to Administer a Server

In this lab, you will:

* Enable Remote Desktop
* Create a shared folder on a remote computer
* Connect to a remote console session
* Create runas shortcuts for administrative tools

Objectives

After completing this lab, you will be able to:

- Enable remote desktop.
- Create a shared folder on a remote computer.
- Connect to a remote console session.
- Create **runas** shortcuts for administrative tools.

Instructions

Ensure that the DEN-DC1, DEN-SRV1 and DEN-CL1 virtual machines are running.

Scenario

You are a systems administrator for Contoso, Ltd. You want to configure a remote console session so that you can use your workstation to view the consoles of both DEN-DC1 and DEN-SRV1. You will also configure shortcuts for Administrative tools that run as Domain Administrator on DEN-SRV1.

Estimated time to complete this lab: 30 minutes

Exercise 1
Enabling Remote Desktop

You will enable Remote Desktop on DEN-SRV1 for remote administration.

Tasks	Specific instructions
1. Log on to DEN-SRV1 as domain Administrator.	■ On DEN-SRV1, press\<RIGHT>ALT+DELETE and log on as **Administrator** with a password of **Pa$$w0rd**.
2. Enable Remote Desktop.	a. Click **Start**, right-click **My Computer** and then click **Properties**. b. Click the Remote tab and then check the **Enable Remote Desktop on this computer** check box.

Exercise 2
Creating a Shared Folder on a Remote Computer

In this exercise, you will create a shared folder on a remote computer by using Computer Management and Remote Desktop Connection.

Tasks	Specific instructions
1. Log on to DEN-CL1 as Paul.	▪ Press <RIGHT>ALT+DELETE and log on as **Paul** with a password of **Pa$$w0rd**.
2. Create a shared folder on DEN-DC1 using MMC1.	a. Use **Run as** to start MMC1 as Contoso\Administrator. b. Under Computer Management (DEN-DC1), click **Shares**. c. Create and share C:\DATA1. d. Configure Administrators to have full access and other users to have read-only access.
3. Create a shared folder on DEN-DC1 using Remote Desktop Connection.	a. Open Remote Desktop Connection and connect to DEN-DC1 as administrator. b. Open Computer Management on the remote computer. c. Create and share C:\DATA2. d. Configure Administrators to have full access and other users to have read-only access.
4. Log off from the remote connection.	▪ Log off from the remote connection.

Exercise 3
Connecting to a Remote Console Session

In this exercise, you will connect to a remote console session by using Remote Desktop Connection.

Tasks	Specific instructions
1. Open Task Manager on DEN-SRV1.	a. Switch to DEN-SRV1. b. Right-click the task bar and then click **Task Manager**.
2. Use Remote Desktop Connection on DEN-CL1 to view the console on the DEN-SRV1 computer.	a. Switch to DEN-CL1. b. Run **MSTSC.exe** with the **/console** switch. c. Log on to the DEN-SRV1 console as **Administrator** with the password of **Pa$$w0rd**.
❓ What happens to the DEN-SRV1 virtual machine while you are viewing the console session from DEN-CL1?	
3. Close Task Manager through Remote Desktop Connection.	a. In the DEN-SRV1 remote window, close **Task Manager**. b. Log off of the remote DEN-SRV1 session. c. Close all windows on DEN-CL1 and then log off.

Exercise 4
Creating runas Shortcuts to Administrative Tools

In this exercise, you will create shortcuts to commonly used administrative tools.

Tasks	Specific instructions
1. On DEN-SRV1, create a shortcut to Computer Management.	a. Log on to DEN-SRV1 as **Administrator** with the password of **Pa$$w0rd**. b. On the desktop create a shortcut to Computer Management using the following: **runas/user:contoso\administrator** **"mmc %windir%\system32\compmgmt.msc"**
2. Create a shortcut to Active Directory Users and Computers.	▪ On the desktop create a shortcut to Active Directory Users and Computers using the following: **runas/user:contoso\administrator** **"mmc %windir%\system32\dsa.msc"**
3. Test each shortcut.	▪ lTest each shortcut and verify that the correct tool appears.
4. Complete the lab exercise.	a. Close all programs and shut down all computers. Do not save changes. b. To prepare for the next module, start the DEN-DC1 and DEN-SRV1 virtual computers.

Module 10: Preparing to Monitor Server Performance

Contents

Overview

* Introduction to Monitoring Server Performance
* Performing Real-Time and Logged Monitoring
* Configuring and Managing Counter Logs
* Configuring Alerts

Introduction

Monitoring server performance is an important part of maintaining and administering an operating system. Routine performance monitoring ensures that you have up-to-date information on computer operation. Performance monitoring also provides data that you can use to predict growth and assess how proposed system configuration changes will affect system operation.

Objectives

After completing this module, you will be able to:

■ Establish a performance baseline.

■ Perform real-time and logged monitoring.

■ Configure and manage counter logs.

■ Configure alerts.

Lesson: Introduction to Monitoring Server Performance

* Why Monitor Performance?
* Multimedia: Creating a Performance Baseline
* Guidelines for Establishing a Baseline

Introduction

This lesson explains the concept of performance monitoring, a baseline, performance objects, and counters. It also describes how to establish a performance baseline.

Lesson objectives

After completing this lesson, you will be able to:

- Explain why administrators monitor performance.
- Explain what a baseline is and when to create one.
- Explain the guidelines for establishing a baseline.

Why Monitor Performance?

* By monitoring performance, you obtain data that you
  can use to:
    * Understand workload and its effect on
      system resources
    * Identify resource-use trends
    * Test proposed configuration changes
    * Diagnose and optimize the system
* Uncover bottlenecks

Introduction

Monitoring performance is a necessary part of preventive maintenance for your server. By routinely monitoring the performance of your server over periods ranging from days to weeks to months, you can establish a baseline for server performance. This information will provide comparative data that will support system analysis and problem solving.

Why monitor performance?

You use performance data to:

- Understand your workload characteristics and their corresponding effect on your system's resources.

- Observe changes and trends in workload characteristics and resource usage so you can plan for future upgrades.

- Monitor the effects of changes or other performance tuning efforts.

- Diagnose problems.

- Identify components or processes to be optimized optimization.

Analysis of performance data and bottlenecks

Analysis of performance data can reveal problems, such as excessive demand on certain resources that results in bottlenecks. A bottleneck exists when the performance of a resource adversely affects the performance of the whole system. Demand on the single resource may become excessive enough to cause a bottleneck of the four subsystems: memory, processor, disk, and network.

Some of the reasons that bottlenecks occur are:

- Subsystems are insufficient, so additional or upgraded components are required. For example, insufficient memory is a common cause of bottleneck.

- Subsystems are not sharing workloads evenly and need to be balanced. For example, an older network card that is installed on a new server may cause a bottleneck.

- A subsystem is malfunctioning and needs to be replaced. For example, abnormally low throughput on a network card may indicate that it is failing.

- A program is monopolizing a particular resource. For example, a program that was written by a consultant may not be sharing memory correctly.

- A subsystem is incorrectly configured. For example, an older multispeed network card may be configured for 10 megabits per second (Mbps) when it should be set to 100 Mbps.

Multimedia: Creating a Performance Baseline

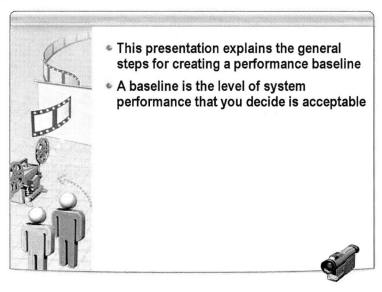

File location

To view the *Creating a Performance Baseline* presentation, open the Web page on the Student Materials compact disc, click **Multimedia**, and then click the title of the presentation.

Objectives

After completing this presentation you will be able to:

- Explain the purpose of a baseline.
- Describe how to use the Performance console.

Key points

Key points from the presentation are summarized in the following list:

- Baseline

   Take samples of counter values every 30 to 45 minutes for a week, during peak, low, and normal operations.

- General steps for creating a baseline

   a. Identify resources

   b. Capture data

   c. Store data

- Four major system resources for performance baselines

   • Memory

   • Processor

   • Physical disk

   • Network

- Performance object

   A performance object is the data generated by a system component or resource. Each performance object provides counters, which represent data about specific aspects of system performance. Performance objects can have multiple instances.

Guidelines for Establishing a Baseline

Introduction

You derive a baseline measurement from a collection of data over an extended period, during varying but typical workloads and network connections. The baseline is a measure of specified resource behavior during normal activity.

Factors to consider when determining a baseline

You should consider the following factors when determining a baseline:

■ When you determine your baseline, it is important to know the type and timing of system load. This helps you associate kinds of load with resource usage and to determine whether the level of performance during those intervals is reasonable. Collect this performance data over an extended period of low, average, and peak usage, to understand acceptable system performance. This determination is your baseline.

Observing performance over time you might see a pattern of performance showing the normal impact of simultaneous logon or logoff (at shift change) or the predictable slowdown during system backup. From observed performance and an understanding of cause and effect, you can determine acceptable performance.

■ Baselines established early in the deployment phase support deployment problem solving.

Employing a baseline

You should consider the following factors when employing a baseline:

■ Establishing a baseline early helps you to quickly identify and resolve system bottlenecks.

■ Use your baseline to watch for long-term changes in usage patterns that require increased capacity.

Lesson: Performing Real-Time and Logged Monitoring

* What Is Real-Time and Logged Monitoring?
* What Is Task Manager?
* What Is the Performance Console?
* Why Monitor Servers Remotely?
* Practice: Performing Real-Time Monitoring

Introduction

The primary monitoring tools in Microsoft Windows Server 2003 are the Performance console and Task Manager.

This lesson describes how to perform monitoring by using Performance and Task Manager.

Lesson objectives

After completing this lesson, you will be able to:

- Explain real-time monitoring and logged monitoring.
- Describe Task Manager.
- Describe the Performance console.
- Explain the reasons for monitoring remote servers from a workstation.
- Monitor real-time performance.

What Is Real-Time and Logged Monitoring?

Real-Time Monitoring

- Monitors the system
- Processes and updates data from the operating system
- Documents the state of memory, processor, storage and network

Logged Monitoring

- Collects and stores data for a span of time
- Detects bottlenecks and records system changes
- Performed in Performance Logs and Alerts

Introduction

Administrators can use logged monitoring to monitor servers on a continuous basis. By configuring logged monitoring, you can establish a performance baseline and use trend analysis to identify server problems. For example, if users complain that an application server is gradually slowing down, you can check that server's log files to support problem analysis.

Administrators must also investigate specific problematic events. By enabling real-time monitoring, administrators can track events for analysis. For example, if a help-desk technician tells you that the printers attached to the print server are printing intermittently, a real-time monitor, such as Task Manager or System Monitor, will greatly aid investigation.

Real-time monitoring

With real-time monitoring, System Monitor processes and updates data counters as soon as the data is received from the operating system. You use real-time monitoring to establish the current state of the four subsystems: memory, processor, disk, and network. For example, if users complain about the slow response time of a client/server application in a situation that caused no previous problems, you can use System Monitor to diagnose the problem.

Logged monitoring

Logged monitoring involves collecting and storing data over time. Use the data to establish a baseline, detect bottlenecks, and recognize gradual system changes Use the Performance Logs and Alerts tool for logged monitoring.

Example of logged monitoring

For example, when your organization acquires a new server, to understand its capabilities, you can configure several counters to track memory usage, CPU usage, disk usage, and network usage. You can use the data that you collect to determine the normal range of counter values for your environment.

You can also set up logs to monitor events over time. This way, you can determine whether events such as backup, domain replication, or evenings and weekend remote connections contribute to server bottlenecks.

What Is Task Manager?

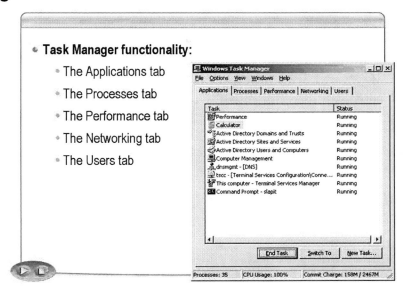

Introduction

Task Manager provides an overview of system activity and performance. It provides information about programs and processes that are running on your computer. It also displays the most commonly used performance measures for processes. You can use Task Manager to perform real-time monitoring.

Task Manager function

Use Task Manager to monitor key performance indicators:

- View open programs status and end programs that are not responding.

- Assess the activity of running processes with up to 15 parameters and view graphs and data about CPU and memory usage.

- View network status when network card is installed.

- See connected users, see what files they are working, and send messages to users.

Task Manager has five tabs:

Applications tab

The **Applications** tab displays the status of open programs. On this tab, you can end, switch to, or start a program.

Processes tab

The **Processes** tab displays information about active processes. For example, you can display information about CPU and memory usage, page faults, handle count, and other parameters.

Performance tab

The **Performance** tab displays a dynamic overview of your computer's performance, including:

- Graphs of CPU and memory usage.

- The number of handles, threads, and processes running on your computer.

- The amount, in kilobytes, of physical, kernel, and commit memory. Physical memory is total memory, kernel memory is the memory that the system kernel and device drivers use, and commit memory is the amount of memory that is allocated to programs and the operating system.

Networking tab

The **Networking** tab displays a graphic representation of network performance. It provides a simple, qualitative indication of the network (or networks) status. The **Networking** tab displays only if a network card is installed.

On this tab, you can view the quality and availability of your network connections.

Users tab

The **Users** tab displays the names of users who have a local or remote session running on the computer. **Client Name** specifies the name of the client computer that the session is started from if it is remote. **Session** is either a console or the name of an RDP session that can be managed in the Terminal Services Manager snap-in.

What Is the Performance Console?

* The Performance console contains System Monitor and Performance Logs and Alerts
* A tool for collecting real-time system performance data
* A tool for managing Logs and Alerts

Introduction

Windows Server 2003 provides the following tools as part of the Performance console for monitoring resource usage on your computer:

- System Monitor
- Performance Logs and Alerts

System Monitor capabilities

With System Monitor, you can collect and view system services hardware resources and the activity data.

With System Monitor you can collect and view the real-time performance data of local or remote computers.

To setup data collection, specify performance objects, performance counters, and performance object instances.

- A *performance object* is a collection of counters associated with a monitored resource or service.

- A *performance counter* is a data item that is associated with a performance object. For selected counters, System Monitor displays a value representing a specific aspect of performance that corresponds to a performance object.

- *Performance object instances* are multiples of the same object type. For example, if a system has multiple processors, the **Processor** object type has multiple instances.

View logged counter data

You can view logged counter data with System Monitor. You can also export logged data to spreadsheet or database for analysis and report generation.

Using System Monitor, you can create graphs, histograms, and reports of the performance counter data. The graph view (default) offers the widest choice of settings.

View	Description
Graph	Supports real-time analysis of system processes
	Employs a time line to display counter data
Histogram	Supports processor bottleneck detection
	Employs a bar chart to display one value per counter instance
Report	Supports counter numerical value monitoring
	Employs a table to display one value per counter instance

Performance Logs and Alerts capabilities

Performance Logs and Alerts support both local and remote computers. Use logging for detailed analysis and record-keeping. Retaining and analyzing log data that is collected over time can be helpful for capacity and upgrade planning.

Collect performance data

With Performance Logs and Alerts, you can collect performance data by using two types of logs: counter logs and trace logs. You can also set an alert on a counter that sends a message, runs a program, or starts a log when the counter's value exceeds or falls below a specified setting.

Define settings

Use Performance Logs and Alerts to define settings for counter logs, trace logs, and alerts. The details pane of the console window shows counter logs and alerts that you have created. You can define multiple counter logs or alerts to run simultaneously. Each counter log or alert represents a saved configuration that you define.

If you configure the log for automatic starting and stopping, a single log can generate many individual log data files. For example, if you generate a log file for each day's activity, one file closes at 11:59 P.M., and a file to record the next day's activity opens immediately after.

Other functions

Data that Performance Logs and Alerts collect can be viewed during collection as well as after collection. Collection occurs regardless of whether any user is logged on to the computer that is being monitored.

You can define start and stop times, file names, file sizes, and other parameters for automatic log generation. You can manage multiple logging sessions from a single console window.

Why Monitor Servers Remotely?

* Prevent performance data distortion
* Monitor multiple servers simultaneously

Why monitor a remote server from a workstation?

The additional load that Task Manager and Performance put on the server can cause misrepresentation of the data that you are collecting. By monitoring the server from a remote location, you reduce the likelihood of this misrepresentation occurring.

Also, administrators are often responsible for many servers making it impractical to monitor each individually.

Options in the Performance console for monitoring a remote server

The Performance console provides the following options that you can use to monitor a remote server:

- You can add objects or counters to a remote server. On the **General** tab, click **Add Objects** or **Add Counters**.

- You can log objects or counters from a computer regardless of where the service is run. Click **Select counter objects from computer** or **Select counters from computer**. Specify the name of the computer that you want to monitor, such as \\MyLogServer.

Counter availability

The counters for monitoring specific applications such as Exchange 2003 or SQL Server™ 2005 are installed on the server with the application. To use application specific counters when monitoring from a workstation, you must specifically install the counters on the workstation. Typically, counters are installed with application management and client tools.

Important If you plan to monitor remote computers, you must have been delegated the appropriate authority to gain access to them.

Practice: Performing Real-Time Monitoring

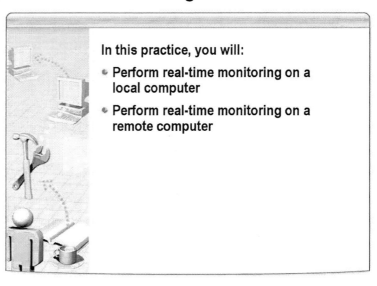

In this practice, you will:

* Perform real-time monitoring on a local computer
* Perform real-time monitoring on a remote computer

Objective

In this practice, you will:

- Perform real-time monitoring on a local computer.
- Perform real-time monitoring on a remote computer.

Instructions

Ensure that the DEN-DC1 and DEN-SRV1 virtual machines are running.

Practice

▶ **Perform real-time monitoring on a local computer**

1. On the DEN-DC1 virtual machine, log on as **Administrator** with a password of **Pa$$w0rd**.

2. Press <RIGHT>ALT+DELETE, and then click **Task Manager**.

3. Click the **Applications** tab. Notice that no applications are running.

4. Click **New Task**, and, in the **Open** box, type **calc** and then click **OK**. Notice that Calculator is now listed as an application.

5. Click the **Processes** tab and find calc.exe in the **Image Name** column. Notice the percentage of CPU utilization and memory usage.

6. Right-click **calc.exe** and then click **End Process**.

7. Click **Yes** to confirm ending the calc.exe process.

8. Click the **Performance** tab and view the level of CPU utilization and memory usage.

9. Close Task Manager.

▶ **Perform real-time monitoring on a remote computer**

1. On the DEN-DC1 virtual machine, click **Start**, point to **Administrative Tools**, and then click **Performance**. Notice that, by default, three counters are being monitored on the local computer: Memory:Pages/sec, PhysicalDisk:Avg. Disk Queue Length, and Processor:% Processor Time.

2. Click the graph and then press **CTRL+E** to create a new counter set (clear the existing counters).

3. Right-click the graph and then click **Add Counters**.

4. In the **Select counters from computer** box, type **DEN-SRV1**.

5. In the **Performance object** box, click **Processor**.

6. Click the **Select counters from list**, click **% Processor Time**, and then click **Add**.

7. In the **Performance object** box, click **Memory**.

8. Click the **Select counters from list**, click **Available MBytes**, and then click **Add**.

9. Click **Close**. Notice that the graph for both objects is fairly level, % Processor Time may show some small spikes in utilization.

10. On the DEN-SRV1 virtual machine, log in as **Administrator** with a password of **Pa$$w0rd**.

11. On the DEN-DC1 virtual machine, look at the changes in the graph. The % Processor Time spiked sharply and Available Mbytes has fallen as part of the logon process.

12. Close **Performance**.

Important   Do not shut down the virtual machines.

Lesson: Configuring and Managing Counter Logs

* What Is a Counter Log?
* Counter Log File Formats
* Why Schedule Counter Logs?
* Practice: Configuring and Managing Counter Logs

Introduction

Use counter logs to gather data about various aspects of performance objects. For example, for the **Memory** object, counter logs gather data about available memory, cache memory, and virtual memory. Counter logs are built into the operating system and continually capture data.

Lesson objectives

After completing this lesson, you will be able to:

- Define counter, counter log, and counter log data.
- Explain the counter log file formats.
- Explain the reasons for scheduling a counter log.
- Configure and manage counter logs.

What Is a Counter Log?

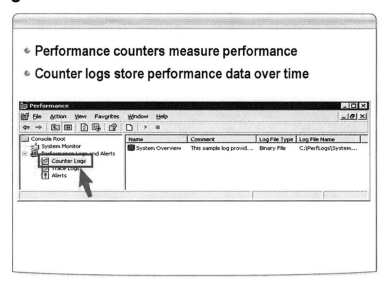

Introduction

Windows Server 2003 collects data about system resources, such as disks, memory, processors, and network components. This data is described as a performance object and is typically named for the component that generates the data. For example, the **Processor** object is a collection of performance data about the processors on your system.

Performance counter

A variety of performance objects are built into the operating system. Each performance object provides performance counters that represent data about specific aspects of a system or service. Counters are used to measure various aspects of performance. For example, the Pages/sec counter provided by the **Memory** object tracks the rate of memory paging.

Counter logs

Counter logs are counters that specify what data is stored in the log file. You use counter logs to select counters to collect performance data. You can use the Performance Logs and Alerts to create counter logs. In the interface, you select counter logs by using the **Counter Logs** option. The right pane of the Performance console window shows counter logs that you have created. You can define multiple counter logs to run simultaneously. Each counter log is a saved configuration that you define.

Counter log information in the Performance console

The following table describes the information about the counter logs that is provided by the columns in the right pane of the Performance console.

Column	Description
Name	The name of the counter log. It describes the type of data you are collecting or the condition you are monitoring.
Comment	Any descriptive information about the counter log.
Log File Type	The log file format that you define.
	For counter logs, this format can be binary, binary circular, text file (comma delimited), text file (tab delimited), or SQL.
Log File Name	The path and base file name that you defined for the files that are generated by this counter log. The base file name is used for automatically naming new files.

Counter log data

Counter log data is the information that you collect automatically from local or remote computers by configuring Performance Logs and Alerts.

Counter log data:

- Can be viewed by using System Monitor.
- Can be exported to spreadsheet programs or databases for analysis and generating reports.
- Is used to compare the values against the counter thresholds to verify that resource usage or other system activity is within acceptable limits.

Counter Log File Formats

Log File Format	Description	When to use
Text File (Comma delimited)	Comma-delimited log file (.csv)	Export to spreadsheet
Text File (Tab delimited)	Tab-delimited log file (.tsv)	Export to spreadsheet
Binary File	Sequential, binary-format log file (.blg)	Record intermittent data instances
Binary Circular File	Circular, binary-format log file (.blg)	Record continuously to same log file
SQL Database	Name SQL database and log set	Collect enterprise level performance data

The following table describes the log file formats that you can use to set file parameters for a counter log.

Log file format	Description	When to use
Text File (Comma delimited)	Defines a comma-delimited log file, with a .csv file extension.	Use this format, for example, to export the log data into a spreadsheet program.
Text File (Tab delimited)	Defines a tab-delimited log file, with a .tsv file extension.	Use this format, for example, to export the log data into a spreadsheet program.
Binary File	Defines a sequential, binary-format log file, with a .blg file extension. Only binary file formats can accommodate instances that are not persistent throughout the duration of the log.	Use this file format to record data instances that are intermittent—that is, stopping and resuming after the log begins to run. Use the **tracerpt** command-line tool to convert binary files into a comma-delimited log file.

(continued)

Log file format	Description	When to use
Binary Circular File	Defines a circular, binary-format log file, with a .blg file extension.	Use this file format to record data continuously to the same log file, overwriting previous records with new data when the file reaches its maximum size. Use the **tracerpt** command-line tool to convert binary files into a comma-delimited log file.
SQL Database	Defines the name of an existing SQL database and log set within the database where the performance data will be read or written.	Use this file format to collect performance data at an enterprise level rather than on a per-computer basis.

Use the text file format or the binary file format if you must export the data to a spreadsheet program later. The binary file format is more compact than the text file format, but you must convert it to the text file format before you export it to a spreadsheet. Use the **tracerpt** command-line tool to convert binary files into a comma-delimited log file. For example, type **tracerpt logfile.blg –o logfile.csv**.

Note Additional information about the **tracerpt** command-line tool can be found on the Tracerpt page of the Microsoft Windows XP Professional Product Documentation Web site.

Why Schedule Counter Logs?

Schedule counter logs to:

- Create a performance baseline
- Determine the effect of replication between domain controllers
- Identify bottlenecks resulting from morning login or evening remote access
- Monitor evening backups for bottleneck
- Scan for bottleneck related system slowdowns

Introduction

Imagine the cost of devoting staff to 24-hour system monitoring. Thankfully, this necessary task can be automated. You can schedule counter logs to create a performance baseline, look for bottlenecks, monitor system events, and collect information about how system events affect the server.

Why schedule counter logs?

You can schedule counter logs to:

- Create a performance baseline.

- Determine the effect on the overall system when replication occurs between domain controllers.

- Determine whether a bottleneck occurs when users log on in the morning.

- Determine whether a bottleneck occurs when users connect remotely in the evening.

- Determine whether Backup causes a bottleneck when it runs in the evening.

- Determine whether a bottleneck occurs during certain times of the day when users complain that the network slows down.

Practice: Configuring and Managing Counter Logs

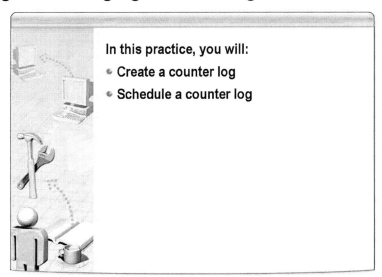

In this practice, you will:
- Create a counter log
- Schedule a counter log

Objective

In this practice, you will:

- Create a counter log.
- Schedule a counter log.

Instructions

Ensure that the DEN-DC1 virtual machine is running.

Practice

▶ **Create a counter log**

1. On the DEN-DC1 virtual machine, click **Start**, point to **Administrative Tools**, and then click **Performance**.
2. Expand **Performance Logs and Alerts** and click **Counter Logs**.
3. Right-click **Counter Logs** and click **New Log Settings**.
4. In the **Name** box, type **PracticeLog** and then click **OK**. Notice that the default location of the log is C:\PerfLogs.
5. Click **Add Counters**.
6. In the **Select counters from computer** box, type **\\DEN-DC1**.
7. In the **Performance object** box, click **Processor**.
8. Click **Select counters from** list, click **% Processor Time**, and then click **Add**.
9. Click **Close**.
10. In the **Interval** box, type **1**.
11. Click the **Log Files** tab.
12. In the **Log file type** box, click **Text File (Comma delimited)**, and then click **OK**.
13. Click **Yes** to create the C:\PerfLogs folder. Notice that PracticeLog has a green icon to indicate it is running.

14. After about one minute, right-click **PracticeLog** and then click **Stop**.

15. To view the contents of the counter log, open the file C:\perflogs\PracticeLog_000001 in Notepad. Notice that the log file has a header row that describes the contents of the file.

16. Close Notepad.

▶ **Schedule a counter log**

1. In **Performance**, right-click **PracticeLog** and then click **Properties**.

2. Click the **Schedule** tab.

3. In the **Stop log** area, click **After**, and set time to 1 minute.

4. In the **Start log** area, click **At**, and set the time to be 2 minutes from now.

5. Click **OK**.

6. Wait two minutes and notice that the icon beside PracticeLog turns green to indicate that it is active.

7. Wait one minute and notice that the icon beside PracticeLog turns red to indicate that it has stopped.

8. Close **Performance**.

Important   Do not shut down the virtual machines.

Lesson: Configuring Alerts

- What Is an Alert?
- Limitations of Alerts
- What Is Event Viewer?
- What Is EventCombMT?
- Practice: Configuring and Viewing Alerts

Introduction

Because administrators cannot constantly monitor all servers in the environment, administrators use alerts keep abreast of system performance that exceeds a set range. Performance Logs and Alerts are also used to collect hardware resource and system performance data.

Lesson objectives

After completing this lesson, you will be able to:

- Explain an alert.
- Explain limitations of alerts.
- Explain what Event Viewer is.
- Explain what EventCombMT is.
- Configure and view alerts.

What Is an Alert?

> * A feature that detects out of range values
> * A counter setting called a threshold
> * A mechanism that:
>   * Logs events
>   * May send a message
>   * May start a counter log
>   * May initiate a program
> * A measure based on baselines

Definition

An *alert* is a feature that detects when a predefined counter value exceeds or falls below a specified setting. The specified setting on the counter is called the *alert threshold*. An action to notify administrators or fix the problem is initiated when an alert is triggered.

Why use alerts?

By using the alert feature, you can define a counter value that triggers actions, such as sending a network message, running a program, or starting a log.

Alerts are useful if you are not actively monitoring a particular counter threshold value but want to be notified when it exceeds or falls below a specified setting so that you can investigate and determine the cause of the change. For example, you can set an alert to notify you when the number of failed logon attempts exceeds a specified number.

You may want to set alerts based on established performance baseline values for your system.

Functions of an alert

You can set an alert on a counter to perform the following functions:

- Make an entry in the application event log.

  For example, enable this option if you want a record of all the events that cause an alert.

- Start a log when the selected counter's value exceeds or falls below the alert threshold.

  For example, a burdened processor indicates a bottleneck, you set an alert to take affect when usage exceeds 85 percent.

- Send a message.

  For example, in the previous bullet, an alert takes effect at 85 percent processor usage, sending the administrator a report.

■ Run a program.

Enable this option if you want a program to run when an event occurs. For example, you may want to trigger database compaction when disk space is getting low.

Note   To send a message, the Messenger service must be running. This service is disabled by default in Windows Server 2003.

Limitations of Alerts

* Permissions constrain alert creation
* Dependent services constrain alert actions
    Example: Messenger service
* Faulty remote connections impair the reliability of alerts

Introduction

Alerts are useful because they are an active way to monitor what is happening on a server, but users need to be aware of their limitations.

Limitations of alerts

Alerts are also subject to limitations some important limitations:

- Security permissions

    Some users are unable to configure alerts. Creating an alert requires administrative permissions on the computer being monitored. When alerts are being configured by someone not logged in with an administrative account, alerts have an option to configure an account with administrative permissions in the **Run As** box.

- Dependent services

    The triggering of alerts is managed by the Performance Logs and Alerts Service, and this service has no dependencies. However the actions specified for an alert may have dependencies.

    For example, if you configure an alert to send a network message to the Administrator, this action is dependent upon the Messenger service. It must be running on the monitored server and on the administrator workstation to enable the message transmission.

- Network communication for remote monitoring

    We noted in an earlier module the benefits of remote performance monitoring, however, this strategy is limited by the quality of the network connection. If there are network communication problems then alerts may not be triggered by the remote server. In addition, if you are monitoring network performance and generating statistics, any connection problem that impedes transmission of data will affect the accuracy of recorded data.

What Is Event Viewer?

* A tool for viewing and configuring event logs
* A way to view the application log
* A collection of log files with a 16 MB default size
* Filter events based on type, source, computer, and time

What is Event Viewer?

With Event Viewer, you can monitor events recorded in event logs. Typically a computer stores events the Application, Security, and System logs. Additional event logs may be created, depending on the computer's role and the installed applications. For example, when you install the DNS service on a computer running Windows Server 2003, a DNS Server log is also created on the server.

Application log

The Application log contains events written by alerts that have been triggered by applications or services running on the computer. Using Event Viewer, you can:

- Configure log settings
- Filter events

Log settings

In the properties of the Application log, the **General** tab allows you to determine log-size limits, action when limits are reached, and clear the log.

The maximum size of the Application log should be high enough to assure important events are not missed. If the Application log size is too small, then a problem occurring on the weekend might fill the entire log and push out the original entries that may provide clues to the cause of the problem. The default application log size of 16 megabytes (MB) is sufficient for most situations.

You configure how events will be logged in the Application log when it has reached its maximum size. You can configure the application log to overwrite events, to only overwrite events older than seven days, or to never overwrite events. If a log is full and overwriting is constrained, no new events can be captured.

Filter events

An Application log may contain thousands of events. Filtering the Application log makes it easier to find relevant information, including alerts. You can configure Application log filtering based on:

- Event type
- Event source
- Computer
- Time

What Is EventCombMT?

* A utility for parsing event logs on multiple servers
* Searching can be based on:
    * Event ID
    * Event type
    * Source
    * Log
* Finds alerts on many servers quickly

What is EventCombMT?

EventCombMT is a multithreaded tool that parses event logs from many servers at the same time, spawning a separate thread of execution for each server that is defined in the search criteria.

Note   EventCombMT is included with the Windows Server 2003 Resource Kit. The Resource Kit tools can be downloaded from the Microsoft Download Center Web site.

Search capabilities

EventCombMT allows you to:

- Define either a single Event ID, or multiple Event IDs to search for.

    You can include a single event ID, or multiple event IDs separated by spaces.

- Define a range of Event IDs to search for.

    The endpoints are inclusive. For example, if you want to search for all events between and including Event ID 528 and Event ID 540, you would define the range as 528 > ID < 540. This feature is useful because most applications that write to the event log use a sequential range of events. This means you can easily get a list of all events generated by a particular application.

- Limit the search to specific event logs.

    You can choose to search the system, application, and security logs. If executed locally at a domain controller, you can also choose to search FRS, DNS and Active Directory® directory service logs.

- Limit the search to specific event message types.

    You can choose to limit the search to error, informational, warning, success audit, failure audit, or success events.

EventCombMT and alerts

An alert writes events to the local Application log. In a multiple-server scenario, it is tedious to check the Application log on each server daily. You can use EventCombMT to simultaneously search many servers for alerts.

Practice: Configuring and Viewing Alerts

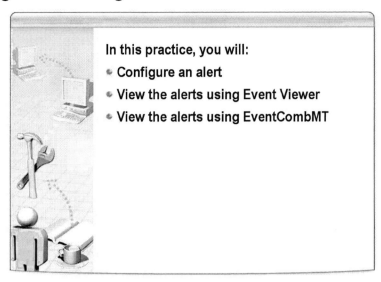

In this practice, you will:
* Configure an alert
* View the alerts using Event Viewer
* View the alerts using EventCombMT

Objective

In this practice, you will:

- Configure an alert.
- View the alerts using Event Viewer
- View the alerts using EventCombMT

Instructions

Ensure that the DEN-DC1 and DEN-SRV1 virtual machines are running.

Practice

▶ **Configure an alert**

1. On the DEN-DC1 virtual machine, click **Start**, point to **Administrative Tools**, and then click **Performance**.
2. Expand **Performance Logs and Alerts** and then click **Alerts**.
3. Right-click **Alerts** and then click **New Alert Settings**.
4. In the **Name** box, type **PracticeCPUAlert**, and then click **OK**.
5. Click **Add**.
6. In the **Select counters from computer** box, type **DEN-DC1**.
7. In the **Performance object** box, click **Processor**.
8. Click the **Select counters from** list, click **% Processor Time**, and then click **Add**.
9. Click **Close**.
10. In the **Limit** box, type **80**.
11. Click the **Action** tab. Notice that writing an alert to the Application log is selected by default.
12. Click the **General** tab.
13. Click **Add**.
14. In the **Select counters from computer** box, type **DEN-SRV1**.

15. In the **Performance object** box, click **Processor**.

16. Click the **Select counters from** list, click **% Processor Time**, and then click **Add**.

17. Click **Close**.

18. In the **Limit** box, type **80**.

19. In the **Run As** box, type **Administrator** and then click **Set Password**.

20. Enter **Pa$$w0rd** in both the **Password** and **Confirm Password** fields and then click **OK**.

21. Click the **Action** tab. Notice that writing an alert to the Application log is selected by default.

22. Click **OK**.

23. Close **Performance**.

24. Press <RIGHT>ALT+DELTE, and then click **Task Manager**.

25. Click the **Performance** tab.

26. Click **Start**, click **Run**, type **D:\2275\Practices\Mod02 \CPULoop.bat**, and then click **OK**. Notice that the CPU Usage rises above 80 percent.

27. After approximately one minute, close the cmd window.

28. Close **Task Manager**.

▶ **View the alerts using Event Viewer**

1. On the DEN-DC1 virtual machine, click **Start**, point to **Administrative Tools**, and then click **Event Viewer**.

2. In the left pane, click **Application**.

3. There are several **Information** events with a source of SysmonLog. Double-click one of them.

4. Read the description portion of the event. It indicates that the \\DEN-DC1\Processor(_Total)\%Processor Time counter was over 80 percent.

5. Click **Cancel** and then close Event Viewer.

▶ **View the alerts using EventCombMT**

1. On the DEN-SRV1 virtual machine, click **Start**, click **Run**, type **\\DEN-DC1\D$\2275\Practices\Mod02\cpuloop.bat**, and then click **OK**. Click **Run** at the security warning.

2. After approximately one minute, close the cmd window.

3. On DEN-DC1, click **Start**, click **Run** and then, in the **Run** dialog box, type **D:\2275\Practices\Mod02\eventcombMT.exe**. Click **OK**.

4. Click **OK** to close the **Simple Instructions** dialog box.

5. Ensure that **contoso.msft** is listed in the **Domain** box.

6. Right-click the text box below **Select To Search/Right Click to Add**. A context menu appears.

7. Click **Get DCs in Domain**. DEN-DC1 appears in the list.

8. In the **Choose Log Files to search** section, clear the **System** check box and select **Application**.

9. Select the **Error, Informational,** and **Warning Event Types** check boxes.

10. In the box before > **ID** <, type **2031**. In the box after > **ID** <, type **2037**.

11. Ensure that **ALL SOURCES** is displayed.

12. Click **DEN-DC1** and then click **Search**.

13. Double-click **EventCombMT.txt** and maximize Notepad. Notice that the file includes event information for DEN-DC1.

14. Close Notepad.

15. Double-click **DEN-DC1-Application_LOG.txt** to view the events recorded.

16. Close Notepad and Windows Explorer.

17. In the EventCombMT utility, click the **Searches** menu, and then click **Save This Search**.

18. Type **CPU Usage**, and then click **OK**.

▶ **To prepare for the next module**

1. Close all programs and shut down all computers. Do not save changes.

2. To prepare for the next module, start the DEN-DC1 virtual computer.

Lab: Preparing to Monitor Server Performance

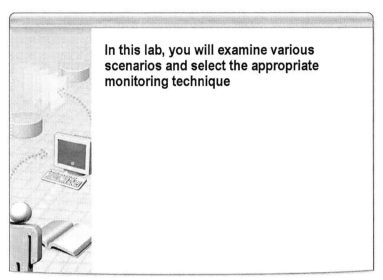

In this lab, you will examine various scenarios and select the appropriate monitoring technique

Objectives

After completing this lab, you will be able to:

- Examine various scenarios and select the appropriate monitoring technique.

Prerequisites

None.

Estimated time to complete this lab: 20 minutes

Exercise 1
Selecting the Appropriate Monitoring Technique

In this exercise, you will select the appropriate monitoring technique based on the following scenarios. R=Real Time, L=Logging, A=Alerts. If more than one technique will work, put your selections in order of preference.

Scenario	Monitoring technique(s)
1. Determine when the hard disk is running out of free space.	
2. Provide management with information that can be used for budgeting purposes.	
3. Determine the number of users that a specific server configuration should support.	
4. Analyze a trend.	
5. Monitor multiple servers.	
6. Determine when to increase capacity.	
7. Find intermittent performance problems.	
8. Investigate why a computer application is slow or inefficient.	
9. Determine when to add additional system resources.	
10. Determine when to upgrade the system.	
11. Determine how a server should be used.	
12. Determine expected response times for specific numbers of users and system use.	
13. Analyze data to find and resolve abnormalities in the system use.	
14. Monitor use over time.	
15. Determine a preventive maintenance schedule for your servers.	
16. Create a baseline for a server.	
17. Monitor the effects of replication.	
18. Troubleshoot a server.	
19. Plan for growth.	
20. Find a slow memory leak.	

(continued)

Scenario	Monitoring technique(s)
21. Find a fast memory leak.	
22. Monitor intermittent disk thrashing.	
23. Monitor continuous disk thrashing	
24. Monitor a remote computer.	
25. Respond to user complaints that a server seems to be running slowly.	
26. Monitor a computer 24 hours a day, seven days a week.	

Microsoft®

Module 11: Managing Data Storage

Contents

Overview

- Managing File Compression
- Configuring File Encryption
- Configuring EFS Recovery Agents
- Implementing Disk Quotas

Introduction

One of your tasks as a systems administrator is to manage the data that you will store on network storage devices. To manage data storage, you can compress files and folders to decrease their size, thereby reducing the amount of space that they use In this module, you will learn when and how to compress files and folders.

To manage data, you must also understand encryption. In this module, you will learn about Encrypting File System (EFS). EFS stores data with a level of security higher than NTFS permissions.

When using EFS, you need a way to recover files when passwords are lost or an account is deleted. In this module, you will learn how to configure an EFS recovery agent.

You will also learn how to administer disk quotas. You use disk quotas to limit the amount of storage space that is available to users on servers running Microsoft® Windows Server™ 2003.

Objectives

After completing this module, you will be able to:

- Manage NTFS file compression.
- Configure file encryption.
- Configure an EFS recovery agent.
- Implement disk quotas.

Lesson: Managing File Compression

* What Is File Compression?
* What Is the compact Command?
* What Are the Effects of Moving and Copying Compressed Files and Folders?
* Best Practices for Compressing Files or Folders
* Practice: Managing File Compression

Introduction

Compressing files and folders decreases their size and reduces the amount of space they use on drives and removable storage devices. Microsoft Windows Server 2003 supports two types of compression: NTFS compression and compression using the Compressed (zipped) Folders feature.

In this lesson, you will learn about these features and how to use them. You will also learn the best practices that are associated with compressing files and folders.

Lesson objectives

After completing this lesson, you will be able to:

- Describe file compression.
- Describe the **compact** command-line tool.
- Describe the effects of moving and copying compressed files and folders.
- Describe the best practices for compressing files and folders.
- Compress a file or folder on an NTFS partition.

What Is File Compression?

* Use compression to save disk space
* Do not use compression for system files and folders
* Compression is configured as an NTFS attribute
* NTFS calculates disk space based on uncompressed file size
* Compressed (zipped) folders are also compressed

File A

File B

Introduction

Use compression when you need more space on your hard-disk drive. Compressing files, folders, and programs decreases their size and reduces the amount of space they use on drives or removable storage devices. You can also compress disk drives.

Windows supports two types of compression: NTFS file compression and Compressed (zipped) Folders. You use Microsoft Windows® Explorer to configure both types.

Uses of compression

You will get the most compression from text files, bitmap files, spreadsheets, and presentation files. You will have less compression with graphic and video files that are already compressed. Avoid compressing system folders and files because this affects the server performance.

NTFS file compression

Volumes, folders, and files on an NTFS volume are either compressed or uncompressed. Compression is configured as an attribute of a file or folder. New files created in a compressed folder are compressed by default. A file can be compressed but have an uncompressed file within it. The compression state of a folder does not necessarily reflect the compression state of files within that folder. For example, you can uncompress some of or all the files in a compressed folder.

When an application or an operating system command requests access to a compressed file, Windows Server 2003 automatically uncompresses the file. When you close or save a file, Windows Server 2003 compresses it again.

Space allocation

When files are copied, NTFS calculates disk space based on the size of the uncompressed file. This is important because files are uncompressed during the copy process and the system must be sure there is enough space. If you copy a compressed file to an NTFS partition that does not have enough space for the uncompressed file, an error message notifies you that there is not enough disk space for the file.

Compressed (zipped) Folders

Files and folders that are compressed using the Compressed (zipped) Folders feature can be compressed on FAT, FAT32, and NTFS drives. A zipper icon identifies files and folders that are compressed by using this feature.

You can open files directly from these compressed folders, and you can run some programs directly from these compressed folders without uncompressing them. You can also move these compressed files and folders to any drive or folder on your computer, the Internet, or your network, and they are compatible with other file-compression programs and files.

Compressing folders by using Compressed (zipped) Folders does not affect the overall performance of your computer. CPU utilization rises only when Compressed (zipped) Folders are accessed to compress a file.

Comparison of compression methods

The two compression methods are compared in the following table.

Attribute	NTFS file compression	Compressed (zipped) Folders
File system	NTFS	NTFS or FAT, FAT32
Compressible objects	Files, folders, and drives	Files and folders
User interaction	Transparent, when saving a file to a folder that is compressed	Manual
Performance	Decrease if system files are compressed	No decrease
Password protection	No	Yes
Encrypt	No	Yes
Change display color	Yes	No

What Is the compact Command?

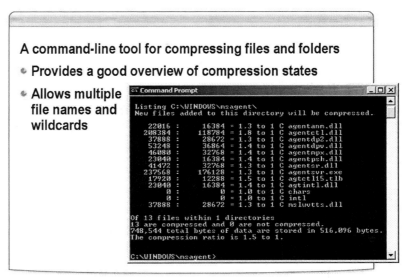

A command-line tool for compressing files and folders
* Provides a good overview of compression states
* Allows multiple file names and wildcards

Definition

Another tool for compressing files and folders is the **compact** command-line tool. This tool allows administrators to write batch scripts to compress files, which can then be scheduled to run at certain times.

Displays compression state of directory

When used without parameters, **compact** displays the compression state of the current directory and any files that it contains. For example, you can use the following command line to compress all files and folders in the Internet Information Services (IIS) directory:

compact /c c:*IIS**.*

Example using multiple parameters

You can use multiple file names and wildcards with **compact**. You must, however, insert spaces between multiple parameters, as shown in the following example:

compact /C | /U] [/S[:*dir***]] [/A] [/I] [/F] [/Q] [***filename*** [...]**

Each parameter is listed and described in the following table.

Parameter	Description
/C	Compresses the files specified. Directories are marked so that files added afterward are compressed.
/U	Uncompresses the specified files. Directories are marked so that files added afterward are not compressed.
/S	Performs the specified operation on files in the specified directory and all subdirectories. The default value is the current directory.
/A	Displays files with the hidden or system attributes. These files are omitted by default.
/I	Continues performing the specified operation even after errors occur. By default, **compact** stops when an error is encountered.
/F	Forces the compress operation on all specified files, even those that are already compressed. Files that are already compressed are skipped by default.
/Q	Reports only the most essential information about the specified pattern, file, or directory. Specifies a pattern, file, or directory.

What Are the Effects of Moving and Copying Compressed Files and Folders?

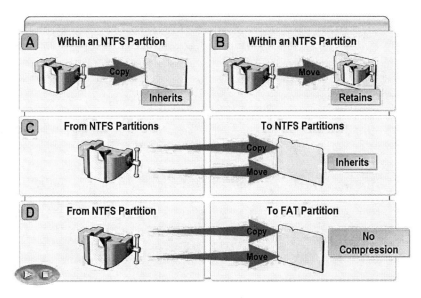

Introduction	Moving and copying compressed files and folders can change their compression state. This lesson examines several move and copy situations and provides you with some basic rules to help you predict outcome.
Copy within an NTFS partition	When you copy a file or folder within an NTFS partition, the file or folder inherits the compression state of the target folder. For example, if you copy a compressed file or folder to an uncompressed folder, the file or folder is automatically uncompressed.
Move within an NTFS partition	When you move a file or folder within an NTFS partition, the file or folder retains its original compression state. For example, if you move a compressed file or folder to an uncompressed folder, the file remains compressed.
Copy between NTFS partitions	When you copy a file or folder between NTFS partitions, the file or folder inherits the compression state of the target folder.
	When copying an NTFS file or a folder to a NTFS folder, the file or folder takes on the compression attribute of the target folder. For example, if you copy a compressed file to an uncompressed folder, the file is uncompressed when it is copied to the folder.
Move between NTFS partitions	When you move a file or folder between NTFS partitions, the file or folder inherits the compression state of the target folder. Because Windows Server 2003 treats a move between partitions as a copy and then a delete operation, the files inherit the compression state of the target folder.

Copying files or folders on NTFS volumes

When you copy a file to a folder that already contains a file of the same name, the copied file takes on the compression attribute of the target file, regardless of the compression state of the folder.

Moving and copying files between FAT16, FAT32, and NTFS volumes

Compressed files that are copied to a FAT or FAT32 partition are uncompressed. This is because compression is not supported on FAT or FAT32 volumes. The same applies to floppy disks because they cannot be formatted with NTFS.

When files are moved or copied from a FAT or FAT32 partition to an NTFS partition. they inherit the compression attribute of the folder into which they are copied.

Note   Unlike NTFS compressed folders and files, Compressed (zipped) Folders can be moved and copied without change between volumes, drives, and file systems. This is because using the Compressed (zipped) Folders creates a new file (with the extension .zip) that is actually copied or moved. The original files retain their attributes and location unless otherwise modified.

Best Practices for Compressing Files or Folders

Introduction	Some files compress better than others, and some files present problems when they are compressed. Consider the following best practices for managing compression on NTFS partitions.

Identify files that will benefit from compression

Because some file types can be compressed more than others, determine which file types to compress based on the anticipated size of the compressed file. For example, because Windows bitmap files contain more redundant data than application executable files, this file type can be compressed more than an .exe file. Bitmaps can often be compressed to less than 50 percent of the original file size, whereas an application file can rarely be compressed to less than 75 percent of its original size.

Do not compress system files

Do not compress system files. If system files are compressed, system performance will suffer because Windows must uncompress the files whenever they are accessed.

Do not compress already compressed file

Do not compress files that are already compressed. This wastes system time and yields no additional disk space.

Compress static data

Compress static data rather than data that changes frequently. Compressing and uncompressing files burdens the system. By choosing to compress files that are accessed infrequently, you minimize the amount of system time that is dedicated to compression and uncompression activities.

Practice: Managing File Compression

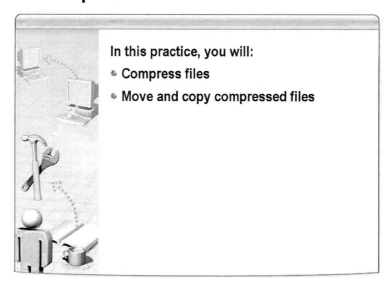

In this practice, you will:
* Compress files
* Move and copy compressed files

Objective

In this practice, you will:

- Compress files.
- Move and copy compressed files.

Instructions

Ensure that the DEN-DC1 virtual machine is running.

Practice

▶ **Compress files**

1. Log on as **Administrator** with a password of **Pa$$w0rd**.
2. Open Windows Explorer.
3. Browse to **D:\2275\Practices\Mod06\Data\Compressed**.
4. Right-click **Compressed** and then click **Properties**.
5. Note the **Size on disk** parameter: ~~9.01 MB~~ /9.02
6. Click **Advanced**.
7. Check the **Compress contents to save disk space** check box, and then click **OK**.
8. Click **Apply**, and then click **OK** to confirm that you want the changes to be made to this folder and all subfolders and files.
9. Note the **Size on disk** parameter: ~~9.01~~ /3.09
10. How much room did you gain by compressing the tax folders? 3γ %.
11. Click **OK**. Notice that the compressed files are now blue.

Practice

▶ **Move and copy compressed files**

1. In Windows Explorer, perform the following file operations in the
   D:\2275\Practices\Mod06\Data\Compressed folder:

File	Action	Destination
C-copybtwn.txt	Copy	C:\Uncompressed
C-copywithin.txt	Copy	D:\2275\Practices\Mod06\Data\Uncompressed
C-movebtwn.txt	Move	C:\Uncompressed
C-movewithin.txt	Move	D:\2275\Practices\Mod06\Data\Uncompressed

2. Record the file compression state results in the following table.

   The drives in the exercise represent NTFS-formatted volumes on the same
   computer.

File	Action	Volume	Folder	File
C-copybtwn.txt	Copy	Different	Uncompressed	
C-copywithin.txt	Copy	Same	Uncompressed	
C-movebtwn.txt	Move	Different	Uncompressed	
C-movewithin.txt	Move	Same	Uncompressed	

3. In Windows Explorer, perform the following file operations in the
   D:\2275\Practices\Mod06\Data\Uncompressed folder:

File	Action	Destination
UC-copybtwn.txt	Copy	C:\Compressed
UC-copywithin.txt	Copy	D:\2275\Practices\Mod06\Data\Compressed
UC-movebtwn.txt	Move	C:\Compressed
UC-movewithin.txt	Move	D:\2275\Practices\Mod06\Data\Compressed

4. Record the file compression state results in the following table.

    The drives in the exercise represent NTFS-formatted volumes on the same computer.

File	Action	Volume	Folder	File
UC-copybtwn.txt	Copy	Different	Compressed	
UC-copywithin.txt	Copy	Same	Compressed	
UC-movebtwn.txt	Move	Different	Compressed	
UC-movewithin.txt	Move	Same	Compressed	

5. Close all open windows and log off of DEN-DC1.

► **To prepare for the next practice**

•   Start the DEN-CL1 virtual machine.

Important   Do not shut down the virtual machines.

Lesson: Configuring File Encryption

* What Is EFS Encryption?
* What Is Public-Key Encryption?
* How EFS Uses Encryption
* How EFS Uses Certificates
* What Are the Effects of Moving and Copying Encrypted Files or Folders?
* Sharing an Encrypted Folder
* Practice: Configuring File Encryption

Introduction

An intruder who has physical access to a computer can easily install a new operating system and bypass the security of the existing operating system. If you realize that the operating system controls access to sensitive data, then you can see the risk to sensitive data. You can add an additional layer of security by encrypting these files with Encrypting File System (EFS). An encrypted file's data is protected even if an intruder has full access to the computer's data storage.

In this lesson, you will learn about encryption, as well as how to manage encryption. You will also learn the effects of moving and copying encrypted files.

Lesson objectives

After completing this lesson, you will be able to:

■ Describe EFS file encryption.

■ Describe public-key encryption.

■ Describe how EFS uses encryption

■ Describe how EFS uses certificates.

■ Describe the effects of moving and copying encrypted files or folders.

■ Describe sharing an encrypted folder.

■ Configure file encryption.

What Is EFS Encryption?

EFS encryption makes data unintelligible without a decryption key

- EFS encrypts data
- Encryption keys are automatically generated if required
- Opening and saving encrypted files is transparent to users
- Use the cipher command to display or alter encryption of folders and files on NTFS volumes

Introduction

An attacker can gain access to a shared system by starting a different operating system. An attacker can also steal a computer, remove the hard disk, install the disk in another system, and gain access to the stored files. Files that are encrypted by using Encrypting File System (EFS), however, appear as unintelligible characters when the attacker does not have the decryption key.

EFS provides file level encryption

EFS provides encryption for files created on NTFS volumes. By using EFS, you bar access to sensitive or confidential data to anyone without a decryption key.

Use EFS to encrypt data

Encryption and decryption are the primary tasks of EFS. The default configuration of EFS requires no administrative effort; users can begin encrypting files immediately. EFS automatically generates an encryption key pair for a user if one does not exist.

Encryption and decryption options available

Several encryption and decryption options are available to users. Users can encrypt and decrypt files by using Windows Explorer, by using the **cipher** command, or by using the shortcut menu accessed by right-clicking a file or folder.

Encrypted folder contents

Folders that are marked for encryption are not actually encrypted. Only the files in the folder are encrypted, as well as any new files that are created in or moved to the folder.

Use EFS to access encrypted data

Authorized users with the appropriate key may access encrypted files just as they do unencrypted files. Thus, when a user accesses an encrypted file that is stored on disk, the user can read the contents of the file in the normal way. When the user saves the file on disk again, EFS saves the changes as encrypted. The process for opening, modifying, and saving encrypted files is completely transparent.

Note   Unauthorized users attempting to access encrypted files will get an access denied message.

Use EFS to decrypt data

You can decrypt a file by clearing the **Encryption** check box in the file's **Properties** dialog box. After it is decrypted, the file remains decrypted until you encrypt it again. There is no automatic re-encryption of a file, even if it exists in a directory that is marked as encrypted.

Authorized users with the appropriate key can decrypt a file either by clearing the **Encryption** check box in the **Properties** dialog box for the file, or by using the **cipher** command.

Display or alter encryption on NTFS volumes with the cipher command
Parameters of cipher

Use the **cipher** command to display or alter the encryption of folders and files on NTFS volumes. Used without parameters, **cipher** displays the encryption state of the current folder and any files it contains.

You can use the **cipher** command with the parameters in the following table to perform the listed tasks.

Example, to encrypt all files in the current directory: **cipher /e /a *.*.**

Parameters	Task description
Use **cipher** with no parameters or with the name of a specific file or folder.	Display the encryption status of files and folders
/e	Set the encryption attribute for folders in the current directory
/e /a	Encrypt files in the current directory
/d	Remove the encryption attribute from folders in the current directory
/d /a	Decrypt files in the current directory
/?	Display all the options that are available with **cipher**

What Is Public-Key Encryption?

* Public key
* Private key
* Certification authorities
* Automated certificate creation

Definition

Public-key encryption, also called *asymmetric encryption*, is an encryption method that uses a public key and private key to encrypt data. Public keys used by a particular user are available to anyone. Private keys must be kept secret by the account that has encrypted the file. A matched public key and private key is referred to as a *key pair*.

Public key characteristics

- Public-key encryption has the following characteristics: Anyone can encrypt data by using a public key, which is available as public information. However, only one account possesses the corresponding private key, so only that account can decrypt the data.

- The account that uses the private key generates the key pair.

- A key pair is created by using a program that generates keys. For example, EFS can be used to create a key pair to encrypt files on your domain.

- The public key, an attribute of the certificate, is widely distributed, in locations such as the Active Directory® directory service, to ensure that other users can obtain the public key for both encryption and digital signing of data.

Private key characteristics

- The private key is never exposed to network users, and is protected either in a user or computer profile, or on a physical device such as a smart card.

Note   EFS uses the public key only for encryption.

Certification authorities

A certification authority (CA) creates certificates for public key cryptography. Windows Server 2003 has the ability to act as a certification authority. When a Windows Server 2003 is used as the certification authority for EFS certificates, the entire certificate creation process can be automated.

How EFS Uses Encryption

* **Symmetric encryption protects the file**
  * Symmetric encryption is strong and fast
* **Public-key encryption protects the symmetric key**
  * A copy is stored for each user
  * A copy is stored for the recovery agent

Introduction

EFS uses a combination of public-key and symmetric-key encryption to ensure that files are protected from all but the most computationally impracticable methods of attack. A symmetric key is used to encrypt the file. Public-key encryption is used to protect the symmetric key.

Symmetric encryption

Symmetric encryption uses the same key to encrypt a file and decrypt a file. This type of encryption is faster and stronger than public key encryption. However, the difficulty of securing the key during a cross-network transfer requires additional security for the symmetric key.

Symmetric is the typical method of encrypting large amounts of data.

Protecting symmetric keys

EFS uses public key encryption to protect the symmetric key that is required to decrypt the file contents. Each user certificate contains a public key that is used to encrypt the symmetric key. Then only the user with the private key can access the symmetric key.

The file encryption process is described below:

1. When a user encrypts a file, EFS generates a file-encryption key (FEK) to encrypt the data. The FEK is encrypted with the user's public key, and the encrypted FEK is then stored with the file. This ensures that only the user who holds the matching EFS Encryption private key can decrypt the file. After a user encrypts a file, the file remains encrypted for as long as it is stored on the disk.

2. To decrypt files, the user can open the file, remove the encryption attribute, or decrypt the file by using the **cipher** command. When this occurs, EFS decrypts the FEK by using the user's private key, and then decrypts the data by using the FEK.

Note In addition to the user that encrypted the file, additional copies of the symmetric key are encrypted with the public key of the recovery agent and any other authorized users.

How EFS Uses Certificates

* **Certificate identifies user**
* **EFS generates a certificate**
  * Requests from CA
  * Self-signed if CA not available
* **EFS renews certificates if required**

Introduction

Each user who logs on to a computer running Windows 2000 or later can encrypt files. The first time the user encrypts a file, EFS generates a unique certificate and key pair for the user. Unless a user sets up sharing for selected users, no one else can access the user's encrypted files.

What is a certificate?

A certificate is a digital statement issued by an authority that vouches for the identity of the certificate holder. A certificate binds a public key to the identity of the person, computer, or service that holds the corresponding private key. Certificates are used by a variety of public key security services and applications to provide authentication, data integrity, and secure communications across networks such as the Internet.

How EFS Uses Certificates

EFS must find a certificate for a user before it will allow the user to access an encrypted file. The method that EFS uses to find and employ certificates to open an encrypted file is described below.

1. When a user sets the encrypted attribute for a file or folder, EFS attempts to locate the user's certificate in the personal certificate store.

2. If the user does not have a certificate that has been authorized for use with EFS, EFS requests a certificate from an available enterprise certification authority (CA).

3. If an enterprise CA is not available, EFS automatically generates its own self-signed certificate for the user.

If the EFS user certificate expires, EFS ensures that the certificate is renewed if possible or, if not, that a new public-private key pair and a new public-key certificate are issued for the user the next time an EFS operation is performed for that user. The private key from an expired certificate can still be used to access previously encrypted files, but the public key from an expired certificate cannot be used to encrypt new files.

What Are the Effects of Moving and Copying Encrypted Files and Folders?

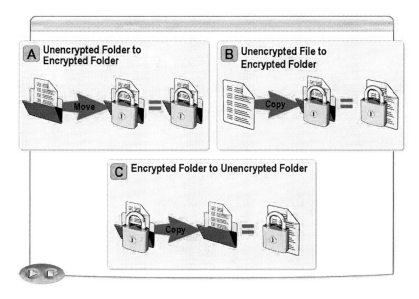

Introduction

All files and folders that are created in a folder marked for encryption are automatically encrypted. Moving and copying encrypted files and folders can change the encryption state of the file or folder This discussion will help you understand the effects of these actions.

Effect of moving encrypted files

If you move a file from an unencrypted folder to an encrypted folder, the file is encrypted.

Effect of copying encrypted files

If you copy an unencrypted file to an encrypted folder, the copied file is encrypted. If you copy an encrypted file from an encrypted folder to an unencrypted folder, the file remains encrypted.

If your access allows you to decrypt a file and you copy the encrypted file from an NTFS volume to a FAT or FAT32 volume, the file becomes unencrypted. If you copy a file from a FAT volume to an encrypted folder on an NTFS volume, the file becomes encrypted. If your access does not allow you to decrypt a file and you attempt to copy or move it to a FAT or FAT32 partition you will receive an access denied error message.

After you encrypt a folder, all files and subfolders that are added to the folder will be encrypted.

Note   For more information about encryption, see the white paper, *EFS*, under **Additional Reading** on the Student Materials compact disc.

Sharing Encrypted Files

* Encrypted files can be shared with local, domain, and trusted domain users
* Groups cannot be authorized for access
* Any user with access can add other users
* Self-signed certificates are difficult for sharing

Introduction

Users can share encrypted files with other local, domain, and trusted domain users. Files can be shared locally on a computer or on the network. Authorizing access to encrypted files is a separate process from NTFS or share permissions. Sharing access to encrypted files involves the configuration of both file system access control list (ACL) permissions, and EFS permissions.

Groups

Because there is no method for issuing a certificate and assigning a key pair for a group, groups cannot be authorized for accessing encrypted files. Only individual user accounts have authorized access to encrypted files.

Authorization

Any user who is authorized to decrypt a file can authorize other users to access the file. Granting access is not limited to the file owner. Caution users to share files only with trusted accounts, because those accounts can authorize other accounts. Removing the Write permission from a user or user group mitigates risk.

Certificates

EFS sharing requires that the users who will be authorized to access the encrypted file have EFS certificates. These certificates can be located in roaming profiles or in the user profiles on the computer on which the file to be shared is stored, or they can be stored in and retrieved from Active Directory.

Self-signed certificates created by EFS are difficult to use for sharing encrypted files because the certificates are stored only on the computer that stores the encrypted files. When files are encrypted on a remote server, a profile is created for the encrypting user on the remote server, and a self-signed certificate is stored there. Each user must import the self-signed certificates of other users to give them access. The file must be exported from the remote server.

If your organization is going to be sharing encrypted files you should configure a certification authority to issue EFS certificates. This provides a central trusted source for certificates and eliminates the need to import user certificates.

Practice: Configuring File Encryption

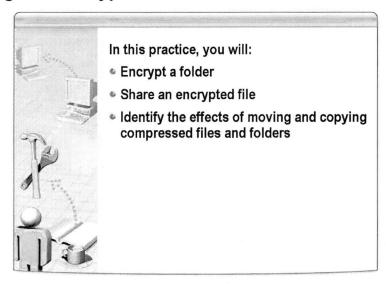

In this practice, you will:
- Encrypt a folder
- Share an encrypted file
- Identify the effects of moving and copying compressed files and folders

Objective

In this practice, you will:

- Encrypt a folder.
- Share an encrypted file.
- Identify the effects of moving and copying compressed files and folders.

Instructions

Ensure that the DEN-DC1 and DEN-CL1 virtual machines are running.

Practice

▶ **Encrypt a folder**

1. On DEN-CL1, log on as **EFS1** with a password of **Pa$$w0rd**.
2. Open Windows Explorer.
3. Browse to **\\DEN-DC1\Data**.
4. Right-click the **Encrypted** folder and then click **Properties**.
5. Click **Advanced**.
6. Check the **Encrypt contents to secure data** check box, and then click **OK**.
7. Click **Apply**.
8. In the **Confirm Attribute Changes** dialog box, click **OK** to confirm that you want the changes to be made to this folder and all subfolders and files.
9. Click **OK**. Notice that the **Encrypted** folder text is colored green.
10. Log off as **EFS1**.
11. Log on to DEN-CL1 as **EFS2** with a password of **Pa$$w0rd**.
12. Open Windows Explorer.
13. Browse to **\\DEN-DC1\Data\Encrypted**.

14. Double-click **E-copybtwn** to open it.

15. Although Notepad opens, access to the file contents is denied. Click **OK** to close the dialog box.

16. Close all open windows.

Practice

▶ **Share an encrypted file**

1. On DEN-DC1, log on as **Administrator** with a password of **Pa$$w0rd**.

2. Click **Start**, click **Run**, type **mmc**, and then click **OK**.

3. Add the Certificates snap-in.

    a. Click **File** and then click **Add/Remove Snap-in**.

    b. Click **Add**.

    c. Double-click **Certificates,** and click **Finish**.

    d. Click **Close** and then click **OK**.

4. Expand **Certificates – Current User**, expand **Trusted People**, and then click **Certificates**.

5. Right-click **EFS1**, point to **All Tasks**, and click **Export**.

6. Click **Next** to start the Certificate Export Wizard.

7. Click **Next** to accept the default export format.

8. In the **File name** box, type **D:\2275\Practices\Mod06\Data\EFS1key.cer** and then click **Next**.

9. Click **Finish**.

10. Click **OK**.

11. On DEN-CL1, open Windows Explorer.

12. Browse to **\\DEN-DC1\Data**.

13. Double-click **EFS1key** and then click **Install Certificate**.

14. Click **Next** to start the Certificate Import Wizard.

15. Click **Next** to let Windows automatically select the certificate store. It will be placed in Trusted People.

16. Click **Finish**. Click **OK**.

17. In the **Certificate** dialog box, click **OK**.

18. In Windows Explorer, browse to **\\DEN-DC1\Data\Encrypted**.

19. Create a text file named **Shared**.

20. Open **Shared**, enter your name, save the file and close Notepad.

21. Right-click **Shared** and then click **Properties**.

22. Click **Advanced**, and then click **Details**.

23. Click **Add**, click **EFS1**, and then click **OK**. Notice that EFS1 and EFS2 are both listed as users.

24. Click **OK** three times to close all dialog boxes.

25. Close Windows Explorer.

26. Log off of DEN-CL1.

Practice

▶ **Identify the effects of moving and copying encrypted files and folders**

1. On DEN-DC1, in Windows Explorer, perform the following file operations in the **D:\2275\Practices\Mod06\Data\Encrypted** folder:

File	Action	Destination
E-copybtwn.txt	Copy	C:\Unencrypted
E-copywithin.txt	Copy	D:\2275\Practices\Mod06\Data\Unencrypted
E-movebtwn.txt	Move	C:\Unencrypted
E-movewithin.txt	Move	D:\2275\Practices\Mod06\Data\Unencrypted

2. Record the file encryption state results in the following table.

   The drives in the exercise represent NTFS-formatted volumes on the same computer.

File	Action	Volume	Folder	File
E-copybtwn.txt	Copy	Different	Unencrypted	
E-copywithin.txt	Copy	Same	Unencrypted	
E-movebtwn.txt	Move	Different	Unencrypted	
E-movewithin.txt	Move	Same	Unencrypted	

3. In Windows Explorer, perform the following file operations in the **D:\2275\Practices\Mod06\Data\Unencrypted** folder:

File	Action	Destination
UE-copybtwn.txt	Copy	C:\Encrypted
UE-copywithin.txt	Copy	D:\2275\Practices\Mod06\Data\Encrypted
UE-movebtwn.txt	Move	C:\Encrypted
UE-movewithin.txt	Move	D:\2275\Practices\Mod06\Data\Encrypted

4. Record the file encryption state results in the following table.

   The drives in the exercise represent NTFS-formatted volumes on the same computer.

File	Action	Volume	Folder	File
UE-copybtwn.txt	Copy	Different	Encrypted	
UE-copywithin.txt	Copy	Same	Encrypted	
UE-movebtwn.txt	Move	Different	Encrypted	
UE-movewithin.txt	Move	Same	Encrypted	

5. Close all open windows.

Important   Do not shut down the virtual machines.

Lesson: Configuring EFS Recovery Agents

* What Is an EFS Recovery Agent?
* Recovering Encrypted Files
* Practice: Configuring EFS Recovery Agents

Introduction

When a user account is deleted the associated certificate is lost as well. Without a recovery agent, that user cannot access encrypted files.

Lesson objectives

After completing this lesson, you will be able to:

- Describe a recovery agent.
- Describe how to recover an encrypted file.
- Export and import a recovery key.

What Is an EFS Recovery Agent?

* Authorized to decrypt data
* Required when users are deleted
* Required when local user passwords are reset
* The recovery key can be exported

Definition

A recovery agent is an individual who is authorized to decrypt data that was encrypted by another user. Recovery agents do not need any other permissions to function in this role. The default recovery agent is the domain administrator. However, this can be delegated to any user.

Uses of data recovery

Data recovery is might be necessary when you need access to data encrypted by an employee who leaves or who loses the private key. Data recovery is available through the Encrypting File System (EFS) as a part of the overall security policy for the system. If your file encryption certificate and associated private key is lost through disk failure, damage, or other reason, the person who is the designated recovery agent can recover the data.

Caution When the password for a local user is reset by an administrator, Windows XP or Windows Server 2003 is unable to read the private key stored in the user's profile. They key must be recovered from a backup or a recovery agent must recover the files.

Special certificates and private key

Each recovery agent has a special certificate and associated private key that allows data recovery wherever the recovery policy applies. If you are the designated recovery agent, you should be sure to use the **Export** command in Certificates in the Microsoft Management Console (MMC) to back up the recovery certificate and the associated private key to a secure location.

After backing them up, you should use Certificates in MMC to delete the recovery certificate. Then, when you need to perform a recovery operation for a user, you should first restore the recovery certificate and associated private key using the **Import** command from Certificates in MMC. After recovering the data, you should again delete the recovery certificate. You do not have to repeat the export process.

Recovering Encrypted Files

* Log on as recovery agent
* Recovery policies define the recovery agent
* Default recovery agent is the domain Administrator account
* Back up the recovery key

Introduction

To recover encrypted files, you must understand which user is configured as the recovery agent. After this is accomplished, log on as that user and decrypt the files.

Recovery policies

A recovery policy is configured locally for stand-alone computers. For computers that are part of a network, a recovery policy is configured at the domain, organizational unit, or individual computer level. These recovery policies apply to all computers running Windows 2000, Windows XP, and Windows Server 2003 operating systems. A certification authority (CA) issues recovery certificates; you use Certificates in Microsoft Management Console (MMC) to manage them.

In a domain environment, the domain Administrator account is automatically configured as a recovery agent.

Adding a recovery agent

The recovery agent is defined through Group Policy. The default recovery agent is defined in the Default Domain Policy. The administrator is the default recovery agent.

When a new recovery agent is added through Group Policy, it is automatically added to all newly encrypted files. However, it is not automatically added to existing encrypted files. The recovery agent for a file is set at the time that the file is encrypted. Therefore an encrypted file must be accessed and saved to update the recovery agent.

Note The best way to update the recovery agent for many files is by using the **cipher /u** command.

Backing up the recovery key

There are two reasons to back up the recovery key:

1. To secure against system failure. The domain administrator key that is used by default for EFS recovery is stored only on the first domain controller in the domain. If anything were to happen to this domain controller, then EFS recovery would be impossible.

2. To make the recovery key portable. The recovery key is not automatically available to the recovery agent on all computers. The recovery key must be installed in the profile of the recovery agent. If roaming profiles are used, then the key will be available to the recovery agent on any computer. However, if roaming profiles are not used, then exporting and importing the recovery key is a method to update the profile of the recovery agent on a particular computer.

Practice: Configuring EFS Recovery Agents

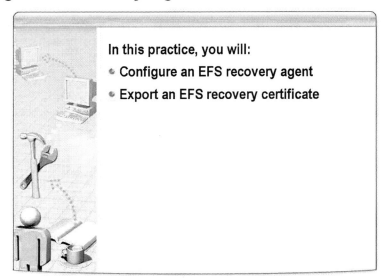

In this practice, you will:

* Configure an EFS recovery agent
* Export an EFS recovery certificate

Objective

In this practice, you will:

- Configure an EFS recovery agent.
- Export an EFS recovery certificate.

Instructions

Ensure the DEN-DC1 and DEN-CL1 virtual machines are running.

Practice

▶ **Configure an EFS recovery agent**

1. On DEN-DC1, log on as **EFS2** with a password of **Pa$$w0rd**.

2. Click **Start**, click **Run**, type **cmd**, and then click **OK**.

3. Type **cipher /r:\\DEN-DC1\data\EFS2recovery** and then press **ENTER**. Type Enter when prompted for a password. This command creates a .cer file to be imported as the recovery agent in Group Policy and a .pfx file to be imported in the profile of the user performing data recovery.

4. Close the command prompt.

5. Log off of DEN-DC1.

6. Log on to DEN-DC1 as the **Administrator** with a password of **Pa$$w0rd**.

7. On DEN-DC1, click **Start**, point to **Administrative Tools**, and then click **Group Policy Management**.

8. Expand **Forest: Contoso.msft**, expand **Domains**, expand **Contoso.msft**, and then click **Default Domain Policy**.

9. Read the **Group Policy Management Console** dialog box that appears, check the **Do not show this message again** check box, and then click **OK**.

10. Right-click **Default Domain Policy** and click **Edit**.

11. Under **Computer Configuration**, expand **Windows Settings**, expand **Security Settings**, expand **Public Key Policies**, and then click **Encrypting File System**.

12. Right-click **Encrypting File System** and click **Add Data Recovery Agent**.

13. Click **Next** to start the **Add Recovery Agent Wizard**.

14. Click **Browse Folders** and select
    D:\2275\Practices\Mod06\Data\EFS2recovery, and then click **Open**.

15. Click **Yes** to install the certificate and then click **Next**.

16. Click **Finish**.

17. Close the **Group Policy Object Editor**.

18. Close **Group Policy Management**.

Practice

▶ **Export an EFS recovery certificate**

1. Click **Start**, click **Run**, type **mmc**, and then click **OK**.

2. Add the Certificates snap-in.

    a. Click **File** and click **Add/Remove Snap-in**.

    b. Click **Add**.

    c. Double-click **Certificates,** and then click **Finish**.

    d. Click **Close** and then click **OK**.

3. Expand **Certificates – Current User**, expand **Personal**, and then click **Certificates**.

4. Right-click the certificate with an intended purpose of **File Recovery**, point to **All Tasks**, and then click **Export**.

5. Click **Next** to start the **Certificate Export Wizard**.

6. Click **Yes, export the private key** and then click **Next**.

7. Click **Next** to accept the default file format.

8. In the **Password** and **Confirm password** boxes, type **Pa$$w0rd** and then click **Next**.

9. In the **File name** box, type
    D:\2275\Practices\Mod06\Data\AdminRecovery.pfx and click **Next**.

10. Click **Finish**.

11. Click **OK**.

12. Close the MMC and do not save console settings.

13. Close all open windows on DEN-DC1 and DEN-CL1.

Important   Do not shut down the virtual machines.

Caution   An EFS recovery key should always be exported directly to removable media and stored in a safe location. Data-recovery tools could be used recover the exported recovery key after it has been deleted if it is stored on a server hard drive.

Lesson: Implementing Disk Quotas

* Multimedia: What Are Disk Quotas?
* What Are Disk-Quota Settings?
* Practice: Implementing Disk Quotas

Introduction

Use disk quotas to manage server resources. Quotas do this by limiting user storage space. You can also use disk quotas to track disk usage by users. In this lesson, you will learn how to use disk quotas and how to set up disk entries.

Lesson objectives

After completing this lesson, you will be able to:

- Explain disk quotas.
- Describe disk-quota settings.
- Implement disk quotas.

Multimedia: What Are Disk Quotas?

* This presentation explains the use of disk quotas as a method for managing data storage space and illustrates how disk quotas operate

* After viewing this presentation, you will be able to explain how to use disk quotas

File location

To view the *What Are Disk Quotas?* presentation, open the Web page on the Student Materials compact disc, click **Multimedia**, and then click the title of the presentation.

Do not open this presentation unless the instructor tells you to.

What Are Disk-Quota Settings?

* Track and control user NTFS volume space
* Restrict storage to quotas
* Trigger log events
* Calculated with uncompressed file size
* Quota entries

Introduction

Administrators must manage the always increasing demand for data storage. You can use disk-quota settings to monitor and manage disk usage. Quotas prevent users from writing additional data to a disk volume after they exceed their quota.

Use disk quotas to track disk space

Quotas need not limit space. You can also use quotas to track the disk-space use of each user. When you do limit space, you can specify whether to log an event when users exceed quota limits or quota warning levels.

Note Quotas are tracked per volume or partition. If there are multiple network fie shares on a volume, then the quotas apply to the sum of all file shares.

Enable quotas on volumes

You can enable quotas on local volumes, network volumes, and removable drives if they are formatted by using NTFS. When you enable disk quotas for a volume, volume usage is automatically tracked for all users from that point on.

File compression does not prevent exceeding quota limits

You cannot use file compression to increase storage capacity within a limit because compressed files are tracked based on their uncompressed size. For example, Windows counts a 50-megabyte (MB) file compressed to 40 MB as 50 MB.

CPU overhead and administration

Enabling disk quotas requires a minimal amount of CPU overhead and no administration after the initial configuration.

Set quotas on remote volumes

You can set quotas on a remote volume by mapping to it by using Windows Explorer or My Computer. You can manage NTFS volumes on remote computers running Windows 2000 and Windows Server 2003. The volumes must be formatted by using NTFS and must be shared from the root folder of the volume.

Overriding quotas for individuals

When quota settings are configured for a volume, they are the default quota values for each user. You can override the quota settings on a per user basis by configuring a quota entry to override the quota settings. For example, you can allow several individual engineers increased quota sizes because they are storing large technical drawings. By default, there is a quota entry for Administrators group allowing unlimited file storage.

Practice: Configuring Quota Limits

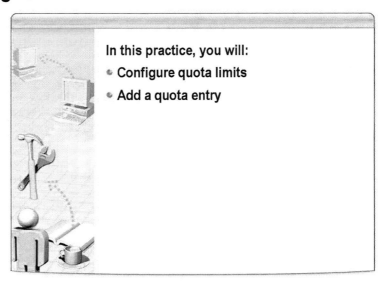

In this practice, you will:
* Configure quota limits
* Add a quota entry

Objective

In this practice, you will:

■ Configure quota limits.

■ Add a quota entry.

Instructions

Ensure that the DEN-DC1 and DEN-CL1 virtual machines are running.

Practice

▶ **Configure quota limits**

1. On DEN-DC1, Click **Start** and then click **My Computer**.
2. Right-click **Allfiles (D:)** and click **Properties**.
3. Click the **Quota** tab.
4. Check the **Enable quota management** check box.
5. Check the **Deny disk space to users exceeding quota limit** check box.
6. Click **Limit disk space to**, type **100** in the box, and click **MB** in the drop-down list.
7. In the **Set warning level to** box, type **90**, and click **MB** in the drop-down list.
8. Check the **Log event when a user exceeds their quota limit** check box.
9. Check the **Log event when a user exceeds their warning level** check box.
10. Click **OK** and click **OK**.

Practice

▶ **Add a quota entry**

1. Right-click **Allfiles (D:)** and click **Properties**.

2. Click the **Quota** tab.

3. Click **Quota Entries**. This is a list of individual quota entries that overrides the defaults set in the previous steps.

4. Click **Quota** and then click **New Quota Entry**.

5. Type **Administrator**, click **Check Names**, and then click **OK**.

6. Click **Do not limit disk usage** and then click **OK**.

7. Close the **Quota Entries for Allfiles (D:)** window.

8. Click **OK**, and then close all open windows.

9. Log off of DEN-DC1 and DEN-CL1.

Important Do not shut down the virtual machines.

Lab: Managing Data Storage

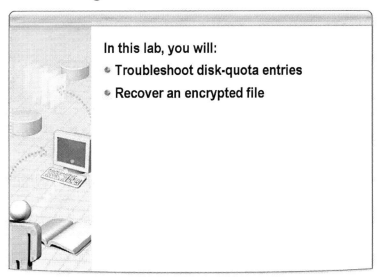

Objectives

After completing this lab, you will be able to:

- Troubleshoot disk-quota entries.
- Recover an encrypted file.

Instructions

Ensure that the DEN-DC1 and DEN-CL1 virtual machines are running.

Scenario

You are the systems administrator for an organizational unit on a large network. After arriving at work one morning, you receive the following requests from your manager:

- You have implemented quotas on data volumes to control the volume of data users were storing. One user, Paul West, is attempting to copy some files between two folders and is getting an error message. Paul needs to copy these files and you must enable him to do so.

- Another systems administrator has deleted some user profiles from the DEN-DC1 server. He did not realize that EFS (without a certification authority) stores encryption keys in profiles on the server with the encrypted files. You must recover these files for the users.

Estimated time to complete this lab: 20 minutes

Exercise 1
Troubleshooting Disk-Quota Entries

You need to configure a disk quota entry for Paul West.

Tasks	Specific instructions
1. Configure a disk-quota entry for Paul West.	a. Log on to DEN-DC1 as **Administrator** with a password of **Pa$$w0rd**. b. Use My Computer to open the properties of **Allfiles (D:)**. c. Click the **Quota** tab in the **Allfiles (D:) Properties** dialog box. d. Configure **Paul West** as a quota entry. e. Configure a limit of **10MB** and warning of **5MB**.
2. Test the disk space as Paul West.	a. Log on to DEN-CL1 as **Paul** with a password of **Pa$$w0rd**. b. Copy **File1**, **File2**, and **File3** from **\\DEN-DC1\Data\Quota** to **\\DEN-DC1\Data\Quota\Project 1**.
3. On DEN-DC1, view the quota status.	a. On DEN-DC1, in **System** event viewer, find the event with source **ntfs**. Notice that a user has hit their threshold limit. b. Copy **File4** and **File5** into the **Project1** folder. You should now get an error message stating that there is not enough free space.
4. Allow Paul West unlimited disk space.	a. Change the Paul West quota entry to unlimited. b. Copy all of the files from the **\\DEN-DC1\Data\Quota** to **\\DEN-DC1\Data\Quota\Project 1**. The copy task should be successful. c. Close all open windows.

Exercise 2
Recovering an Encrypted File

In this exercise, you recover an encrypted file.

Tasks	Specific instructions
1. Create an encrypted file logged on as **Paul West**.	a. Ensure that you are logged on to DEN-CL1 as **Paul** with a password of **Pa$$w0rd**. b. Create a text file in **\\DEN-DC1\Data\Encrypted** named **Recover.txt**. c. Put some information in the text file. d. Log off of DEN-CL1.
2. On DEN-DC1, log on as **Administrator** and Delete the Paul West profile.	a. Log on to DEN-DC1 as **Administrator** with a password of **Pa$$w0rd**. b. Open **System Properties**. c. Delete the **Paul West** profile. d. Restart DEN-DC1.
3. On DEN-CL1, open Recover.txt.	a. Log on to DEN-CL1, as **Paul**. b. Attempt to open the **\\DEN-DC1\Data\Encrypted\Recover.txt** file. This action will fail because the profile with the private key required for decryption is missing. c. Close all open windows.
4. On DEN-DC1, decrypt the file.	a. Log on to DEN-DC1 as **Administrator** with a password of **Pa$$w0rd**. b. Browse to **D:\2275\Practices\Mod06\Data\Encrypted**. c. Decrypt **Recover.txt**.
5. On DEN-CL1, open Recover.txt.	▪ On DEN-CL1, as Paul, attempt to open the **\\DEN-DC1\Data\Encrypted\Recover.txt** file. This action will be successful because the file is decrypted.
6. Encrypt Recover.txt	a. Encrypt the file again. b. Close all windows and log off.
7. Complete the lab exercise.	a. Close all programs and shut down all computers. Do not save changes. b. To prepare for the next module, start the DEN-DC1 virtual computer.

Microsoft®

Module 12: Managing Disaster Recovery

Contents

Overview

- ❖ **Preparing for Disaster Recovery**
- ❖ **Backing Up Data**
- ❖ **Scheduling Backup Jobs**
- ❖ **Restoring Data**
- ❖ **Configuring Shadow Copies**
- ❖ **Recovering from Server Failure**

Introduction

This module helps you prepare for a computer disaster. Microsoft® Windows Server™ 2003 includes several features that support data loss prevention. It also includes tools that allow you recover when data loss occurs. Understanding these features is essential to developing and implementing an effective disaster protection and recovery plan.

Objectives

After completing this module, you will be able to:

- Prepare for disaster recovery.
- Back up data.
- Schedule backup jobs.
- Restore data.
- Configure a shadow copy.
- Recover from server failure.

Lesson: Preparing for Disaster Recovery

* What Is Disaster Recovery?
* Disaster Recovery Preparation Guidelines

Introduction

This lesson introduces the components of disaster recovery and the methods of recovering data after a disaster occurs. This lesson also provides recommended guidelines that will help you to develop your own disaster recovery plan.

Lesson objectives

After completing this lesson, you will be able to:

- Describe recovery plan components.
- List the guidelines for creating a disaster recovery plan.

What Is Disaster Recovery?

* Resuming operations after a disaster
* Implementing a disaster recovery plan:
  * Replacing damaged components
  * Restoring data
  * Testing before resuming

Introduction

A sudden catastrophic loss of data is a computer disaster. The business world depends on mission-critical data more than ever. As a result, organizations place greater emphasis on protecting their information assets from data loss and server failure.

Disaster recovery

Disaster recovery is the process that allows normal business operations to resume as quickly as possible after a disaster. Disaster recovery seeks to restore data and services to the state before the disaster occurred.

Disaster-recovery considerations

For each operating system and application that you introduce to your environment, answer the following questions about disaster recovery:

Disaster-recovery item	Considerations
Recovery plan	• What are the possible failure scenarios?
	• What data is critical?
	• How often should you perform backups?
	• How long will you save the backups?
	• How fast must data be restored from backup to prevent unacceptable downtime?
	• Where will you store the backups to allow access by the appropriate people?
	• If the responsible systems administrator is gone, is there someone else who knows the proper passwords and procedures to perform backups and, if necessary, to restore the system?

(*continued*)

Disaster recovery item	Considerations
Hardware	• How many, what kind, and where are individual computer components, such as hard disks and controllers, processors, and RAM?
	• How many, what kind, and where are external components such as routers, bridges, switches, cables, and connectors?
	• Are the critical hardware and services redundant?
Data restoration	• To what storage device, will you send the backup?
	• When will you perform backups, while users are working, or when the system is offline?
	• Will you perform the backups manually or schedule them to be performed automatically?
	• How long will you save the backups?
	• How often is the critical data updated?
Testing	• How will you verify automated backups ?
	• How will you ensure the usability of backups?

Determine questions based on your situation   This is not a complete list; you must determine other questions based on your particular situation.

Disaster-Recovery Preparation Guidelines

- Develop a backup strategy
- Test your backup strategy and assess its product
- Include an alternate backup that is stored offsite
- Backup System State data
- Install the Recovery Console as a startup option
- Store the installation CD for accessibility in a crisis

Introduction

You should develop and thoroughly test a disaster recovery plan. When testing the plan, apply the results to as many failure scenarios as possible.

Guidelines

Use the following guidelines to prepare for disaster recovery:

- Create a disaster recovery plan for performing regular backup operations.

  Review and incorporate a plan for backing up all your files on a regular basis. Keep a log of every update in your disaster-recovery plan.

- Test your backup files and your backup plan.

  Testing your backup files and recovery plan is an important part of being prepared for disaster recovery. Testing must include the following tasks:

  - Test your uninterruptible power supply (UPS) on the computers running Windows Server 2003 and on hubs, routers, and other network components.

  - Perform full or partial restorations from your daily, weekly, and monthly backup media.

- Keep two sets of backed-up files: one onsite, for accessibility, and one offsite, for security.

  The backup should be available for restoration to another computer. This can be achieved with network shared folders or with removable media.

  If possible, make a copy of your backup sets every day and store them separately, one onsite and one offsite. That way, if a catastrophic event, such as a fire, destroys all your computers and onsite backup sets, you can restore all your data later. If all your backups are offsite, then the restore process will be very time-consuming because every time you need to recover a file, you must get the backup files from the offsite location.

- Create a backup of the System State data.

  System State data is the collection of system-specific data used by Windows Server 2003 to load, configure, and run the operating system. (System State data is discussed in more detail later on in this module) Create a backup copy of the System State data in case the hard disk on the server fails and cannot be recovered. This backup is required to properly restore your operating system to a new hard disk.

- Install the Recovery Console as a startup option.

  The Recovery Console is a minimal version of the Windows Server 2003 operating system that you can use to start Windows Server 2003 when severe startup problems prevent the server from booting. To allow rapid access to the Recovery Console in a crisis, install the Recovery Console on your computer. This adds the Recovery Console to the list of available operating systems.

- Keep the installation CD-ROM accessible.

  Keep the installation CD-ROM where it can be easily found. You can start the computer from the CD-ROM and then use the Recovery Console or Automated System Recovery.

Lesson: Backing Up Data

* Overview of Backing Up Data
* Who Can Back Up Data?
* What Is System State Data?
* What Is the Backup Utility?
* Types of Backup
* What Is ntbackup?
* What Is Automated System Recovery?
* Practice: Backing Up Data

Introduction

Backing up your data prevents data loss when the original files are lost. Windows Server 2003 includes a backup utility, Backup, that backs up data by copying designated files to storage media. You can also use Windows Server 2003 to back up your server by using Automated System Recovery.

Lesson objectives

After completing this lesson, you will be able to:

- Describe the process of backing up data.

- List those who can back up data.

- Describe the backup of System State data.

- Describe the Backup utility.

- List the various types of backup.

- Describe the **ntbackup** command-line tool.

- Describe an Automated System Recovery set.

- Backup files.

Overview of Backing Up Data

Backups:
- Copy data to alternate media
- Prevent data loss
- Require the following considerations:
  - Which files need back up?
  - What is the backup frequency?
  - What is the need for network backup?

Back Up Data

Introduction

Backup is a single process of copying files and folders from one location to another. Regularly backing up the data on server and client computer hard disks prevents data loss due to disk-drive failures, power outages, virus infections, and other such incidents. If a data loss occurs, and you have performed regular backups based on careful planning, you can restore the lost data, whether it is in one file or on an entire hard disk.

Types of data to back up

The general rule for backing up is, if you cannot get along without it, back it up.

Critical data is the information that your organization needs to survive. If files are accidentally lost or corrupted, you can use the most recent backup to restore this data.

System State data defines the configuration of the server's operating system. If accidental changes occur or if System State data is lost, you can restore System State data from a backup.

How frequently to back up

The following factors determine backup frequency:

- How critical is the data to the organization? You back up critical data more often than data of less importance.

- How frequently is the data changed? For example, if users create or modify reports only on Fridays, a weekly backup for these files is sufficient.

When to use a network backup

Perform a network backup when the critical data is stored on multiple servers. The following table describes the advantages and disadvantages of a network backup.

Advantages	Disadvantages
Backs up the entire network	Users must copy their important files to the servers
Requires less storage	Cannot back up the registry on remote computers
Less media to manage	Increases network traffic
One user can back up data	Requires greater planning and preparation

Who Can Back Up Data?

- **File owners and users with read permissions**
- **Users with rights to the backup files and directories**
- **Groups on local servers:**
  - Administrators
  - Backup operators
  - Server operators

Introduction

You must have certain permissions or user rights to back up and restore files and folders.

Permissions and user rights

To successfully back up and restore data on a computer running Windows Server 2003, you must have the appropriate permissions and user rights, as described in the following list:

- Users can back up the files and folders for which they have assigned ownership, as well the files they have permission to read.

- Users that are assigned the Backup Files and Directories right are able to backup files on the specified servers.

- Users that are assigned the Restore Files and Directories right are able to restore files on the specified servers.

- Members of the local or domain local Administrators, Backup Operators, and Server Operators groups can back up and restore all files, regardless of the assigned NTFS permissions. Server operators can back up all domain controllers. By default, members of these groups have the following user rights: Backup Files and Directories and the Restore Files and Directories.

Restrict access

You can restrict access to a backup by selecting **Allow only the owner and the Administrator access to the backup data** in the **Backup Job Information** dialog box. If you select this option, only an administrator or the person who created the backup file can restore the files and folders.

Separate backup and restore user rights

For security reasons, many organizations prefer to separate the backup and restore user rights into two groups as follows:

1. Create a Backup group and a Restore group by using Active Directory Users and Computers.

2. Add one set of members to the Backup group and another set of members to the Restore group.

3. Assign the Backup group the right to **Backup files and directories** using a Group Policy object (GPO).

4. Assign the Restore group the right to **Restore files and directories** using a GPO.

Location of the Backup files and directories GPO setting

The Backup files and directories GPO setting and Restore files and directories GPO setting are located in the following area of a group policy object:

Computer Configuration

   Windows Settings

      Security Settings

         Local Policies

            User Rights Assignment

What Is System State Data?

System-specific data that must be backed up as a unit

Component	Included in System State
Registry	Always
Boot files, including system files	Always
Certificate Services database	If it is a Certificate Services server
Active Directory directory service	If it is a domain controller
SYSVOL Directory	If it is a domain controller
Cluster service information	If it is within a cluster
IIS metadirectory	If it is installed
System files that are under Windows File Protection	Always

Definition

The System State is the collection of system-specific data that must be backed up as a unit and is maintained by the operating system. The computer uses these system files to load, configure, and run the operating system.

System State components

Backup refers to the following system files as the System State data.

Component	Included in System State?
Registry	Always
Boot files, Com+ Class Registration, including the system files	Always
Certificate Services database	If Certificate Services is installed
Active Directory® directory service	If it is a domain controller
SYSVOL directory	If it is a domain controller
Cluster service information	If it is within a cluster
IIS metadirectory	If IIS is installed
System files that are under Windows File Protection	Always

Back up System State data

When you back up or restore the System State data, all the System State data for the relevant system is backed up or restored. You cannot back up or restore individual components of the System State data because of dependencies among the System State components. However, you can restore the System State data to an alternate location. If you do this, only the registry files, SYSVOL directory files, Cluster database information files, and system boot files are restored to the alternate location. Active Directory, the Certificate Services database, and the COM+ Class Registration database are not restored if you designate an alternate location when you restore the System State data.

Note   To restore system state data on a domain controller you must start the computer in Directory Services Restore Mode.

What Is the Backup Utility?

Use Backup Utility to:
- Back up files and folders
- Back up System State data
- Schedule a backup
- Restore data

Back up open files with Volume Shadow Copy

Back up to various media types

Back Up Data

Corrupted Data

Restore Data

Introduction

The Windows Server 2003 backup utility, Backup, is designed to protect data from accidental loss resulting from the failure of your hardware or storage media.

Use to manage backup

You can use Backup to:

- Back up files and folders.
- Back up System State data.
- Schedule a backup job.
- Restore data.

You can use the Backup Wizard to back up the entire contents of a server, selected portions of the server contents, or the System State data.

Volume shadow copy

You can use Backup to create shadow copy backups of volumes and exact copies of files, including all open files. For example, databases that are held open exclusively and files that are open due to operator or system activity are backed up during a volume shadow copy backup. In this way, files that changed during the backup process are copied correctly.

Volume shadow copy backups ensure that:

- Applications can continue to write data to the volume during a backup.
- Open files are not omitted during a backup.
- Backups can be performed at any time, without locking out users.

Some applications manage storage consistency differently while files are open, which can affect the consistency of the files in the backup. For critical applications, consult the application documentation or your provider to gain a complete understanding of the recommended backup method. When doubt occurs during a backup, quit the application and resolve any questions before performing the backup.

Volume shadow copy is enabled by default. If you disable this option, some files that are open or in use during the backup might be skipped. It is recommended that you do not disable this option.

Storage devices   The Backup utility supports a variety of storage devices and media, including tape drives, logical drives, removable disks, and recordable CD-ROM drives.

Types of Backup

* Some backup types use the archive attribute
* Some backup types work together

Type	Files backed up	Clears archive attribute
Normal or Full	Selected files and folders	Yes
Copy	Selected files and folders	No
Differential	Selected files and folders that were modified after the last normal backup	No
Incremental	Selected files and folders that changed after the last normal or incremental backup	Yes
Daily	Selected files and folders that changed during the day	No

Introduction

Because system needs vary greatly, Windows Server 2003 provides five backup alternatives in the Backup utility. The table below describes each alternative and specifies which data is backed up.

Backup archive attributes

Some backup types use the **archive** attribute, which indicates that a file was modified since the last backup. When a file is modified, the **archive** attribute is set to show that the file needs to be backed up. If these files are backed up by Normal or Incremental, the **archive** attribute is cleared or reset.

Backup types

Backup provides five backup types: Normal, Copy, Differential, Incremental, and Daily. Each of these backup types targets specific file categories for backup, such as files that have changed since the last backup or all files in a specific folder.

The following table presents the backup types, the function of each type, whether the backup type clears **archive** attributes, and tips for using the backup type.

Type	Description
Normal	Backs up all selected files, regardless of the setting of the **archive** attribute, and clears the archive attribute on each backed up file.
	If the file is modified later, the archive attribute is reset to indicate that the file needs to be backed up.
	To establish a baseline for future backups, perform a Normal backup the first time you create a backup set.
Copy	Identical to a Normal backup except that it does not change the **archive** attribute, which allows you to perform other types of backups on the files later.
	Use a Copy backup to create an additional backup tape or disk without disturbing the **archive** attributes.

(continued)

Type	Description
Differential	Creates backup copies of files that have changed since the last backup. The presence of the **archive** attribute indicates that the file was modified and only files with this attribute are backed up. However, the **archive** attribute on files is not modified. This allows you to perform other types of backups on the files later.
	Because a Differential backup does not clear archive attributes, if you perform two Differential backups on a file, the file is backed up each time.
	Differential backups use more media than Incremental backups, but when you restore, you need only the media that contains the files from the Normal backup and the most recent Differential backup. The Differential backup method is slower than the Incremental backup method for backup but faster for restore.
Incremental	Designed to create backups of files that have changed since the most recent normal or Incremental backup. The presence of the **archive** attribute indicates that the file was modified, and only files with this attribute are backed up. When a file is backed up, the **archive** attribute is cleared.
	Because an Incremental backup clears **archive** attributes, if you perform two Incremental backups in a row on a file, the file is not backed up the second time.
	Incremental backups use the minimum amount of media and also save time in a backup by not copying all of the files that have changed since the last full backup. However, restoring a disk after Incremental backups may be inconvenient because some files needing restoration will be on the Normal backup and other files will be on the Incremental backups. The Incremental method backs up faster than the Differential method but restores more slowly.
Daily	Backs up files by using the modification date on the file itself; the Daily method disregards the current state of the archive attribute. The Daily backup does not change the **archive** attributes of files. If a file was modified on the same day as the backup, the file is backed up.

Important   Your backup plan can combine various backup types. If you combine backup types, it is critically important to understand the **archive** attribute. Incremental and Differential backups check for and rely on the **archive** attributes.

Backup scenarios

You perform a normal backup on Monday and Incremental backups on Tuesday through Friday. If your disk fails on Saturday, you must restore the hard disk with Monday's backup and then complete the restore process by using the Tuesday-through-Friday backups in the order that they were written.

You perform a normal backup on Monday and differential backups on Tuesday through Friday. If your disk fails on Saturday, you must restore the hard disk using Monday's backup followed by Friday's backup.

Workers in your organization are required to save their work to a server every hour. Management wants to limit the amount of data that is lost due to a server failure to one hour. To accomplish this, you perform a normal backup on Monday, a differential backup the other four days, and a daily backup every hour.

What Is ntbackup?

* Use the ntbackup command-line tool to:
    * Back up System State data
    * Back up files
    * Back up using batch files
* Understand the ntbackup limitations
    * Backs up whole folders, not selected files
    * Does not accommodate wildcard characters

Definition

In addition to Backup, Windows Server 2003 provides a command-line tool, **ntbackup**, that you can use to back up and restore data. Just like Backup, it can back up files and folders, as well as System State data. However, unlike Backup, **ntbackup** can be used in batch files.

Use the command prompt or batch file

You can perform backup operations from a command prompt or from a batch file by using the **ntbackup** command, followed by various parameters.

Bach files have two important limitations when used to back up your data:

■ When using the **ntbackup** command, you can back up entire folders only. You cannot designate individual files for backup. However, you can designate a backup selection file (.bks file) from the command line, which contains a list of files that you want to back up. You must use the GUI version of the Backup utility to create backup selection files.

■ The **ntbackup** command does not support the use of wildcard characters. For example, typing ***.txt** does not back up files with a .txt extension.

Ntbackup syntax

To back up files by using **ntbackup**:

■ At the command-line prompt, type:

ntbackup backup [systemstate] "@bks *file name*" **/J** {*"job name"*} [**/P** {*"pool name"*}] [**/G** {*"guid name"*}] [**/T** { *"tape name"*}] [**/N** {*"media name"*}] [**/F** {*"file name"*}] [**/D** {*"set description"*}] [**/DS** {*"server name"*}] [**/IS** {*"server name"*}] [**/A**] [**/V:**{**yes|no**}] [**/R:**{**yes|no**}] [**/L:**{**f|s|n**}] [**/M** {*backup type*}] [**/RS:**{**yes|no**}] [**/HC:**{**on|off**}] [**/SNAP:**{**on|off**}]

■ To back up the System State to E:\SysState.bkf:

ntbackup backup systemstate /J SysState /F E:\SysState.bkf

- To backup the C:\MOC directory:

ntbackup backup C:\MOC /J MOC /F E:\MOC.bkf

Parameter	Definition
systemstate	Initiates a backup of the System State data. When you select this option, the backup type is forced to normal or copy.
@bks *file name*	Specifies the name of the backup selection file (.bks file) to be used for this backup operation. The at (@) character must precede the name of the backup selection file. A backup selection file contains information about the files and folders you have selected for backup. You must create the file by using the graphical user interface (GUI) version of Backup.
/J {*"job name"*}	Specifies the job name to be used in the backup report. The job name usually describes the files and folders you are backing up in the current backup job.
/P {*"pool name"*}	Specifies the media pool from which you want to use media. This is usually a subpool of the Backup media pool, such as 4mm DDS. If you select this parameter, you cannot use the **/A**, **/G**, **/F**, or **/T** command-line options.
/G {*"guid name"*}	Overwrites or appends to this tape. Do not use this switch in conjunction with **/P**.
/T {*"tape name"*}	Overwrites or appends to this tape. Do not use this switch in conjunction with **/P**.
/N {*"media name"*}	Specifies the new tape name. Do not use **/A** with this switch.
/F {*"file name"*}	Logical disk path and file name. Do not use the **/P**, **/G**, or **/T** switch with this switch.
/D {*"set description"*}	Specifies a label for each backup set.
/DS {*"server name"*}	Backs up the directory service file for the specified Microsoft Exchange server.
/IS {*"server name"*}	Backs up the Information Store file for the specified Microsoft Exchange server.
/A	Performs an append operation. Use either **/G** or **/T** with this switch. Do not use this switch in conjunction with **/P**.
/V:{**yes**|**no**}	Verifies the data after the backup is complete.
/R:{**yes**|**no**}	Restricts access to this tape to the owner or members of the Administrators group.

(*continued*)

Parameter	Definition
/L:{f|s|n}	Specifies the type of log file: **f**=full, **s**=summary, **n**=none (no log file is created).
/M {*backup type*}	Specifies the backup type. It must be one of the following: normal, copy, differential, incremental, or daily.
/RS:{yes|no}	Backs up the migrated data files located in Remote Storage. The /RS command-line option is not required to back up the local Removable Storage database that contains the Remote Storage placeholder files. When you back up the %systemroot% folder, Backup automatically backs up the Removable Storage database as well.
/HC:{on|off}	Uses hardware compression, if available, on the tape drive.
/SNAP:{on|off}	Specifies whether the backup should use a volume shadow copy.

Note For more information about how to use **ntbackup** command-line parameters, see Microsoft Knowledge Base article 814583 on the Microsoft Help and Support Web site.

What Is Automated System Recovery?

* A recovery option in the Backup utility
* Operating system backup
* Does not include data files
* Creates a floppy disk with configuration information

To back up all data, choose the All information option

 Automated System Recovery Wizard
The ASR Preparation wizard helps you create a two-part backup of your system: a floppy disk that has your system settings, and other media that contains a backup of your local system partition.

Introduction

Automated System Recovery (ASR), in the Backup utility, helps you to recover a system that does not start. ASR contains two parts: backup and recovery. ASR also creates a floppy disk that is used to store disk configurations during the ASR recovery procedure.

ASR restores operating system

Typically, after installing or upgrading to Windows Server 2003, you create a set of ASR disks. The ASR process enables you to restore an installation of Windows Server 2003 to the condition of the operating system at the time that you created the ASR backup set.

ASR Backup Wizard

The ASR Backup Wizard backs up the System State data, system services, and the boot and system volumes. The ASR Backup Wizard also creates a floppy disk, which contains information about the backup, the disk configurations, including basic and dynamic volumes, and the restore procedure. The ASR Backup Wizard does not back up volumes other than the boot and system volumes.

Backup or Restore Wizard

The Backup or Restore Wizard provides several backup options. The **All information on this computer** option backs up all data on the computer in addition to the System State data and the operating system components. This option also creates a system recovery disk that you can used to restore Windows in case of a disk failure.

Practice: Backing Up Data

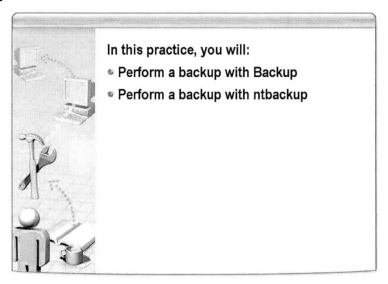

In this practice, you will:
- Perform a backup with Backup
- Perform a backup with ntbackup

Objective

In this practice, you will:

- Perform a backup with Backup
- Perform a backup with ntbackup

Instructions

Ensure that the DEN-DC1 virtual machine is running.

Practice

▶ **Perform a backup with Backup**

1. Log on to DEN-DC1 as **Administrator** with a password of **Pa$$w0rd**.
2. Click **Start**, point to **All Programs**, point to **Accessories**, point to **System Tools**, and click **Backup**.
3. Click **Advanced Mode** and click the **Backup** tab.
4. Expand **D:\2275\Practices**, and then check the **MOD07** check box.
5. In the **Backup media or file name** box, type **D:\MOD07.bkf**
6. Click **Start Backup**.
7. Click **Replace the data on the media with this backup** and click **Start Backup**.
8. When the backup is complete, click **Report**.
9. Read the report then close Notepad.
10. Click **Close** and close Backup.

Practice

▶ **Perform a backup with ntbackup**

1. Open a command prompt.

2. In the command window, type:
   ntbackup backup D:\2275\Practices\Mod07 /j ntbackup /f d:\MOD072.bkf

   This command backs up the **D:\2275\Practices\Mod07** folder as **D:\MOD072.bkf**.

3. Verify the backup completed.

   a. Type **D:** and press ENTER.

   b. Type **dir** and press ENTER. **MOD072.bkf** should be listed and the same size as **MOD07.bkf**.

4. Close the command prompt.

Important Do not shut down the virtual machine.

Lesson: Scheduling Backup Jobs

- What Is a Scheduled Backup Job?
- What Are Scheduled Backup Options?
- Best Practices for Backup
- Practice: Scheduling Backup Jobs

Introduction

A systems administrator responsible for backing up files and folders must take care to schedule backups appropriately. Using your organization's backup plan, schedule your backups so that they contain the most complete and up-to-date set of files by using the most efficient method.

Lesson objectives

After completing this lesson, you will be able to:

- Describe a scheduled backup job.
- List backup schedule options.
- List best practices for backup.
- Schedule a backup job by using Backup.

What Is a Scheduled Backup Job?

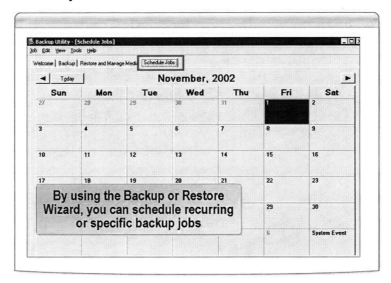

Introduction

Most backups occur outside of regular business hours; it is a good practice to perform backups on a consistent and predictable schedule. Backups are ideal to run as scheduled jobs because they are routine work done at inconvenient times. Scheduling backups ensures that they are not forgotten and avoid requiring staff at odd hours.

Two ways to schedule a backup job

Try to schedule a backup job to occur at regular intervals or during periods of relative inactivity on a network.

You can schedule a backup job two ways:

- When you create a new backup job in Backup
- By using the **Scheduled Jobs** tab in Backup to schedule a previously saved backup job

What Are Scheduled Backup Options?

Schedule options	Executes the job:
Once	At a specific time on a specified date
Daily	At a specified time each day
Weekly	At a specified time on specified weekdays
Monthly	At a specified time on a specified day each month
At startup	The next time the system is started
At logon	The next time the job owner logs on
When idle	After the system is idle for a specified period

Introduction

Windows Server 2003 provides several options to help you schedule your backup job.

Backup options

The following table describes the options that are available for scheduling backup jobs.

Schedule options	Executes the job:
Once	At a specified time on a specified date
Daily	At a specified time each day
Weekly	At a specified time on each specified day of the week
Monthly	At a specified time on a specified day each month
At system startup	The next time the system is started
At logon	The next time the job owner logs on
When idle	After the system is idle for a specified period

Best Practices for Backup

- Develop a backup strategy and test it
- Train appropriate personnel
- Backup volume and System State data simultaneously
- Create an Automated System Recovery Backup set
- Make copies
- Perform trial restorations
- Secure media
- Use the default Volume Shadow Copy backup

Introduction

You can protect your organization from data loss with a backup plan that employs the backup best practices.

Best practices

Apply these best practices as you develop your backup plan:

- Develop backup strategies and test them.

  A good plan ensures that you can quickly recover your data if it is lost.

- Train appropriate personnel.

  On minimum-security and medium-security networks, assign backup rights to one user, by using Group Policy, and assign restore rights to a different user. Identify and train alternate administrators with rights to perform the restore tasks when the administrator is unavailable.

  On a high-security network, only administrators should restore files.

- Back up volumes and the System State data at the same time. This action allows you to be prepared in the unlikely event of a disk failure.

- Create an Automated System Recovery backup set.

  Always create an Automated System Recovery (ASR) backup set when the operating system changes, for example, whenever you install new hardware and drivers or apply a service pack. An ASR backup set can help you to recover from a server failure. ASR protects only the System State files, so you must back up data volumes separately.

- Create a backup log.

  Always create a backup log for each backup, and then print the logs for reference. Keep a book of logs to help you locate specific files. The backup log is helpful when you restore data; you can print it or read it from any text editor. Also, if the media containing the backup set catalog is corrupted, the printed log can help you locate a file.

- Make copies of the backup media.

  Keep at least three copies of the media. Keep at least one copy offsite in a properly controlled environment.

- Perform trial restorations.

  Perform a trial restoration on a regular basis to verify that your files are properly backed up. A trial restoration can uncover hardware or media corruption problems that do not show up when you verify software.

- Secure media.

  Secure the media. It is possible for someone to access the data from a stolen medium by restoring the data to another server for which they are an administrator.

- Use the default Volume Shadow Copy backup.

  Do not disable the default Volume Shadow Copy backup method. If you disable this method, open files that are being used by the system during the backup process will be skipped during the backup.

Practice: Scheduling Backup Jobs

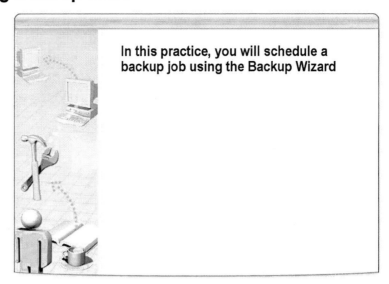

In this practice, you will schedule a backup job using the Backup Wizard

Objective

In this practice, you will schedule a backup job using the Backup Wizard.

Instructions

Ensure that DEN-DC1 virtual machine is running.

Practice

▶ **Schedule a backup job by using the Backup Wizard**

1. Click **Start**, point to **All Programs**, point to **Accessories**, point to **System Tools**, and click **Backup**.

2. Click **Advanced Mode**, and then click the button beside **Backup Wizard (Advanced)**.

3. Click **Next** to begin the Backup Wizard.

4. Click **Back up selected files, drives, or network data** and click **Next**.

5. Expand **My Computer**, expand **D:\2275\Practices**, check the **MOD07** check box, and click **Next**.

6. In the **Choose a place to save your backup** box, click **D:**.

7. In the **Type a name for this backup** box, type **MOD07**, and click **Next**.

8. Click the **Advanced** button.

9. Click **Next** to select a normal backup.

10. Check the **Verify data after backup** check box and click **Next**.

11. Click **Replace the existing backups** and click **Next**.

12. Click **Later**, type **MOD073** in the **Job name** box, and click **Set Schedule**.

13. Change the **Start time** to 5 minutes from now and click **OK**.

14. In the **Run as** box, type **CONTOSO\Administrator**, type **Pa$$w0rd** in the **Password** and **Confirm password** boxes, and then click **OK**.

15. Click **Next**.

16. In the **Run as** box, type **CONTOSO\Administrator**, type **Pa$$w0rd** in the **Password** and **Confirm password** boxes, and then click **OK**.

17. Click **Finish**.

18. Close Backup.

19. Click **Start**, point to **Control Panel**, point to **Scheduled Tasks**, and click **MOD073**. This is the task that runs the backup job you just created.

20. Read the options in the **Run** box. These options correspond with options you selected when creating the backup job.

21. Click **Cancel** and wait for the backup job to run.

Important   Do not shut down the virtual machine.

Lesson: Restoring Data

* What Is Restoring Data?
* Guidelines for Restoring Data
* Practice: Restoring Data

Introduction

The second part of the disaster recovery process involves restoring the backup data.

Lesson objectives

After completing this lesson, you will be able to:

- Describe how to restore data.
- Describe guidelines for restoring data.
- Restore data with Backup.

What Is Restoring Data?

Restoring data rewrites:

* Files and folders

* System State data

The ASR Restore:

* Reads recovery data for disk configuration

* Restores book disk signatures, volumes, and partitions

* Installs a recovery version of Windows

* Initiates the restore from backup

Restore Data

Introduction

When you use Backup to create a duplicate copy of the data on your hard disk and then archive the data on another storage device, such as a hard disk or a tape, you can use the Restore feature in Backup to easily restore the data.

Restore files and folders

Using Backup, you can restore the archived files and folders to your hard disk or any other disk that you can access.

Back up and restore data on FAT or NTFS volumes

You can use Backup to back up and restore data on either FAT (file allocation table) or NTFS file system volumes. However, restore data backed up from an Windows Server 2003 NTFS volume, to a Windows Server 2003 NTFS volume. This practice avoids the loss of both data and file and folder features, such as permissions, Encrypting File System (EFS) settings, disk quota information, mounted drive information, and Remote Storage information.

Restore System State data

You can use Backup to restore the System State data. If the System State data was backed up on a computer and that computer system fails, you can rebuild the computer with the original Windows Server 2003 compact disc and the System State data.

ASR Restore

You can access the restore part of ASR by pressing F2 when prompted in the text mode portion of Windows setup. ASR reads the disk configurations from the floppy disk and restores the entire disk signatures, volumes, and partitions on the disks that are required to start the computer. ASR then installs a simple installation of Windows and automatically starts to restore from backup by using the ASR backup set that you created by using the ASR Backup Wizard.

Guidelines for Restoring Data

- Plan and test restoration strategies
- Set permissions for systems administrators
- Verify connections to each restore location
- Ensure access to network based media
- Consider data recovery for EFS files restored at alternate locations

Introduction

After backing up your files and employ the best practices while developing a backup plan, you must create a restoration plan. The following checklist includes recommended best practices for creation of your organization's restoration plan.

Guidelines for restoring data

Restoration plan best practices include the following:

- Develop restoration strategies and test them.

  Remember to keep a record of your backup and restoration plans for reference in the event of data loss.

- Be sure that all appropriate systems administrators have the necessary permissions.

- Verify that you can connect to all shared folders on computers under your restoration plan.

  You can use the default user rights of the Backup Operators group to restore your organization's data and system files, or you can segregate backup and restore permissions by individuals.

- Ensure that you have access to network-based media and to the server where the data is to be restored.

  As part of your restoration plan, be sure to test your access to the storage media with the backed-up files.

- To restore files manually, use the Backup utility and select the appropriate files or folders.

  Because you may need to restore only certain files, use the Backup utility to test the procedure that you will use to select and restore only those files.

- If you are restoring EFS files on a system where the private key for the encrypted data is inaccessible, send the files to a designated recovery agent.

  For files that are inaccessible due to encryption, perform a test by sending the files to a designated recovery agent.

Practice: Restoring Data

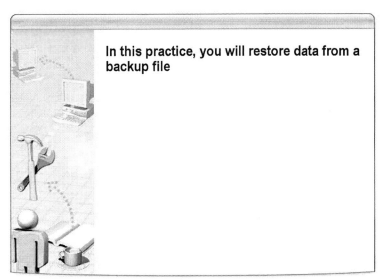

In this practice, you will restore data from a backup file

Objective

In this practice, you will restore data from a backup file.

Instructions

Ensure that the DEN-DC1 virtual machine is started.

Practice

▶ **Restore data from a backup file**

1. Open Windows Explorer, and delete the **D:\2275\Practices\MOD07** folder.

2. Click **Start**, point to **All Programs**, point to **Accessories**, point to **System Tools**, and then click **Backup**.

3. Click **Advanced Mode** and click the **Restore and Manage Media** tab.

4. On the **Restore and Manage Media** tab, expand **File**, expand **MOD07.bkf**, and expand **D:**. You can see that only the MOD07 folder structure exists in this backup.

5. Check the **D:** check box, and then click **Start Restore**.

6. Click **OK**.

7. When "Restore is complete" appears in the **Restore Progress** dialog box, click **Close**, and then close the Backup utility.

8. In Windows Explorer, press F5 to refresh the screen, and then verify that the **D:\2275\Practices\MOD07** folder has been restored.

9. Close Windows Explorer.

▶ **To prepare for the next practice**

- Start the DEN-CL1 virtual machine.

Important   Do not shut down the virtual machine.

Lesson: Configuring Shadow Copies

* What Are Shadow Copies?
* Previous Versions Client Software for Shadow Copies
* Shadow Copy Scheduling
* What Is Restoring Shadow Copies?
* Best Practices for Using Shadow Copies
* Practice: Configuring Shadow Copies

Introduction

In Windows Server 2003, you can use Shadow Copies of Shared Folders as a data recovery tool. The Previous Versions client software saves iterative versions of files and folders.

Lesson objectives

After completing this lesson, you will be able to:

■ Describe shadow copies.

■ Describe the Previous Versions client software for shadow copies.

■ Describe scheduling shadow copies.

■ Describe restoring shadow copies.

■ List best practices for using shadow copies.

■ Configure Shadow Copies.

What Are Shadow Copies?

* Shadow copies provide iterative versions of network folders
* Use shadow copies to:
  * Recover files
  * Review previous versions
* Shadow copies are:
  * Enabled per volume
  * Not a replacement for regular backups
  * Allocated storage limits versions

Definition

A shadow copy is a feature of the Windows Server 2003 family that provides point-in-time, read-only copies of files on network shares. With Shadow Copies of Shared Folders, you can view the contents of network folders as they existed at various points in time. To view Shadow Copies of Shared Folders, you must install the client software.

Shadow copy scenarios

You can use shadow copies in the following three scenarios:

- Recover files that were accidentally deleted.

  This scenario is the network equivalent of a short-term local backup and restore. If a user accidentally deletes a file, the user can open a previous version of the file and copy it to a safe location.

- Recover files that were accidentally overwritten.

  Shadow Copies of Shared Folders can be very useful in environments where new files are commonly created by opening an existing file, making modifications, and then saving the file with a new name. For example, you might open a financial-modeling spreadsheet, make modifications based upon new assumptions, and then save the spreadsheet with a new name to create a new spreadsheet. The problem arises when you forget to save the file by using a new name, thereby erasing the original work. You can use Shadow Copies of Shared Folders to recover the previous version of the file.

- Allow version-checking while working on documents.

  You can use Shadow Copies of Shared Folders during the normal work cycle to check the differences between two versions of a file. For example, you might want to know "What did this paragraph say this morning before I started to rewrite it?"

Shadow copy characteristics

The following characteristics apply to shadow copies:

- Configuring shadow copies is not a replacement for creating regular backups. Shadow copies may not be able to recover corrupted files, and cannot recover files if a volume fails.
- Shadow copies are read-only. You cannot edit the contents of a shadow copy.
- Shadow copies are enabled on a per-volume basis. You cannot enable shadow copies on specific shared resources.
- After shadow copies are enabled on a volume, shadow copies are enabled for all shared folders on that volume.
- Shadow copies track changes to files, they do not make copies of files.

Shadow copies storage

The minimum amount of storage space for shadow copies is 100 megabytes (MB). The default maximum storage size is 10 percent of the source volume or the volume being copied, but you can change the maximum size at any time. When the storage limit is reached, the oldest versions of the shadow copies are deleted and cannot be restored.

Allocate storage space

When determining the amount of space to allocate for storing shadow copies, you must consider how many files are being changed, the size of the files, and the number of changes being performed. If too little space is allocated, some previous versions will be lost.

Store shadow copies on a different volume

You can also store shadow copies on a different storage volume. However, changing the storage volume deletes the shadow copies. To avoid this problem, verify that the storage volume that you initially select is large enough to handle your present and future needs.

Note For more information about shadow copies, see the Volume Shadow Copy Presentation on the Microsoft Web site.

Previous Versions Client Software for Shadow Copies

* Previous Versions client software is stored on the server

  %systemroot%\system32\clients\twclient\x86 directory

* Use to access previous versions of files

Introduction

The ability to access shadow copies of files is not built into client computers. The Previous Versions client software must be installed on each client that requires access to shadow copies of files.

Client software for shadow copies

The installation files for the Previous Versions client software are located on the server in the %Systemroot%\system32\clients\twclient\x86 directory. You can distribute the client software in a variety of ways; consider the various options before deployment. Windows Server 2003 provides several tools, such as Group Policy, that can make deploying and maintaining the client software easier.

Viewing shadow copies

Shadow copies are snapshots of files taken at a specific point in time to retain multiple versions. Shadow copies are not available for files stored on client computers, only Windows Server 2003. Shadow copies can be viewed from both servers and clients.

Locations of shadow copy views

Access to shadow copies differs between server and client.

- On the server, access shadow copies of shared folders through the **Shadow Copies** tab of the **Local Disk Properties** dialog box.

- On the client, access shadow copies (called previous versions) through the **Previous Versions** tab of the shared folder **Properties** dialog box.

Alert users

It is recommended that you place the client software on a shared resource and then send an e-mail message to users that describes the function of the software and how to install it.

For example, you may want to inform users that:

- A new feature, Previous Versions, is enabled on the following file share: *\\server\sharedresource*.

- Files are scheduled to be copied at 7:00 A.M. and noon, Monday through Friday. Remember that these copies do not reflect modifications made to these files after these copy times.

- Saving your work frequently is still the best way to ensure that your work is not lost.

- To use Previous Versions, install the client software located at *\\server\sharedresource* and double-click **twclient.msi**.

Note For more information about installing software using Group Policy, see Course 2279, *Planning, Implementing, and Maintaining a Microsoft Windows Server 2003 Active Directory Infrastructure*.

Shadow Copy Scheduling

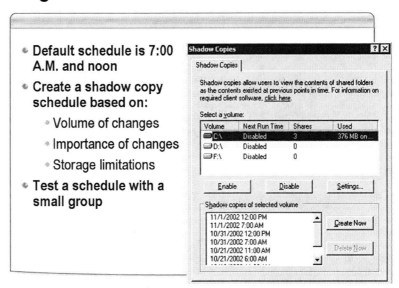

- Default schedule is 7:00 A.M. and noon
- Create a shadow copy schedule based on:
  - Volume of changes
  - Importance of changes
  - Storage limitations
- Test a schedule with a small group

Introduction

When you enable Shadow Copies of Shared Folders, a default schedule is created. Although this schedule may work for your organization, evaluate the work habits of your users to confirm its suitability to your needs.

Create a shadow copy schedule

Consider how many changes there are to your data and how important it is to capture them all. The default schedule is 7:00 A.M. and noon, daily. In most organizations this schedule captures changes before daily work begins and again during the lull at lunch hour. However, if the work day starts at 6 A.M., you may want to change the first shadow copy to 5 A.M. If losing a half day of changes would severely affect your users, you might want to create a shadow copy every hour.

If you increase the number of scheduled shadow copies, consider how often copies can be added without requiring additional storage. Before deploying Shadow Copies of Shared Folders, it is recommended that you create a plan that specifies where to store the shadow copies and what the storage limits are. You can store up to 64 shadow copies per volume. When this limit is reached, the oldest shadow copy is deleted and cannot be retrieved.

Deploy a small test group

You may want to create an initial schedule and deploy it for a small group to test whether your schedule creates enough shadow copies while staying within your storage limits. Also, consider asking your users about their work habits and when they think that a shadow copy would be beneficial. For example, if there is a shift change at 3 P.M., that would be a good time to capture changes.

Scenario

You have enabled Shadow Copies for Shared Folders on all file servers and are using the default schedule. Your organization has a flexible schedule that allows employees to work any time between 7:00 A.M. and 7:00 P.M. Many users create files between noon and 7:00 P.M.

Question: Are these files protected by shadow copies if users save them every hour?

Answer: The files of users who modify and save their files between noon and 7:00 P.M. are not saved by shadow copies until 7:00 A.M. the next day. To protect their files, set up a schedule to create shadow copies of their files every hour from 7:00 A.M. to 7:00 P.M. every weekday. Depending on storage limits, this schedule provides the users with up to five days of shadow copies.

What Is Restoring Shadow Copies?

A server saved copy of a file or folder is restored to the client

Characteristics of Shadow Copies	
If...	**Then**
No previous versions	The file was not modified after the last save
Restoring a folder	The current version is deleted
Restoring a file	File permissions are not changed
Properties does not include a Previous Versions tab	Shadow copies might not be enabled
Copying a file	File permissions are set to default

Introduction

After you create a shadow copy, you can use it to restore shared files and folders to a previous version.

Note   You can restore a shadow copy only from a client.

Restored files and folders using previous versions

If no previous versions are listed on the Previous Versions tab, the file has not changed since the oldest copy was made.

Restoring overwrites the current version

Restoring a previous version overwrites the current version. If you restore a previous version of a folder, the folder is restored to its state at the date and time that you selected. Any changes that you made to files in the folder before that time are lost.

If you do not want to delete the current version, use the **Copy** command to copy the previous version to a different location.

Example of a previous version folder

For example, the current version of a folder contains files A, B, and C. The previous version of the folder contained only files A and B. After you restore the previous version, the folder contains the previous version of file A, the previous version of file B, and the current version of file C.

File permissions are not changed

When you restore a file, the file permissions are not changed. Permissions remain the same as they were before you restored the file. When you copy a previous version of a file, the permissions are set to the default permissions for the directory where the copy of the file is placed.

Best Practices for Using Shadow Copies

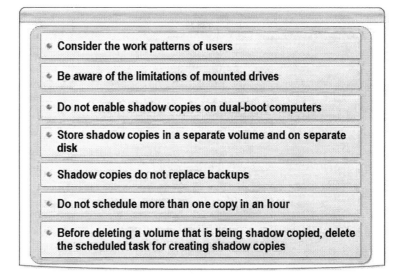

* Consider the work patterns of users

* Be aware of the limitations of mounted drives

* Do not enable shadow copies on dual-boot computers

* Store shadow copies in a separate volume and on separate disk

* Shadow copies do not replace backups

* Do not schedule more than one copy in an hour

* Before deleting a volume that is being shadow copied, delete the scheduled task for creating shadow copies

Introduction

Shadow copies can help you restore lost or corrupt data files. Best practices are designed to help you gain the maximum benefit from this important resource.

Best practices

Consider these best practices when you configure shadow copies and create a shadow copy schedule:

- Adjust the shadow copy schedule to fit the work patterns of your users.

- Be aware of mounted drive limitations.

  Mounted drives are not included when shadow copies are made for a volume. If you want shadow copies enabled on a mounted drive, it must be done separately from the volume to which the drive is mounted. Clients cannot access previous versions on a mounted drive if it is through a share with mount points. However, clients can access previous versions if they have access through a share on the mounted drive.

Note For more information about Volume Shadow copies and mounted drives see Microsoft Knowledge Base article 812547 on the Microsoft Help and Support Web site.

- Do not enable shadow copies on computers with a dual-boot configuration.

  If you have enabled a dual-boot configuration on a computer running an earlier operating system (such as Microsoft Windows NT® 4.0), the shadow copies that persist during the reboot may be corrupted and unusable when the computer is started in Windows Server 2003.

- Select a separate volume on another disk as the storage area for shadow copies.

  Using a separate volume on another disk provides better performance and is recommended for heavily used file servers.

■ Creating shadow copies is not a substitute for regular backups.

Use Backup in coordination with shadow copies to provide your best restoration scenario.

■ Do not schedule copies to occur more often than once per hour. The default schedule is set for 7:00 A.M. and noon. If you decide that you need copies to be made more often, make sure you allot enough storage space and that you do not schedule copies to be made so often that server performance is degraded.

■ If you delete the volume but not the shadow copy task, the scheduled task fails and an Event ID: 7001 error is written to the event log. Delete the shadow copy task before deleting the volume to avoid filling the event log with these errors.

Practice: Configuring Shadow Copies

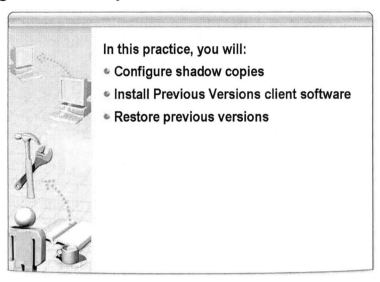

In this practice, you will:
* Configure shadow copies
* Install Previous Versions client software
* Restore previous versions

Objective

In this practice, you will:

- Configure shadow copies.
- Install Previous Versions client software.
- Restore previous versions.

Instructions

Ensure that the DEN-DC1 and DEN-CL1 virtual machines are running.

Practice

▶ **Configure shadow copies**

1. On DEN-DC1, click **Start**, point to **Administrative Tools**, and click **Computer Management**.

2. Right-click **Shared Folders**, point to **All Tasks**, and then click **Configure Shadow Copies**.

3. Click the **D:** volume and then click **Enable**.

4. In the **Enable Shadow Copies** dialog box, click **Yes**.

5. Click **Settings**, and then click **Schedule**.

6. Check the **Sat** and **Sun** check boxes. This configures a 7 A.M. shadow copy to also run on Saturday and Sunday.

7. In the Schedule drop-down list, click item **2**. This selects the 12 P.M. shadow copy schedule.

8. Check the **Sat** and **Sun** check boxes. This configures the 12 P.M. shadow copy to also run on Saturday and Sunday.

9. Click **OK** and click **OK**.

10. Click **OK** and close **Computer Management**.

Practice

▶ **Install Previous Versions client software**

1. On DEN-DC1, click **Start**, point to **Administrative Tools**, and click **Computer Management**.

2. Expand **Shared Folders**, right-click **Shares**, and click **New Share**.

3. Click **Next**, in the **Folder path** box, type **C:\Windows\system32\clients\twclient\x86**, and then click **Next**.

4. Type **ShadowClient** in the **Share name** box, and click **Next.**

5. Click **Finish** and click **Close**.

6. Close **Computer Management**.

7. On DEN-CL1, log on as **Administrator** with a password of **Pa$$w0rd**.

8. Click **Start**, click **Run**, type **\\DEN-DC1\ShadowClient\twcli32.msi** and then click **OK**.

9. Click **Finish** and then log off of **DEN-CL1**.

10. Log on to DEN-CL1 as **Paul** with the password of **Pa$$w0rd**.

Practice

▶ **Restore previous versions**

1. On DEN-CL1, click **Start**, click **Run**, type **\\DEN-DC1\Data**, and then click **OK**.

2. Create a text file named **Shadow**.

3. Double-click **Shadow** to edit it, type **Version1**, save the file, and close Notepad.

4. On DEN-DC1, click **Start**, point to **Administrative Tools**, and click **Computer Management**.

5. Right-click **Shared Folders**, point to **All Tasks**, and then click **Configure Shadow Copies**.

6. Click the **D:** volume and click **Create Now**. This forces a shadow copy to be taken. This is done in the classroom because the default schedule for shadow copies is 7A.M. and 12 noon only.

7. Click **OK** and close **Computer Management**.

8. On DEN-CL1, double-click **Shadow** to edit it, add a second line **Version2**, save the file, and close Notepad.

9. Right-click **Shadow** and click **Properties**.

10. Click the **Previous Versions** tab. Notice that the previous version is here.

11. Click **Copy**, click **My Documents**, and click **Copy**.

12. Click **OK**.

13. In Windows Explorer, click **My Documents**.

14. Double-click **Shadow** to edit it. This is the original version of the file.

15. Close **Notepad** and close the Explorer window.

Important   Do not shut down the virtual machines.

▶ **To prepare for** the **next practice**

• To prepare for the next practice, start the DEN-SRV1 virtual machine.

Lesson: Recovering from Server Failure

- ● What Is Safe Mode?
- ● What Are Safe Mode Options?
- ● What Is Last Known Good Configuration?
- ● What Is the Recovery Console?
- ● What Is a Windows Startup Disk?
- ● How Startup Files Function
- ● Selecting Disaster-Recovery Methods
- ● Practice: Recovering from Server Failure

Introduction

If a server fails, Windows Server 2003 provides you with several options for restoring the computer. Understanding these options and their functions can help you to restore a server to working condition.

Lesson objectives

After completing this lesson, you will be able to:

- Explain safe mode and when it is appropriate.
- Describe safe mode options.
- Explain Last Known Good Configuration and when its use is appropriate.
- Describe the Recovery Console and when its use is appropriate.
- Describe the Windows startup disk.
- Explain how startup files function.
- Explain how to select a disaster-recovery method.
- Use server recovery methods.

What Is Safe Mode?

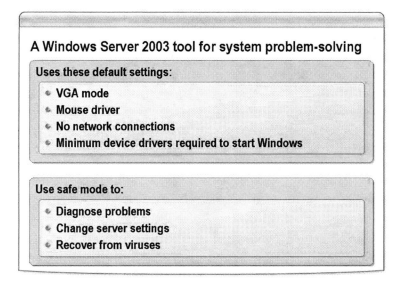

A Windows Server 2003 tool for system problem-solving

Uses these default settings:

- VGA mode
- Mouse driver
- No network connections
- Minimum device drivers required to start Windows

Use safe mode to:

- Diagnose problems
- Change server settings
- Recover from viruses

Definition

If your computer does not start, you may be able to start it in safe mode. In this mode, Windows uses default settings, video graphics adapter (VGA) mode, the mouse driver, no network connections, and only the device drivers required to start Windows.

Start a computer using Safe Mode

If your computer does not start after you install new software, new hardware, or a new driver, you may be able to start it with minimal services in safe mode and then change your computer settings, remove newly installed software from startup, or remove a hardware driver that is causing the problem. If necessary, you can reinstall a service pack or the entire operating system.

Use Safe Mode to diagnose problems

Safe mode helps you diagnose problems. If a symptom does not reappear when you start in safe mode, you can eliminate the default settings and minimum device drivers as possible causes. If a newly added device or a changed driver is causing problems, you can use safe mode to remove the device or reverse a change.

Safe mode is often used when recovering from a virus infection. Starting only the minimum drivers ensures that a virus is not in memory when the system is cleaned.

What Are Safe Mode Options?

Option	Description	Use
Safe Mode	**Loads only basic files and drivers**	**When Windows is not starting in Normal mode**
Safe Mode with Networking	**Loads only basic files and drivers, plus network connections**	**To access troubleshooting tools that are on the network**
Safe Mode with Command Prompt	**Loads only basic files, drivers, and a command prompt interface**	**When Safe Mode will not start properly**

Introduction

There are three different Safe Mode options in the Advanced Startup Options that you can use to troubleshoot problems. Each option is suited to a different set of circumstances.

Note   To display the advanced startup options, press F8 during the operating system selections phase of the startup process in Windows Server 2003.

Safe Mode

Safe Mode loads only the basic devices and drivers that are required to start the computer, including the mouse, keyboard, mass storage devices, base video, and the standard, default set of system services. This option also creates a log file.

This mode is used to troubleshoot most problems because it provides access to all of the standard GUI administrative tools while minimizing the running services. Typical problems include poorly written drivers and bad services. In Safe Mode, drivers can be changed and services can be disabled.

The Windows installer service is not functional in Safe Mode, so installing and removing most applications is not possible.

Safe Mode with Networking

Safe Mode with Networking loads the same basic set of drivers and services as Safe Mode, but also includes networking drivers. This option also creates a log file.

This mode is used when network drivers are not suspect and troubleshooting tools on the network are required. For instance, a computer may need to obtain a virus removal tool from a network file share.

Safe Mode with Command Prompt

Safe Mode with Command Prompt loads the same basic set of drivers and services as Safe Mode, but does not load the GUI. This option also creates a log file.

This mode is typically used only when Safe Mode is unable to start properly. If Safe Mode with Command Prompt starts properly and Safe Mode does not then there is likely a problem with the display subsystem in Windows.

What Is Last Known Good Configuration?

* Restores registry information and drivers
* Resolves startup problems after a change
* Does not solve problems caused by corrupted or missing drivers or files
* Logging on updates the Last Known Good Configuration

Definition	The Last Known Good Configuration startup option uses the registry information and drivers that Windows saved at the last successful logon. When you use this option to start a server, any changes made to driver settings or other system settings since the last successful logon are lost. Use this option only when the configuration is incorrect.
Registry restore	When Last Known Good Configuration is selected, the information for the registry subkey HKEY_LOCAL_MACHINE\SYSTEM\CurrentControlSet is restored. Also, if you updated any device drivers, using Last Known Good Configuration restores the previous drivers.
Resolve startup problems	Using Last Known Good Configuration can help you resolve startup or stability problems. For example, if a Stop error occurs immediately after you install a new application or device driver, you can restart the computer and use Last Known Good Configuration to recover from the problem. It does not solve problems that are caused by corrupted or missing drivers or files.
Updating Last Known Good Configuration	Windows Server 2003 only updates Last Known Good Configuration information in the registry when the operating system starts in normal mode and a user logs on successfully.
	Logging on to the computer in safe mode does not update the Last Known Good Configuration. Therefore, using Last Known Good Configuration remains an option if you cannot resolve your problem by using safe mode.

What Is the Recovery Console?

```
Includes:

  * A minimal version of Windows Server 2003
  * A command-line interface

Allows administrators to:

  * Enable or disable device drivers or services
  * Copy files from the installation CD for the operating
    system, or copy files from other removable media
  * Create a new boot sector or new master boot record
    (MBR)
```

Definition

The Recovery Console is a minimal version of the Windows Server 2003 operating system that you can use to start Windows Server 2003 when severe startup problems prevent the server from booting. It provides a command-line interface and a set of commands that you can use to repair damaged system components, such as a damaged boot sector, that prevent you from starting the computer any other way.

Starting the Recovery Console

You can start the Recovery Console from the Windows Server 2003 Setup program or from the operating system section screen at startup. To start the Recovery Console from the Windows Server 2003 Setup program, boot the computer using the Windows Server 2003 compact disk. When prompted to choose whether to set up Windows Server 2003 or repair an existing installation, select the repair option.

The Recovery Console must be manually installed into the operating system selection screen. To install the Recovery Console locally, run **D:\i386\winn32.exe /cmdcons**, where D: is your CD-ROM drive.

If Windows Server 2003 has been updated with Service Pack 1 then the Recovery Console must be installed from updated installation files. For more information see Microsoft Windows Server 2003 Service Pack 1 Installing and Deploying Updates on the Windows Server 2003 Web site.

Logging in

When you start the Recovery Console, you must specify which installation of Windows Server 2003 you wish log on to, even on a server with a single-boot configuration. Then, you must log on using the local Administrator account.

On a domain controller, the local Administrator account is often referred to as the Directory Services Restore Mode (DSRM) administrator and the password is set when Active Directory® directory service is installed. This password is not synchronized with the domain Administrator account. In Windows Server 2003, use **ntdsutil** to reset the DSRM administrator password. In Windows 2000, use **setpwd** to reset the DSRM administrator password.

Use to perform repair tasks

You use the Recovery Console to perform the following repair tasks:

- Enable and disable services that prevent Windows Server 2003 from starting.
- Read and write files on a local drive, including drives that are formatted with the NTFS file system. The Recovery Console recognizes and enforces NTFS permissions.
- Format hard disks.
- Repair a boot sector.
- Copy files and system files from a floppy disk or compact disc.

Recovery Console commands

When you run the Recovery Console, you can get help on the available commands by typing **help** at the command prompt and then pressing ENTER.

The following table describes the commands available in the Recovery Console.

Command	Description
attrib	Displays the attributes of the files in the current folder
batch	Executes commands specified in a text file
bootcfg	Repairs boot configuration and recovery
chdir (cd)	Displays the name of the current folder or changes the current folder
chkdsk	Checks a disk and displays a status report
cls	Clears the screen
copy	Copies a single file to another location
delete (del)	Deletes one or more files
dir	Displays a list of files and subfolders in a folder
disable	Disables a system service or a device driver
diskpart	Manages partitions on your hard disks
enable	Starts or enables a system service or a device driver
exit	Exits the Recovery Console and restarts your computer
expand	Expands a compressed file
fixboot	Writes a new partition boot sector onto the system partition
fixmbr	Repairs the master boot record of the partition boot sector
format	Formats a disk
help	Displays a list of the commands that you use in the Recovery Console
listsvc	Lists all available services and drivers on the computer
logon	Logs on to a Windows Server 2003 installation
map	Displays the drive letter mappings
mkdir (Md)	Creates a folder
more	Displays a text file

(*continued*)

Command	Description
rmdir (rd)	Deletes a folder
rename (ren)	Renames a single file
systemroot	Sets the current folder to the Systemroot folder of the system to which you are currently logged on
type	Displays a text file

What Is a Windows Startup Disk?

* **Allows Windows startup on a computer with a faulty boot sequence**
  * Damaged boot sector
  * Damaged master boot record (MBR)
  * Missing or damaged Ntldr or Ntdetect.com files
  * Incorrect Ntbootdd.sys driver
* **Includes:**
  * Ntldr
  * Ntdetect.com
  * Boot.ini
  * Ntbootdd.sys

all attributes
www. bootdisk.com

Definition

A Windows startup disk allows you to start the operating system on a computer running Windows Server 2003 that has a faulty boot sequence.

Use a Windows startup disk to work around the following startup problems:

- Damaged boot sector
- Damaged master boot record (MBR)
- Missing or damaged Ntldr or Ntdetect.com files
- Incorrect Ntbootdd.sys driver

The Windows startup disk must include the Ntldr, Ntdetect.com, and Boot.ini files. It may also require ntbootdd.sys, which is the device driver for your hard disk controller renamed to ntbootdd.sys.

Note   The attributes of the Ntldr, Ntdetect.com, and Boot.ini files are typically set to system, hidden, and read-only. You do not have to reset these attributes for the startup disk to work, but you must reset them if you copy these files to the hard disk.

Using the Windows startup disk

To use a Windows startup disk, place it in the floppy drive and boot from it. After starting the system from the floppy disk Windows is loaded from the hard drive.

A Windows startup disk was a common repair tool in Windows NT. However, the Recovery Console eliminates the need for a Windows startup disk. The Recovery Console allows the necessary access to repair all of the problems that a Windows startup disk solves.

How Startup Files Function

Introduction

If your server fails to start, and you must start the computer temporarily, start it by using the Windows startup disk. If the problem is caused by one of the three boot files, you will be able to run the server normally.

Function of the boot files

The boot files function as follows.

1. After the power-on self test (POST) loads the system BIOS into memory, the BIOS reads the contents of the master boot record (MBR). The MBR takes control, finds the active partition, and loads the boot sector from the active partition.

2. The boot sector program reads the root directory and loads Windows Server 2003 Loader (NTLDR).

3. NTLDR loads the basic memory configuration and switches to 32-bit mode (protected mode). NTLDR then places itself into high memory to free as much memory space as possible.

4. NTLDR reads boot.ini to find the operating system. If boot.ini is not present, NTLDR assumes that Windows Server 2003 is in the C: \Windows directory.

5. NTLDR switches back to 16-bit mode and loads ntdetect.com, which is a 16-bit application. NTDETECT determines the computer's physical environment. This determination occurs every time Windows Server 2003 starts, so the environment can change for each boot.

6. NTLDR loads into memory and reads the resource map that NTDETECT builds.

7. NTLDR switches the system back to protected mode. NTLDR then sets up the ring 0 mode for the kernel and loads the proper kernel (NTOSKRNL) for the computer. NTLDR pulls in the proper Hardware Abstraction Layer (HAL) and all boot drivers. Everything that NTDETECT collects becomes the HKEY_LOCAL_MACHINE/HARDWARE Registry key.

8. NTLDR starts the run process for NTOSKRNL.

Selecting Disaster-Recovery Methods

Tool	Use When
Safe Mode	**A problem prevents the normal Windows Server 2003 startup**
Last Known Good Configuration	**The configuration is incorrect**
Backup	**You need to create a duplicate copy of data on your hard drive and then archive the data on another storage device**
Recovery Console	**You cannot fix the problems by using one of the startup methods**
Automated System Recovery (ASR)	**Other repair operations fail**

Introduction

To recover your system, you can use Safe Mode, Last Known Good Configuration, Backup, Recovery Console, ASR, or some combination of these tools, as well as others such as shadow copies. Follow the recommended best practices when you use these disaster recovery solutions.

Disaster recovery tools

The following table lists disaster recovery tools in the preferred order of use, from tools that present little or no risk to data, to those that might cause data loss.

Disaster recovery tool	Function
Safe Mode	Use when a problem prevents Window Server 2003 from starting normally.
	Safe mode is a startup option that disables startup programs and nonessential services to create an environment that is useful for troubleshooting and diagnosing problems.
Last Known Good Configuration	Use only in cases of incorrect configuration. By using Last Known Good Configuration, you recover by reverting back to a previous configuration that worked. This also serves to remove the most recent driver and registry changes.
Backup	Use Backup to create a duplicate copy of data on your hard drive and then archive the data on another storage device.
	Backup is a tool for saving and restoring data, including System State data.

(continued)

Disaster recovery tool	Function
Recovery Console	Use if you cannot fix the problems by using one of the startup methods.
	The Recovery Console is used if Windows cannot be started.
Automated System Recovery (ASR)	Use to restore an operating system from a backup.
	Use this option instead of reinstalling Windows because ASR restores system settings and critical files on the system and boot partitions.
	Because the ASR process formats disks, consider this a last resort to be used when other repair operations such a restoring system state or the Recovery Console are not effective.

Note   For more information about how to select the correct recovery tool or combination of tools to correct the specific disaster you encounter, see Appendix E, "Which Recovery Tool Do I Use?"

Practice: Recovering from Server Failure

In this practice, you will:

• Recover using Safe Mode and Last Known Good Configuration

• Install the Recovery Console

Objective

In this practice, you will:

■ Recover using Safe Mode and Last Known Good Configuration

■ Install the Recovery Console

Instructions

Ensure the DEN-DC1 and DEN-SRV1 virtual machines are running.

Practice

▶ **Recover using Safe Mode and Last Known Good Configuration**

1. Log on to DEN-SRV1 as **Administrator** with a password of **Pa$$w0rd**.

2. On DEN-SRV1, click **Start**, click **Run** dialog box, type **\MOC\2275\Practices\Mod07\install.bat** and then click **OK**.

3. After the computer restarts, log on as Administrator.

4. Note the unusual behavior. What does the computer do?

_____

5. When the computer restarts, press **F8** to access the Windows Advanced Options Menu.

6. Select **Last Known Good Configuration** and press ENTER.

7. Press ENTER to start Windows Server 2003, Enterprise Edition

8. Log on as **Administrator**.

9. Did this work? Why or why not?

_____

10. When the computer restarts, press F8 to access the Windows **Advanced Options** Menu.

11. Select **Safe Mode** and press ENTER.

12. Press ENTER to start the computer.

13. Log on as **Administrator**.

14. Click **OK** to close the **Safe Mode** dialog box.

15. Did this work? Why or why not?

_____

16. Click **Start** menu and click **Search**.

17. In the **All or part of the file name** box, type **bootme**, and click **Search**.

18. In the **Search Results** dialog box, delete the **bootme** file in the Windows folder.

19. Restart your computer, and then log on as **Administrator**. Does the problem appear to be solved?

_____

▶ **Install the Recovery Console**

1. On DEN-DC1, click **Start**, click **Run** dialog box, type **C:\win2k3\i386\winnt32.exe /cmdcons** and then click **OK**. A copy of the Windows Server 2003 installation CD-ROM is located in C:\win2k3.

2. Click **Yes** to install the Recovery Console.

3. Click **Skip this step and continue installing Windows** and click **Next**.

4. Click **OK** to close the **Windows Server 2003, Enterprise Edition Setup** dialog box.

5. Restart **DEN-DC1**.

6. When the computer restarts, select **Microsoft Windows Recovery Console** and press ENTER.

7. Type **1** and press ENTER to select C:\WINDOWS as the Windows Server 2003 installation.

8. Type **Pa$$w0rd** as the password and press ENTER.

9. Type **help** and press ENTER.

10. Press the SPACEBAR to scroll through the list.

11. Type **listsvc** and press ENTER.

12. Press the SPACEBAR to scroll through the list.

13. Type **dir** and press ENTER.

14. Press the SPACEBAR to scroll through the list.

15. Type **exit** and press ENTER to exit the Recovery Console and restart Windows.

_____

Important   Do not shut down the virtual machines.

Lab: Managing Disaster Recovery

In this lab, you will:

* Back up System State data

* Recover from a corrupt registry by using Last Known Good Configuration

* Recover from a corrupt registry by restoring System State data

Objectives

After completing this lab, you will be able to:

- Back up System State data.

- Recover from a corrupt registry by using Last Known Good Configuration.

- Recover from a corrupt registry by restoring System State data.

Instructions

Ensure that the DEN-DC1 and DEN-SRV1 virtual machines are running.

Estimated time to complete this lab: 50 minutes

Exercise 1
Backing Up the System State Data

In this exercise, you will use the Backup Wizard to back up the System State data for your computer.

Tasks	Specific instructions
1. Back up the System State data.	a. Log on to DEN-DC1 as **Administrator** with a password of **Pa$$w0rd**. b. Start **Backup** in **Advanced** mode. c. On the **Backup** tab, select **System State**. d. Save the backup as **D:\SysState.bkf**. e. Start the backup. f. When the backup completes, close the **Backup Utility**.

Exercise 2
Recovering from a Corrupt Registry by Using Last Known Good Configuration

In this exercise, you will recover from a nonresponsive computer. The cause of this problem was the installation of a software package that modified the registry. (The source for this exercise is Microsoft Knowledge Base article 317246.)

Tasks	Specific instructions
1. Install the software.	a. Log on to DEN-SRV1 as **Administrator** with a password of **Pa$$w0rd**. b. Using Windows Explorer, browse to **C:\MOC\2275\Labfiles\Lab07** and then double-click **inst_01.bat**.
❓	What happens when the computer restarts? _____
❓	What do you need to do to recover from this disaster? _____
2. Repair the system.	a. Reset the virtual machine from the Action menu. b. Access the Windows Advanced Options menu. c. Choose the appropriate recovery method. d. Repair the system.
3. Log on as **Administrator**.	▪ Log on as **Administrator** with a password of **Pa$$w0rd**.

Exercise 3
Recovering from a Corrupt Registry by Restoring System State Data

In this exercise, you will recover from a nonresponsive mouse. The cause of this problem was the installation of a software package that modified the registry. (The source for this exercise is Microsoft Knowledge Base article 317246.)

Tasks	Specific instructions
1. Install the software.	a. On DEN-DC1, open Windows Explorer, browse to **D:\2275\Labfiles\Lab07**, and then double-click **inst_04.bat**. b. When the computer restarts, log on to the domain as **Administrator**.
❓ What do you need to do to recover from this disaster?	
2. Recover from a corrupt registry using Last Known Good Configuration.	a. Press **CTRL+ESC** to open the **Start** menu and restart the computer. b. Access the Windows **Advanced Options** menu. c. Select **Last Known Good Configuration** to resolve this problem. d. Log on to the domain using the **Administrator** account. Did this resolve the problem?
3. Recover from a corrupt registry by restoring System State data using the keyboard. Use the following keys to navigate in the Backup program: ALT+TAB CTRL+ESC TAB ENTER CTRL+TAB SPACEBAR Up arrow Down arrow Right arrow Left arrow	a. Access the Windows **Advanced Options** menu. b. Select **Directory Services Restore Mode**. c. Open the **Start** menu by pressing CTRL+ESC. d. Use the arrow keys to start **Backup**. e. Use keyboard commands to restore the system state backup **D:\SysState.bkf**.
4. Confirm the problem is fixed.	■ Log on as **Administrator** with a password of **Pa$$w0rd**.
5. Complete the lab exercise.	a. Close all programs and shut down all computers. Do not save changes. b. To prepare for the next module, start the DEN-DC1 virtual computer.

Course Evaluation

Your evaluation of this course will help Microsoft understand the quality of your learning experience.

At a convenient time before the end of the course, please complete a course evaluation, which is available on the Metrics That Matter page of the Knowledge Advisors Web site at http://www.metricsthatmatter.com/ MTMStudent/ClassListPage.aspx?&orig=6&VendorAlias=survey.

Microsoft will keep your evaluation strictly confidential and will use your responses to improve your future learning experience.

Microsoft®

Module 13: Maintaining Software by Using Windows Server Update Services

Contents

Overview

- ❖ **Introduction to Windows Server Update Services**
- ❖ **Installing and Configuring Windows Server Update Services**
- ❖ **Managing Windows Server Update Services**

Introduction

This module introduces Microsoft® Windows Server Update Services (WSUS), a tool for managing and distributing software updates that resolve known security vulnerabilities and other stability issues in Microsoft Windows® 2000 and newer operating systems, as well as other Microsoft applications. This module also describes how to install the client and server components of WSUS. It also provides necessary information about managing the WSUS infrastructure.

Objectives

After completing this module, you will be able to:

- Describe Microsoft WSUS.
- Install and configure servers to use WSUS.
- Manage WSUS.

Lesson: Introduction to Windows Server Update Services

* Multimedia: Windows Server Update Services
* What Is Microsoft Update?
* What Is Automatic Updates?
* What Is Windows Server Update Services?
* Windows Server Update Services Process

Introduction

Traditionally, systems administrators keep systems up-to-date by frequently checking the Microsoft Update Web site or the Microsoft Security Web site for software updates. Administrators manually download available updates, test the updates in their environments, and then distribute the updates manually or by using their traditional software-distribution tools.

By using WSUS, administrators can perform these tasks automatically.

This lesson describes WSUS and explains how it works with Microsoft Update and Automatic Updates.

Lesson objectives

After completing this lesson, you will be able to:

* Describe WSUS.
* Describe Microsoft Update.
* Describe Automatic Updates.
* Describe how WSUS is used.
* Describe the WSUS process.

Multimedia: Windows Server Update Services

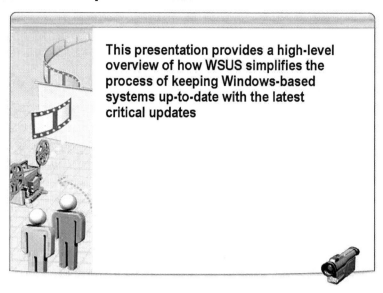

File location

To view the *Windows Server Update Services* presentation, open the Web page on the Student Materials compact disc, click **Multimedia**, and then click the title of the presentation.

What Is Microsoft Update?

Microsoft Update is a Microsoft Web site that includes:

- ☼ Updates for Microsoft Windows operating systems, software, and device drivers
- ☼ Updates for Microsoft applications
- ☼ New content that is added to the site regularly

Definition

Microsoft Update is a Web site that helps keep your systems up-to-date. Use Microsoft Update to obtain updates for Windows operating systems and applications, updated device drivers, and software. New content is added to the site regularly, so you can always get the most recent updates to help protect your server and the client computers on your network.

What are updates?

Updates can include security fixes, critical updates, and critical drivers. These updates resolve known security and stability issues in Microsoft Windows 2000, Windows XP, and Windows Server™ 2003 operating systems. The Microsoft Update site also has updates for applications such as Microsoft Office, Microsoft Exchange Server and Microsoft SQL Server.

Update categories

The categories for the Windows operating system updates are:

- *Critical updates*. Security fixes and other important updates to keep computers current and networks secure.

- *Recommended downloads*. Latest Windows and Microsoft Internet Explorer service packs and other important updates.

- *Windows tools*. Utilities and other tools that are provided to enhance performance, facilitate upgrades, and ease the burden on systems administrators.

- *Internet and multimedia updates*. Latest Internet Explorer releases, upgrades to Microsoft Windows Media® Player, and more.

- *Additional Windows downloads*. Updates for desktop settings and other Windows features.

- *Multilanguage features*. Menus and dialog boxes, language support, and Input Method Editors for a variety of languages.

- Deployment guides and other software-related documents are also available.

What Is Automatic Updates?

Definition

Automatic Updates is a configurable option in Windows. It can download and install operating system updates without any user intervention. The updates can be downloaded from the Microsoft Update Web site or a WSUS server. Configuration of Automatic Updates can be controlled centrally by the administrator.

Automatic Update options

Automatic Updates gives you flexibility to decide how and when updates will be installed. The options are:

- *Automatic*. Updates downloaded automatically and installed at a scheduled time. This option installs updates for all users and is recommended. If the computer is turned off at the scheduled update time, Windows will install the updates the next time you start your computer. This option is recommended.

- *Download updates for me, but let me choose when to install them*. Updates are downloaded automatically, but they are not installed until an administrator chooses to install them.

- *Notify me but do not automatically download or install them*. Updates are not downloaded or installed automatically. The notifications are only shown to administrators logged on to the local machine.

- *Turn off Automatic Updates*. There will be no notifications when updates are available for your computer. This option is not recommended.

Notification of available updates

After a download is complete, an icon appears in the notification area with a message that the updates are ready to be installed. When you click the icon or message, Automatic Updates guides you through the installation process.

If you choose not to install a specific update that has been downloaded, Windows deletes its files from your computer. If you later change your mind, you can download it by opening the **System Properties** dialog box, clicking the **Automatic Updates** tab, and then clicking **Offer updates again that I've previously hidden**.

Note If required, the version of Automatic Updates is upgraded the first time a WSUS server is contacted.

Digital signatures

To ensure that the programs you download from Microsoft Update are from Microsoft, all files are digitally signed. The purpose of digital signatures is to ensure the authenticity and integrity of the signed files. Automatic Updates installs a file only if it contains this digital signature.

Automatic Updates client deployment

The following operating systems include the required version of Automatic Updates:

- Windows 2000 Service Pack 3 (SP3)
- Windows XP SP1
- Windows Server 2003

Note For more information about deploying Windows Server Update Services, see the white paper, *Deploying Microsoft Windows Server Update Services*, under **Additional Reading** on the Web page on the Student Materials compact disc.

What Is Windows Server Update Services?

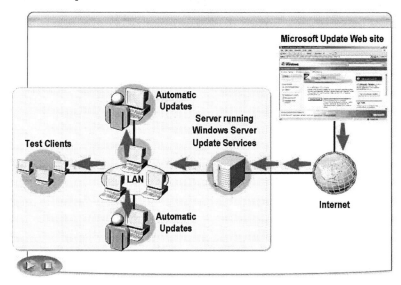

Definition

WSUS is an optional component for Windows 2000 Server or Window Server 2003 that can be downloaded from the Microsoft Web site. It acts as a central point on your network for distributing updates to workstations and server.

Supported software

WSUS has the ability to deliver updates for all Microsoft products. However, at this time, WSUS provides updates for the following:

- Windows 2000 and newer operating systems
- Microsoft Office
- Exchange Server
- SQL Server

Server component

You install the server component of WSUS on a server running Windows 2000 Server or Windows Server 2003 inside your corporate firewall. The firewall must be configured to allow your internal server to synchronize content with the Microsoft Update Web site whenever critical updates for Windows are available. The synchronization can be automatic, or the administrator can perform it manually.

Synchronized updates must be approved before they can be installed by client computers. This allows testing of updates with corporate applications before distribution. This is a key benefit over Microsoft Update.

Client component

Automatic Updates is the client software that downloads and installs updates from a WSUS server. The client must be configured with the location of a WSUS server. The location can be configured through registry edits or through Group Policy. Using Group Policy is strongly recommended.

Note WSUS is not intended to serve as a replacement for enterprise software-distribution solutions, such as Microsoft Systems Management Server or Microsoft Group Policy–based software distribution. Many customers use solutions such as Microsoft Systems Management Server for complete software management, including responding to security and virus issues, and these customers should continue using these solutions. Advanced solutions such as Microsoft Systems Management Server provide the ability to deploy all software throughout an enterprise, in addition to providing administrative controls that are critical for medium-size and large organizations.

Windows Server Update Services Process

Introduction

The process for using WSUS involves both the server running WSUS and the client computers on a network. If both are configured, the administrator can review the update packages and approve them for installation.

Server-side processes

The server-side process occurs as follows:

1. The server running WSUS runs a scheduled synchronization with Microsoft Update and receives new update packages.

2. The systems administrator reviews the new packages and determines whether testing is required.

   a. If testing is required, the administrator sends the new packages to be tested. This can be done by manually by downloading the updates on a test system or approving the updates for a test group.

   b. If testing is not required, the administrator proceeds to step 3.

3. Administrator approves the new packages of updates.

Client-side processes

The client-side process occurs as follows:

1. Automatic Updates on client computers check the server running WSUS daily and download new approved updates packages from either the server running WSUS or the Microsoft Update Web site.

2. At the scheduled update time, Automatic Updates checks to determine whether the administrator is logged on.

   a. If logged on, the administrator sees a status balloon on the desktop and decides whether to defer or run the installation.

   b. If the administrator is not logged on, step 3 is performed.

Note By using Group Policy, you can configure Automatic Updates to allow nonadministrative users to defer installing updates.

3. The scheduled installation job begins, and Automatic Updates installs new or changed packages.

4. Automatic Updates checks whether the new packages require a restart of the server or client.

    a. If a restart is required, the system restarts after all the packages are installed.

    b. If no restart is required, the installation is completed.

5. Automatic Updates waits for the next scheduled check.

Lesson: Installing and Configuring Windows Server Update Services

* WSUS Deployment Scenarios

* Server Requirements for Windows Server Update Services

* Automatic Updates Configuration

* Practice: Installing and Configuring Windows Server Update Services

Introduction

WSUS consists of both client-side and server-side components to provide a basic solution to critical update management.

This lesson explains how to install and configure the client-side and server-side components of WSUS.

Lesson objectives

After completing this lesson, you will be able to:

- Describe WSUS deployment scenarios.
- Describe server hardware and software requirements for WSUS.
- Describe Automatic Updates configuration.
- Install and configure WSUS.

WSUS Deployment Scenarios

Introduction	To allow for varied situations, you can deploy a WSUS server in several scenarios. You can choose the deployment scenario that is most appropriate for your organization. The decision factors may include the number of locations in your network or the speed of your Internet connection.
Single WSUS server	In a single-site network, a single WSUS server can be sufficient to support as many as 5,000 clients. This is suitable for most single-site networks.
Independent WSUS servers	In a multiple-site network, you can configure multiple independent WSUS servers are each location. This requires that each site use its own Internet connection to download the updates. Having each site download its own updates reduces the load on wide-area network (WAN) links as compared to using a centralized server to download updates.
	Independent WSUS servers are also managed independently. This scenario is best suited to organizations with distributed IT support.
Replica WSUS servers	Another option for multiple-site networks it to use replica WSUS servers. Replica WSUS servers download their updates and configuration information from a central WSUS server. This allows the approval of updates to be centralized for multiple servers.
	In this scenario, only one server is exposed to the Internet and it is the only server that downloads updates from Microsoft Update. This server is set up as the upstream server—the source from which the replica server synchronizes.
Disconnected WSUS servers	For organizations that do not allow servers to communicate directly with the Internet, you can deploy disconnected WSUS servers. In this scenario, you can set up a server running WSUS that is connected to the Internet but isolated from rest of the network. After downloading, testing, and approving the updates on the isolated server, an administrator would then export the update metadata and content to external storage, and then, from the external storage, import the update metadata and content to servers running WSUS within the intranet.

Server Requirements for Windows Server Update Services

- **Hardware requirements**
  - Pentium III 1GHz or higher
  - 1 GB of RAM
  - 30 GB of hard disk space
- **Software requirements**
  - Windows 2000 Server or Windows Server 2003
  - IIS 5.0 or later
  - BITS
  - Microsoft .NET Framework 1.1 SP1
  - Internet Explorer 6.0 SP1 or later

Introduction

You install the server component of WSUS by using a Windows Installer package that installs the necessary server files and configures Internet Information Services (IIS). To ensure that your server can support WSUS, check the hardware and software capabilities of your server.

Hardware server requirements

The following are the recommended hardware requirements for a server with as many as 500 clients.

- Pentium III 1 gigahertz (GHz) or faster
- 1 gigabyte (GB) of RAM
- 1 GB of hard disk space on the system volume
- 30 GB of hard disk space for security packages
- Hard disks must be formatted with NTFS

Software server requirements

Each server running WSUS requires the following software:

- Windows 2000 Server or Windows Server 2003
- IIS 5.0 or later
- Windows SQL Server 2000 Desktop Engine (WMSDE) for deployments up to 500 clients
- Microsoft SQL Server 2000 for deployments over 500 clients
- Background Intelligent Transfer Service (BITS) 2.0
- Microsoft .NET Framework 1.1 Service Pack 1
- Internet Explorer 6.0 Service Pack 1 or later

Note   WMSDE is included when WSUS is installed on Windows Server 2003. Deployments on Windows 2000 must use a free download of MSDE or Microsoft SQL Server 2000.

Note   For more information about server requirements for WSUS, see the white paper, *Deploying Microsoft Windows Server Update Services*, under **Additional Reading** on the Web page on the Student Materials compact disc.

Automatic Updates Configuration

* **Configure Automatic Updates by using Group Policy**
* **Requires updated wuau.adm administrative template**
* **Requires:**
  * Windows 2000 SP3
  * Windows XP SP1
  * Windows Server 2003

Introduction

Group Policy is the most appropriate way to configure the settings for Automatic Updates. It allows configuration to be centralized and distributed to all WSUS client computers without any user interaction.

Updating Group Policy administrative templates

WSUS enables some Automatic Updates options that were not available in older versions of the Automatic Updates client. As a consequence, the default Group Policy settings that are included with Windows Server 2003 do not allow configuration of all the options in the current Automatic Updates client that is used with WSUS.

Group Policy settings are based on administrative templates (.adm files). These templates contain lists of registry keys, available options and descriptions. **Wuau.adm** is the template for Automatic Update settings. The latest version of **wuau.adm** is available in Windows XP SP2 and Windows Server 2003 SP1.

If a Group Policy object is created on a server without the latest version of **wuau.adm,** then some WSUS options will not be available.

Administrative control by using policies

Administrator-defined configuration options that are defined by Group Policy always take precedence over user-defined options. Also, **Automatic Updates** options in Control Panel are disabled on the target computer when administrative policies are set.

The Group Policy object (GPO) setting for Automatic Updates is located in the Computer Configuration\Administrative Templates\Windows Components\Windows Update folder.

Group Policy settings for Automatic Updates

Some of the Group Policy settings for Automatic Updates are:

- Specify intranet Microsoft update service location
- Automatic Updates detection frequency
- Allow Automatic Updates immediate installation
- Delay Restart for scheduled installations
- Allow nonadministrators to receive update notifications

Requirements for the client computer

Client computers must be running the updated Automatic Updates client and Windows 2000 (Service Pack 3), Windows XP (Service Pack 1), or Window Server 2003.

Practice: Installing and Configuring Windows Server Update Services

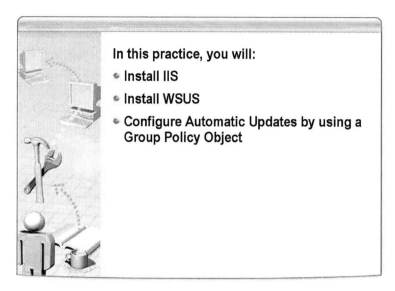

In this practice, you will:
- Install IIS
- Install WSUS
- Configure Automatic Updates by using a Group Policy Object

Objective

In this practice, you will:

- Install IIS.
- Install WSUS.
- Configure Automatic Updates by using a Group Policy object.

Instructions

Ensure that the DEN-DC1 virtual machine is running.

Practice

▶ **Install IIS**

1. Log on DEN-DC1 as **Administrator** with a password of **Pa$$w0rd**.
2. Click **Start**, point to **Control Panel**, and then click **Add or Remove Programs**.
3. Click **Add/Remove Windows Components**.
4. In the **Components** box, select the **Application Server** check box, and then click **Next**.
5. Click **Finish**.
6. Close Add or Remove Programs.

▶ **Install WSUS**

1. Open Windows Explorer.

2. Browse to **D:\2275\Practices\Mod08**.

3. Double-click **WSUSSetup**.

4. Click **Next** to begin the Microsoft Windows Server Update Services Setup Wizard.

5. Click **I accept the terms of the License agreement** and then click **Next**.

6. Ensure that the **Store updates locally** check box is selected and the path is configured for **D:\WSUS**, and then click **Next**.

7. Click **Next** to accept the default of **Install SQL Server desktop engine (Windows) on this computer**.

8. Ensure that **Use the existing IIS Default Web site** is selected and click **Next**. Take note of the Web sites used for management and obtaining updates.

9. Click **Next** to accept the default of this server being a standalone WSUS server.

10. Read the installation summary and then click **Next**. The installation will take about 10 minutes.

11. Click **Finish**.

12. Complete the **New Connection Wizard** with the following settings:

   • Connect to the Internet

   • Connect using a broadband connection that is always on.

13. Open **Internet Explorer**.

14. Check the **In the future, do not show this message** check box and click **OK**.

15. In the Address bar type **HTTP://DEN-DC1/Wsusadmin**. Press **Enter**.

16. In the **User name** box type **Administrator**, in the **Password** box type **Pa$$w0rd**, and click **OK**.

17. Add **http://DEN-DC1** to the list of trusted Web sites and close the Internet Explorer dialog box. Notice that this is the management interface for WSUS.

18. Close **Internet Explorer** and close all open windows.

▶ **Configure Automatic Updates by using a Group Policy object**

1. Click **Start**, point to **Administrative Tools**, and click **Group Policy Management**.

2. Expand **Forest: Contoso.msft**, expand **Domains**, and expand **Contoso.msft**.

3. Right-click **Contoso.msft** and click **Create and link a GPO here**.

4. In the **Name** box, type **WSUS** and then click **OK**.

5. Right-click **WSUS** and click **Edit**.

6. Under **Computer Configuration**, expand **Administrative Templates**, expand **Windows Components**, and click **Windows Update**.

7. Double-click **Configure Automatic Updates**.

8. Click **Enabled**, in the **Configure automatic updating** box, select **4 – Auto download and schedule the install**, and then click **OK**.

9. Double-click **Specify intranet Microsoft update service location**.

10. Click **Enabled**, type **http://DEN-DC1** in the **Set the intranet update service for detecting updates** box and the **Set the intranet statistics server** box, and click **OK**.

11. Close **Group Policy Object Editor**.

12. Close **Group Policy Management**.

13. Close all open windows.

▶ **To prepare for the next practice**

•   Start the DEN-CL1 virtual machine.

Important   Do not shut down the virtual machines.

Lesson: Managing Windows Server Update Services

* Windows Server Update Services Administration Web Site
* How Synchronization Works
* Managing Computer Groups
* Approving Updates
* Using Reports
* Backing Up and Restoring Windows Server Update Services
* Guidelines for Deploying Updates
* Practice: Managing Windows Server Update Services

Introduction

As an administrator, you decide whether to install updates immediately after they are downloaded, or to test the updates first. This lesson discusses how to view the synchronized content, as well as how to approve and install the updates.

It is important to have your WSUS configuration backed up and ready to restore in the event of a disaster. This lesson also describes what portions of WSUS need to be backed up and how to do it.

Lesson objectives

After completing this lesson, you will be able to:

* Describe the features and function of the WSUS administration Web site.
* Describe how synchronization works.
* Describe computer groups and how to manage them.
* Describe how updates are approved.
* Describe how to use reports.
* Describe the backup and restore process for WSUS.
* Describe guidelines for deploying updates.
* Manage WSUS.

Windows Server Update Services Administration Web Site

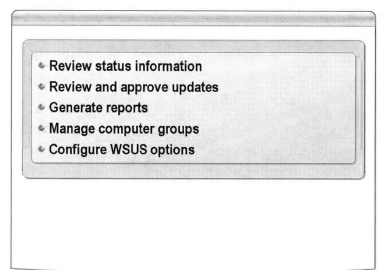

- Review status information
- Review and approve updates
- Generate reports
- Manage computer groups
- Configure WSUS options

Administrative tasks for managing WSUS

These are the five primary administrative tasks for managing WSUS.

- Review status information, such as computers requiring updates.
- Review and approve updates for distribution to clients.
- Generate reports on the status of updates, computers, synchronization, and WSUS settings.
- Manage computers and computer groups.
- Configure WSUS options for synchronization, automatic approval, and assigning computers to groups.

WSUS administrative Web site

All WSUS configuration is performed by using the WSUS administration Web site. The WSUS administration Web site is located at http://*servername*/WSUSAdmin, where *servername* is the DNS name of the server on which WSUS is installed.

You can access these pages on a corporate intranet by using Microsoft Internet Explorer 5.5 or later. If you try to connect to the administration Web site with a version of Internet Explorer earlier than version 5.5, an error page appears, reminding you to upgrade Internet Explorer.

Note To view this Web site, you must be a local administrator on a computer that is running WSUS.

How Synchronization Works

Introduction	Servers running WSUS are updated with a process called synchronization. This process compares the WSUS server software with the Microsoft Update Web site's latest release. Administrators can choose to configure these updates to proceed automatically or they can perform this process manually.
Synchronization schedule	The default setting for the synchronization schedule is manual. This means that an administrator must manually choose to download new updates to the WSUS server. This is appropriate for disconnected WSUS servers only. For other WSUS servers, synchronization should be scheduled.
	Schedule synchronization occurs once per day at a time selected by an administrator. Daily synchronization ensures that the WSUS server has the latest updates. After synchronization an administrator must still approve the updates before they are distributed to clients.
Products and update classifications	An administrator can select specific products and update classifications to limit unnecessary downloads. By default, only critical updates and security updates are downloaded.
	If a server is configured for WSUS, but requires a systems administrator to manually synchronize the updates, the updates remain on the Microsoft Update Web site until the administrator reviews and approves them.
Update source	You can synchronize content on your WSUS server from the Microsoft Update Web site or from another installation of WSUS. The update source you select will depend on how you have planned your deployment of WSUS. An independent WSUS server will synchronize content from the Microsoft Update Web site, while a branch office replica WSUS server will synchronize from a head-office WSUS server.
Update languages	You can limit the updates that are downloaded based on the language of the update. This reduces the bandwidth used for downloads and reduces disk space required for storing updates. The default configuration downloads updates in all languages.

Managing Computer Groups

- Computers are automatically added
- Default computer groups
  - All Computers
  - Unassigned Computers
- Client-side targeting

How computer groups are used	Computer groups are used by WSUS to control which updates are applied to which computers. This allows you to stage deployment of updates to reduce load on the network. Computer groups make it convenient to test updates on a few specific computers before distributing the updates to the entire organization.
Client computers	Client computers are listed on the Computers page of the WSUS administration site. They are automatically added to this page after they contact the WSUS server for the first time.
	A computer is never removed from WSUS server automatically. If you reconfigure a computer to use a different server, you must manually remove it from the original WSUS server.
Default computer groups	All new computers are added to the All Computers group and the Unassigned Computers group automatically. The All Computers group provides a convenient way to apply updates to every computer that is using a WSUS server. The Unassigned Computers group lets you see which computers using the WSUS server might be new and need to be added to a group. After computers are added to an administrator created group then they are no longer a part of Unassigned Computers.
Adding computers to computer groups	Computers can be added to groups manually in WSUS administration site or automatically through client-side targeting. Client-side targeting is done by using Group Policy settings. If the computers in your organization are organized into organization units (OUs) based on department, it is easy to configure a Group Policy for each OU that defines which computer group those computers should be a member of.

Approving Updates

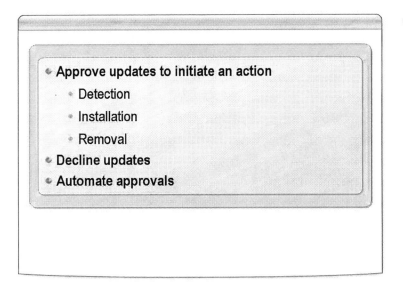

- **Approve updates to initiate an action**
  - Detection
  - Installation
  - Removal
- **Decline updates**
- **Automate approvals**

Introduction

After updates have been synchronized to a WSUS server, you must approve them to initiate a deployment action. When you approve an update, you are essentially telling WSUS what to do with it.

Approving an update

Your choices for approving an update are Install, Detect only, Remove, or Decline. When you approve an update, you specify a default approval setting for the All Computers group, and any necessary settings for each computer group in the **Approve Updates** dialog box. If you do not approve an update, its approval status remains Not approved and your WSUS server performs no action for the update. The exceptions to this are Critical Updates and Security Updates, which by default are automatically approved for detection after they are synchronized.

Detection

When you approve an update for detection, the update is not installed. Instead, WSUS checks whether the update is compliant with or needed by computers in the groups you specify for the **Detect only approval** option. The detection occurs at the scheduled time that the client computer communicates with the WSUS server.

After detection you can view how many computers do not have the update installed and need it. If the number of needed for an update is zero, then all client computers are up-to-date.

Installation

The **Install approval** option installs the update for selected computer groups. In a default installation of WSUS, updates are not downloaded to the WSUS server until they are approved for installation.

When an update is approved for installation, you can configure a deadline. The date specified in a deadline forces an update to be installed on client computers by that time. This overrides clients configured to only notify of available updates.

Removal

If an update causes problems after being approved for installation it can be removed by approving it for removal. This is particularly important if you have automated installation approval for certain classifications of updates.

Declining updates

You can choose to decline any updates that are not relevant for your environment. A declined update is removed from the list of available updates.

Automating approvals

The process for testing and approving new updates can be slow in many organizations. Some organizations have found that there is less risk in applying critical updates and security updates immediately than waiting for the testing process to be complete. This ensures that new viruses do not take advantage of flaws before updates are installed.

WSUS has the ability to automatically approve updates for detection or installation. By default critical updates and security updates are approved for detection and WSUS updates are approved for installation. Automatic approvals can be configured to apply only to certain computer groups.

Using Reports

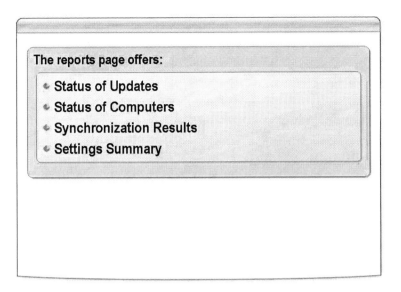

The reports page offers:

- Status of Updates
- Status of Computers
- Synchronization Results
- Settings Summary

Introduction

Reports provide a quick way to get an overview of an update status, computer status, synchronization results, and WSUS configuration. You can also print reports so that you can take them to status meetings and include them with network status reports.

Reports

The reports page offers four preconfigured reports:

- Status of Updates

  This report shows the status of updates for a particular computer group. For each update it shows how many computers have installed the update, need the update, or failed to install the update. This report can also be filtered based on update status such as updates that have failed to install.

- Status of Computers

  This report shows the status of updates on individual computers in a computer group. For each computer it shows how many updates are installed, needed or failed. This report can also be filtered based on update status such as computers with failed updates.

- Synchronization Results

  This report summarizes synchronization information including status of the last synchronization, synchronization errors, and new updates. This report can be filtered to limit the relevant timeframe.

- Settings Summary

  This report lists the current configuration of the WSUS server. This is useful for general documentation, comparing server configurations, and disaster recovery.

Backing Up and Restoring Windows Server Update Services

- **Use the Backup Utility**
- **Backup database**
  - Stop MSSQL$WSUS service
  - Contains metadata, configuration information, and client computer information
- **Updates folder**

Introduction

Although WSUS does not provide a built-in backup tool, you can use the Backup utility that is available on all servers running Windows 2000 or Windows Server 2003 to easily back up and restore both the WSUS database and update file storage folder.

WSUS database

When the WSUS database is backed up, the MSSQL$WSUS service should be stopped. If this service is running during a backup there is a risk the backup will be inconsistent.

The WSUS database contains the following information:

- Update metadata, including information about updates. Metadata is also where end-user license agreements (EULAs) are stored.

- WSUS server configuration information, which includes all settings for your WSUS server. These are options you specified through the WSUS console and settings configured by WSUS automatically during setup.

- Information about client computers, updates, and client interaction with updates. You can access this information through the WSUS console when you view status and run reports on update status and client computer status.

Note If you are using a full version of Microsoft SQL Server 2000 for your database, which is not installed by WSUS, you can use SQL Server Enterprise manager as an alternative to the Backup utility.

Updates folder

The updates folder contains all of the updates that have been downloaded and stored on the WSUS server. By default, update files are stored in the %systemdrive%\WSUS\WSUSContent folder on your WSUS server. If you have chosen to store update files on Microsoft Update, you do not have to back up the update file storage folder on your WSUS server.

Guidelines for Deploying Updates

* Use computer groups for testing

* Configure an initial test group

* Configure a business testing group

* Deploy updates one department at a time

* Remove problem updates

Introduction

Due to the complex interdependencies between operating system components and corporate applications, it is strongly recommended that all updates be tested before deploying them to WSUS clients. This is particularly important for custom designed or in-house applications which may not be as well written as commercially available applications.

Guidelines

Use the following guidelines to install updates on the client computers on your network:

- Use computer groups for testing.

    Computer groups let you control which computers are approved to install updates. Using computer groups to install updates on test computers avoids the hassle of downloading updates for testing through a separate process.

- Configure an initial test group.

    Create a test group of nonproduction computers for testing updates. These computers should match your production environment as closely as possible. This initial testing can be performed by the IT group or designated business users. In this testing you can identify obvious problems with installation or functionality. At this stage a problem update will have no impact on production.

- Configure a business testing group.

    Recruit power users from different business groups to act as test groups before distributing updates to all users. Power users will be able to provide detailed functional testing of applications. This will catch application specific errors. At this stage a problem update will affect a limited group of users in production.

- Deploy updates one department at a time.

  Deploying updates to one department at a time will reduce the scope of a problem if an update causes a problem. Testing can also be done on a per department basis because they typically have unique applications.

- Remove problem updates.

  If an update causes problems, mark it for removal. This will uninstall the update. Be aware that some updates cannot be uninstalled.

Practice: Managing Windows Server Update Services

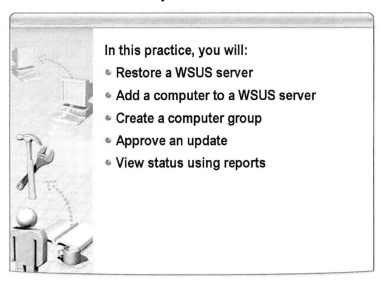

In this practice, you will:
- Restore a WSUS server
- Add a computer to a WSUS server
- Create a computer group
- Approve an update
- View status using reports

Objective

In this practice, you will:

- Restore a WSUS server.
- Add a computer to a WSUS server.
- Create a computer group.
- Approve an update.
- View status using reports.

Instructions

Ensure that the DEN-DC1 and DEN-CL1 virtual machines are running.

Practice

▶ **Restore a WSUS server**

1. If necessary, log on to DEN-DC1 as **Administrator** with a password of **Pa$$w0rd**.
2. Click **Start**, click **Run**, type **net stop mssql$wsus**, and then click **OK**.
3. Click **Start**, point to **All Programs**, point to **Accessories**, point to **System Tools**, and then click **Backup**.
4. Click **Advanced Mode** and click the **Restore and Manage Media** tab.
5. Click the **Tools** menu and then click **Options**.
6. Select **Always replace the file on my computer**. Click **OK**.
7. Right-click **File** and click **Catalog file**.
8. In the **Open** box, type **D:\2275\Practices\Mod08\WSUSBackup.bkf**, and then click **OK**.
9. Expand **File**, expand **WSUSBackup.bkf** and then select the check box next to **D: Allfiles**.

10. Click **Start Restore** and then click **OK**. This backup restores the updates folder that contains installation files for updates and the SQL database to the D: drive.

11. Click **Close** and close **Backup**.

12. Click **Start**, click **Run**, type **net start mssql$wsus**, and then click **OK**. Wait a couple of minutes before proceeding to the next step.

► **Add a computer to a WSUS server**

1. Log on to DEN-CL1 as **Administrator** with a password of **Pa$$w0rd**.

2. Click **Start**, click **Run**, type **cmd**, and then click **OK**.

3. Type **gpupdate /force** and press ENTER. This ensures that the latest Group Policy settings are applied to this computer.

4. Type **wuauclt.exe /detectnow** and press ENTER. This forces the Automatic Updates client to communicate with the WSUS server to register the computer.

5. Close the command prompt.

► **Create a computer group**

1. On DEN-DC1, click **Start**, point to **All Programs**, and click **Internet Explorer**.

2. In the **Address** Bar, type **http://DEN-DC1/WSUSadmin** and press ENTER.

3. In the **User name** box, type **administrator** and, in the **Password** box, type **Pa$$w0rd**, and then click **OK**.

4. Click **Computers**. Notice that DEN-CL1 is among the computers listed.

5. Click **Create a computer group**.

6. In the **Group name** box, type **HO-Clients**, and then click **OK**.

7. Click **den-cl1** and then click **Move the selected computer**.

8. In the **Computer group** box, click **HO-Clients**, and then click **OK**.

9. In the **Groups** area, click **HO-Clients**. Notice that DEN-CL1 is now in this computer group.

► **Approve an update**

1. On DEN-DC1, click **Updates**.

2. Scroll down and select **Security Update for Windows XP (KB885835)** and then click **OK** to the warning.

3. Click **Change approval**.

4. In the **Approval** box, select **Install**, and then click **OK**.

5. On DEN-CL1, click **Start**, click **Run**, type **wuauclt.exe /detectnow** and click **OK**. This forces DEN-CL1 to contact the WSUS server.

▶ **View status using reports**

1. On DEN-DC1, click **Reports**.

2. Click **Settings Summary**.

3. Scroll down and read the settings for your WSUS server.

4. Click **Reports**.

5. Click **Status of Updates**.

6. In the **Computer group** box, select **All Computers**.

7. Select the **Needed** and **Unknown** check boxes and then click **Apply**. This shows how many computers need updates and how many computers are unknown; meaning that they have not yet reported their update status.

8. Click **Reports**.

9. Click **Status of Computers**.

10. In the **Computer group** box, select **All Computers**.

11. Select the **Needed** and **Unknown** check boxes and click **Apply**.

12. Expand **den-cl1.contoso.msft** to see the status of each update for DEN-CL1.

Note   You may have to wait up to 15 minutes for DEN-CL1 to report its status. Once it has reported its status, you will see the number of updates needed for the client.

---

13. Close Internet Explorer.

▶ **To prepare for the lab**

• Start the DEN-SRV1 virtual machine.

Lab: Maintaining Software by Using Windows Server Update Services

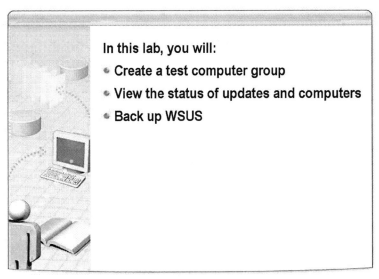

In this lab, you will:
* Create a test computer group
* View the status of updates and computers
* Back up WSUS

Objectives

After completing this lab, you will be able to:

- Create a test computer group.

- View status of updates and computers.

- Back up WSUS.

Instructions

Ensure that the DEN-DC1, DEN-CL1 and DEN-SRV1 virtual machines are running.

Estimated time to complete this lab: 25 minutes

Exercise 1
Create a Test Computer Group

In this exercise, you will create a test computer group and place DEN-SRV1 in it.

Tasks	Specific instructions
1. Add DEN-SRV1 as a computer in WSUS.	a. Log on DEN-SRV1 as **Administrator**. b. Run **GPupdate /force**. c. Run **wuauclt.exe /detectnow**.
2. Open the WSUS Administration Web site.	a. If necessary, log on to DEN-DC1 as **Administrator**. b. Open the WSUS Administration Web site.
3. Create a Test computer group.	a. Create a computer group named **Test**. b. Add DEN-SRV1 to the Test computer group.
4. Approve an update for the Test group.	▪ Approve the most current update for **Microsoft Windows Installer 3.1** for the **Test** group. Hint: You will need to change the view to all updates which have been synchronized at any time.

Exercise 2
View the Status of Updates and Computers

In this exercise, you will view the status of updates and computers.

Tasks	Specific instructions
1. View update status.	a. If necessary, open the WSUS Administration Web site. b. Click **Reports**. c. View the Status of Updates that are needed or unknown for the computer group **Test**.
2. View computer status.	a. Click **Reports**. b. View the Unknown status of Computers for the computer group Test. c. Notice that DEN-SRV1 reports unknown updates.

Exercise 3
Back up WSUS

In this exercise, you will back up the WSUS database and updates.

Tasks	Specific instructions
1. Stop the database service.	▪ On DEN-DC1, stop the MSSQL$WSUS service.
2. Back up the updates and database.	▪ Use **Backup** in System Tools to: • Back up D:\WSUS\MSSQL$WSUS\Data. • Back up D:\WSUS\WsusContent. • Back up to file D:\WSUS.bkf.
3. Start the database service.	▪ Start the MSSQL$WSUS service.
4. Complete the lab exercise.	a. Close all programs and shut down all computers. Do not save changes. b. To prepare for the next module, start the DEN-DC1 virtual computer.

Microsoft®

Module 14: Securing Windows Server 2003

Contents

Overview

- Introduction to Securing Servers
- Implementing Core Server Security
- Hardening Servers
- Microsoft Baseline Security Analyzer

Introduction

Security is no longer the responsibility of a specific person in the Information Technology (IT) department. Every administrator must understand how to secure servers to prevent them and their data from harm. This module introduces you to securing Microsoft® Windows Server™ 2003.

Objectives

After completing this module, you will be able to:

- Describe how servers are secured.
- Explain core server security.
- Harden servers in various roles.
- Use Microsoft Baseline Security Analyzer.

Lesson: Introduction to Securing Servers

- Security Challenges for Small and Medium-Sized Businesses
- Fundamental Security Trade-Offs
- What Is the Defense-in-Depth Model?
- Microsoft Windows Server Security Guidance

Introduction

Organizations now know that effective security is essential to their business operations. The big question is how to implement security. This lesson describes the challenges to implementing security and the trade-offs that must be made.

This lesson also describes the defense in depth model for security analysis and provides some sources of security information from Microsoft.

Lesson objectives

After completing this lesson, you will be able to:

- Describe security challenges for small and medium-sized businesses.
- List fundamental security trade-offs.
- Explain the defense-in-depth model.
- List sources of Microsoft security information.

Security Challenges for Small and Medium-Sized Businesses

Introduction

The security threats that are encountered by small and medium-sized businesses are unique from the security threats encountered by larger businesses. Smaller organizations typically have fewer formal procedures and fewer resources devoted to security.

Security challenges

Security challenges that are encountered by small and medium-sized businesses include:

- *Servers that have a variety of roles.* In businesses with limited resources, servers can have multiple roles. You can easily apply multiple security templates to a server, but the templates can conflict. When a server performs multiple roles, it is more difficult to protect that server. In addition, a server performing multiple roles presents a larger attack surface. If a security breach occurs, all the roles that are performed by that server can be compromised.

  For example, many small businesses have deployed Microsoft Windows Small Business Server 2003, which operates as a domain controller, Exchange server, file server, database server, remote-access server, and possibly a firewall. Servers that provide a variety of services should be isolated from the Internet, and all unnecessary services and applications disabled or uninstalled.

- *Limited resources to implement secure solutions.* If a business has limited resources, it might not be able to provide components for a secure solution. Implementing multiple firewalls is an example of an expensive solution that might not be financially feasible.

- *Internal or accidental threat.* Internal compromise of systems, either malicious or accidental, accounts for a high percentage of attacks on small business and enterprise networks worldwide. Attackers usually find their attacks easier to perform if they have internal access to the network (either personal access or access by means of an unsuspecting or compromised accomplice).

■ *Lack of security expertise.* Smaller IT departments may lack personnel that have appropriate security expertise. Not having the appropriate expertise can lead to overlooked security issues. In this situation, using standard security templates can be beneficial.

■ *Physical access negates many security measures.* Physical access to a system can allow an attacker to execute utilities, install malicious programs, change configurations, remove components, and cause physical damage. Always lock servers in a secure room and require visible identification of anyone authorized to be in the server room.

■ *Legal consequences.* Security breaches can have legal consequences. Depending on the state or country that has jurisdiction over the organization, a business may face legal liability resulting from a breach of its server security. Examples of such legislation include the Sarbanes-Oxley Act of 2002, which requires full compliance by all public firms in the United States by the second half of 2005, the Health Insurance Portability and Accountability Act of 1996 (HIPAA), the Gramm-Leach-Bliley Act (GLBA), California Senate Bill (SB) 1386, and Directive 95/46/EC of the European Parliament and of the Council of 24 October 1995.

■ *Using older systems.* Older systems might not support security configurations without an upgrade. If older systems are not upgraded, the risk of a security breach is greater than it is for newer systems.

Security facts

Security is essential for small organizations and large organizations. Consider the following:

■ Many computer users do not properly update their antivirus software definitions.

■ Spyware infects many computers, which can cause extremely slow performance, excessive pop-up ads, hijacked home pages, and loss of personal information including account passwords. Often users are unaware that their computers are infected.

■ Some organizations do not have an effective strategy for applying security updates. Other organizations do not apply updates due to concerns that they will break applications.

Note For more information about the unique security issues that are encountered by small businesses, see the "Security Guide for Small Business" document under **Additional Reading** on the Student Materials compact disc.

Fundamental Security Trade-Offs

Introduction

When you plan your network security strategy, consider the fundamental security trade-offs that are involved.

Goals

The goals for a computer system or network vary depending on your role in the system. Consider the goals for security administration and network administration:

- The goal of security administration is to safeguard network resources by restricting access to them.

- The goal of network administration is to ensure that users can access all the network applications and programs that they need to do their jobs.

Security vs. usability

The first fundamental security trade-offs that you must consider are security versus usability:

- When you install an application on any operating system, you enable additional functionality, which may make the system less secure because it increases the attack surface of the system. The attack surface of a system is the available opportunities to compromise the system.

- You can make technology more secure but, by doing so, you may make the technology less usable.

- The most secure system is one that is disconnected and locked in a safe. Such a system is secure, but not usable.

Security vs. low cost   The next trade-off to consider is low cost versus security:

- In an ideal world, where resources are unlimited, most companies would choose to make their networks as secure and usable as possible. In the real world, however, cost is often a significant factor that affects the amount of security and usability that can be achieved.

- You may be familiar with the principle of "good, fast, and cheap—you get to choose any two." The principle of fundamental security trade-offs is similar: "secure, usable, and cheap—you get to choose any two." It is possible to have both security and usability, but there is a cost in terms of money, time, and personnel.

Note   For more information about fundamental security trade-offs, see the "Security Management—The Fundamental Tradeoffs" article on the Microsoft TechNet Web site.

What Is the Defense-in-Depth Model?

* Increases an attacker's risk of detection
* Reduces an attacker's chance of success

Layer	
Data	ACLs, encryption, EFS
Application	Application hardening, antivirus
Host	OS hardening, authentication
Internal Network	Network segments, IPSec
Perimeter	Firewalls
Physical Security	Guards, locks
Policies, Procedures, & Awareness	Security documents, user education

Introduction

A security strategy for an organization is most effective when data is protected by more than one layer of security. A defense-in-depth security model uses multiple layers of defense so that, if one layer is compromised, it does not necessarily mean that the attacker will be able to access all the resources on your network. A defense-in-depth model increases an attacker's risk of detection and reduces an attacker's chance of success.

Base layers

The defense-in-depth model consists of a series of interconnected layers. The base layers of the defense-in-depth model are:

■ *Policies, procedures, and awareness layer.* This foundational layer affects every other defense-in-depth layer. Components in this layer include security policies, security procedures, and security education programs for users.

■ *Physical security layer.* This layer wraps around the remaining five core layers. Components in this layer include security guards, locks, and tracking devices.

Core layers

There are many tools, technologies, and best practices you can use to protect each of the five core layers. Examples include:

■ *Perimeter layer.* Hardware or software firewalls, or both, and virtual private networks that use quarantine procedures.

■ *Internal network layer.* Network segmentation, Internet Protocol security (IPSec), and network intrusion-detection systems (NIDS).

- *Host layer.* Server and client operating system hardening practices, strong authentication methods, update management tools, and host-based intrusion-detection systems (HIDS).

- *Application layer.* Application hardening practices and antivirus and antispyware software.

- *Data layer.* Access control lists (ACLs), encryption, and the Encrypting File System (EFS).

This module focuses on securing your Windows-based servers. Security methods and practices discussed in this module relate primarily to the application, host, and internal-network layers.

Important   Remember that server security is only *part* of the overall security strategy of your organization.

Microsoft Windows Server Security Guidance

- Threats and Countermeasures Guide
- Windows Server 2003 Security Guide
- Default Access Control Settings in Windows Server 2003
- Security Innovations in Windows Server 2003
- Technical Overview of Windows Server 2003 Security Services

Introduction

One of the best sources of information on securing servers running Windows is Microsoft. Microsoft provides several documents that contain prescriptive guidance on how to secure computers running Windows Server 2003.

Documents

Security documents available from Microsoft include:

- *Threats and Countermeasures Guide.* Provides a reference to many of the security settings that are available in the current versions of the Microsoft Windows operating systems.

- *Windows Server 2003 Security Guide.* Focuses on providing a set of easy to understand guidance, tools, and templates to help secure Windows Server 2003 in many environments. This guide provides background information about risks, methods to mitigate those risks, and information about the impact of those methods beyond mitigating the risk.

- *Default Access Control Settings in Windows Server 2003.* Describes the default security settings for components of the Microsoft Windows Server 2003 operating system. These components include the registry, file system, user rights, and group membership. This white paper also details the implications of these settings for developers and system administrators, and provides answers to frequently asked questions.

- *Security Innovations in Windows Server 2003.* Describes the security feature enhancements in Windows Server 2003 and outlines how they facilitate business scenarios such as building a secure Web application platform, providing secure mobile access, and streamlining identity management across the enterprise.

- *Technical Overview of Windows Server 2003 Security Services.* Discusses the tools and processes that deliver important security benefits to organizations deploying Windows.

Lesson: Implementing Core Server Security

* Core Server Security Practices
* Recommendations for Hardening Servers
* Windows Server 2003 SP1 Security Enhancements
* What Is Windows Firewall?
* Post-Setup Security Updates
* What Is the Security Configuration Wizard?
* Practice: Implementing Core Server Security

Introduction

This topic explores the components of core server security. The security recommendations in this section apply to *all* servers in a Windows 2000– or Windows Server 2003–based network environment. In addition, this section also provides an overview of the security enhancements available in Windows Server 2003 Service Pack 1 (SP1).

Lesson objectives

After completing this lesson, you will be able to:

* Describe core server security practices.
* List recommendations for hardening servers.
* Explain Windows Server 2003 SP1 technologies enhancements.
* Explain what Windows Firewall is and describe its features.
* Describe post-setup security updates.
* Explain what the Security Configuration Wizard is.
* Implement core server security.

Core Server Security Practices

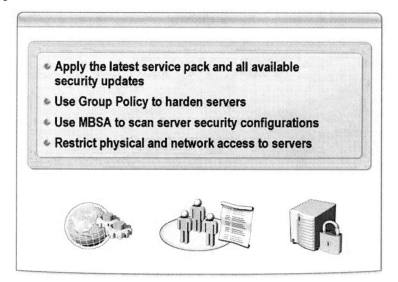

- Apply the latest service pack and all available security updates
- Use Group Policy to harden servers
- Use MBSA to scan server security configurations
- Restrict physical and network access to servers

Introduction

There are several core server security practices. The following is not an exhaustive list; however, it contains some of the more common fundamental server security practices. You may already be using many, if not most, of these core security practices on your network servers.

Important The security practices and measures recommended in this lesson apply to *all* servers in a Windows 2000– or Windows Server 2003–based network environment, including member servers, domain controllers, servers that perform specific roles, and stand-alone servers.

Apply updates and service packs

Applying the latest service pack and available security updates is important because:

- Service packs increase operating system security and stability.

- Most attacks against servers exploit vulnerabilities that have been previously reported and fixed in a service pack or in an operating system security update.

- Computers that do not have the latest service pack and security updates installed are vulnerable.

Use Group Policy

Use Group Policy to harden servers. By using Group Policy, you can:

- Disable services that are not required. Any service or application is a potential point of attack. Therefore, disable or remove all unneeded services to reduce the attack surface.

- Implement secure password policies. You can strengthen the password and account lockout policy settings for a domain controller, member server, or stand-alone server by applying the settings in an appropriate security template.

- Disable LAN Manager and NTLMv1 authentication and storage of LAN Manager hashes. LAN Manager and NTLMv1 are authentication methods required by pre-Windows 2000 clients. Implementing this practice may prevent access by pre-Windows 2000 clients, so you must ensure that you can configure these settings without disabling the functionality that you require.

Use MBSA

Use Microsoft Baseline Security Analyzer (MSBA) to scan server security configurations. MSBA can perform local or remote scans of computers running Windows to identify missing security updates and potential configuration issues. MBSA displays the results of the scan in a Web-based report.

Restrict server access

Use the following guidelines to restrict physical and network access to servers:

- Store servers in a locked room. Use card-key locks or cipher locks on the entrance to the locked room.

- Prevent domain controllers from starting to an alternate operating system by disabling floppy drives, universal serial bus (USB) ports, and CD-ROM drives.

- Allow only trusted personnel to have access to servers. Establish security practices for service administrators and data administrators to ensure that only personnel who require access to servers for their job have access.

- Assign only the permissions and user rights that are necessary to each user in your organization.

Build on core practices

Consider the previous core server security practices a baseline to which you can add advanced server security practices. Examples of advanced server security practices include applying customized security templates to servers and manually configuring IPSec port filtering based on server roles.

Note For more information about core server security practices, see the "Windows Server 2003 Security Guide" on the Microsoft TechNet Web site.

Recommendations for Hardening Servers

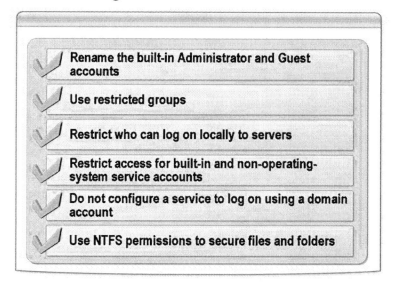

- Rename the built-in Administrator and Guest accounts
- Use restricted groups
- Restrict who can log on locally to servers
- Restrict access for built-in and non-operating-system service accounts
- Do not configure a service to log on using a domain account
- Use NTFS permissions to secure files and folders

Introduction

Consider implementing the following recommendations for hardening all servers on your Windows Server 2003–based network:

Built-in accounts

Recommendations for managing built-in accounts include:

- Renaming the built-in Administrator and Guest accounts, and changing their descriptions. Renaming these accounts to use unique names can make it easier to identify attempted attacks against these accounts. In almost all cases, the Guest account should be disabled.

- Assigning long and complex passwords or passphrases to the built-in Administrator and Guest accounts.

- Using scripts or third-party utilities to periodically verify local passwords on all workstations and servers in the enterprise.

- Using different passwords for the built-in Administrator and Guest accounts on each server so that a compromise of one of these accounts on one server does not enable an attacker to compromise additional servers.

Restricted groups

Use restricted groups to limit the memberships of administrative groups. By using the Restricted Groups option in Active Directory® directory service, you can ensure that administrative groups contain only authorized users.

Log on locally

Restrict the users who can log on locally onto the servers. Use Group Policy to configure user rights so that only authorized administrators can log on locally onto the servers.

Restrict access

Restrict access to the system for built-in and service accounts other than the system service accounts. Configure user rights assignments as follows:

- Deny access to this computer from the network for the Built-In Administrator, Support_388945a0 (the account that is used for remote assistance), Guest accounts, and all service accounts other than the system service accounts.

- Deny logon as a batch job for the Support_388945a0 and Guest accounts.

- Deny logon using Terminal Services for the Built-In Administrator, Support_388945a0, Guest accounts, and service accounts other than the system service accounts.

Services

Do not configure a service to log on by using a domain account. Whenever possible, use a local account for each service. In addition, do not use the same user account name and password for a service on multiple servers.

Use NTFS

Use NTFS permissions to secure files and folders. Convert any FAT or FAT32 volumes to NTFS, and then apply the appropriate permissions to the files and folders on those volumes.

Windows Server 2003 SP1 Security Enhancements

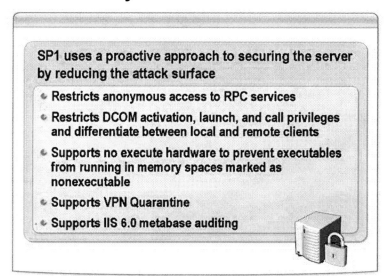

SP1 uses a proactive approach to securing the server by reducing the attack surface

- Restricts anonymous access to RPC services
- Restricts DCOM activation, launch, and call privileges and differentiate between local and remote clients
- Supports no execute hardware to prevent executables from running in memory spaces marked as nonexecutable
- Supports VPN Quarantine
- Supports IIS 6.0 metabase auditing

Introduction

The primary objective of Windows Server 2003 SP1 is to increase server security. Instead of focusing on update management to respond to threats after they have been discovered, SP1 takes a more proactive approach of reducing the attack surface on the server.

RPC configuration

Microsoft Windows operating systems rely on remote procedure call (RPC) services to run. Many of these RPC services are accessible to anonymous network users. Service Pack 1 makes RPC interfaces more secure by enabling the **RestrictRemoteClients** and the **EnableAuthEpResolution** registry keys.

The **RestrictRemoteClients** registry key enables you to modify how the computer will accept connections on all RPC interfaces to eliminate remote anonymous access to RPC interfaces on the system. If you restrict access to the RPC services to only authenticated users, then you must configure the **EnableAuthEpResolution** registry key on each client so that it will use NTLM authentication when connecting to the RPC Endpoint Mapper.

Important   You can configure both the **RestrictRemoteClients** and the **EnableAuthEpResolution** registry entries by using Group Policy if your servers and clients are members of an Active Directory domain.

Note   RPC clients that use the named pipe protocol sequence (**ncacn_np**) are exempt from all restrictions discussed in this section. The named pipe protocol sequence cannot be restricted due to several significant backward-compatibility issues.

DCOM configuration   With DCOM, an anonymous remote client can ask a DCOM server to perform a task that normally requires authentication. Some Component Object Model (COM) servers allow unauthenticated remote access and can be called by anyone, including unauthenticated users. Service Pack 1 addresses this issue by using:

- New computerwide restrictions that apply to DCOM activation, launch, and call privileges that differentiate between local and remote clients. By default, everyone is granted local launch, local activation, and local call permissions, which should enable all local scenarios to continue to work without change. In addition, all authenticated users are granted remote call permissions by default, which allow most common server applications to function properly if the client is not anonymous. The default configuration grants only administrators remote activation and launch permissions.

- More specific COM permissions that allow individual COM servers to restrict the rights that are available to users. There are four new launch permission levels for COM servers: local launch, remote launch, local activate, and remote activate. There are two new access permission levels for COM servers: local calls and remote calls. The default permission levels will work properly for almost all situations.

Note   For more information about DCOM configuration enhancements, see Changes to Functionality in Microsoft Windows Server 2003 Service Pack 1 on the Microsoft Web site.

No-execute support   For both 32-bit and 64-bit systems, support for "no execute" hardware eliminates one of the broadest and most exploited methods of information attack. Service Pack 1 allows Windows Server 2003 to use functionality built in to computing hardware from such companies as Intel and Advanced Micro Devices to prevent malicious code from launching attacks that originate from areas of computer memory that should have no code running in it.

VPN quarantine   VPN quarantine automatically provides the means for limiting network access for computers on virtual private networks (VPNs) that do have the most current security updates.

IIS 6.0 metabase auditing   The metabase is the XML-based, hierarchical store of configuration information for Internet Information Services (IIS) 6.0. IIS 6.0 metabase auditing allows network administrators to see which user accessed the metabase in case it becomes corrupted.

What Is Windows Firewall?

* Enabled by default in new installs
* Audit logging to track firewall activity
* Boot-time security
* Global configuration
* Port restrictions based on the client network
* On with no exceptions
* Exceptions list
* Group Policy support

Definition

Windows Firewall is a software-based firewall for Windows XP and Windows Server 2003. Windows Firewall provides protection for computers that are connected to a network by preventing unsolicited inbound connections through Transmission Control Protocol/Internet Protocol (TCP/IP) version 4 (IPv4) and TCP/IP version 6 (IPv6).

Windows Firewall features

Some of the changes to Windows Firewall include:

- *Enabled by default for new installations of Windows Server 2003 SP1.* Provides more network protection by default for Windows Server 2003. Windows Firewall blocks all outside sources from connecting to the computer with the exception of those that are identified on the exception list.

- *Audit logging.* Enables customers to track changes that are made to Windows Firewall settings and to see which applications and services requested a port to be opened. After you enable audit logging, audit events are logged in the security event log. Auditing the activity of Windows Firewall is part of a defense-in-depth strategy that allows customers to react quickly to attacks on their systems.

- *Boot-time security.* In earlier versions of Windows, there was a period of time between when the computer would accept network connections and when Internet Connection Firewall (ICF) started to provide protection on the network. During this brief period of time, the computer was on the network and unprotected by Internet Connection Firewall. With boot-time security, only such basic networking functions as Domain Name System (DNS), Dynamic Host Configuration Protocol (DHCP), and communication with a domain controller are allowed. Other networking functions are disabled until the firewall service starts.

- *Global configuration.* In earlier versions of Windows, Internet Connection Firewall was configured on a per-interface basis. This meant that each network connection had its own firewall policy, making it difficult to synchronize policy between connections. With global configuration, whenever a configuration change occurs, the change applies to all network connections. When you create new connections, the configuration is applied to them also. The global policy makes it easier for users to manage their firewall policy across all network connections. It also makes it easier to configure network applications.

- *Port restrictions based on the client network.* Traditionally, when a service listens on a port it is open to incoming traffic from any network location, such as a local network or the Internet. With Windows Firewall, you can configure the port to receive only network traffic with a source address from the local subnet, from specific IP addresses or from specific subnets, or from both.

- *On with no exceptions operational mode.* You can configure Windows Firewall to allow unsolicited incoming traffic to provide server services. However, if you discover a security issue in one or more of the services or applications that are running on the computer, you can switch into a client-only mode, which is called "On with no exceptions." Switching into this client-only mode configures Windows Firewall to prevent unsolicited inbound traffic without having to reconfigure the firewall. In this mode, all static ports are closed and any existing connections are dropped. Viruses, worms, and attackers look for services to exploit. When in this operational mode, Windows Firewall helps to prevent such types of attacks from succeeding.

- *Windows Firewall exceptions list.* An application that needs to accept connections from the network can be added to the Windows Firewall exceptions list. Only administrators can add an application to the exceptions list. When an application is on the Windows Firewall exceptions list, only the necessary ports are opened, and they are opened only for the duration that the application is accepting connections on those ports.

- *Group Policy Support.* With Windows Server 2003 SP1, you can configure every Windows Firewall configuration option by using Group Policy. Examples of the new configuration options available include:

  - Define program exceptions

  - Allow local program exceptions

  - Allow Internet Control Message Protocol (ICMP) exceptions

  - Prohibit notifications

  - Allow file and printer sharing exception

  - Allow logging

  - You can also use Security Configuration Wizard to configure the Windows Firewall settings

Post-Setup Security Updates

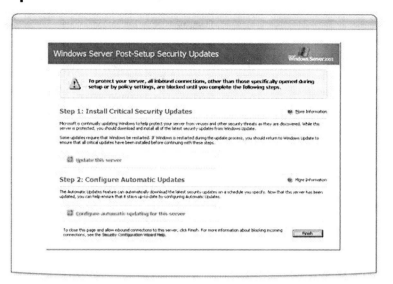

Introduction

Post-Setup Security Updates (PSSU) is designed to protect the server from risk of infection between the time the server is first started and the application of the most recent security updates from Windows Update.

PSSU

To protect the server, Windows Firewall is enabled during a new installation of any version of Windows Server 2003 Service Pack 1. If Windows Firewall is enabled and the administrator did not explicitly enable it by using an unattended-setup script or Group Policy, PSSU opens the first time an administrator logs on. Inbound connections to the server are blocked until the administrator has clicked the **Finish** button on the **PSSU** dialog box; this allows the administrator to download and install updates securely from Windows Update. If the administrator set exceptions to the firewall by using Group Policy or by enabling Remote Desktop during installation, inbound connections assigned to these exceptions remain open.

PSSU:

- Is not available from the **Start** menu.

- Does not appear when the server is being upgraded from the following operating systems:

  - Windows 2000 to Windows Server 2003 with Service Pack 1

  - Windows Server 2003 to Windows Server 2003 with Service Pack 1

- Is displayed when the server is being upgraded from Microsoft Windows NT® 4.0 to Windows Server 2003 with Service Pack 1.

- Does not apply to installations of Windows Server 2003 that use either an unattended setup script or an application of a Group Policy that enables or disables Windows Firewall.

What Is the Security Configuration Wizard?

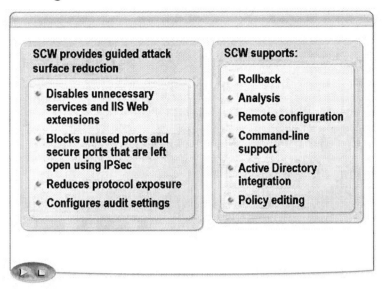

Definition

The Security Configuration Wizard (SCW) provides guided attack surface reduction for servers running Windows Server 2003 SP1. When you run the wizard, it asks a series of questions to determine the server role or roles, and then uses a roles-based metaphor that is driven by an extensible XML knowledge base that defines the services, ports, and other functional requirements for more than 50 different server roles. Any functionality that is not required by the roles that the server is performing will be disabled.

Reduce attack surface

To reduce attack surface, the wizard allows administrators to:

- Disable unnecessary services.
- Disable unnecessary IIS Web extensions.
- Block unused ports, including support for multihomed scenarios.
- Secure ports that are left open by using IPSec.
- Reduce protocol exposure for Lightweight Directory Access Protocol (LDAP), LAN Manager, and server message block (SMB).
- Configure audit settings with a high signal-to-noise ratio.
- Import Windows security templates for coverage of settings that are not configured by the wizard.

SCW features

In addition to role-based, guided security policy authoring, SCW also supports:

- *Rollback.* Returns the server to the state that it was in before the SCW security policy was applied, which can be useful when applied policies disrupt service expectations.

- *Analysis.* Verifies that servers are in compliance with expected policies.

- *Remote access.* Supports remote access for configuration and analysis operations.

- *Command-line support.* Enables remote configuration and analysis of groups of servers.

- *Active Directory integration.* Supports deploying SCW policies by using Group Policy.

- *Editing.* Enables modification of a security policy that is created by using SCW as necessary, such as when server roles are redefined.

Practice: Implementing Core Server Security

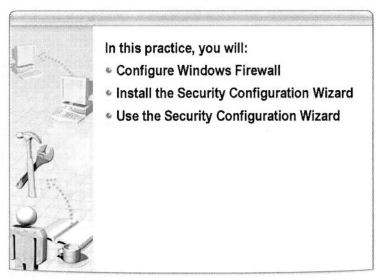

In this practice, you will:
* Configure Windows Firewall
* Install the Security Configuration Wizard
* Use the Security Configuration Wizard

Objective

In this practice, you will:

- Configure Windows Firewall.
- Install the Security Configuration Wizard.
- Use the Security Configuration Wizard.

Instructions

Ensure that the DEN-DC1 virtual machine is running.

Practice

▶ **Configure Windows Firewall**

1. On DEN-DC1, log on as **Administrator** with a password of **Pa$$w0rd**.
2. Click **Start**, point to **Control Panel**, and click **Windows Firewall**.
3. Click **Yes**, to start the Windows Firewall/ICS service.
4. Click **On**.
5. On the **Exceptions** tab, select the **Remote Desktop** check box.
6. Click **Edit**. This shows the ports allowed by the Remote Desktop rule.
7. Click **Change scope**, click **My network (subnet) only** and then click **OK**. This limits communication with Remote Desktop to only computers on the same subnet as the server. Click **OK**.
8. On the **Advanced** tab, in the **Security Logging** area, click **Settings**.
9. Select the **Log dropped packets** check box, and then click **OK**.
10. Click **OK** to close Windows Firewall.

▶ **Install the Security Configuration Wizard**

1. On DEN-DC1, click **Start**, point to **Control Panel**, and then click **Add or Remove Programs**.

2. Click **Add/Remove Windows Components**.

3. Scroll down in the **Components** box, select the **Security Configuration Wizard** check box., and then click **Next**.

4. If prompted for the location of the Service Pack 1 CD-ROM, use **C:\win2k3\I386**.

5. Click **Finish**.

6. Close **Add or Remove Programs**.

▶ **Use the Security Configuration Wizard**

1. Click **Start**, point to **Administrative Tools**, and then click **Security Configuration Wizard**.

2. Click **Next** to begin the Security Configuration Wizard.

3. Ensure that **Create a new security policy** is selected, and then click **Next**.

4. Ensure that DEN-DC1 is the server to be used as a baseline for the policy, and then click **Next**.

5. Click **View Configuration Database**.

6. Scroll through and read the list of Server Roles, Client Features, Services, Ports, Applications, and Administration and Other Options.

7. Close **SCW Viewer** and then click **Next** twice.

8. Click **Next** again to accept the installed roles.

9. Click **Next** to accept the installed client features.

10. Click **Next** to accept the installed administration and other options.

11. Click **Next** to accept the additional services.

12. Ensure that **Do not change the startup mode of the service** is selected and then click **Next**.

13. Scroll through the list of changed services and note which ones are being disabled.

14. Click **Next**.

15. Click **Next** again to start configuring network security.

16. Scroll through the list of ports that will be opened and click **Next**.

17. Click **Next** again to accept the list of ports that will be opened.

18. Check the **Skip this section** check box, and then click **Next** to skip configuring registry settings.

19. Check the **Skip this section** check box, and then click **Next** to skip configuring audit policies.

20. Check the **Skip this section** check box, and then click **Next** to skip configuring Internet Information Services.

21. Click **Next** to begin saving the security policy.

22. In the **Security policy file name** box, type
C:\WINDOWS\security\msscw\Policies\NewDC.xml and then click **Next**.

23. Click **Apply now**, and then click **Next**.

24. When the application of the security policy is complete, click **Next**.

25. Click **Finish**.

26. Restart DEN-DC1.

Important   Do not shut down the virtual machines.

Lesson: Hardening Servers

- What Is Server Hardening?
- What Is the Member Server Baseline Security Template?
- Security Threats to Domain Controllers
- Implement Password Security
- Security Templates for Specific Server Roles
- Best Practices for Hardening Servers for Specific Roles
- Practice: Hardening Servers

Introduction

This lesson shows you how to implement server hardening to protect data and services.

Lesson objectives

After completing this lesson, you will be able to:

- Explain server hardening.
- Describe the Member Server Baseline Security template.
- List security threats to domain controllers.
- Explain the importance of password security.
- Describe using security templates for specific server roles.
- Use best practices for hardening servers for specific roles.
- Harden a server.

What Is Server Hardening?

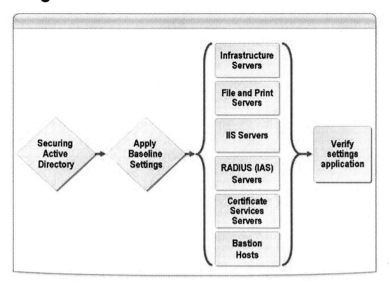

Definition

Server hardening is the process of securing a server by implementing security settings that are specific to the servers' role. For example, you can restrict the right to log on locally to a server to only administrators.

Server hardening process

The server hardening process is as follows:

1. Secure Active Directory. This includes creating an organizational unit (OU) structure that is appropriate for delegating administrative permissions and then delegating permissions. It is also common to create separate OUs for servers that fulfill similar roles. This allows easy implementation of Group Policy to configure server security.

2. Apply a set of baseline security settings to all servers in the domain. For member servers, use the Member Server Baseline security template. For domain controllers, use the Domain Controller security template.

3. After you apply baseline security settings, you can use various security templates and Group Policy to apply additional, incremental security settings to servers that perform specific roles, such as infrastructure servers, file servers, print servers, and IIS servers. These incremental security settings are different for each type of server role.

4. After you apply security settings to servers, you can use GPResult on a computer running Windows Server 2003, or use the Local Security Policy snap-in on a computer running Windows 2000 Server to verify that these settings have been applied correctly.

What Is the Member Server Baseline Security Template?

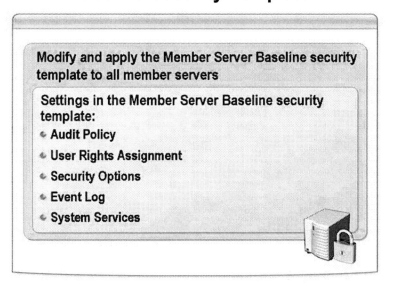

Modify and apply the Member Server Baseline security template to all member servers

Settings in the Member Server Baseline security template:
- Audit Policy
- User Rights Assignment
- Security Options
- Event Log
- System Services

Introduction

You can apply baseline security settings to all member servers by using the Member Server Baseline security template that is included with the Windows Server 2003 Security Guide.

After you modify this template to meet the needs of your organization and test the template's security configurations by using your organization's business applications, import this template's settings into a Group Policy object (GPO) and link the GPO to the Member Servers OU.

Note Do not apply the member server template to domain controllers; instead, apply the domain controller template to the Domain Controllers OU.

Member Server Baseline security template security settings

The Member Server Baseline security template contains numerous security settings, including:

- *Audit Policy settings.* Specify the security events that are recorded in the Event Log. You can monitor security-related activity, such as who attempts to access an object when a user logs on to or logs off a computer, or when changes are made to an Audit Policy setting.

- *User Rights Assignment settings.* Specify users or groups that have logon rights or privileges on the member servers in the domain.

- *Security Options settings.* Used to enable or disable security settings for servers, such as digital signing of data, administrator and guest account names, floppy-disk drive and CD-ROM drive access, driver installation behavior, and logon prompts.

- *Event Log settings.* Specify the size of each event log and what actions to take when each event log becomes full. There are several event logs that store logged security events, including the Application log, the Security log, and the System log.

- *System Services settings.* Specify the startup type and permissions for each service on the server.

Note For more information about security templates and to obtain a comprehensive set of security templates, download the *Windows Server 2003 Security Guide* from the Microsoft Download Center Web site.

Security Threats to Domain Controllers

- Modification of Active Directory data
- Password attacks against administrator accounts
- Denial-of-service attacks
- Replication prevention attacks
- Exploitation of known vulnerabilities

Introduction

Domain controllers are central to the security of a Windows Server 2003 network. They hold a copy of the Active Directory database which contains user credentials and other network information. Domain controllers are a tempting target for hackers because of the information that they contain.

Threats

Domain controllers are targets for specific security threats, including:

- *Modification or addition of Active Directory objects.* If attackers can compromise a domain controller, they can make whatever changes that they want to Active Directory. This includes creating a user account for their purposes, and adding that user account to any group in the domain.

- *Password attacks.* If attackers can gain access to a domain controller, they can back up the Active Directory database by performing a System State backup or by copying the Active Directory database and logs to another computer. The attacker can use the backup of the domain controller restore a remote computer and then initiate an offline password attack.

- *Denial-of-service attacks.* Attackers can prevent users from performing authentication by executing denial-of-service (DoS) attacks against domain controllers. Denial-of-service attacks typically take advantage of security vulnerabilities for which updates have not been installed. Denial-of-service attacks can also result when account lockout thresholds are turned off or set too low. DNS servers are logical targets of denial-of-service attacks because when a DNS server is disabled, a potentially large number of clients is prevented from finding a domain controller.

■ *Replication prevention attacks.* If attackers are able to disrupt replication between domain controllers, they might be able to prevent the application of GPOs, which secure domain controllers. For example, if you modify the GPO that is applied to all domain controllers and the GPO is not replicated to all domain controllers, some of the domain controllers will not have the new security settings applied. Also, if DNS resource records are modified or deleted, a domain controller might not be able to find its replication partners. Likewise, if wide-area network (WAN) links are blocked, replication traffic might not be able to reach domain controllers at remote sites.

■ *Exploitation of known security issues.* Attackers might be able to compromise a domain controller that is not kept up to date with the latest service packs and security updates. For example, if the latest service packs are not applied to a domain controller, attackers might be able to disable the domain controller by performing a buffer-overflow attack. The result of such an attack could be to prevent the domain controller from responding to any network requests. Worse, a buffer overflow might allow attackers to modify configuration and take control of a domain controller.

Implement Password Security

* Use complex passwords to help prevent
  security breaches
* Do not implement authentication protocols that require
  reversible encryption
* Disable LM hash value storage in Active Directory

Introduction

One important step to increase domain controller and domain security is to implement password security.

Complex passwords

You should require complex passwords for all user accounts. A long, complex password is very difficult to for hackers to discover. To enable complex passwords, enable the Password Must Meet Complexity Requirements setting on a GPO that is assigned to the domain. When this setting is enabled, passwords must be at least six characters in length and consist of at least three of the following four forms:

- English uppercase letters
- English lowercase letters
- Numbers
- Nonalphanumeric characters, such as punctuation marks or symbols

---

Important Before you require users to use complex passwords, you may need to provide some training on how to remember these passwords. You can teach users to use passphrases (for example, "AnewPa$$word4me!") or use mnemonic tricks to create and remember complex passwords. (For example, "To be or not to be" becomes 2Bee0rkNOT2b?.)

Reversible encryption

Do not implement protocols that require passwords to be stored in a reversibly encrypted format, such as Challenge Handshake Authentication Protocol (CHAP) or digest authentication for Web applications. A password that is stored in this format is more susceptible to password attacks if attackers gain physical access to a domain controller.

LAN Manager hash values

Disable LAN Manager (LM) hash values in the Active Directory database. When you set a password that contains fewer than 15 characters, Windows generates both a LAN Manager hash and a Windows NT LAN Manager (NTLM) hash of the password. A password that is stored in an LM hash value is more susceptible to password attacks. You can disable the storage of passwords in this format by enabling the Network Security: Do Not Store LAN Manager Hash Values On Next Password Change Group Policy setting in Security Options.

Security Templates for Specific Server Roles

Introduction

In an Active Directory environment, there are member servers that perform specific server roles. You can organize these servers by creating an appropriate child OU for each server role under the Member Servers OU. For example, you might have a File Servers OU and a Print Servers OU under the Member Servers OU in your OU hierarchy.

Applying templates

To harden member servers you can apply the Member Server Baseline security template to all member servers. In addition to this security template, you can apply incremental, role-based security settings to servers that perform specific roles. You accomplish this by modifying the settings in a role-based security template, importing the settings within this template into a GPO, and then linking the GPO to the OU for the specific server role.

The *Windows Server 2003 Security Guide* includes security templates for the following specific server roles:

- Infrastructure server
- File server
- Print server
- Internet Information Services (IIS) server
- Internet Authentication Service (IAS) server
- Certificate services server
- Bastion host

Multiple roles

If you need to combine roles for some of the servers in your environment, you can customize security templates so that the appropriate combination of services and security options is configured for the servers that perform multiple roles.

Note   The *Windows Server 2003 Security Guide* can be found on the Microsoft TechNet Web site.

Best Practices for Hardening Servers for Specific Roles

Introduction

Hardening servers for specific roles includes applying the appropriate security templates and manually configuring server settings for the role. Most of the recommended security settings are applied to role-based servers by using the Member Server Baseline security template and, incrementally, by using a role-based security template.

Best practices

Consider the following best practices when hardening servers for specific roles:

- *Modify templates as needed for servers with multiple roles.* Servers that perform multiple roles require a customized template that specifically configures the server's security settings to enable it to perform multiple roles. You may need to start with the pre-configured template for one of the roles the server performs, and then modify the template so that services and other security settings required by the additional role are correctly configured in the template. Be sure to preserve the original template so you can revert to it if required.

- *Enable only services that are required for the role.* Any that is service not required by the server to fulfill its assigned role should be disabled.

- *Enable service logging to capture relevant information.* Consider enabling logging for critical services that are required by the server role. For example, enable DHCP logging for a DHCP server.

- *Use IPSec filtering to block all ports except the specific ports needed, based on server role.* For more information about the specific ports that should be allowed on a server for a specific role, see the appropriate chapter in the *Windows Server 2003 Security Guide.*

- *Secure service accounts and well-known user accounts.* Do not configure a service to log on by using a domain account unless absolutely necessary. Rename the built-in Administrator and Guest accounts and change their descriptions. In addition, assign long and complex passwords to these built-in accounts. Finally, use different passwords for these accounts on each server so that a compromise of one of these accounts on one server does not enable an attacker to compromise additional servers.

Practice: Hardening Servers

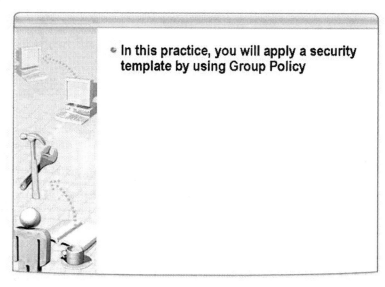

- In this practice, you will apply a security template by using Group Policy

Objective

In this practice, you will:

- Apply a security template by using Group Policy.

Instructions

Ensure that the DEN-DC1 virtual machine is running.

Practice

▶ **Apply a security template through Group Policy**

1. On DEN-DC1, log on as **Administrator** with a password of **Pa$$w0rd**.

2. Click **Start**, point to **Administrative Tools**, and then click **Group Policy Management**.

3. Expand **Forest: Contoso.msft**, expand **Domains**, expand **Contoso.msft**, and then expand **Domain Controllers**.

4. Right-click **Domain Controllers**, and click **Create and Link a GPO Here**.

5. In the **Name** box, type **DC Security** and then click **OK**.

6. Click **DC Security** and then click **OK** to clear the dialog box.

7. Right-click **DC Security** and click **Edit**.

8. Under **Computer Configuration**, expand **Windows Settings**, right-click **Security Settings**, and click **Import Policy**.

9. Select **D:\2275\Practices\Mod09\Security Templates\Enterprise Client – Domain Controller.inf**, and then click **Open**.

10. Close the Group Policy Object Editor.

11. Close Group Policy Management.

Important Do not shut down the virtual machines.

Lesson: Microsoft Baseline Security Analyzer

* What Is MBSA?
* MBSA Benefits
* How MBSA Works
* MBSA Scan Options
* Practice: Microsoft Baseline Security Analyzer

Introduction

The Microsoft Baseline Security Analyzer (MBSA) tool is used to identify security weaknesses in Windows networks. It is available from Microsoft at no charge and is an essential tool for security analysis.

Lesson objectives

After completing this lesson, you will be able to:

- Describe MBSA.
- List MBSA considerations.
- Describe how MBSA works.
- Describe MBSA scan options.
- Use Microsoft Baseline Security Analyzer.

What Is MBSA?

* Scans systems for:

  * Missing security updates

  * Potential configuration issues

* Works with a broad range of Microsoft software

* Allows an administrator to centrally scan multiple computers simultaneously

MBSA is a free tool, and can be downloaded from the Microsoft TechNet Web site

---

Definition

The MBSA, which includes a graphical and command-line interface, can perform local or remote scans of computers running Windows to identify missing security updates and potential configuration issues. MBSA displays the results of the scan in a Web-based report.

MBSA features

MBSA runs on computers running Windows XP, Windows 2000, and Windows Server 2003 and will scan for missing security updates and potential configuration issues on a broad range of Microsoft software. MBSA scans for:

- Missing security updates and updates on these products:

  - Microsoft BizTalk® Server 2000, 2002, and 2004

  - Microsoft Commerce Server 2000 and 2002

  - Microsoft Content Management Server 2001 and 2002

  - Microsoft Exchange Server 5.5, Exchange 2000 Server, and Exchange Server 2003

  - Microsoft Host Integration Server 2000 and 2004

  - Microsoft Internet Explorer 5.01 and later versions

  - Internet Information Services (IIS) 4.0, IIS 5.0, IIS 5.1, and IIS 6.0

  - Microsoft Data Access Components (MDAC) 2.5, 2.6, 2.7, and 2.8

  - Microsoft Virtual PC

  - MSXML 2.5, 2.6, 3.0, and 4.0

  - Microsoft Office 2000, Office XP, and Office 2003 (for local scans only)

- Microsoft SNA Server 4.0
- Microsoft SQL Server™ 7.0 and SQL Server 2000 (including Microsoft Data Engine)
- Microsoft Windows Media® Player 6.4 and later versions
  Microsoft Windows NT 4.0, Windows 2000, Windows XP (including SP 2), and Windows Server 2003
- Potential configuration issues on these products:
  - Internet Explorer 5.01 and later versions
  - IIS 4.0, IIS 5.0, and IIS 6.0
  - Office 2000, Office XP, and Office 2003
  - SQL Server 7.0 and 2000
  - Windows NT 4.0, Windows 2000, Windows XP, and Windows Server 2003

MBSA will not run on computers running Windows NT 4.0. However, it can be used to remotely scan a computer running Windows NT 4.0 when run from a supported operating system. Other benefits of MBSA:

- An administrator can use MBSA to centrally scan multiple computers simultaneously.
- MBSA requires minimal configuration.
- MBSA is available as a free download from the Microsoft Web site.
- MBSA version 2 integrates with Windows Server Update Services (WSUS).

MBSA Benefits

MBSA reports important vulnerabilities:

- Password weaknesses
- Guest account not disabled
- Auditing not configured
- Unnecessary services installed
- IIS product vulnerabilities
- IE zone settings
- Automatic Updates configuration
- Windows XP firewall configuration

Introduction

In addition to detecting missing security updates, MBSA scans for numerous security issues and weaknesses. These include weak passwords and common configuration errors.

Weak passwords

MBSA performs a password test on each local user account on the computer. This check is not performed on domain controllers. MBSA identifies common password vulnerabilities, such as:

- Blank passwords
- Passwords that are the same as the corresponding user account names
- Passwords that are the same as the corresponding machines
- Passwords that use the word "password"
- Passwords that use the words "admin" or "administrator"

Important   The password scan is resource-intensive; skipping the password scan dramatically increases performance, especially when scanning over the network.

Configuration errors

MBSA checks for other important security issues, such as:

- Whether the Guest account is disabled
- Whether there are any user accounts that have nonexpiring passwords
- Whether auditing is configured
- Whether the computer is properly restricting anonymous access
- Unnecessary services that are installed on the system
- IIS security issues

- Internet Explorer zone settings and Enhanced Security Configuration checks for Windows Server 2003
- Office macro security
- Automatic Updates configuration
- Internet Connection Firewall (ICF) and Windows Firewall configuration

How MBSA Works

The MSSecure.xml file

The file MSSecure.xml is the list of security weaknesses that is used by MBSA to scan for problems. This file can be obtained automatically by using MBSA or downloaded manually when an Internet connection is not available.

The MSSecure.xml contains:

- Security bulletin names
- Product-specific updates
- Version and checksum information
- Registry keys changes
- Microsoft Knowledge Base article numbers

MBSA process

How MBSA works:

1. Run MBSA and specify the target computers to scan.
2. MBSA downloads the MSSecure.cab file containing MSSecure.xml and verifies its digital signature.

   MBSA attempts to contact the Microsoft Download Center to obtain this file; alternatively, the file can be downloaded and copied to the computer that initiates the scan and then placed in the MBSA installation folder.
3. MBSA scans the target systems for operating systems, operating system components, and applications.
4. MBSA parses the MSSecure.xml file to see if updates are available.
5. MBSA checks the system to see if required updates are missing.
6. MBSA generates a time-stamped report that lists any security updates missing from your system.

Note   You can manually download the MSSecure.cab file from the Microsoft Download Web site. MBSA Version 2 uses Wsusscan.cab instead of MSSecure.cab.

MBSA Scan Options

MBSA has three scan options:

- MBSA graphical user interface (GUI)
- MBSA standard command-line interface (mbsacli.exe)
- HFNetChk scan (mbsacli.exe /hf)

Introduction

You can use MBSA through a graphical user interface (GUI) or either of two command-line interfaces: the MBSA standard command-line interface or the HFNetChk scan interface. The GUI is used most often by administrators because it is easy to use.

The MBSA standard command-line interface is used in batch files. The HFNetChk scan interface is used for backwards compatibility with scripts created for HFNetChk.

Graphical user interface

When you use the MBSA graphical user interface, you initiate the scan from a GUI interface and MBSA generates a report that you can view in the same interface.

Standard command-line interface

You can use standard command-line interface to perform the same types of scans as the GUI version of MBSA. You can use the command-line interface to scan for missing security updates as well as for potential configuration issues.

When you run MBSA from the command line, you can specify numerous options, such as a range of IP addresses of the computers to be scanned, the various security issues for which you want MBSA to scan, and the manner in which you want the output from the scan to be displayed. The output from a command-line interface scan is displayed as text in the command-line window.

One of the advantages of using the command-line interface is that MBSA can be run from a script, which enables you to run scans on a schedule or use other tools to automate the use of MBSA in your environment.

To see the full list of available MBSA command-line switches, type **mbsacli /?** at a command prompt.

HFNetChk interface

The HFNetChk scan interface is an MBSA command-line interface parameter that enables MBSA to emulate the HFNetChk tool. This scan option can be used only to scan for missing security updates.

The HFNetChk scan, like the standard MBSA command-line interface, displays scan results as text in the command-line window.

Note By default, the command-line and HFNetChk scans perform checksum checking, which is turned off by default on MBSA GUI scans.

Practice: Microsoft Baseline Security Analyzer

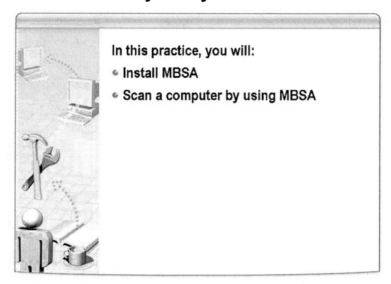

In this practice, you will:
- Install MBSA
- Scan a computer by using MBSA

Objective

In this practice, you will:

- Install MBSA.
- Scan a computer by using MBSA.

Instructions

Ensure that the DEN-DC1 virtual machine is running.

Practice

▶ **Install MBSA**

1. If necessary, log on to DEN-DC1 as **Administrator** with a password of **Pa$$w0rd**.

2. Open Windows Explorer.

3. Browse to **D:\2275\Practices\Mod09** and double-click **MBSASetup-EN**.

4. Click **Next** to begin the MBSA setup.

5. Click **I accept the license agreement**, and then click **Next**.

6. Click **Next** again to accept the default installation folder.

7. Click **Install**, and then click **OK**.

8. Copy **MSSecure_1033.cab** from the **D:\2275\Practices\Mod09** folder to the **C:\Program Files\Microsoft Baseline Security Analyzer** folder.

9. Close Windows Explorer.

▶ **Scan a computer using MBSA**

1. On the desktop, double-click **Microsoft Baseline Security Analyzer 1.2.1**.

2. Click **Scan a computer**.

3. In the **Computer name** box, type **CONTOSO\DEN-DC1**.

4. Click **Start scan**.

5. Scroll down to an item with a yellow X beside it and click **Result details**. This shows why the item was marked with a yellow X.

6. Close the window with the result details.

7. Click **How to correct this**, read the contents of the pop-up window, and close the pop-up window.

8. Close Microsoft Baseline Security Analyzer.

▶ **To prepare for the next lab**

1. Start the DEN-SRV1 virtual machine.

2. Start the DEN-CL1 virtual machine.

Important   Do not shut down the virtual machines.

Lab: Securing Windows Server 2003

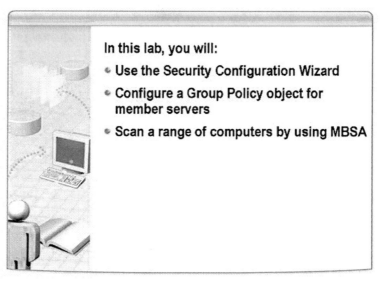

In this lab, you will:

● Use the Security Configuration Wizard

● Configure a Group Policy object for member servers

● Scan a range of computers by using MBSA

Objectives

After completing this lab, you will be able to:

■ Use the Security Configuration Wizard.

■ Configure a Group Policy object for member servers.

■ Scan a range of computers by using MBSA.

Instructions

Ensure that the DEN-DC1, DEN-SRV1, and DEN-CL1 virtual machines are running.

Scenario

As the system administrator for a mid-sized organization you are exploring your options for securing servers and workstations. You are testing the Security Configuration Wizard, Group Policy objects, and MBSA to compare the differences in their capabilities.

Estimated time to complete this lab: 30 minutes

Exercise 1
Using the Security Configuration Wizard

In this exercise, you will install and run the Security Configuration Wizard.

Tasks	Specific instructions
1. Install the Security Configuration Wizard.	a. Log on to DEN-SRV1 as **Administrator** with a password of **Pa$$w0rd**. b. Open **Add or Remove Programs**. c. Open **Add/Remove Windows Components**. d. Select the **Security Configuration Wizard** component. If required, Windows Server 2003 SP1 is located in **C:\win2k3\i386**.
2. Run the Security Configuration Wizard.	a. Open the **Administrative Tools** menu and click **Security Configuration Wizard**. b. Create a new policy and accept the default settings as presented by the wizard. c. Save the setting in the default location called **NewMember.xml**. d. Apply the settings to the server. e. Restart DEN-SRV1.

Exercise 2
Configuring a Group Policy Object for Member Servers

In this exercise, you will configure a group policy object for member servers.

Tasks	Specific instructions
1. Create an OU for member servers.	a. Log on to DEN-DC1 as **Administrator** with a password of **Pa$$w0rd**. b. Open **Active Directory Users and Computers**. c. Create an OU called **MemberServers**. d. Move the **DEN-SRV1** computer object into the **MemberServers** OU.
2. Create a Group Policy object for member servers.	a. Open **Group Policy Management**. b. Create and link a GPO to **MemberServers** called **Member Security**. c. Edit the **Member Security** GPO.
3. Import a security template into the Group Policy object for member servers.	a. Expand **Computer Configuration\Windows Settings**, and then click **Security Settings**. b. Import the **D:\2275\Practices\Mod09\Security Templates\Enterprise Client – Member Server Baseline.inf** template into the newly created GPO. c. Close all open windows.

Exercise 3
Scanning a Range of Computers by Using MBSA

In this exercise, you will scan all computers on a subnet by using MBSA.

Tasks	Specific instructions
1. Scan a range of computers from DEN-DC1.	a. On DEN-DC1 start **MBSA**. b. Click the **Scan more than one computer** link. c. Use an IP range of **10.10.0.1** to **10.10.0.20**.
2. View the reports for all computers.	a. Click **Pick a security report to review**. b. Click the first report in the list. c. Click Next security report.
3. Complete the lab exercise.	■ Close all programs and shut down all computers. Do not save changes.

Course Evaluation

Your evaluation of this course will help Microsoft understand the quality of your learning experience.

To complete a course evaluation, go to the Metrics That Matter page of the Knowledge Advisors Web site at http://www.metricsthatmatter.com/MTMStudent/ClassListPage.aspx?&orig=6&VendorAlias=survey.

Microsoft will keep your evaluation strictly confidential and will use your responses to improve your future learning experience.

Index

Special Characters

Notes

Notes

Notes

Notes

MSM2273BCP/C90-04743